NO MAN'S
MISTRESS

Also by Mary Balogh

More than a Mistress
One Night for Love

NO MAN'S
MISTRESS

MARY BALOGH

DELACORTE PRESS

Published by
Delacorte Press
Random House, Inc.
1540 Broadway
New York, New York 10036

Library of Congress Cataloging in Publication Data
Balogh, Mary.
No man's mistress / Mary Balogh.
p. cm.
ISBN 0-385-33529-6
I. Title.
PR6052.A465   N6 2001
823'.914—dc21
2001028313

Manufactured in the United States of America

Published simultaneously in Canada

August 2001

10 9 8 7 6 5 4 3 2 1

BVG

NO MAN'S
MISTRESS

1

The picturesque village of Trellick, nestled in a river valley in Somersetshire, was usually a quiet little backwater. But not on this particular day. By the middle of the afternoon it appeared that every villager and every country dweller for miles around must be out-of-doors, milling about the village green, enjoying the revelries.

The maypole at the center of the green, its colored ribbons fluttering in the breeze, proclaimed the occasion. It was May Day. Later, the young men would dance about the maypole with the partners of their choice, as they did with great energy and enthusiasm every year.

Meanwhile, there were races and other contests to draw attention to the green. Pitched about its perimeter were tented booths with their offerings of appetizing foods, eye-catching baubles, and challenging games of skill or strength or chance.

The weather had cooperated in magnificent fashion with warm sunshine and a cloudless blue sky. Women and girls had discarded shawls and pelisses they had worn in the morning. A few men and most boys remained in their shirtsleeves after engaging in one of the more strenuous contests. Tables and chairs had been carried from the church hall onto the lawn outside so that tea and cakes could be served in full view of all the merriment. Not to be out-done, on an adjacent side of the village green the Boar's Head had its own tables and benches set up outside for the convenience of those folk who preferred ale to tea.

A few strangers, on their way past the village to destinations un-known, stopped off for varying periods of time to observe the fun and even in some cases to participate in it before continuing their journeys.

One such stranger was riding slowly down toward the green from the main road when Viola Thornhill glanced up from serving tea to the Misses Merrywether. She would not have seen him over the heads of the crowd if he had not been on horseback. As it was, she paused for a second, more leisurely look.

He was clearly a gentleman, and a fashionable one at that. His dark blue riding coat looked as if it might have been molded to his frame. His linen beneath it was white and crisp. His black leather breeches clung to his long legs like a second skin. His riding boots looked supple and must surely have been made by the very best of boot makers. But it was not so much the clothes as the man inside them who attracted and held Viola's appreciative attention. He was young and slim and darkly handsome. He pushed back his tall hat even as she watched. He was smiling.

"You ought not to be serving *us*, Miss Thornhill," Miss Prudence Merrywether said, a customary note of anxious apology in her voice. "*We* ought to be serving *you*. You have been rushed off your feet all day."

Viola reassured her with a warm smile. "But I am having so much fun," she said. "Are we not fortunate indeed that the weather has been so kind?"

When she looked again, the stranger had disappeared from view, though he had not ridden on his way. His horse was being led away by one of the lads who worked in the inn stables.

"Miss Vi," a familiar voice said from behind her, and she turned to smile at the small, plump woman who had touched her on the shoulder. "The sack race is ready to begin, and you are needed to start it and award the prizes. I'll take the teapot from you."

"Will you, Hannah?" Viola handed it over and hurried onto the green, where a number of children were indeed wriggling into sacks and clutching them to their waists. Viola helped the stragglers and then directed them all as they hopped and shuffled into a roughly even line along the appointed starting point. Adults crowded about the four sides of the green to watch and cheer.

Viola had set out from home early in the morning looking lady-like and elegant in a muslin dress and shawl and straw bonnet, her hair in a neatly braided coronet about her head beneath it. She had even been wearing gloves. But she had long ago discarded all the accessories. Even her hair, slipping stubbornly out of its pins during the busy morning of rushing hither and yon, had been allowed finally to hang loose in a long braid down her back. She was feeling flushed and happy. She could not remember when she had enjoyed herself more.

"Get ready," she called, stepping to one side of the line of children. "Go!"

More than half the racers collapsed at their very first leap, their legs and feet all tangled up in sacking. They struggled to rise, to the accompaniment of good-natured laughter and shouted encouragement from relatives and neighbors. But inevitably there was one child who hopped across the green like a grasshopper and crossed the finish line before some of her less fortunate fellow contestants had recovered from their tumble.

Viola, laughing merrily, suddenly found herself locking eyes with the dark, handsome stranger, who was standing at the finish line, his own laughter emphasizing his extraordinary good looks. He looked her over frankly from head to toe before she turned away, but she discovered with pleased surprise that she felt amused, even exhilarated by his appreciation rather than repelled. She hurried forward to give out the prizes.

It was time then to hasten into the inn, where she was to judge the pie-baking contest with the Reverend Prewitt and Mr. Thomas Claypole.

"Eating pie is thirsty work," the vicar declared more than half an hour later, chuckling and patting his stomach after they had sampled every pie and declared a winner. "And if my observations have been correct, you have not had a break all day, Miss Thornhill. You go over to the church lawn now and find a table in the shade. Mrs. Prewitt or one of the other ladies will pour you tea. Mr. Claypole will be pleased to escort you, will you not, sir?"

Viola could have done without the escort of Mr. Claypole, who because he had proposed marriage to her at least a dozen times during the past year appeared to believe that he had some claim on her and the right to speak plainly to her on any number of issues. The best that could be said of Thomas Claypole was that he was worthy—a solid citizen, a prudent manager of his property, a dutiful son.

He was dull company at best. Irritating company at worst.

"Forgive me, Miss Thornhill," he began as soon as they were seated at one of the tables beneath the shade of a huge old oak tree and Hannah had poured their tea. "But you will not mind plain speaking from a friend, I daresay. Indeed, I flatter myself that I am more than a friend."

"What criticism of a perfect day do you have, then, sir?" she asked, setting her elbow on the table and her chin in her hand.

"Your willingness to organize the fête with the vicar's committee and to work hard to see that it runs smoothly is admirable indeed," he began, while Viola's eyes and attention drifted to the stranger, whom she could see drinking ale at a table outside the inn. "It can do nothing but earn my highest esteem. However, I have been somewhat alarmed to discover that today you look almost indistinguishable from any country wench."

"Oh, do I?" Viola laughed. "What a delightful thing to say. But you did not mean it as a compliment, did you?"

"You are hatless and your hair is down," he pointed out. "You have *daisies* in it."

She had forgotten. One of the children had presented her with a bunch gathered from the riverbank earlier in the day, and she had pushed the stems into her hair above her left ear. She touched the flowers lightly. Yes, they were still there.

"I believe it is *your* straw bonnet that is lying on the back pew of the church," Mr. Claypole continued.

"Ah," she said, "so *that* is where I left it, is it?"

"It should be protecting your complexion from the harmful rays of the sun," he said with gentle reproof.

"So it should," she agreed, finishing her tea and getting to her feet. "If you will excuse me, sir, I see that the fortune-teller is setting up her booth at last. I must go and see that she has everything she needs."

But Mr. Claypole would not have recognized a dismissal if it had doubled up into a fist and collided with his nose. He rose too, bowed, and offered his arm. Viola took it with an inward sigh of resignation.

Actually, the fortune-teller was already doing a brisk business, as Viola had been able to see from across the green. What she had also noticed, though, was that the stranger had strolled over to the throwing booth, which had been popular with the young men earlier in the afternoon. He was talking with Jake Tulliver, the blacksmith, when Viola and Mr. Claypole drew near.

"I was about to close down the booth, seeing as how we have run out of prizes," Jake said, raising his voice to address her. "But this gentleman wants a try."

"Well, then," she said gaily, "we will have to hope he does not win, will we not?"

The stranger turned his head to look at her. He was indeed tall, almost a full head taller than she. His eyes were almost black. They gave his handsome face a somewhat dangerous look. Viola felt her heartbeat quicken.

"Oh," he said with quiet assurance, "I *will* win, ma'am."

"Will you?" she asked. "Well, there is nothing so very surprising about that. Everyone else has won too, almost without exception. Hence the embarrassing lack of prizes still to give away. I daresay the targets were set too close. We must remember that next year, Mr. Tulliver."

"Set them back twice as far," the stranger said, "and I will still win."

She raised her eyebrows at the boast and looked at the metal candlesticks—the old set from the church vestry—which had been toppling all too readily before the ball the contestants had been hurling at them.

"Are you sure?" she asked. "Very well, then, sir, prove it. If you win—four out of the five must fall with just five throws, you understand—then we will return your money. It is the best we can do. All of today's proceeds go to the vicar's charities, you see, so we cannot afford to offer cash prizes."

"I will pay twice the entry fee," the stranger said with a grin that made him look both reckless and boyish. "And I will knock all five candlesticks down at twice their present distance. But I must insist upon a prize, ma'am."

"I believe we might safely offer the church spire without fear of denuding the church," she said. "It cannot be done."

"Oh, it can and will," he assured her, "if the prize is to be those daisies you wear above your ear."

Viola touched them and laughed. "A valuable prize indeed," she said. "Very well, sir."

Mr. Claypole cleared his throat. "You will permit me to point out that wagers are inappropriate to what is essentially a church fête, sir," he said.

The stranger laughed into Viola's eyes, almost as if he believed it was she who had spoken.

"Let us make sure that the church benefits well from this wager, then," he said. "Twenty pounds for the church whether I win or lose. The lady's daisies for me if I win. Move back the targets," he instructed Jake Tulliver, while he set a few banknotes down on the booth counter.

"Miss Thornhill." Mr. Claypole had taken her by the elbow and was speaking earnestly into her ear. "This will not do. You are drawing attention to yourself."

She looked about to see that indeed people who had been awaiting their turn outside the fortune-teller's booth and had overheard the exchange were beginning to gather around. And their interest was attracting more. A number of people were hurrying across the green toward the throwing booth. The gentleman was removing his coat and rolling up his shirtsleeves. Jake was repositioning the candlesticks.

"This gentleman has donated twenty pounds to the vicar's fund," Viola called gaily to the gathering crowd. "If he knocks down all five candlesticks with five throws of the ball, he will win . . . my daisies."

She gestured toward them and laughed with the crowd. But the stranger, she saw, did not. He was rolling the ball in his hands, concentrating on it, and squinting ahead to the candlesticks, which now looked an impossible distance away. He could not possibly win. She doubted he could knock over even one.

But one toppled over even as she was thinking it, and the crowd applauded appreciatively.

Jake handed the stranger the ball again, and he concentrated on it as before. A hush fell on the gathered crowd, which had swelled even more in size.

A second candlestick teetered, looked as if it were about to right itself, and fell with a clatter.

At least, Viola thought, he had not totally humiliated himself. He looked more than handsome in his shirtsleeves. He looked... well, very male. She desperately wanted him to win his bet. But he had set himself a nearly impossible task.

Again he concentrated.

The third candlestick fell.

The fourth did not.

There was a collective moan from the crowd. Viola felt absurdly disappointed.

"It would seem, sir," she said, "that I get to keep my flowers."

"Not so hasty, ma'am." His grin was back and he held out his hand for the ball. "The wager was for five candlesticks down with five throws, was it not? Did it state that one had to go down with each throw?"

"No." She laughed when she understood his meaning. "But you have only one throw left, and two candlesticks are standing."

"Oh ye of little faith," he murmured with a wink, and Viola felt a pleased fluttering of awareness low in her abdomen.

Then he was concentrating again, and the crowd was being shushed by those who realized he had not yet admitted defeat, and Viola's heart was beating right up into her ears.

Her eyes widened with incredulity and the crowd erupted into a roar of wild cheering as the ball hit one upright candlestick, glanced sideways off it as it fell, and demolished the fifth with a satisfying crack.

The gentleman turned, bowed to his audience, and then grinned at Viola, who was clapping and laughing and realizing that this was by far the most exhilarating moment of the day.

"That bouquet is forfeit, I believe, ma'am," he said, pointing to her daisies. "I will claim them for myself."

She stood still while his fingers detached the small bunch of daisies from her hair. His laughing eyes did not waver from her own—they were a very dark brown, she could see now. His skin looked sun-bronzed. His body heat and a musky cologne reached out to envelop her. He carried the daisies to his lips, bowed with careless grace, and pushed the stems into a buttonhole of his shirt.

"A lady's favor at my breast," he murmured. "What more could I ask of the day?"

But she had no chance to respond to such blatant flirtation. The Reverend Prewitt's hearty voice intruded.

"Bravo, sir!" he exclaimed, stepping forward from the crowd, his right hand extended. "You are a regular good sport, if you will permit me to say so. Come over to the church lawn and my wife will pour you a cup of tea while I tell you about the charities that will benefit from your generosity."

The stranger smiled into Viola's eyes with a hint of reluctance and moved away with the vicar.

"I am vastly relieved," Mr. Claypole said, taking Viola by the elbow again as the crowd drifted away to sample other attractions, "that the Reverend Prewitt was able to cover up for the vulgarity of that display, Miss Thornhill, focused as the whole wager was on your person. It was not seemly. Now perhaps—"

She gave him no chance to complete his thought. "I do believe, sir," she said, "your mother has been beckoning you for the past ten minutes."

"Why did you not say so before?" He looked sharply in the direction of the church and hurried off without a backward glance. Viola looked at Hannah, who was standing close by, raised her eyebrows, and laughed aloud.

"Miss Vi," Hannah said, shaking her head, "he is as handsome as sin. And twice as dangerous, if you were to ask me."

Clearly she was not talking about Mr. Claypole. "He is just a stranger passing through, Hannah," Viola said. "It was a very generous donation, was it not? Twenty pounds! We must be thankful that he broke his journey at Trellick. Now I am going to have my fortune told."

But fortune-tellers were all the same, she reflected when she came out of the booth some time later. Why could they not aim for at least some originality? This one was a gypsy with a reputation for being able to predict the future with remarkable accuracy.

"Beware of a tall, dark, handsome stranger," she had said after consulting her crystal ball. "He can destroy you—if you do not first snare his heart."

Tall, dark, and handsome indeed! Viola smiled at a child who had stopped to show her his new spinning top. What a lamentable cliché.

And then she spotted the stranger again, striding away from the church lawn in the direction of the inn stables. Ah, he was leaving, then. Continuing on his way while there was still some daylight left.

A tall, dark, handsome stranger. She laughed softly.

The sun was already low in the western sky. From the direction of the inn she could hear the fiddlers tuning their instruments. A couple of men were checking the ribbons about the maypole, making sure they were not tangled. She watched and listened with a certain wistfulness. The maypole dancing was always the joyful, exuberant climax of the May Day celebrations. But it was one activity in which she would have no part. It was not viewed as a genteel activity by the upper-class families of the village and neighborhood. A lady might watch, but she might not participate.

But no matter. She *would* watch and enjoy doing so, as she had last year—her first May Day at Trellick. In the meantime, she was expected at the vicarage for dinner.

By the time Viola stepped out of the vicarage again, darkness had fallen and bonfires were burning on three sides of the village green to provide light for the dancing. The fiddlers were playing, and young people were already twirling about the maypole in a merry, energetic dance. Viola declined an invitation to accompany the Reverend and Mrs. Prewitt as they strolled around the green. Instead, she moved onto the now-deserted church lawn to enjoy the spectacle alone.

It was amazingly warm for a spring evening. She had draped her shawl about her shoulders, but she did not really need it. Her bonnet was probably still on the back pew of the church. Hannah, her maid, once her nurse, had brushed out her hair before dinner and left it unbraided, tied back at the nape of her neck with a ribbon. It was more comfortable that way. Mr. Claypole would be scandalized indeed if he could see her, but fortunately he had taken his mother and his sister home at dusk.

The fiddling stopped and the dancers dispersed to the edges of the green to catch their breath and choose new partners. The moon was almost at the full, Viola saw, tipping back her head. The sky was brilliantly star-studded. She inhaled deeply of the clean country air, closed her eyes, and breathed a silent prayer of thanksgiving. Who could have predicted just two years ago that she would ever be living in a place like this? Belonging here, accepted here, generally liked here. Her life might have been very different now if . . .

"Now, what are you doing hiding here," a voice asked, "when you should be out there dancing?"

Her eyes snapped open. She had neither seen nor heard his approach. She had seen him go to the inn stables earlier and had assumed that he had long ago resumed his journey. She had assured herself that she was not disappointed. Why should she be, after all? He was merely an attractive stranger, who had passed briefly through her life and engaged her in a harmless flirtation over a bunch of wild daisies.

But here he was standing in front of her, awaiting her answer, his face in shadows. *Awaiting her answer.* She suddenly realized what it was he had said.

. . . you should be out there dancing.

It would be the perfect ending to a perfect day. Twirling about the maypole. Dancing with the handsome stranger. She did not even want to know who he was. She wanted the mystery preserved so that she could look back on this day with unalloyed pleasure.

"I have been waiting for the right partner, sir," she said. And then, more outrageously, as she lowered her voice, "I have been waiting for *you*."

"Have you indeed?" He reached out a hand. "Well, here I am."

She dropped her shawl heedlessly to the grass and placed her hand in his. It closed firmly about her own before he led her away.

It was all pure enchantment after that. The green was lit by the flickering flames of the bonfires. The air was full of the pungent smell of wood smoke. Young men were already leading their partners forward and claiming the bright dangling ribbons. But the stranger secured two and put one in Viola's hand, his teeth flashing white in the darkness. And then the fiddles were scraping out a merry tune and the dance began—the light, tripping, intricate steps, the circular clockwise motion, the twirling and dipping and weaving while ribbons twined together and then miraculously untwined again, the pulsing, steady rhythm that thrummed with the blood through veins; the stars wheeling overhead; the fires crackling, throwing faces into mysterious shadow one moment, illuminating the gay animation in them the next; the spectators around the edges of the green clapping in time to the fiddles and the dancers.

And the focus of the enchantment—the handsome, long-legged stranger, still in his shirtsleeves, the wilting bunch of daisies adorning one buttonhole, dancing with light-footed grace and vibrant energy and merry laughter. And watching her own exuberance. As if the very universe revolved about the two of them just as surely as they circled the maypole.

Viola was breathless when the music ended and so happy that she thought she might well burst with it. And regretful too that now, finally, this magical day was at an end. Hannah would be eager to return home. The day had been as busy for her as it had been for Viola. She would not make her maid feel obliged to stay longer—though that generous impulse was quickly abandoned, at least temporarily.

"You look as if you would welcome a glass of lemonade," the stranger said, setting a hand at the small of her back and leaning down to smile into her face.

Tea was no longer being served on the church lawn. But two tables had been left outside, a large bowl of lemonade and a trayful of glasses on each. Not much of it was being drunk. Most of the older generation had gone home, and the younger people seemed to prefer the ale being served at the inn.

"I would indeed," she agreed.

They did not speak as they crossed the green and then the road to the church lawn and the table beneath the oak tree where she had found shade from the sun after judging the pie contest. He ladled out a glassful of lemonade for her and watched as she drank it, grateful for its tart coolness. Behind her, out of sight beyond the massive trunk of the old oak, the fiddlers were playing again, the sound of their brisk music mingling with the sounds of voices and laughter. Ahead she could see moonlight gleaming on the surface of the river, which flowed past the village behind the church.

It was a scene she concentrated deliberately upon remembering.

When she had finished drinking, he took the empty glass from her hand and set it on the table. It was on the tip of her tongue to ask him if he was not thirsty himself. But there was a certain spell, a certain tension between them that words might break. She had no wish to break it.

She had had no real girlhood—not after the age of nine, at least. No chance to steal away into the shadows for an innocent, clandestine tryst with a beau. There had been no chance for romance or even for light, harmless flirtation. At the age of five-and-twenty she

suddenly felt like the girl she might have grown into, had her life
not changed forever more than half a lifetime ago. She liked being
that girl, however fleetingly.

He slid one arm about her waist and drew her against him. With
the other hand he grasped her hair below the ribbon and pulled on
it with just enough pressure to tip back her head. Moonlight and
tree branches were dappled across his face. He was smiling. Did he
always smile, this stranger? Or was he merely indulging today, amid
strangers he would never see again, in his own escape from more
sober reality?

She closed her eyes when his face dipped down, and he kissed
her.

It did not last long. It was not by any means a lascivious kiss.
Although his lips parted over her own, he made no attempt to plun-
der her mouth. His one hand remained splayed firmly against the
back of her waist, while the other cupped the ribbon at her neck.
She did not for one second lose herself in passion, though she knew
she could swoon into it if she chose. She would not so waste a single precious moment. What she did instead was carefully and deliberately savor and memorize each sensation. She felt his long,
hard-muscled, leather-clad thighs against the softness of her own,
his abdomen hard against hers, his chest firm against her breasts.
She felt the moist intimacy of his lips, the warmth of his breath
against her cheek. She breathed in the mingled scents of cologne
and leather and man, and tasted on his mouth ale and something
unidentifiable that must be the very essence of him. She heard music, voices, laughter, water flowing, a single owl hooting—all from a
vast distance away. She twined her fingers in his thick, soft hair and
felt with the other hand the well-developed muscles of his shoulder
and upper arm.

Beware of a tall, dark, handsome stranger.

She drank her brief, clandestine draft of youthful romance from
the brim to the very dregs. And then, when he raised his head and

loosened his hold on her, she accepted the fact that the day was ended.

"Thank you for the dance." He chuckled. "And for the kiss."

"Good night," she said softly.

He looked down at her for a few moments longer. "Good night, my country lass," he said in answer, and strode past her, back in the direction of the green.

2

❧

*T*rellick was a pretty village. He had seen that yesterday, gazing down on it as the main road dipped into the river valley. This morning, as he stood at the taproom window inside the Boar's Head sipping coffee, Lord Ferdinand Dudley noticed the whitewashed, thatched cottages with their neat, colorful flower gardens on two sides of the green. On the riverside stood the stone church, with its tall, slender spire and spacious lawn, in the middle of which stood a great old oak tree. The vicarage, its gray stone walls ivy-covered, was beside the church. He could not see the water from where he stood, just as he could not see the row of shops next to the inn, but he could see the forest of trees on the far side of the river, a pleasantly rural backdrop for the church and village.

He wondered where exactly Pinewood Manor was. He knew it must be reasonably close, since Bamber's solicitor had mentioned Trellick to him as the nearest village. But how close? And how large was it? What did it look like? A cottage like one of those opposite? A house like the vicarage? A larger building, as its name implied? A dilapidated heap? No one had seemed to know, least of all Bamber himself, who had not appeared to care much either.

Ferdinand fully expected the dilapidated heap.

He could have asked for directions yesterday, of course—it was what he had ridden into the village to do, after all. But he had not done so. It had been well into the afternoon and he had persuaded himself that viewing Pinewood for the first time would be better left until the morning. The gaiety of the village fête into which he had ridden had been partly responsible for that decision, of course, as well as that country lass with the enticingly swinging braid whose laughing eyes he had met across the village green after the children's sack race. He had wanted to stay and enjoy himself—and see more of her.

Just two weeks ago he had not even heard of Pinewood. Now here he was on the verge of seeing it, and wondering what exactly there would be to see. A fool's errand, Lord Heyward, his brother-in-law, had predicted of his journey. But then, Heyward was never strong on optimism, especially where the escapades of Angeline's two brothers were concerned. He did not have a high opinion of the Dudleys, even though he had married one of them.

He ought not to have kissed that woman last night, Ferdinand thought uneasily. He was not in the habit of indulging in flirtations with innocent country wenches. And he suspected that she might be more than just a country wench. What if Pinewood Manor turned out to be very close, after all—and not in ruins? What if he should decide to stay there for a while? She might even turn out to be the vicar's daughter. It was entirely within the realm of possibility, since she had clearly been one of the prime movers of the festivities— and she had stepped out of the vicarage during the evening. He had not asked who she was. He did not even know her name.

Devil take it, but he hoped she was not the vicar's daughter. And he hoped Pinewood was not so very close. That stolen kiss might yet prove an embarrassment.

Of course, she had been pretty enough to tempt a saint—and Dudleys had never been candidates for sainthood. Her dark red hair and perfect features in an oval face would give her a claim to extraordinary beauty even if one considered her only from the neck up. But when one added the rest of her to the picture . . . Ferdinand blew out his breath and turned from the window. *Voluptuous* was one word that leaped to mind. She was tall and slim but generously curved in all the right places. He had had evidence of that with his body as well as his eyes.

The memory itself was enough to make him uncomfortably warm.

He went in search of the landlord to ask about Pinewood. Then he summoned his valet, who had arrived with his coach and baggage in the middle of last evening, an hour after his groom had arrived with his curricle.

An hour later, freshly shaven and wearing clean riding clothes and boots so shiny that he could almost see his face in them, Ferdinand was riding across the river via a triple-arched stone bridge beyond the vicarage. Pinewood Manor, the landlord had assured him, was very close indeed. The river formed the boundary of its park on two sides, in fact. Ferdinand had not asked for further details. He wanted to see for himself what the place was like. He noticed suddenly that a number of the trees on the other side of the river were pines. *Pine*wood, of course. There was a footpath between the trees and the river, stretching away to his right until it was lost to view around a sharp bend in the river beyond the village.

It all looked very promising, but he must not get his hopes up prematurely.

It did not matter anyway, he told himself. Even if Heyward's gloomy predictions proved correct, he would be no worse off than he had been two weeks ago. All he would have missed was a week or so of the London Season and the arrival in town of his brother Tresham with his wife and children.

Ferdinand's spirits continued to rise when he found himself riding along a winding driveway shaded by overhanging trees—a driveway wide enough to accommodate even the grandest of carriages and displaying no sign of being overgrown from disuse.

He burst into song, as he sometimes did when alone, serenading the trees around him and the blue sky above. " 'Now is the month of Maying, when merry lads are playing. Fa-la-la-la-la, la-la-la-laaa. Fa-la-la-la-la-la-la. Each with his bonny lass.' "

But both the song and his forward motion came to an abrupt pause as he rode into the bright sunlight clear of the band of trees and found himself at the foot of a wide lawn. It was bisected by the driveway, which curved off to the left before it reached the house in the near distance.

House. Ferdinand whistled through his teeth. It was definitely more than that. It was closer to being a mansion, though that might be something of an exaggeration, he admitted, thinking of the imposing grandeur of Acton Park, his childhood home. Nevertheless, Pinewood was an impressive gray stone manor set in a sizable park. Even the stables and carriage house toward which the driveway turned were not negligible in size.

A flicker of movement to his left drew Ferdinand's eyes to two men, who were busy cutting the grass with scythes. It was only then that the neat, well-kept appearance of the lawn struck him. One of the men turned to gaze curiously at him, leaning both arms on the long handle of his scythe as he did so.

"That is Pinewood Manor?" Ferdinand pointed with his whip.

"Aye, 'tis, sir," the man agreed, respectfully touching his forelock.

Ferdinand rode onward, feeling somewhat euphoric. He resumed his singing as soon as he judged himself to be out of earshot of the grass cutters, though perhaps not with quite such cheerful abandon. " 'A-a-dancing on the grass,' " he sang, picking up the song where he had left it off. " 'Fa-la-la-la-laaa.' " He held the high note and noticed that the lawn did not stretch right up to the doors of the manor but ended before a low, neatly clipped box hedge with what looked like a formal garden beyond it. And unless he was much mistaken, there was a fountain in that garden. One that worked.

Why the devil had Bamber been so careless of such an apparently substantial property? Was the house a mere empty shell beyond the respectable outer facade? It was surely damp and horridly dilapidated from disuse, but if that was all that was wrong with it, he would count himself well blessed indeed. Why let the prospect of a little mildew dampen his spirits? He finished the verse of his song with a flourish.

" 'La-la-la-la-laaa.' "

There was a cobbled terrace before the front doors of the manor, he noticed as he approached the stables. The formal garden, consisting of graveled walks, box hedges, and neat floral borders, was below it, at the foot of three broad steps. He was surprised, as he dismounted by the stables, to be met by a young lad coming out of one of the stalls.

The Earl of Bamber had never lived at this manor in remote Somersetshire or even visited it, if he was to be believed. He had denied any knowledge of it. Yet he seemed to have been spending money on its upkeep. Why else were there two gardeners at work on the lawn and a groom in the stables?

"Are there servants at the house?" he asked the lad curiously.

"Aye, sir," the boy told him as he prepared to lead the horse away. "Mr. Jarvey will see to you if you knock on the door. That was a right fine display of ball throwing, if you will pardon me for saying so, sir. I could only hit three of them candlesticks myself, and they was much closer when I tried."

Ferdinand grinned his acknowledgment of the compliment. "Mr. Jarvey?"

"The butler, sir."

There was a *butler*? Curious indeed. Ferdinand nodded affably, strode across the terrace to the double front doors of the manor, and rattled the knocker.

"Good morning, sir."

Ferdinand smiled cheerfully at the respectably black-clad servant who stood between the opened doors, a look of polite inquiry on his face.

"Jarvey?" Ferdinand asked.

"Yes, sir." The butler bowed respectfully and opened the doors wider before stepping to one side. His professional glance had obviously informed him that he was confronting a gentleman.

"Pleased to make your acquaintance," Ferdinand said, stepping inside and looking around with frank interest.

He found himself standing in a square, high-ceilinged hall with a tiled floor. The walls were tastefully hung with landscape paintings in gilded frames, and a marble bust of stern Roman aspect stood on a marble stand in an alcove opposite the door. There was an oak staircase with an ornately carved banister to the right, doors leading into other apartments to the left. The appearance of the hall certainly boded well for the rest of the house. Not only was it light, pleasingly designed, and tastefully decorated, but it was also clean. Everything gleamed.

The butler coughed with polite inquiry as Ferdinand strode to the center of the hall, his boots clicking on the tiles, and turned slowly about, his head tipped slightly back. "How may I help you, sir?"

"You may have the master bedchamber prepared for my use tonight," Ferdinand said, giving the man only half his attention, "and some luncheon conjured up an hour or so from now. Is that possible? Is there a cook here? Cold meat and bread will do if there is nothing else."

The butler regarded him with unconcealed astonishment. "The master bedchamber, sir?" he said stiffly. "I beg your pardon, but I have not been informed that you are expected."

Ferdinand chuckled good-naturedly and gave his full attention to the matter at hand. "I gather not," he said. "But then I was not informed that I was to expect *you*. I suppose the Earl of Bamber has not written or got anyone else to write for him?"

"The earl?" The butler sounded even more astonished. "He has never had anything to do with Pinewood Manor, sir. He—"

That was just like Bamber. To have known nothing about the place, not even that there were servants here. Not to have warned anyone that Lord Ferdinand Dudley was on his way here. But then, he had not appeared to know that there was anyone to warn. What a ramshackle fellow!

Ferdinand held up one hand. "You must be a devoted retainer indeed, then," he said, "if you have kept the manor and grounds in such fine order when he never comes to call you to account. Has he always paid the bills without question? I daresay you have grown to think of the house almost as your own, in which case you will soon wish me to the devil. All that is to change, you see. Allow me to introduce myself. I am Lord Ferdinand Dudley, younger brother of the Duke of Tresham, and the new owner of Pinewood."

Suddenly the truth of it took on a new reality to him. This was *his*. And it really did exist. In more than just name. There really was a manor and a park, and presumably farms as well. He was a member of the landed gentry.

The butler stared at him with stiff incomprehension. "The new owner, sir?" he said. "But—"

"Oh, I assure you the change of ownership is all legal," Ferdinand said briskly, his eye taken by the chandelier overhead. "*Is* there a cook? If not, I had better take my meals at the Boar's Head until there is. In the meantime, you may give the order about the master bedchamber while I take a look around. How many indoor servants are there?"

The butler did not answer his question. Another voice spoke instead. A female voice. A low, husky voice, which immediately sent shivers of recognition up Ferdinand's spine.

"Who is it, Mr. Jarvey?" she asked.

Ferdinand turned his head sharply. She was standing on the bottom stair, her left hand resting on the newel post. She looked altogether different today, dressed as she was in a dark green high-waisted walking dress, which hugged her magnificent figure in all the right places, her hair pulled back rather severely from her lovely face and braided into a coronet about her head. Today there was no mistaking the fact that she was no girl, but a woman. And no village wench, but a lady. For a moment she looked vaguely familiar, even apart from yesterday's acquaintance, but he was not at leisure to pursue that impression.

"Lord Ferdinand Dudley, ma'am." The butler, stiff and correct, made his name sound as if he were close blood kin to Satan.

Oh, Lord! Bamber had not given any hint about people being in residence. Had he *forgotten?* All the signs had been punching Ferdinand in the nose like a giant fist for the past half hour, but idiot that he was, he had recognized not a one of them. The house was *occupied.* And of all people, by the woman he had kissed last night. Possibly by her husband too. He had a pained mental image of pistols at dawn, grass for breakfast.

She had stepped down onto the tiled floor and was hurrying toward him, her right arm extended in greeting. She was smiling. And devil take it, but she was beautiful. He licked lips suddenly turned dry. There was no sign of a husband thundering down the stairs behind her.

"You!" she exclaimed. Then she seemed to hear the echo of what her butler had said to her and her smile faltered. "*Lord* Ferdinand Dudley?"

He took her outstretched hand in his and bowed over it, clicking his heels as he did so. "Ma'am," he murmured. *Bloody hell,* he added silently.

"I supposed that you had continued your journey this morning," she said. "I expected never to see you again. Do you have far to go?

But how delightful that you have called on me first. Someone told you where I live? Do come up to the drawing room. Mr. Jarvey will have refreshments sent up. I was on my way out for a walk, but I am so glad you came before I left."

Where I live. His mind latched on to those three words. She *did* live here. She thought he had come to call on her on the strength of yesterday's acquaintance. Lord, what rotten bad luck. He dredged up a smile from somewhere deep inside himself, bowed again, and offered his arm.

"It would be my pleasure, ma'am," he said, instead of simply telling her what was what and having done with it.

This would teach him to avoid village fêtes and pretty country lasses, Ferdinand thought as she took his arm and led him toward the staircase. He tried to stuff aside the memory of her dancing with gay animation about the maypole on the village green, her face vibrant and beautiful in the firelight, her thick hair bouncing and swaying against her back below its confining ribbon. And of the kiss he had incautiously maneuvered, during which he had held her very shapely body flush against his own.

Devil take it!

3

❧

*H*e had come! He was tall and lithe and elegant in crisply clean riding clothes different from yesterday's. He was smiling and handsome, and he was *Lord Ferdinand Dudley*. She remembered how the arm through which her own was now loosely linked had felt holding her close the night before. She remembered how his mouth had felt on her own.

He had come!

It was absurd, as well as undesirable, to imagine that he had come courting. He was merely a stranger passing through, who had danced with her and kissed her, discovered her identity, and come to pay a courtesy call. No, more than that, surely. He must have felt the sheer romance of the maypole dance and its aftermath, as she had. He had come to see her once more before riding on.

He had come!

Viola led Lord Ferdinand Dudley into the drawing room and indicated a chair beside the marble fireplace. She took one opposite him and smiled at him again.

"How did you discover my identity?" she asked. It warmed her to know that he had made the effort.

He cleared his throat and looked uncomfortable. How gratifying that she could discompose a *lord*. Her eyes sparkled with amusement.

"I asked the landlord of the Boar's Head for the direction to Pinewood Manor," he said.

Ah, so he had known yesterday who she was? She had not known his identity or sought to discover it. But she was glad he had come to introduce himself before riding on. She was glad their encounter yesterday had meant something to him, as it had to her.

"The fête was a great success," she said. She wanted him to talk about it, to mention their lovely dance.

"Quite so." He cleared his throat again and flushed. But before he could continue, the door opened and the parlormaid brought in a tray of coffee and set it down in front of Viola before bobbing a curtsy and leaving. Viola poured two cups and rose to set one down on the table beside Lord Ferdinand. He watched her in silence.

"Look here, ma'am," he blurted as she resumed her seat. "Has Bamber not written to you either?"

"The Earl of Bamber?" She stared at him in surprise.

"I beg your pardon, ma'am," he continued, "but Pinewood is no longer his, you see. It is mine. As of two weeks ago."

"Yours?" What *was* this? "But that is impossible, my lord. Pinewood Manor is mine. It has been for almost two years."

He reached into an inner pocket of his riding coat to draw out a folded sheet of paper, which he held out to her. "Here is the deed to the manor. It is now officially in my name. I am sorry."

She looked at it blankly without reaching for it, and foolishly all she could think of was that she had been mistaken. He had *not* come to call on her. At least, not because of yesterday. The contest for her daisies, the dance about the maypole, the kiss beneath the old oak had meant nothing whatsoever to him. Today he had come with the intention of ousting her from her home.

"It is a worthless piece of paper," she told him through lips that felt suddenly stiff. "The Earl of Bamber has made off with the price you paid for it, Lord Ferdinand, and is laughing at you from some safe distance. I suggest you find him and take up the matter with him." She felt the stirring of anger—and fright.

"There is nothing to take up," Lord Ferdinand told her. "The legality of the document is not in question, ma'am. It has been attested to by both Bamber's solicitor and my brother's—he is the Duke of Tresham. I was careful to verify the authenticity of my winnings."

"*Winnings?*" Oh, yes, of course. She knew his type—yes, indeed she did. He was the brother of the Duke of Tresham, with all of a younger son's weaknesses and vices—boredom, shiftlessness, extravagance, insensitivity, arrogance. He was probably impoverished too. But yesterday she had chosen to be beguiled by a handsome face and a virile male body, and to be flattered by his attentions. He was a gambler of the very worst kind, one who played deep without any concern for the human consequences of his addiction. He had won property that was not even his opponent's to lose.

"At cards," he explained. "There are any number of witnesses to the fact that Pinewood was fairly won. And I *did* have the document checked very thoroughly. I am indeed sorry for this inconvenience to you. I had no idea there was someone living here."

Inconvenience!

Viola leaped to her feet, her cheeks flooding with hot color, her eyes flashing. How dare he!

"You may take your *document* with you and toss it into the river as you leave," she said. "It is worthless. Pinewood Manor was willed to me almost two years ago. The Earl of Bamber may not have liked it, but there was nothing he could do to prevent it. Good day to you, my lord."

But Lord Ferdinand Dudley, although he too got to his feet, made no move to leave the room and her life, as any decent gentleman would have done. He stood before the fireplace looking large and unyielding and unsmiling. All his false geniality had been abandoned.

"On the contrary, ma'am," he said, "it is you who are going to have to leave. I will, of course, grant you sufficient time to gather your belongings and arrange for a destination, since Bamber has not seen fit to give you decent notice. You are a relative of his, are you? I suppose you should go to Bamber Court, then, unless somewhere else leaps to mind. He will hardly refuse you admittance, will he, though I daresay he is still in London. His mother lives there all the time, though, I believe. She will doubtless welcome you."

His words filled her with icy terror. Her nostrils flared. "Let me make one thing very clear to you, Lord Ferdinand," she said. "This is my home. You are a trespasser here and an unwelcome one, despite . . . well, despite yesterday. I understand clearly now that you are a gamer and an opportunist. I had evidence of those weaknesses yesterday but did not realize they were habitual. I do not doubt that you are also any number of other unsavory things. You will leave immediately. I will be going nowhere. I am already at home. Good day to you."

He gazed at her with those almost black eyes, which were quite unfathomable. "I will be taking up residence as soon as you have had time to pack up your belongings and remove yourself, ma'am," he said. "I would advise you not to delay too long. You would certainly not wish to be forced to spend any night beneath the roof of a single gentleman who is also a gamer and an opportunist, among other unsavory vices."

And she had danced about the maypole with this cold, unfeeling, obstinate man the night before and thought it surely the most glorious experience of her life? She had kissed him and thought she would warm herself with the memory for the rest of her life?

"I will simply not allow you to do this," she said. "How dare you expose me to public attention yesterday by wagering on my—my *daisies!* How dare you haul me onto the green to dance about the *maypole!* How dare you maul my person and k-*kiss* me as if I were a common milkmaid!"

His brows snapped together and she realized with some satisfaction that she had finally rattled him. "Yesterday?" he barked at her. "*Yesterday?* You accuse me of common assault when you *flirted* with me from the moment your eyes first alighted on me?"

"And how *dare* you have the audacity to come here today to invade my home and privacy, you . . . you Bond Street fop! You conscienceless rake! You callous, dissolute gamer!" She had lost control of both the situation and herself, she knew, but she did not care. "I know your sort, and I will *not* allow you to ignore my very existence. Get out of here!" She pointed toward the door. "Go back to London and your own kind, where you belong. We do not need you here."

He raised his eyebrows haughtily—and then lifted one hand and ran his fingers through his hair. He sighed out loud.

"Perhaps, ma'am," he suggested, "we should discuss this matter like civilized beings instead of scrapping like a couple of ill-bred children. Your presence here has taken me by surprise. You know, it was unpardonable of Bamber not to have informed you that the property is no longer his. You of all people should have been the first to know. But—I beg your pardon—does he *know* you are living here? I mean . . . well, he did not *say* anything about you."

She regarded him scornfully. There was nothing to discuss, civilly or otherwise. "It is quite immaterial to me whether he knows or not," she said.

"Well," he said, "he should have informed both you and me, and so I shall tell him when I see him. It is a dashed awkward thing that I have descended on you like this without warning of any kind. Accept my apologies, ma'am. Is he a close relative of yours? Are you fond of him?"

"My affections would be sadly misplaced if I were," Viola said. "A man of *honor* surely does not pledge at a card game what does not belong to him."

He took one step closer to her. "Why do you claim that Pinewood is yours?" he asked. "You said it was willed to you?"

"When the Earl of Bamber died," she said. "This man's father."

"Were you there for the reading of the will?" he asked. "Or were you informed of the bequest by letter?"

"I had the earl's promise," she said.

"The old earl?" He was frowning. "He promised to leave you Pinewood? But you have no proof that he kept his promise? You were not there for the reading? You received no letter from his solicitor?" He shook his head slowly. "You have been hoaxed, I am afraid, ma'am."

Her clasped hands felt cold and clammy. Her heartbeat was thudding against her eardrums. "I was not there for the reading of the will," she said, "but I trust the word of the late Earl of Bamber, my lord. He promised me when I came here two years ago that he would change his will. He lived for more than a month after that. He would neither have changed his mind nor procrastinated. No one belonging to the present earl has been here or communicated in any way with me. Is that not proof enough that he knew very well the property is mine?"

"Why do you not have the deed in your possession, then?" he asked. "Why did both Bamber's solicitor and my brother's assure me that the property was indeed his before he wagered it and lost it to me?"

Viola's stomach somersaulted queasily. But she dared not give in to terror. "I have never thought about it," she said curtly. "The deed is merely a piece of paper. I trusted the word of the late Earl of Bamber. I still do. Pinewood is mine. I do not intend to discuss the matter further with you, Lord Ferdinand. I do not need to. You must leave."

He stared at her, the long fingers of one hand drumming a tat-
too against the outside of his thigh. He was not going to go away
quietly. Had she expected that he would? She had known from her
first sight of him yesterday that he was a dangerous man. He was
one who was accustomed to having his own way, she guessed. And
he was the Duke of Tresham's brother? The duke was a notoriously
ruthless man, whose will no one dared cross.

"There is an easy way to settle the matter," he said. "We can
send for a copy of the old earl's will. But I would not hold out any
hope of its saying what you wish it to say, if I were you, ma'am. If
the old earl did indeed make you such a promise—"

"If? *If?*" Viola took an incautious step forward so that she was
almost toe-to-toe with him.

He held up a staying hand. "Then I am afraid he did not keep it.
There can be no doubt about it. I made very certain, before I left
London to come down here, that Pinewood was Bamber's to lose. It
is now mine."

"He had no right to wager away the house," she cried, "when it
did not belong to him. It is *mine*. It was left to me."

"I can understand your agitation," he told her. "This was dashed
irresponsible of Bamber—both Bambers: the father for making a
promise he did not keep, the son for forgetting you were here. If I
had only known of your existence, I could at least have given you
ample notice before I came here in person. But I did not know, and
so here I am, eager to acquaint myself with my new property. You
really are going to have to leave, I'm afraid. There is no sensible alternative, is there? We cannot *both* live here. But I'll give you a week.
Will that be long enough? I'll sleep at the inn in Trellick during that
time. Do you have somewhere else to go? *Could* you go to Bamber
Court?"

Viola clenched her hands even tighter. She could feel her fingernails digging into her palms. "I have no intention of going anywhere," she told him. "Until I see that will and it is proved to me

that I am not named in it, this is where I belong. This is my house. My home."

He sighed, and she realized that he was too close for comfort. But she would not take a step back. She tilted her head and looked him straight in the eye—and had a flashing memory of standing even closer to him just the evening before. Could he possibly be the same man?

Beware of a tall, dark, handsome stranger. He can destroy you.

"If there is nowhere," he said with what she might have interpreted as kindness had the words not been so brutal, "I'll send you to London in my own carriage. I'll send you to my sister, Lady Heyward. No, on second thought, Angie is too scatterbrained to offer any practical assistance. I'll send you to my sister-in-law, the Duchess of Tresham, then. She will gladly offer you shelter while she helps you find some suitable and respectable employment. Or a relative willing to take you in."

Viola laughed scornfully. "Perhaps the Duchess of Tresham could do that for *you*, my lord," she suggested. "Find you respectable employment, that is. Gamblers frequently find their pockets to let, I understand. And gamblers are invariably gentlemen who have nothing more meaningful to do with their lives."

He raised his eyebrows and looked at her in some astonishment. "You *do* have a sharp tongue," he said. "Who are you? Have I seen you somewhere before? Before yesterday, that is?"

It was entirely possible. Though no one else in the neighborhood of Pinewood had. That had always been a large part of its charm. The only twinge of alarm she had felt at first downstairs—it seemed laughable now—had come with Mr. Jarvey's introduction of yesterday's handsome stranger as Lord Ferdinand Dudley—a member of the *ton*, possibly someone who lived much of his life in London and had perhaps done so for several years. She guessed that he must be in his late twenties.

"Viola Thornhill," she told him. "And I have never seen you before yesterday. I would have remembered."

He nodded, but his brows were still knitted in thought. He was obviously trying to remember where it was he had seen her before, if anywhere. She could have offered a few suggestions, though it was true she had never seen him before yesterday.

"Well," he said briskly, shaking his head, "I will take myself off back to Trellick, Miss Thornhill. It is Miss, not Mrs.?" She inclined her head. "For seven nights, though I must beg leave to intrude upon you here in the daytime. If you need my assistance in planning your journey, feel free to ask for it."

He strode past her across the room, all masculine arrogance and energy and power. Yesterday's dream transformed into today's nightmare. She looked after him with intense hatred.

"Lord Ferdinand," she said as his hand closed about the door-knob, "I do not believe you heard me a moment ago. Until I have seen that will, I am going nowhere. I will be remaining here in my own house and my own home. I will not give in to bluster and bullying. If you were a gentleman, you would not even ask it of me."

When he turned, she could see that she had angered him. His eyes looked very black. His brows had drawn together. His nostrils were flared, making his nose look sharper, almost hooked, and his lips were set in a grim line. He looked altogether more formidable than he had a moment before. Viola glared defiantly at him.

"If I were a *gentleman*?" he said, so softly that despite herself she felt a shiver of apprehension curl about her spine. "If you were a *lady*, ma'am, you would accept with grace what has happened through no fault of mine. I am not answerable for the failure of the late earl to keep his promise to you, or for his son's choosing to bet an estate instead of money on the outcome of a card game. The simple fact is that Pinewood Manor is *mine*. It was my plan a moment ago to inconvenience myself out of deference to your sensibilities and the awkwardness of your situation. It is no longer my plan. I will be taking up residence here immediately. It is *you* who will stay

at the Boar's Head tonight. But as a *gentleman,* I will send a maid with
you and have the bill sent to me."

"I will be sleeping here, in my own house, in my own bed," she
told him, holding his gaze.

The air fairly crackled with the clashing of their wills.

His eyes narrowed. "Then you must share the house with me,"
he told her. "With someone you have accused of being less than a
gentleman. Perhaps, as well as being a dissolute gamer, I am also
possessed of unbridled sexual appetites. Perhaps last evening gave
you only the glimmering of a hint of what I am capable of when
my passions are aroused. Are you sure you wish to put your person
and your reputation at such risk?"

She might have laughed if she had not been so incensed.

She took long, angry strides toward him until she was close
enough to point a finger at him and jab it against his chest, like a
blunt dagger, as she spoke. Her voice shook with fury.

"If you so much as attempt to lay one lascivious finger on me,"
she told him, "you may be surprised to discover that your sexual appetites will die an ignominious death and remain dead for all time.
Be warned. I am no man's mistress. I am no man's abject victim, to
be threatened and coerced into whimpering submission. I am my
own mistress, *my lord,* and I am mistress of Pinewood. I will remain
here tonight and every night for the rest of my life. If you truly believe you have a claim to the house, then I daresay you will stay here
too. But I can guarantee that soon you will be glad enough to leave.
You are a rake and a town fop and would be quite incapable of living more than a week in the country without expiring of boredom.
I will endure you for that week. But I will not be bullied or threatened sexually without retaliating in ways you would not enjoy. And
I will not be removed from my rightful home." She stabbed at his
chest one more time—it was a remarkably solid chest. "And now, if
you please, I wish to leave the room in order to resume my interrupted plan of walking out and taking the air."

He stared at her with the same angry expression—with perhaps also a suggestion of shock?—for several moments before standing aside, whisking open the drawing room door, and gesturing with a flourish toward the landing beyond it, while sketching her a mocking bow.

"Far be it from me to hold you against your will," he said. "But I in my turn can guarantee that within a week, or two at the most, you will be forced to abandon your rash determination to share a bachelor establishment with a rake. I will send for that damned will."

Viola ignored the blasphemy with cold civility and swept from the room. He had the deed of Pinewood, she thought as she climbed the stairs to her room. Something was terribly wrong. She had no written proof, only the word of a man long dead. But strangely, foolishly, the thought that crowded all else from her mind was that he—Lord Ferdinand Dudley, that is—had not known she lived here. He had made no attempt to discover who she was. He had not cared enough. Yesterday had meant nothing to him.

Well, it had not meant anything to her either!

4

*V*iola did not, after all, go out walking. She sat for a long
time on the window seat in her bedchamber. Hers was
fortunately not the master bedchamber—at least they
were not to fight over that and perhaps insist upon sharing the same
bed. She had always preferred her present room, with its cheerful
Chinese wallpaper and draperies and screens and its view over the
back of the house rather than the front, over the kitchen garden and
greenhouses, over the long avenue beyond them, culminating in the
tree-dotted hill half a mile away.

Pinewood was hers. No one else had even been interested in
it until it had become the subject of a card game. Lord Ferdinand
Dudley would not be interested either once he recovered from
the novelty of having won it. He was a city man, a dandy, a
fop, a gamer, a rake—and probably many more nasty things.
Once he went back to London, he would forget all about Pinewood
again.

Once he went back to London . . .

Viola got to her feet, smoothed out her dress, straightened her shoulders, and left her room, bound for the kitchen.

"Yes, it is true," she said in answer to all the anxious, inquiring looks turned her way as soon as she walked in. They were all there—Mr. Jarvey; Mr. Paxton, the steward; Jeb Hardinge, the head groom; Samuel Dey, the footman; Hannah; Mrs. Walsh, the cook; Rose, the parlormaid; Tom Abbott, the head gardener. They must have been holding a meeting. "Though I do not believe it for a minute. Lord Ferdinand Dudley claims to be the new owner of Pinewood. But I have no intention of leaving. Indeed, I have every intention of persuading Lord Ferdinand to go away again."

"What do you have in mind, Miss Vi?" Hannah asked. "Oh, I *knew* that man was trouble the minute I set eyes on him. Too handsome for his own good, he is."

"How difficult can it be," Viola asked, "to convince a town tulip that the life of a country squire is not for him?"

"I can think of a few ways without even taxing my brains, Miss Thornhill," Jeb Hardinge said.

"So can I," Mrs. Walsh agreed grimly.

"Let's hear some of these ideas, then," Mr. Paxton suggested, "and see if we can come up with a plan."

Viola sat down at the kitchen table and invited everyone to join her.

A short while later, Viola was walking into the village. She was far too restless to sit still in any vehicle when she might be striding along, trying to keep up with the pace of her teeming thoughts.

How very different two days could be. Yesterday's dream had been very pleasant while it had lasted—more than pleasant. She had lain awake half the night reliving the dance about the maypole, when she had felt more vigorously alive than she had since she did not know when. And reliving his kiss and the feel of his lean man's body against her own.

More fool her, for allowing herself to indulge in dreams, she thought, lengthening her stride. Maybe that gypsy fortune-teller had not been so far off the mark, after all. She should have taken more heed. She should have been more wary.

She stopped first at the vicarage and found both the Reverend and Mrs. Prewitt at home.

"My dear Miss Thornhill," Mrs. Prewitt said when her house-keeper had ushered Viola into the parlor, "what a delightful sur-prise. I fully expected that you would remain at home, exhausted, today."

The vicar beamed at her. "Miss Thornhill," he said. "I have just now finished adding the proceeds from the fête. You will be de-lighted to know that we surpassed last year's total by almost exactly twenty pounds. Is that not significant? So you see, my dear, your daisies were sacrificed to a good cause."

He and his wife laughed over his joke as Viola took her seat.

"It was an extremely generous donation," Mrs. Prewitt said, "es-pecially when one remembers that the gentleman was a stranger."

"He called on me this morning," Viola told them.

"Ah." The vicar rubbed his hands together. "Did he indeed?"

"He claims to be the rightful owner of Pinewood." Viola clasped her hands tightly in her lap. "Most provoking, is it not?"

Both her listeners stared blankly at her for a moment.

"But I was under the impression that Pinewood was yours," Mrs. Prewitt said.

"It *is*," Viola assured them both. "When the late Earl of Bamber sent me here almost two years ago, he changed his will so that it would be mine for the rest of my life. However, the present earl had the deed and chose to wager away the property in a *card* game at a *gaming hell* a short while ago, and lost it." She did not know where the card game had been played, but she chose to assume it had been at the shabbiest, most notorious hell.

"Oh, dear me," the vicar commented, looking down in some concern at his visitor. "But his lordship could not wager away property that does not belong to him, Miss Thornhill. I hope the gentleman was not too disappointed to learn how he had been deceived. He seemed pleasant enough."

"In a *card* game?" Mrs. Prewitt was more satisfyingly shocked than her husband. "We were deceived in him yesterday, then. I did think it very forward of him, I must confess, Miss Thornhill, to make you dance with him about the maypole when he had not been formally presented to you. What a dreadful turn you must have had when he called on you with his claim this morning."

"Oh, I have not allowed him to upset me greatly," Viola assured them. "Indeed I have a plan to persuade him that he would find life at Pinewood vastly uncomfortable. You may both help me if you will..."

A short while later she was outdoors again and continuing the round of visits she had planned. Fortunately everyone was at home, perhaps understandably so after such a busy day yesterday.

Her final call was at the cottage of the Misses Merrywether, who listened to her story with growing amazement and indignation. She had disliked Lord Ferdinand Dudley from the moment she first set eyes on him, Miss Faith Merrywether declared. His manners had been far too easy. And no true gentleman removed his coat in the presence of ladies, even when he was engaged in some sport on a hot day.

He was extremely handsome, Miss Prudence Merrywether conceded, blushing, and of course he had that charming smile, but one knew from experience that handsome, charming gentlemen were never up to any good. Lord Ferdinand Dudley was certainly not up to any if his intention was to drive their dear Miss Thornhill away destitute from Pinewood.

"Oh, he will not drive me away," Viola assured both ladies. "It will be the other way around. *I* shall get rid of *him.*"

"The vicar and Mr. Claypole will see what can be done on your behalf, I am sure," Miss Faith said. "In the meantime, Miss

Thornhill, you must come and live here. You will not be at all in the way."

"That is extremely kind of you, ma'am, but I have no intention of leaving Pinewood," Viola said. "Indeed, it is my plan to—"

But the description of her plan had to be deferred to a more convenient moment. Miss Prudence was so shocked at the mere idea of her returning to the house when there was a single gentleman in residence there that Miss Faith, made of sterner stuff herself, had to send in a hurry for their young maid to fetch burned feathers and hartshorn in order to prevent her sister from swooning dead away. Viola meanwhile chafed her wrists.

"There is no telling what such a libertine might attempt," Miss Faith warned Viola after the crisis had passed and a still-pale Miss Prudence was propped against cushions sipping weak, sweet tea, "if he were to get you alone with no servants in attendance. He might even attempt to *kiss* you. No, no, Prudence, you must not go off again; Miss Thornhill will not return to Pinewood. She will remain here. We will have her things sent for. And we will lock all our doors from now on, even during the daytime. And bolt them too."

"I will be perfectly safe at Pinewood," Viola assured both sisters. "You must not forget that I am surrounded there by my own loyal servants. Hannah has been with me all my life. Besides, Lord Ferdinand will be leaving soon. He is about to discover that life in the country is simply not for him. You can both help me if you will . . ."

On the whole, Viola thought as she made her way homeward, she was pleased with her afternoon's visits. At least all the villagers with whom she was closely acquainted had heard her side of the story before he had had a chance to tell his own. And those she had not told would soon find out for themselves. News and gossip traveled on the wind, she sometimes thought.

As far as those families who lived in the country were concerned, well, she would be able to talk to several of them this evening when she dined at Crossings with the Claypoles.

Lord Ferdinand Dudley would dine alone at Pinewood. Viola smiled with sheer malice. But thinking of the man only served to remind her that she could no longer approach her home with the usual glad lifting of her spirits. She looked ahead up the lawn toward the house and wondered if he was standing at one of the windows, watching her. She wondered if she would encounter him as soon as she entered the house—in the hall, on the stairs, in the upper corridor.

It was intolerable to know that a stranger had invaded her most private domain. But there was no help for it, for the moment at least. And she could not afford to allow her footsteps to lag. She had an evening engagement to prepare for.

She was striding along the terrace from the stable side of the house several minutes later, determined not to tiptoe fearfully into her own home, when she was met by the sight of him striding onto it from the opposite direction. They both abruptly stopped walking.

He was still in his riding clothes. He was hatless. He looked disorientingly male in what she had made into her own essentially female preserve. And he was clearly making himself right at home. He must have been down by the river or out behind the house, inspecting the kitchen gardens and the greenhouses.

He bowed stiffly.

She curtsied stiffly—and then hurried on her way to the house without looking at him again. Whether he was coming in behind her or was still rooted to the spot or had gone to jump into the fountain, she neither knew nor cared.

"Mr. Jarvey," she said, seeing him pacing about the hall looking unaccustomedly lost. "Have Hannah come up to me, please."

She continued on her way upstairs, assuring herself with every step that she hurried only because there was little time left before she must leave for Crossings.

If only he were not so handsome, she thought. Or so young.

If only she had not flirted with him yesterday. Not that she had really *flirted*, of course. It had been her duty as a member of the fête committee to be pleasant to everyone, villager and stranger alike. She had merely been amiable.

Viola sighed as she hurried along the upper corridor in the direction of her bedchamber. A spade might as well be called a spade. She had flirted with him.

She *wished* she had not.

She would not allow her mind even to touch upon that kiss. But she could feel the hardness of his thighs against her own and the warm softness of his lips parted over her own, and she could smell his cologne all the time she kept her mind off that particular incident.

" 'Each with his bonny lass.' "

Ferdinand determinedly clamped his teeth together after singing just the one phrase and drew a leather-bound book randomly off a library shelf. He had sung the song with cheerful gusto as he approached the house for the first time many hours before. But it had stuck in his unconscious mind, as songs sometimes do, so that he had caught himself singing or humming snatches of it ever since, until he was heartily sick of it. It was a ridiculous song, anyway, with all its interminable fa-la-las.

And he was definitely not in the mood for music. He was rattled. And annoyed too—with himself because he had allowed *her* to dampen his spirits, with *her* because she had done the dampening. And with Bamber—no, make that plural. He was furious with the Bambers, father and son. What the devil sort of responsible heads of the family had either of them been? The one had sent her here with promises he had forgotten to honor—or had had no intention of honoring in the first place—and the other seemed unaware of her very existence.

He himself had allowed her to dig in her heels and put him in the embarrassing situation of sharing a house with an unmarried young lady. And a damned gorgeous one too, though that had nothing to say to the matter. He should have kicked her out. Or stayed at the Boar's Head himself until that infernal will could arrive and convince her that she had no claim to the property.

Ferdinand ran his fingers through his hair and glanced at the letters on the desk, sealed and ready to go in the morning. Perhaps he should simply go and get the will himself. Better yet, he should go and send it to her with a trusty messenger and a formal notice to quit. He would return after she had left.

But it would seem so damnably *weak* to turn tail and run and let someone else do his dirty business for him. It was just not the way he did things. It was not the Dudley way. If she could be stubborn, he could be ten times more so. If she was willing to risk her reputation by living here with him unchaperoned, on her own head be it. He was not going to worry *his* conscience over it.

He should go to bed before she returned from her dinner party, Ferdinand thought. He had no particular wish to encounter her again tonight—or ever again, if it came to that. But dash it all, it was not even midnight. He looked about him at the tastefully furnished library, with its cozy sitting area about the fireplace, its elegant desk, and its small but superior collection of books, which he had noticed were not even dusty. Did that mean she was a reader? He did not want to know. But he liked the library. He could feel right at home here.

Once she was gone.

He had not wanted to play for the wretched property in the first place, Ferdinand recalled, replacing the book on the shelf when it became obvious that his mind was too distracted to allow him to read tonight. He had never been much interested in card playing. He preferred physical sport. He liked the sort of extravagant dares with which the betting books at the various gentlemen's clubs always

abounded—particularly the ones that involved him in the perform-
ance of some dangerous or daring physical feat.

He had played that night at Brookes's up to the limit he always
privately allowed himself, and then he had risen to leave. There was
a party he had half promised to look in on. But Leavering, who had
accompanied him to the club, was just then being called away by the
news that his wife was in childbed and likely to deliver at any moment, and Bamber, loud and obnoxious in his cups—as he invariably was, damn him—was accusing the prospective papa of making
a lame excuse to leave with his winnings before he, the drunken earl,
had had a chance to win them back. His luck was changing, he had
declared. He could feel it in his bones.

Ferdinand had caught his friend by the arm just when the scene
was threatening to turn ugly and was beginning to attract attention.
He had offered to take Leavering's place and had tossed five hundred pounds onto the table.

A few minutes later he had been exclaiming in protest over the
signed voucher Bamber had cast onto the table in place of money. It
had represented the promise of property that no one in the card
room had ever heard of—it was certainly not Bamber's principal
seat or any of his better known secondary properties. Somewhere
called Pinewood Manor in Somersetshire. Somewhere probably
nowhere near as valuable as the five hundred pounds Ferdinand had
thrown in, one of the players had warned.

Ferdinand would not have played any man for his home—no true
gentleman would. But Pinewood was apparently some subsidiary, in-
ferior property. And so he had played—and won. And discovered
the next day from both Bamber's solicitor and Tresham's that
Pinewood really did exist and really was his. When in a pang of conscience, despite everything, he had called on Bamber the day after
that to offer the return of the property in exchange for some mone-
tary settlement of the gaming debt, the earl, nursing a colossal hang-
over from some orgy the previous night, had announced that talking

made his head feel as if it were about to explode. Dudley would doubtless humor him by going away. And he was certainly welcome to Pinewood, which Bamber was unlikely to miss, having never set eyes on the place or seen a penny in rents to his knowledge.

And so Ferdinand had set out with a clear conscience to discover and inspect his new property. He had never owned, or expected to own, any land. He was the son of a duke, it was true, and enormously wealthy, to boot—his father had left him a generous portion, and both his mother and her sister had left him their not-insignificant fortunes on their deaths. But he was a younger son. Tresham had inherited Acton Park and all the other estates with the ducal titles.

Drat! Ferdinand thought suddenly, lifting his head and listening. The knocker had rattled against the front door and it was being opened. There was the sound of voices in the hall. More than one. More than two. Either all the servants had come upstairs to greet her return, or else she had brought people back with her. At almost midnight?

His first impulse was to stay where he was until they were all gone. But that butler fellow knew he was in here, and a Dudley could not have it said that he had skulked out of sight rather than establish from the outset that he was master of his own domain. He trod purposefully across the library and opened the door.

There were five persons standing in the hall—Jarvey, a small, plumpish woman who looked like a maid, Viola Thornhill, and two strangers, a man and a woman. The man was not entirely a stranger, though. He was the dry stick who had given it as his opinion yesterday that wagering was inappropriate to a church fête.

They all looked his way. Viola Thornhill herself did so by glancing over her shoulder at him, her eyebrows raised, her lips slightly parted. She was wearing a green silk opera cloak, the wide hood spread becomingly over her shoulders, her head with its high coronet of dark red braids bare of any covering or adornment.

Damn! Where the devil had he seen her before this trip to the hinterlands?

"Good evening." He stepped into the hall. "Will you present me, Miss Thornhill?"

The maid disappeared upstairs. The butler melted into the background. The three remaining people all gazed at him with undisguised hostility.

"This is Miss Claypole," Viola Thornhill said, indicating the tall, thin woman of indeterminate age. "And her brother, Mr. Claypole."

She did not introduce him to them. But then, it was probably unnecessary. He had doubtless formed the chief topic of conversation for the evening. Ferdinand bowed.

Neither visitor veered from the upright.

"This will not do, sir," Claypole said with pompous severity. "It is extremely improper for you, a single gentleman, to be occupying the home of a single, virtuous lady."

Ferdinand's right hand found the gilded handle of his quizzing glass and raised it to his eye. "I agree with you," he said curtly after a significant pause. "Or would if your facts were correct. But they are topsy-turvy, my good fellow. It is the single, virtuous female who is occupying *my* home."

"Now, see here—" Claypole took one aggressive stride toward him.

Ferdinand dropped his glass on its ribbon and held up his hand. "Take a damper," he advised. "You do not want to go that route, I do assure you. Certainly not in the presence of ladies."

"You have no need to rush to my defense, Mr. Claypole," Viola Thornhill said. "Thank you both for escorting me home in the carriage, but—"

"You will but me no buts, Viola," Miss Claypole said in strident tones. "This scandalous situation calls for an act of demonstrable propriety. Since Lord Ferdinand Dudley has chosen to remain at Pinewood instead of removing decently to the inn, then I will remain here as your chaperon. Indefinitely. For as long as I am needed. Humphrey will have a trunk of my things sent over in the morning."

Some of the tension had drained out of Claypole's body and flushed face. He had clearly realized how foolhardy it would be to come to blows. Ferdinand turned his attention to the sister.

"I thank you, ma'am," he said, "but your presence here will be quite unnecessary. I cannot answer for Miss Thornhill's reputation, but I can answer for her virtue. I have no intention of having my wicked way with her as soon as we are alone together—alone except for a number of servants, that is."

Miss Claypole appeared to add an extra couple of inches to her height as she inhaled audibly.

"Your vulgarity is boundless," she said. "Well, sir, I am here to guard Miss Thornhill's reputation as well as her virtue. I would not trust you one inch farther than I could see you. We have been informed today—my mother, my brother, and I—that you forced her to dance *about the maypole* with you last evening. Do not think to deny it. There were any number of witnesses."

"Bertha—" Viola Thornhill began.

Ferdinand had his glass to his eye again. "In that case," he said, "I will not perjure myself by denying it, ma'am. Now, I believe you and your brother are leaving?"

"I will not leave this house unless I am thrown bodily out," the lady said.

"You tempt me, ma'am," Ferdinand told her quietly. He turned his attention to Claypole. "Good night, sir. You *will* take Miss Claypole with you when you leave?"

"Miss Thornhill." Claypole possessed himself of one of her hands. "Do you see now the foolishness of insisting upon returning here? Was not my mama right? Bertha is your friend. I flatter myself that I am more than just a friend. Come back with us to Crossings until this matter can be settled."

"Thank you again, but I will not leave my own home, sir," she said. "And you must not upset yourself on my behalf, Bertha. I have Hannah and the other servants. I do not need a female companion."

"It is a good thing too," Ferdinand said briskly. "Because you won't be having one. Not in this house."

She looked at him with raised eyebrows and then turned away again to bid her companions good night.

"This is highly improper—" Claypole began.

"Good night." Ferdinand strode to the double doors, opened them with a flourish while Jarvey still hovered uncertainly in the background, and gestured toward the darkness outside.

They went unwillingly, but they did go. They had little choice without risking violence. The woman might have been game, Ferdinand judged, but the man certainly would not have been.

"I suppose," he said after he had closed the door behind them, turning on Viola Thornhill, who was removing her cloak and handing it to the butler, "he is your beau?"

"Do you?" she said. "Thank you, Mr. Jarvey, you will not be needed again tonight."

Ferdinand could have argued, since Jarvey was now *his* servant, but he would not appear petty.

"Claypole is a craven jackass," he said. "If the situation were reversed, I would have drawn the cork of any man who insisted on your being unchaperoned if you remained here. And then I would have dragged you out of here whether you wished to go or not."

"How comforting," she said, "to know that I am sharing a house with a caveman. I presume, my lord, that would have been by the hair, while you flourished a club in the other hand? Such a manly image."

He wished she had not removed her cloak. The darker green evening gown she wore beneath it was not in any way indecent. It fell in soft, shimmering folds from beneath her bosom to her ankles, and the bodice, though low, would have looked almost conservative in a London ballroom. But the garment did nothing whatsoever to hide the alluring curves of the woman beneath it. And he knew just what those curves felt like pressed to his own body, dammit.

Lord! Perhaps he should have stayed at the Boar's Head after all, stubbornness notwithstanding.

"What you are doing," he said, "is insisting upon sharing a house with a man who knows what is what. And it is not at all the thing for you to be here with me. That idiot was right about that, at least."

She had crossed the hall to the staircase. She turned with her foot on the bottom stair.

"What, Lord Ferdinand?" she said. "Are you considering ravishing me after all, then? Must I race for my room? At least I must be thankful that I have a head start on you."

She had a saucy tongue. He had noticed it before.

"Believe me, ma'am," he said, "if I wanted to catch you, you would not even make it to the top of the staircase."

She smiled sweetly at him. "Did you enjoy your dinner?"

It was a strange question to ask at such a moment—until he understood the reason. They had both been out for the evening. She had had a dinner engagement, a fact he had learned with considerable relief, until the butler had informed him that since Miss Thornhill had not been expected to dine at home, all there was in the house to set on the dinner table for him was the leftover beef from two days ago, their having all dined in the village the evening before, his lordship would understand. But even though the beef still looked and smelled and even tasted unspoiled, the butler suggested that he should perhaps bear in mind that the weather *had* been unseasonably warm. And the pantry had never kept the food as cool as the cook would like, the butler had added as an aside. And no one could ever discover where the flies all managed to get in.

Ferdinand had announced his intention of dining at the Boar's

Head. The food there had not been quite as appetizing as it had been yesterday, nor the service quite as prompt or friendly, but he had put those facts down to tiredness on the part of the staff after a day of celebrating.

Now, with a simple question, Viola Thornhill had made all clear to him. He must be a fool not to have realized sooner. He was already—both at Pinewood and in the village—carrying around the label of local enemy number one, was he?

"Extremely well, thank you," he said. "Did you?"

She smiled again and turned to climb the stairs without saying another word. In the light of the hall candles, the satin of her gown shimmered over the feminine sway of her hips.

Devil take it, but it was a hot night for May.

5

❦

erdinand might have been convinced that he had not slept all night had he not been woken so rudely while it was still dark. He shot out of bed rather as if a spring had broken through the mattress, catapulted him in an upward arc, and brought him down flat on his feet beside the bed.

"The devil!" he exclaimed, running the fingers of one hand through his disheveled hair. "What in thunder?" He had no idea what had disturbed him. For the moment he could not even recall where he was.

And then the raucous noise was repeated. He strode across to the open window, flung back the curtains, and thrust out his head. Dawn was the merest smudge of gray on the eastern horizon. He shivered in the predawn chill and for once wished he wore a night-shirt to bed. *There* it was, he saw as he glared downward, strutting along the terrace before the house as if it owned the universe.

A cockerel!

"Go to the devil!" Ferdinand instructed it, and the bird, startled out of its arrogant complacency, scuttled halfway along the terrace before recovering its dignity and crowing again.

Cock-a-doodle-doooo.

Ferdinand in his turn scuttled back to bed after closing both the window and the curtains. He had been unable to fall asleep after coming to bed at midnight. Partly, of course, that had been due to his knowledge that he was sharing his house with an unmarried young lady—who also happened to be voluptuous beauty personified—and had refused to allow her a companion to lend a measure of respectability to the situation. Mainly, though, it was because of the silence. He had lived all his adult years in London, ever since coming down from Oxford seven years before, at the age of twenty. He was unaccustomed to silence. He found it unnerving.

Why was a cockerel allowed to run loose so close to the house? he wondered suddenly. Was he to be woken thus every night (one could hardly call it morning, after all)? He thumped his pillow, which was about the most lumpy, uncomfortable specimen of pillowhood he had ever encountered, and tried to burrow his head into such a position in it that instant sleep would be induced.

Five minutes later he was still very wide awake.

He was remembering how she had looked in that shimmering satin evening gown. He was remembering how her shapely body had felt pressed against his own body, behind the oak tree in the village. And he thought about the fact that she was sleeping in a room not far from his own.

Ferdinand made the sudden discovery that it was the heaviness of the bedcovers that was preventing him from falling back to sleep. He pushed them aside, turned his hot pillow and thumped it again, tried to find a soft, cool nook for his head, failed miserably, and shivered in the chilly air, which was assaulting his naked body on three sides. The blankets were out of reach unless he sat up to grab them.

Devil take it, his sleep had been ruined. And she was entirely to blame. Why had she not taken herself off as any decent woman would, or at least taken the week he had offered before he lost his temper, so that he might now be sleeping the peaceful sleep of the just at the Boar's Head in Trellick? Bedamned to her, he thought unchivalrously. She was going to have to learn who was master at Pinewood, and the sooner the better. Today she would learn—when today came. He grimaced as he looked about his bed-chamber, into which not even the suggestion of daylight had yet penetrated.

He sat up on the side of the bed and thrust both hands through his hair again. Dammit, in his more normal life he often had not even gone to bed at this hour. Yet here he was, getting up. To do what, for God's sake? Eat his breakfast? It would serve those servants right—they had *deliberately* sent him off to the village for his dinner last evening—if he went downstairs, loudly demanding food. But they would probably just slap that cold green beef on a plate for him. Read, then? He was not in the mood. Write some letters? But he had scribbled off notes to Tresham and Angie last evening to be sent this morning with the letter to Bamber.

Ferdinand got to his feet, stretched, yawned until his jaws cracked, and shivered. He would go out for a ride and blow away some cobwebs before coming back and laying down the law. He *enjoyed* early morning rides, after all, he told himself grimly and not altogether truthfully. Anyway, he thought as he strode off in the direction of his dressing room, this hardly qualified as early morning. It was still the middle of the night, for God's sake.

He found his riding clothes in one of the wardrobes without ringing for his valet, dressed, and headed for the outdoors without stopping to shave. He had raced the sun, he saw grimly. Although it was no longer quite dark out, the world was lit only by a very gray twilight. It suited his mood to perfection.

He stalked off to the stables in the fervent hope that there would be a few sleepy grooms there to bark at.

*   *   *

The cockerel had awakened Viola even though her room was at the
back of the house. But then, of course, she had been expecting it
and had been sleeping lightly in anticipation of it. It seemed impossible to her that anyone in the house, especially someone whose
room overlooked the terrace, could have slept through the alarum.
She had chuckled with open malice when, ten or fifteen minutes
later, she had heard a door open farther along the corridor and the
sound of booted feet receding in the direction of the staircase.

And then she had dozed off again.

"His lordship was out the door, fit to be tied, not fifteen minutes
after the first cock-crow," Hannah reported later as she helped Viola
dress and braided and coiled her hair. "In a proper rage he was, apparently, when he took his horse out. And then he went galloping
off, cursing and scowling, the Lord knows where. You stay out of his
way, Miss Vi. You let us servants handle everything this morning."

"But I can hardly wait to witness his rage for myself, Hannah,"
Viola assured her. "I would not miss this morning for any consideration. Perhaps by noon he will be on his way back to London and
we will be rid of him."

Hannah sighed as she straightened the combs and brushes on
the dressing table. "I wish it could be that easy, lovey," she said.

So did Viola. There was a yawning empty feeling somewhere in
the region of her stomach that she was trying hard to ignore. This
was not a game she played with Lord Ferdinand Dudley, after all.
Her home, her income, her hard-won peace, her very identity were
severely at risk.

Viola was seated at the breakfast table later, still eating, when he
strode into the dining room. Even though she had been expecting him
and had steeled herself to having her privacy invaded, her heart felt as

if it were hammering against her ribs. If this had to be happening at all, why could he not be an old man or an ugly man or in some way an unappealing man? Why should she be made to feel as if the very essence of maleness had just filled the room to suffocate her?

He had obviously come straight from his ride. His buff riding breeches hugged his long, well-muscled legs like a second skin. His boots must have been freshly polished last night and still shone. He was wearing a well-tailored brown riding coat with a white shirt beneath. She had spent enough years in London to recognize in him a regular top sawyer, an out-and-outer, as other gentlemen would call him. His dark hair was tousled from his hat and the outdoors. His face glowed with healthy color.

He was also smiling and looking annoyingly good-humored.

"Good morning, Miss Thornhill." He sketched her a bow. "And what a beautiful morning it is. I was awoken by a cockerel crowing beneath my window and so was out riding in time to watch the sun rise. I had forgotten how exhilarating life in the country can be."

He rubbed his hands together and looked about the room, hunger written all over his face. The sideboard was empty. So was the table, except for Viola's plate and cup and saucer. There were no servants present. He looked a little less cheerful.

"Good morning, my lord." Viola smiled placidly. "And to think that I tiptoed past your room a short while ago, believing that you must be sleeping on late in the country air. It *is* chilly in here, is it not? I'll have the fire lit and your breakfast brought up. I took the liberty of ordering what I thought you might like." She got to her feet and pulled on the bell rope beside the sideboard.

"Thank you." He took the chair at the head of the table, which she had left vacant for him, as she did not want the morning cluttered with unnecessary wrangling over precedence.

She still had eggs and sausage and toast on her plate—a far larger breakfast than her usual fare of toast and coffee. She picked up her knife and fork and continued eating, chewing each mouthful with slow relish, even though everything suddenly tasted like straw.

"The avenue behind the house must be delightful for walking as well as riding," he said. "The grass is well kept, and the trees on either side are as straight as two lines of soldiers on parade. It is a marvel of nature how they can hide an army of birds, is it not, so that one hears a thousand voices and yet is unable to see a single chorister until one of them decides to fly from one branch to another?"

"I have always enjoyed strolling there," she said.

"One can see for miles around from the top of the hill," he said. "I would have loved it as a boy. It reminds me a little of the hills at Acton Park, where I grew up. I would have been king of the castle and held it against all comers. Correction." He grinned, and Viola was unwillingly reminded of the dashing stranger at the fête. "I daresay my brother would have been king and I would have been his loyal henchman. But henchmen have the more exciting life, you know. They fight dragons and assorted other villains, while the king merely sits on his throne looking bored and supercilious and issuing orders and cursing foully."

"Gracious! Is that what your brother used to do?" She almost laughed.

"Elder brothers can be an abomination."

But Viola had no wish to hear about his childhood or his family. She did not want to see his boyish grin. She wanted him in a towering rage. She wanted *him* cursing foully. He was rather more frightening this way. Did he know it? Was this behavior deliberate? A cat toying with a mouse? He was drumming his fingertips on the table, though, and glancing at the door, sure signs that he did not feel as relaxed or as cheerful as he looked.

Viola popped a forkful of egg into her mouth.

"They are certainly taking their time in the kitchen," he said after a short silence. "I must have a word with Jarvey."

How dare he! Mr. Jarvey was *her* butler. The old Earl of Bamber had employed him specifically to serve her. But it was not part of her plan to quarrel with this man just yet.

"Does it seem a long wait to you?" She looked at him in cheerful surprise. "I am so sorry. The kitchen is at an inconvenient distance and the stairs are steep. Mr. Jarvey is not as young as he used to be and sometimes has trouble with his legs. The cook is a little slow too—and absentminded. But good servants are not easily come by in the country, you know, and one is wise to keep what one has even if it does not quite measure up to town standards."

The door opened as she spoke and the butler appeared, an uncovered plate in one hand, a vast tankard of ale in the other. Viola gazed at both with admiration. How had Mrs. Walsh been able to pile the plate so high without everything sliding off? And where had she found such an enormous and hideous tankard? As Mr. Jarvey set his load down on the table, she could see eggs, sausages, kidneys, and bacon as well as slices of toast balancing on one edge of the plate. But the pièce de résistance was a large, thick beefsteak, which must surely have been shown briefly on both sides to the fire and then slapped onto the plate. It was swimming in red juice.

She transferred her gaze to Lord Ferdinand's face, which looked somewhat astonished for a moment.

"I was sure you would enjoy a hearty country breakfast after a vigorous ride, my lord," she said—and remembered too late that she was supposed to have thought him still fast asleep in his bed as a result of the country air.

"Yes, indeed." He rubbed his hands together again, in apparent glee.

Was it possible that such a breakfast really did look appetizing to him? She waited with bated breath for him to taste it. But there was another detail to be taken care of without delay.

"Mr. Jarvey," she directed, "would you light the fire? His lordship is chilly."

The butler bent with agility to the task while Lord Ferdinand watched him. Viola hoped he was not noticing that there was no sign of creaky knees. And then she watched covertly as he speared a kidney with his fork and popped it in his mouth. She could have crowed with glee when he set his knife and fork down with a clatter.

"The food is cold," he said in astonishment.

"Oh, dear." She looked at him with apologetic concern. "I am so accustomed to it that I did not think to warn you. I daresay the cook prepared your food some time ago and forgot—again—to keep it warm in the oven until you came in. Is that what happened, Mr. Jarvey? Perhaps you would have it warmed up and brought back when it is ready. Will you wait for half an hour or so, my lord?"

The fire in the hearth crackled to life, and the butler straightened up and took one step forward.

"No, no." Lord Ferdinand held up one staying hand. "Never mind. I really do not need such a large breakfast. The toast will do me well enough. Fortunately, toast is appetizing even when cold. Normally I would prefer coffee to ale—perhaps you will remember that tomorrow, Jarvey?" He picked up a slice of toast and bit into it. It made a loud, crunching noise, suggesting to Viola that it was stone cold and crisp enough to smash into smithereens if he accidentally dropped it.

Viola, glancing toward the fireplace, raised her napkin to her nose and controlled her own reactions until Lord Ferdinand began to cough.

"Oh, dear," she said. The fireplace was belching smoke. "There must be a bird's nest in the chimney again. That is forever happening. And it always takes *days* to fetch a sweep to clean it out." She coughed into her napkin and felt her eyes begin to sting. "There is no chimney sweep in the village, you see, and the nearest town is eight miles away."

"One can only hope," Lord Ferdinand said, jumping to his feet and hurrying across the room to throw first one and then the other window wide, "that the nest is empty at this particular moment. Otherwise I daresay we can enjoy roast bird for dinner."

Something in his tone alerted Viola. He *knew* at last. He understood. But he was not going to lose his temper as she had hoped. He was going to play out the game, perhaps on the theory that good humor would annoy her far more than scowls and bellows. He was perfectly right too, of course. But it did not matter. At least he would understand now what he was facing—his lone person, and perhaps those of his handful of servants, pitted against a houseful of people bent on making his life as uncomfortable as they possibly could. She wondered how he had enjoyed his pillows last night.

"Sometimes," she said, shivering despite herself as a fresh breeze from the outdoors fluttered the edges of her napkin and wrapped itself about her person like an icy cloak, "I believe that the few advantages of living in the country are far outweighed by the disadvantages. You may leave, thank you, Mr. Jarvey. We must simply hope that the day will be warm enough that we can live without fires in only a moderate degree of discomfort."

The butler made for the door.

"Don't leave yet, Jarvey," Lord Ferdinand instructed him, staying close to the window. "Find me a good stout groom or gardener, will you? One with a head for heights? Perhaps one who is familiar with the rooftop and the chimneys? I daresay there *is* such a person. I would wager on it, in fact. I will go up there with him when I have finished my ale and see if we can rescue the poor homeless birds. Unless it is too late for them, of course, as undoubtedly it is for their nest."

Viola's eyes were watering and aching quite abominably. He was going to be a worthy foe, she realized with a sinking heart. Well, they would see who would win the final victory. He was grossly outnumbered. And she was no mean foe herself. She had far more to lose than he, after all—a thought that conspired to make her egg sit quite uncomfortably in her stomach.

"You will fall and kill yourself," she predicted before indulging in a prolonged coughing fit into her napkin. What on earth had Eli stuffed up the chimney? And why should she care if Lord Ferdinand came to grief?

"You must not fear for my safety, ma'am," he said as the butler slipped from the room. "One of my more notable escapades, though admittedly it was back in my salad days, was in response to a wager that I could not move from one end of a long London street to the other without once touching the ground. The dare was made more interesting by the fact that it was a wet, windy, moonless night, and there was a time limit of one hour. I did it in forty-three minutes."

"I suppose," she said more tartly than she intended, "you rode your horse."

"And took forty-three minutes?" He chuckled. "Alas, the men who issued the dare considered that possibility in advance. No form of conveyance was allowed except my feet. I did it over the rooftops."

"You have won my warmest admiration, my lord," she said, getting to her feet and doing nothing to hide her scorn.

"Where are you going?" he asked.

She raised her eyebrows and looked coolly at him through the gradually dispersing smoke haze. "My movements are none of your affair, my lord," she said—and then wished she had chosen different words. His eyes moved down her body, stripping her of clothes as they proceeded—or so it seemed. She clamped her teeth together and glared.

"Perhaps after I have dealt with the chimney," he said, "you will take a walk with me, Miss Thornhill."

"To show you the park?" she asked incredulously. "It is my private domain and is shown only to privileged visitors."

"Of which number I am not one," he said.

"Right."

"But I am not a visitor, am I?" he asked in that soft voice that insisted on curling itself about her spine despite all her determination not to be cowed by him.

"If you wish to find your way around the park, ask someone else to show you," she said, turning to the door.

"And find myself abandoned in a field with an ill-tempered bull?" he said. "Or in quicksand beside the river? I was not asking for a guided tour. I wish to talk with you, and the outdoors seems like the best venue. We need to forget the fun and games, Miss Thornhill, and come to some decision about your future—which will not be spent at Pinewood, by the way. There is no point in postponing the inevitable. Even if you insist upon staying here until a copy of the old earl's will arrives, you are going to have to deal with reality after that event. It would be best for you to be prepared. Walk with me."

She looked back at him over her shoulder. He had begun with a request but had ended with an order. He was so typical of his type. Lesser mortals existed merely to perform his will.

"I have household duties to perform," she said. "After that I will stroll down on the river walk. If you care to join me there, Lord Ferdinand, I will not turn you away. But you will be my guest. You will not issue commands to me—not now or ever. Is that understood?"

He folded his arms and reclined back against the windowsill, looking both relaxed and elegant as he did so. His lips were pursed and there was something that might have been amusement—or was it merely contempt?—lurking in his eyes.

"English has always been my first language," he said.

It was clear he did not intend to say anything else. She left the room, realizing as she did so that all the tricks she and the servants had dreamed up so far had only challenged him and caused him to dig in his heels, more determined than ever to stay. It had been perfectly predictable, of course. Games and tricks must be the breath of life to a bored London beau.

Well, they would see what he would do about everything else that was in store for him today.

What would she dream up next? Ferdinand wondered as he leaned back against the windowsill without making any attempt to put out the fire. It would burn itself down soon and he was well enough removed from the worst effects of the smoke. After last night's dinner offering, he should have been more alert to the significance of a cockerel apparently gone astray from the home farm and of a cold, undercooked breakfast. But it had taken the smoking chimney to open his eyes—or rather, to make them smart and water.

She actually thought she could drive him away.

His vigorous ride had blown away his irritation at being woken at such an ungodly hour. And toast—even cold, slightly burned toast—had always been sufficient to satisfy his hunger at breakfast. Smoking chimneys were simply a challenge. As for the threat of spoiled beef and flies' eggs last evening—well, he could take a joke as well as the next man. Indeed, he was tempted to join in the horseplay and dream up a few schemes of his own to convince Miss Viola Thornhill that it really was not a comfortable thing to be sharing a bachelor establishment with a man. He could easily tramp mud through the house, leave mess and mayhem behind him wherever he went, acquire a few unruly dogs, wander about the house only half dressed, forget to shave . . . well, he could be endlessly irritating if he chose.

But the trouble was, this was no game.

The devil of it was that he was feeling sorry for her this morning. And guilty, for God's sake, as if *he* were the villain of the piece. The very silliness of this morning's amateurish pranks—and yesterday's—was proof of how desperate she was.

She had shown no inclination to accept his offer to send her to Jane, Duchess of Tresham, his sister-in-law. She had not jumped for

joy at the prospect of going to Bamber Court. She had not suggested any alternatives of her own. She seemed markedly unwilling
to face up to reality. What else could he suggest? He was going to
have to think of something. The only thing he was sure of was that
he did not have the stomach to throw her out bodily or have her
forcibly removed by a magistrate or constable. He had always been
the weak member of the Dudley family in that respect, he thought
uneasily. No backbone. But dammit, he felt *sorry* for her. She was a
young innocent in the process of having all her comfort and security ripped away from her.

Ferdinand shook off his dilemma and pushed himself away
from the windowsill. First things first. There being no hot coffee to
tempt him to sit down at the table again—and he had to admit that
the sight of that beefsteak made his stomach feel decidedly rebel-
lious—it was time to go roof climbing.

After going belowstairs to discuss the day's menu with Mrs. Walsh,
Viola went to the library, where she intended to spend time bringing the household books up to date. But there was a letter on the
desk, one that must have arrived with the morning post. She
snatched it up and looked eagerly at the handwriting. *Yes!* It was
from Claire. She was tempted to break the seal and read the contents without further delay, but of course the house was no longer
her own. He might walk in upon her at any moment and ask one of
his impertinent questions, as he had after breakfast. *Where are you going?* It was demeaning, to say the least.

Viola slid the unopened letter into the side pocket of her morning dress. There would be more privacy outdoors.

But the outdoors did not look particularly private when she
stepped out through the unattended front doors. In fact, the box
garden below the terrace was dotted with people—the butler, the

head groom, the head gardener and both his assistants, the footman, Rose, Hannah, two male strangers who must be Lord Ferdinand's servants—all standing stock-still facing the house and gazing skyward. Rose had one hand over her eyes, a pointless affectation, since her fingers were spread.

No, Viola thought, correcting her first impression as she stood looking at them all for a moment, it was not skyward they were gazing, but *roofward.* Of course!

"It still don't make no sense why he didn't send for the sweep," she heard one of the undergardeners say to the other. "It don't make no sense to clean a chimney from the top."

"Eli'll fall right through and crack his skull in the hearth, you mark my words," the other predicted with ghoulish relish.

"Aye. *And* burn all his hair off."

Viola went down to join them at a run. He really had gone up there? He had not been bluffing? He and Eli, the groom's young apprentice? She did not want to look. She had no head for heights and could not imagine how anyone did.

"Hush your babbling!" the head gardener instructed his subordinates. "You'll distract their attention."

Viola turned and looked upward—and her legs turned to jelly. The attic window was opened wide onto the small balcony beyond it. But none of the tall chimneys could be reached from there. The rest of the roof was steeply sloped and covered with gray slates, which looked as smooth as an egg and twice as slippery. Lord Ferdinand Dudley and Eli were standing on the balcony, the former with his hands on his hips and his head tipped back to survey the roof above him. He had shed both his riding coat and his waistcoat.

"Jeb," Viola said in a loud whisper, "how did Eli plug the chimney? From below or from above?" She had assumed the former. She would never have consented to allowing him to clamber over the roof, putting his life at risk.

"The rags would have caught on fire if they were too low, Miss Thornhill," the groom explained to her. "He went up after he fetched the cockerel. Swore afterward that he didn't have the head to do it again, mind. But his lordship made him go."

Well, they had not stepped away from the relative safety of the flat balcony yet. The whispering and shushing were unnecessary.

"Eli!" Viola called, bracketing her mouth with her hands so that the sound of her voice would carry better. "Come down from there immediately before you break your neck. I do not care what Lord Ferdinand says to the contrary."

They both looked down. Viola could just imagine how precarious their safety looked from up there. It was bad enough from below.

"Come down!" she called again. "Both of you."

Even across the distance Viola could see Lord Ferdinand's grin as he set a hand on the boy's shoulder and said something that could not be heard from below. And then he swung first one long leg and then the other over the low rail that separated the balcony from the slate roof. He began the climb upward, using both his hands and his feet. Eli stayed where he was.

Rose stifled a shriek, and Mr. Jarvey admonished her sotto voce.

Viola would have sat down on the bench that circled the fountain if she could have moved the necessary six feet to reach it. As it was, she had to stand still, both hands pressed over her mouth. The fool! The imbecile! He would fall and break every bone in his body, and she would have his death on her conscience forevermore. That was probably what he wanted.

But he reached the peak of the roof without mishap. He pulled himself up beside the chimney that connected with the dining room fireplace among others and peered over the top of it—it reached up to his chest.

Foolish man. *Idiot* man!

"It won't do no good," Jeb Hardinge muttered. "He won't be able to reach down far enough."

Then Rose shrieked, the butler scolded, and Lord Ferdinand Dudley braced his hands on top of the chimney, pulled himself up until he could sit on the edge of it, and swung his legs to the inside.

"He won't be happy till he's killed himself," Hannah said.

"He's a jolly good sport, I must say," the footman observed, but Viola only half heard him. Lord Ferdinand Dudley was disappearing—had disappeared—inside the chimney.

He would fall through and kill himself. He would get stuck and die a slow and horrible death. If he survived, she would kill him with her bare hands.

It was probably two minutes, but felt more like two hours, before he reappeared—or at least a blackened version of him did. His face looked as black as his hair. His shirt was gray. He held aloft a fistful of blackened rags with a black hand and grinned down at his audience, his teeth startlingly white even from such a distance.

"Not a bird's nest after all," he called out, "but some mysterious flying object, doubtless from the moon." He dropped the rags, which tumbled in slow disorder down over the roof and drifted off its edge to litter the terrace below.

How was he going to get down?

He did it in a matter of moments, loping carelessly, for all the world as if he were descending a grassy slope to a soft lawn below. When he reached the railing and the balcony where Eli still stood, he vaulted over the railing and turned to wave one hand. The boy was laughing and applauding.

"He has pluck. One must grant him that," Jeb Hardinge said.

"A jolly good sport," the footman agreed.

"He might have made Eli do it, like he threatened," the head gardener added, "but he did it himself. You won't find too many gents what would be as sporting as that."

"The thing of it is, you see," one of the strangers said, watching his master and Eli disappear through the attic window, "his lordship can't bear to stand by watching while someone else has all the fun. This was *nothing*. I could tell you—"

But Viola had heard enough. "Mr. Jarvey," she said coldly before setting off with purposeful strides for the terrace. "Perhaps it is time everyone got back to work?"

They were all admiring that act of utter foolhardiness. He was winning them over. Jolly good sport, indeed!

She marched into the house and up the stairs to the bedroom floor. She would have continued on up to the attic, but he was down already, standing with Eli on the clean, costly carpet of the corridor. If there was any soot left in the chimney, she would be surprised to hear it. It was surely all adorning his person.

"That was a reckless and disgusting display!" she cried, not reducing her pace until she was three feet in front of him. "You might have *killed* yourself!"

He grinned again. How could he possibly succeed in looking handsome and virile even at such a moment? The fact that he did merely fanned her ire.

"And *look* at the mess you are making on my carpet!"

"You may get back to the stables, lad," he told Eli. "And if you set so much as one toenail on that roof ever again, you will have a thrashing at my hands to look forward to when you come back down. Do you understand?"

"Yes, m'lord." And while Viola watched, outraged, the boy grinned cheekily at Lord Ferdinand and cast him a look of pure hero worship before turning and running down the stairs.

"You may eat your dinner tonight in both comfort and warmth, ma'am," Lord Ferdinand said, turning his attention back to Viola.

"Now, if you will excuse me, I must go and face my valet's wrath. He will not be amused by the appearance of my boots."

"You did it deliberately," she said, her eyes narrowing, her hands closing into fists at her sides. "You made sure that everyone knew you were going up there before you went. You made sure you would be playing to an audience. You risked life and limb just so that everyone would gaze in admiration and call you a *jolly good sport*."

"No!" His eyes danced with merriment. "Is that what they were saying?"

"Life is nothing but a game to you," she cried. "You are probably *glad* you found me here and that I refused to leave. You are probably *glad* that everyone here is set on your discomfort."

"You must understand," he said, "that I have always been able to resist almost every temptation except a challenge. When you threw down the gauntlet, Miss Thornhill, I picked it up. What did you expect?"

"But this is not a game!" Her fingernails were digging painfully into her palms.

His almost-black eyes regarded her out of his blackened face. "No, it is not," he agreed. "But then, I was not the one who planned or executed the pranks, was I, ma'am? If there is a game afoot, you cannot expect me not to play it, you know. And I always play to win. You may wish to remember that. Give me half an hour or so. I am going to need a bath. Then we will take that walk you agreed to."

He turned and strode away. Viola watched him until his bedchamber door closed behind him. There was a decidedly grubby spot on the carpet where he had stood, she could see.

I always play to win.

He has pluck.

A jolly good sport.

She felt like throwing a major tantrum. Or weeping self-pityingly into her handkerchief. Or committing murder.

She did none of the three. Instead, she turned on her heel and made her way back downstairs. She was going outside to read her letter. She would go down onto the river walk. If he cared to, he could find her there. But she was not going to wait for him like an obedient scion.

6

❦

She was reading when he found her. At least, she was folding up a letter, probably the one that had been on the library desk earlier. She was sitting on the grassy bank well north of the house, between the path and the river, her light muslin dress spread about her, her hair in its neat braided coronet. She was surrounded by daisies and buttercups and clover. She looked the perfect picture of beauty and innocence, at one with her surroundings.

Ferdinand felt wretched. He had heard that the late Earl of Bamber was a decent sort, though he had not known him personally. But obviously the man had been as much of a loose screw as his son.

She did not look up as he approached, though she surely must have heard him. She was slipping her letter into her pocket. Did she imagine he was going to snatch it away from her to read himself? His annoyance returned.

"Hiding from me, Miss Thornhill?"

She turned her head to look up at him. "With not a single tree to duck behind for cover?" she said. "If I chose to hide from you, my lord, you would not find me."

He stood on the grass beside her while she turned her gaze toward the river and beyond, her arms clasped about her updrawn knees. He would have preferred to walk with her, but she showed no inclination to get to her feet. He could hardly conduct a reasonable conversation with her, towering over her as he was. He sat down not far from her, one leg stretched out before him, an arm draped over the raised knee of the other.

"You have had a day and a night to think," he said. "You have had a chance to consult with your friends and neighbors. Although I have sent a request for a copy of the will to be sent down here, I believe you must realize now that Pinewood never was yours. Have you come to any decision about your future?"

"I am staying here," she said. "This is my home. This is where I belong."

"Your friends were right last night," he said. "Your reputation is severely at risk for as long as you stay here with me."

She laughed softly and plucked a daisy. He watched her split its stem with her thumbnail and then pluck another daisy to thread through it.

"If you are worried about propriety," she said, "perhaps you are the one who should go away. You have no right to Pinewood. You won its title in a *card game* at a gaming hell. Doubtless you were so drunk that you did not even know it until the next day."

"The gaming hell was Brookes's," he explained. "An eminently respectable gentlemen's club. And one would have to be a fool to gamble while foxed. I am no fool."

She gave him that low laugh again for answer—he recognized scorn in it—and her daisy chain acquired another link.

"The will may take a week to get here," he said. "If Bamber decides to send it or a copy of it, that is. He may choose to ignore my request. I really cannot have you staying here indefinitely, you know." Good Lord, her reputation would be in tatters, if it was not already. He would be expected to make reparation. And he knew what *that* meant. He was going to find himself leg-shackled to her if he was not very careful.

The very thought of a leg shackle was enough to make him break out in a cold sweat, warm May sunshine notwithstanding.

"Why are you so sure that the old earl meant to leave Pinewood to you?" he asked her. "Apart from the fact that he apparently promised to do so, that is."

"That he *did* do so," she corrected.

"That he did promise, then," he said. "Why would he promise such a thing? Were you a favorite niece or cousin?"

"He *loved* me," she said with quiet vehemence, plucking a number of daisies that were within her reach all at once and setting them down on the grass beside her before resuming her work.

"That does not always mean—"

"And I loved *him*," she added. "Perhaps you have never loved or been loved, Lord Ferdinand. Love encompasses trust. I trusted him. I still do. I always will. He said that Pinewood was to be mine, and I do not doubt for one moment that it is."

"But the will?" He frowned and watched her hands. She had slim, delicate fingers. "If it gives proof that he did not keep his word, then you will have to accept the fact that he let you down."

"Never!" Her hands paused and she turned her head to glare at him. "All that will have been proved is that someone has tampered with it. Destroyed it, perhaps. I will never lose my trust in him because I will never stop loving him or knowing beyond any doubt that he loved me."

Ferdinand was silent, shaken by the passion with which she spoke of the love between herself and the old Earl of Bamber. What relationship had they had, for God's sake?

"That is a serious charge," he said. "That someone changed the will, I mean."

"Yes," she agreed. "It is." The daisy chain grew longer.

He did not really want to know more about her. He did not want her to become more of a person to him than she already was. He felt bad enough about her as it was. For a minute or two he fought his curiosity. A few stray curls of dark red hair lay enticingly against the back of her neck.

"Did you grow up in the country?" he asked despite himself.

"No." He thought for a few relieved moments that she would not elaborate, but she did. "I grew up in London. I spent all my life there until I came here almost two years ago."

"That must have been a shock to the system," he said.

"It was." She had denuded the grass within reach of daisies. She sat holding the two ends of the chain. "But I loved it from the first moment."

"Are your parents still living?" But if they were, why the devil were they not here with her? Or why was she not with them?

"My mother is."

"Were you very young when your father died?" he asked.

She spread the daisy chain across her lap, the ends trailing onto the grass on either side of her. Very deliberately she was arranging the daisies so that the blossoms all faced upward.

"My mother married my stepfather when I was nine," she said. "He died when I was eighteen—in a gaming hell brawl. He had been accused of cheating, and I daresay there was justice in the charge." Her voice was emotionless.

"Ah," he said. What else was there to say? He had won the home she had thought was hers in a card game. What a cruel irony of fate that must seem to her.

"I hated him," she said, meticulously continuing her task. "I could never understand why my mother doted on him."

"Do you have any memories of your real father?" he asked, being drawn inexorably into an interest in her life.

"Oh, yes." Her voice became more husky, as if she had forgotten his presence. Her hands fell still on the daisy chain. "I adored him. I used to watch for his coming home and run to meet him—sometimes right out onto the street even before he could come inside. My mother used to scold and remind me I must behave like a lady, but he used to snatch me up and twirl me about and tell me it was the loveliest welcome any man could wish for."

She laughed softly at the memory. Ferdinand sat very still. He felt almost as if he held his breath, eager to hear more, but suspecting that she would stop if she recalled to whom she was speaking.

"He used to take me on his knee while he and Mama talked," she said. "I would sit there patiently, because I knew that my turn would come. And even while he was taking no particular notice of me, I could feel the solid safety of his presence and smell the snuff he always used. And he would play absently with my fingers, his own hands large and capable. When he *did* turn his attention to me, he used to listen to all my little, insignificant pieces of news as if there were nothing more interesting in the world, and often he would have me read to him from my books. Sometimes *he* would read to me, but after a while he would always change the words of my favorite stories until I got indignant and corrected him. Then I would catch him winking at Mama. He used to call me his princess."

But he had died before she was even nine. The childhood idyll had ended. Ferdinand did not know why he should feel sad for her. It was a long time ago.

"It is important to be loved during one's childhood, is it not?" he said.

She turned her head to look at him then. "You must have been loved," she said. "You had two parents, did you not? And a brother to play with. And a sister?"

"We fought as fiercely as only Dudleys know how," he said with a grin. "But we were allies too whenever there was someone outside

our threesome to terrorize. There was always someone—usually a
tutor, sometimes a gamekeeper or a village notable—who had
somehow incurred our wrath."

"You had a country home in which to grow up," she said, "and
parents to love you and each other."

What a naïve assumption, he thought.

"Oh, they loved each other, all right," he said. "When one of
them was at Acton Park, the other was in London. They alternated.
They rarely spent more than a few hours in each other's company.
Though I suppose I should be grateful that they did spend those
few hours together at least three times in their married life. My
brother, my sister, and I might not exist otherwise."

She was carefully joining together the ends of her chain.

"They had a perfectly civilized relationship," he said. "Really
quite typical of married couples of the *ton*."

"How cynical you sound," she said. "Were you hurt by their
near-estrangement?"

"Why should I have been?" He shrugged. "We were always quite
happy when our father was away. He had been a hellion like us and
so there was no deceiving him. And no escaping the birch cane he
kept propped against the desk in his study. The one thing I was always grateful for was that my brother was his favorite and therefore
was thrashed more often than I was."

"Your mother was kinder?" she asked.

"Our mother was bored by us," he said. "Or perhaps it was just
the countryside that bored her. We did not see much of her—at
least, my brother and sister did not. I was her favorite. She used to
take me to London with her when I was old enough."

"You must have enjoyed that," she said.

He had hated it. It had brought about his early loss of innocence. It seemed to him that he had always known that his father
kept mistresses. Somehow he had known—though he believed

Tresham and Angie had not—that the poor relative living at Dove Cottage on the estate was no relative at all, but one of the mistresses. It was why they had not been allowed to visit her, of course, even though the cottage was below their beloved wooded hills and close to the pool where they bathed in summer despite the fact that they were strictly forbidden to do so.

What he had not known until he went to London with his mother, whom he had adored, was that she too had lovers—legions of cicisbei who assembled in her dressing room both morning and evening to observe all but the most intimate stages of her toilette before squiring her about to all the routs and parties with which the London Season abounded, and a number of particular favorites with whom she shared a bed, though never at the house. She was never vulgar, his mother.

Infidelity in marriage, for both wives and husbands, was very much the norm in the *ton*, he had learned early. The vows brides and their grooms exchanged in the nuptial service were a sham. Marriages were for financial and dynastic alliances.

Ferdinand wanted none of it. The very idea of marriage sickened him. And unlike the naïve and gullible Miss Viola Thornhill, he did not believe in love and trust. Oh, he loved Tresham and Tresham's wife and children. He loved Angie and was even fond of Heyward. But not blindly, as Miss Thornhill loved and trusted. Perhaps after this disillusionment she would harden her heart and learn to trust no one but herself.

"Yes, I enjoyed it," he said in answer to her observation.

They seemed to have nothing more to say to each other after that. Ferdinand sat looking at her. He was annoyed with himself. He had sought her out so that they could talk about her future, make some sort of definite decision about her leaving. Instead they had talked about their childhoods. There was a light breeze blowing. It was lifting the short curls at her neck. He felt an absurd—

and hastily quelled—desire to brush them aside with his hand and set his lips there.

"What are you planning to do with that daisy chain?" he asked her, getting to his feet.

She looked down at it as if she were noticing it for the first time. "Oh," she said.

He reached down a hand and helped her to her feet. He took the chain from her and looped it over her head.

"My wholesome country lass," he murmured, and bent his head to kiss her on the lips. He raised his head again sharply, but too late, of course. What sort of a blithering idiot had he turned into for that brief, thoughtless moment?

Color flamed in her cheeks, and her eyes sparked. He waited with an inward grimace for the crack across the cheek he fully expected—he would not defend himself, since he had undoubtedly been in the wrong. But she kept her hands to herself.

"Lord Ferdinand," she said, her voice cold and quavering, "you may have grounds for believing that Pinewood is yours. But I am not part of the package. My person is my own property. I believe I have said this before, but I say it again, lest you did not believe me the first time. I am no man's mistress. I am my own."

She turned and strode away, not along the river path but across it and up the steep bank beyond, to disappear over the top.

The devil! Ferdinand thought. What in thunder had possessed him? He had come out here to be firm, to assert himself, to get rid of the woman, and he had ended up kissing her and murmuring something so deucedly embarrassing that he did not care to remember the exact words.

My wholesome country lass.

Each word taken separately was enough to make him wince for a week.

Lord, but she had certainly been transformed before his eyes. A daisy-bedecked country lass one moment, a frosty, tight-lipped lady the next.

He wished suddenly that he could be as iron-willed and ruthless as Tresham would undoubtedly be in a situation like this. The woman would have been gone yesterday, forgotten today.

How the devil was he going to get rid of her?

He set off back along the river path, feeling all the frustration of having settled nothing but only compounded his problems. What he needed to do was sit down quietly somewhere and think for a few hours. Make plans. And then carry through on them. But as soon as he set foot inside the house, he knew that he was not going to get what he needed—not for a while anyway. The hall seemed crammed to capacity with people, all of whom turned at his entrance and gazed expectantly at him.

"Jarvey?" Ferdinand singled out the butler and raised his eyebrows in inquiry.

"Mr. Paxton is awaiting your return in the library, my lord," Jarvey told him. "And there are a number of persons who are requesting an audience with you."

"Paxton?"

"Pinewood's steward, my lord," Jarvey explained.

Ferdinand glanced about at all the silent persons who awaited an audience with him, and turned in the direction of the library.

"I had better see him, without further delay, then," he said.

Viola walked in the avenue until she felt she had calmed down sufficiently to risk meeting other people. She had *talked* with him, almost as if he were a friend. She had let him *kiss* her. Yes, she had allowed it. She had known somehow as soon as he took the daisy chain from her hands and looped it over her head that he was going to do it. She could have stopped him. But she had not. All the time he had been sitting beside her, half reclined on the grass, she had fought the effects of his attractiveness on her breathing, her heartbeat, her nerve endings.

She did not want to find him attractive. She wanted to hate him. She *did* hate him.

She turned her mind determinedly to her letter, slipping her hand into her pocket and closing her fingers about it. The answer was no—again.

"We are all very much obliged to you for your kind invitation," Claire had written. "You must know how we long to see you again after so long. Two years is *too* long a time. But Mama has asked me to express our deepest regrets on her behalf and to explain why we cannot go. She feels that she owes too much to our uncle, especially now that he has been generous enough to send Ben to school. She feels that she must stay here and help out as best she can. But she misses you dreadfully, Viola. We all do."

Viola felt bereft. She felt not so much her loneliness—she had learned to hold that at bay with her various activities and friendships at Pinewood—as her terrible aloneness. They would never come. Why did she keep on hoping they would?

It had been her dearest dream when she had come to Pinewood that soon her mother would recover from her anger and forget the dreadful quarrel they had had over Viola's accepting the earl's gift, that she would come to live with her daughter and bring Claire and the twins, Maria and Benjamin—Viola's half siblings—with her. But her mother was not ready to forgive her, at least not to the extent of coming here.

Mama and the children—though Claire was fifteen already and the twins twelve—did not have a home of their own. Viola's stepfather had died when she was eighteen and left nothing to his family except debts, which Uncle Wesley, Mama's brother, had paid off. He had taken them all to live at the coaching inn he owned, and they had remained there ever since.

"I am working now," Claire had continued. "Uncle Wesley has

been showing me how to keep the account books, as you once did. He has said that he may let me serve in the coffee room too now that I am fifteen. I am happy to work for him, but what I really want to do is be a governess as you were, Viola, and help support the family with my earnings."

They had been proud of her, both Mama and her uncle, Viola recalled. Uncle Wesley had been disappointed when she had first announced that she would be leaving the inn, but he had understood her desire to help support her family. Two years ago her mother had not been able to understand why she was so eager to leave respectable, interesting, well-paid employment in order to accept charity. Charity, she had called the gift of Pinewood. . . .

"It feels good to help out," Claire had written. "Uncle Wesley really is most generous. Ben's school fees are considerable. In addition, he has bought new books for Maria, who is learning from Mama and is becoming more of a scholar than I ever was, and new clothes for her too. He bought me new shoes even though the old ones would have done for a while longer."

Only Uncle Wesley knew that the money for Ben's education and for many of the extra family expenses came from Pinewood rents. He had not wanted to be part of the deception. He did not want to take credit where it was not due. But Viola had pleaded with him in a letter she had written soon after coming to Somersetshire. Mama would never accept anything that came from Pinewood. But Viola needed to keep on helping her family. Claire and Ben and Maria must have a chance at a decent life.

"Bless you, dearest Viola," the letter had concluded. "Since we cannot go to Pinewood, can you not come to London for a visit? Please?"

But she had never been able to bring herself to go back there. The very thought made her shudder.

Upset over her encounter with Lord Ferdinand, and upset too over this letter, Viola gave in to a rare moment of self-pity and heard a gurgling in her throat. She swallowed determinedly. She did miss her family dreadfully. She had not seen them for two years, not since that dreadful quarrel she had had with her mother. Her one consolation had been that she was doing them some good while she lived here. But how would she continue to help out if Pinewood was no longer hers?

How would she be able even to support herself?

Panic tied her stomach in queasy knots as she turned her steps back toward the house. How she hated Lord Ferdinand. It was not just Pinewood he was trying to take away from her. It was everything. And how she hated herself for not merely turning a cold face away from him on the riverbank just a short while ago.

She might have gone into the house through the back door, since it was the closest entrance from the avenue. But she walked around to the front. She wanted to see if the plans for the rest of the day were being put into effect. Somehow she expected to find the hall deserted. But it was not. It was filled with people. Far more than she had expected or even hoped for. Was there a tenant farmer or a laborer who was *not* here?

Viola smiled broadly as all the men touched their forelocks or bowed awkwardly to her, and the few women bobbed curtsies. But they all grinned back at her in mass acknowledgment of the conspiracy afoot.

"Good morning," she said brightly.

Was it still morning? It certainly would not be by the time he had dealt with every petitioner and complainer who had demanded audience with the new owner of Pinewood. And before he could begin to admit them, he would have to listen to the speech of welcome and orientation that Mr. Paxton had doubtless stayed up half the night preparing. Mr. Paxton could be alarmingly ponderous when he set his mind to it. Lord Ferdinand would be fortunate indeed if he had time to snatch some luncheon before all the afternoon callers began to arrive to pay their respects to their new neighbor.

The Reverend Prewitt would talk about the church choir and next Sunday's sermon, Mrs. Prewitt about the ladies' sewing circle and the new kneelers they were busy making. The schoolmaster would drone on about the leaking schoolroom roof and the necessity of teaching something meaningful to the older pupils at the same time as he instructed the younger ones in the recitation of the alphabet. The Misses Merrywether would talk about the flower show coming up in the summer and the attempts of certain villagers to grow new or better strains of various blooms. Mrs. Claypole, Mr. Claypole, and Bertha—well, the Claypoles would simply be themselves. Mr. Willard had a bull who he claimed was in a state of deep depression over the demise—by butchering—of his favorite cow. Mr. Willard could—and would—wax marvelously eloquent on the subject of his cattle.

Mr. Codaire could put anyone to sleep on the subject of roads and toll gates and new methods of paving. Fortunately for Viola, he knew it and had offered it up as a suitable topic with which to regale the ears of Lord Ferdinand Dudley when the Codaires called upon him. Mrs. Codaire had just read a book of sermons she was sure his lordship would enjoy hearing paraphrased. And the Misses Codaire, aged sixteen and seventeen, had suggested accompanying their mama and papa and *giggling* at every available opportunity. Since the sight of a handsome young man was always opportunity enough for those girls even without an extra incentive, Viola was confident that they would grate upon every adult nerve in Pinewood's drawing room, most particularly upon those of Lord Ferdinand Dudley.

By this time tomorrow, Viola thought hopefully as she retired to her room, where she planned to spend a cozy afternoon reading, he might well be on his way back to London, having realized that country living would drive him mad within a week. He would still be the owner in the eyes of the law, she supposed, but chances were that he would never come back. If he tried to take the rents for himself, she would simply ignore him until he stopped asking. By this time tomorrow she might have her home to herself again.

And by this time tomorrow pigs might also have learned to fly, she thought with a sigh.

Viola did not leave her room until dinnertime. She had steeled herself to dine with him, consoling herself with the conviction that at least she would have his grumblings to listen to and enjoy. But the dining table was set for only one person, and the butler was standing behind Viola's usual chair at the head of the table, waiting to seat her.

"Where is Lord Ferdinand?" she asked him.

"He said he would dine at the Boar's Head, ma'am."

"I daresay," she said, smiling with relief and preparing unexpectedly to enjoy the meal, "he has had enough of making polite conversation for one day."

"I suppose so, ma'am," Mr. Jarvey agreed with a smirk, ladling soup into her bowl.

"Has he enjoyed his day, do you think?" She was feeling almost lighthearted.

"He *seemed* in a good enough humor whenever I stepped into the drawing room to announce another visitor," Mr. Jarvey told her. "He was smiling and talking and greeting the new arrivals as if he couldn't think of any better way to be spending his time. But I daresay that was just his cunning, so that I would not see that we had him bothered."

"Yes," Viola agreed. "I am sure you are right." But she would have far preferred to hear that he had been looking bored or irritable or weary or thunderous. "Have you spoken with Mr. Paxton?"

"His lordship demanded to see the estate books and then wanted to know who kept them so neat and precise, ma'am," Mr. Jarvey said. "Mr. Paxton told me he asked a number of questions that were more intelligent than what Mr. Paxton had expected. His lordship took the books upstairs with him when he left. He said he wanted to study them more closely. And then instead of having all those people sent into the library one by one, he took a chair out into the middle of the hall, his lordship did, and sat down and talked to everyone at once. I was there, ma'am, and you will be pleased to hear that he doesn't seem to know the first thing about farming. He is a downright ignoramus, in fact."

"Indeed?" Viola said, vexed that Lord Ferdinand had thought of a way of saving himself from being overwhelmed by numbers, but also pleased that his presence in the hall had allowed the butler to be witness to all his inadequacies and embarrassment.

"Yes, indeed, ma'am," the butler said. "But he does know how to listen, he does, and he knew just exactly what questions to ask. He can tell a joke too. He had everyone laughing more than once. Even I almost smiled at the one about the town rake and the country parson. It seems that—"

"Thank you, Mr. Jarvey," Viola said firmly. "I am not really in the mood for jokes."

"No, ma'am." Mr. Jarvey retreated into his more normal poker-faced manner as he cleared away her empty soup bowl.

Viola felt guilty then for being so surly. But really! Was he winning everyone over? Could not everyone see that he was a practiced charmer, who would do anything to cut the support from under her feet so that she would have no choice but to leave?

The thought destroyed the little appetite she had.

Perhaps he would stay late at the inn tonight and get obnoxiously drunk. Perhaps he would make a spectacle of himself and show himself in his true colors. Perhaps she would even hear a commotion from the direction of the Boar's Head when she came out of the church after choir practice this evening. How very satisfying that would be. All the other choir members would hear it too.

But that faint, uncharitable hope was dashed an hour later when Viola left the horse and gig at the vicarage stables and walked into the church. She was almost late. Every other member of the choir was already present.

So was Lord Ferdinand Dudley.

7

❧

*I*t had not taken Ferdinand long to understand what was going on. His day had been planned for him with meticulous care, beginning with the cockerel crowing at the very crack of dawn. It was probably intended to end with the world's worst dinner at Pinewood. If his breakfast was any indication of the cook's ingenuity in serving up culinary stomach-churners, he would be better off eating at the Boar's Head, even if he was not exactly welcome there either.

The strange thing was, he thought as he ate his steak and kidney pie in a private parlor at the inn, that he had almost enjoyed the day. Almost, but not quite. There was Viola Thornhill, the thorn in his conscience, to spoil his fun. But the morning horseplay had been entertaining once he had adjusted his mind and body to being up even before the proverbial lark. And he had found his talk with Paxton and his cursory perusal of the estate books interesting. He looked forward to learning more. It was already evident to him that in two years the estate had developed from a run-down, slovenly kept, unprosperous business to just the opposite. Paxton was obviously an able steward.

He had enjoyed talking with the estate laborers and tenants, distinguishing real problems from petty complaints, observing the various personalities, picking out those who were leaders, those who were followers. He had enjoyed joking with them and watching their initial hostility begin to thaw. Paxton, of course, had not been so easily swayed. He was loyal to Miss Thornhill.

Afternoon visits had always been something to avoid. But today's had been vastly amusing, especially since each caller had come with the express purpose of boring his head off.

The thing was, though, that he had long been fascinated with new developments in road construction. And talk of cattle could easily be turned into talk about horses, one of Ferdinand's favorite topics. Ladies who formed sewing circles were naturally interested to learn that the infant Lord Ferdinand had once talked his nurse into teaching him to knit and that within a week he had produced a scarf that had grown progressively narrower as he gradually dropped stitches but that had stretched the whole length of the nursery when laid flat on the floor after he had finished it. As for the pupil at the village school who had asked the schoolmaster for Latin lessons—well, Ferdinand had graduated from Oxford with a degree in Latin and Greek. Perhaps he could offer his services as a teacher.

All the people he had met today, of course, had been determined not to like him. Many probably still did not and perhaps never would. Their hostility was a tribute to Viola Thornhill, who appeared to have won everyone's respect and even affection in the two years she had been at Pinewood. But Ferdinand did not despair. He had never had difficulty relating to all kinds of people, and he had always been gregarious.

He rather thought he was going to enjoy life in the country.

The vicar had said there was to be a practice for the church choir tonight. His wife had even invited Ferdinand to join them, though she had said it in such a way that he knew she did not expect him to accept. But why not? he thought, pushing away half the suet pudding he had been brought for dessert. He did not want to return to Pinewood yet. That would mean either making conversation with Miss Thornhill in the drawing room or slinking off to hide in a room where she was not—and he had never been a slinker. Neither did he want to spend another whole evening drinking in the taproom.

The choir practice it would be, then.

The practice was not in the church itself, he discovered as soon as he opened the door and stepped inside. But he could hear the sound of a pianoforte being thumped upon and followed it down a steep flight of stone steps to the church hall below, a gloomy apartment with a few windows high on three of the four walls. There were fifteen or twenty people gathered in groups, talking. None of them was taking any notice of the pianist, a thin woman of indeterminate age and faded, frizzed fair hair, who was peering at the music propped before her through small wire-framed spectacles. She was one of the spinster sisters who had called during the afternoon with the vicar and his wife, Ferdinand recalled—Merryfield? Merryheart? *Merrywether*—that was it. While her sister had talked at great, droning length about the growing of prize blooms, this one had apologized whenever she had been able to work a word into the conversation, assuring Lord Ferdinand Dudley that he could not possibly be interested in such rural concerns but must be simply longing to return to town.

"It is in four parts," she was saying to no one in particular but with every appearance of extreme anxiety as Ferdinand's eyes alighted on her. "Oh, dear, can we manage four parts?"

Perhaps someone would have answered her had not everyone at the same moment noticed the new arrival and fallen silent.

"I have accepted my invitation, you see, sir," Ferdinand said, sin-

gling out the vicar and striding toward him, his right hand outstretched.

The Reverend Prewitt appeared slightly flustered, but gratified.
"That is very obliging of you, I am sure, my lord," he said. "Do you
sing?"

But Ferdinand had no chance to answer. There was a slight stir
among the choir members, whose eyes had all moved from
Ferdinand himself to some point beyond his left shoulder. He
turned to see Viola Thornhill coming down the stairs, a look of
pure astonishment on her face. She was part of the choir too?

He bowed as he looked up at her—and something snatched at
the edges of his memory again. Damn, but he had seen her somewhere. She was looking rather regal, her chin raised, her face a mask
of controlled dignity—a far cry from the laughing lass of the
maypole.

"Lord Ferdinand," she said, stepping down onto the stone floor
of the hall, "I did not expect to find *you* here."

"I trust you had a pleasant day, ma'am," he said. "The vicar's
wife was kind enough to invite me to choir practice."

She looked at the clergyman with what might have been silent reproach, and Ferdinand turned away to address the pianist.

"You were saying as I came in, Miss Merrywether," he said, "that
the piece of music before you is in four parts. It that a problem?"

"Oh, not a *problem*, exactly, my lord," she assured him, her voice
breathless with apology for bothering him with such a slight concern. "But Mr. Worthington is our only tenor, you see. Not that I
am saying he does not have a fine voice, for he does. Very fine indeed. It is just that—well, he does not like to sing alone, and I do
not blame him, I am sure. I would certainly not wish to do it. Not
that I have a tenor voice, of course, being a woman, but—"

"He is easily distracted by the basses and sings along with
them," a round woman Ferdinand had not encountered before said
more bluntly.

There was general laughter.

"We have never claimed to be professional singers," the vicar added. "But what we lack in musicality we make up for in enthusiasm."

"And volume," someone else added, to the accompaniment of more laughter.

"All we can ask of ourselves," the vicar said genially, "is that we make a joyful noise unto the Lord."

"You would not enjoy listening to us," Viola Thornhill told Ferdinand.

Smiling into her eyes, he offered his services. "I sing tenor," he said quite truthfully. He had sung with a university choir and enjoyed the experience enormously. "No one has ever accused me of having extraordinary talent, but I have never noticed particularly pained expressions on the faces of those within earshot of my singing voice either. Shall Worthington and I put our heads and our voices together and see if we can hold our own against the basses?" Worthington, a balding, freckled redhead, was one of the tenant farmers who had camped out in his hall during the morning, he recalled.

"We would not put you to so much trouble, my lord," Miss Thornhill said firmly. "You surely wish to—"

He did not wait to hear what it was he would wish.

"But it is no trouble at all," he assured everyone. "I love nothing better than an evening of music, especially when I may be a participant rather than a mere listener. However, I must ask if I am being presumptuous—are there auditions?"

That question drew a burst of hilarity from most of the choir members. Even Miss Merrywether tittered.

"No one with a desire to sing with us has ever been turned away, my lord," the vicar assured him. "We should get started, then."

It was certainly not a particularly musical group. Someone who

was nominally a contralto was tone deaf but sang heartily nevertheless, one of the sopranos sang with a shrill vibrato, the bass section
proceeded under the apparent assumption that it was their primary
function to drown out the rest of the choir, and Mr. Worthington
did indeed display a tendency to join forces with them when he was
not inventing a tune all of his own. Miss Merrywether was heavy-
handed on the pianoforte, and the conductor slowed or speeded up
the rhythm with bewildering and unpredictable frequency.

But despite it all, music was created.

Ferdinand amused himself by imagining the reactions of his
friends if they could see him now. They would bundle him up and
cart him off to Bedlam as a raving lunatic. Tresham would fix him
with one of his famous black stares. No—perhaps not. Tresham
had been playing the pianoforte again during the past few years—
since his marriage, in fact—instead of smothering his talent as he
had done most of his life. Their father had brought them up to the
belief that the most deadly of all sins for a Dudley male was anything that hinted at effeminacy. Music, art, an overindulgence in intellectual pursuits—all had been ruthlessly stamped out, with the
aid of that infamous birch cane when necessary.

Ferdinand had enjoyed both the singing and the company. And
obviously he had cooled the hostility of at least a few of the neighbors with whom he was going to have to consort during future
years. It was the habit of several of the male members of the choir,
it seemed, to take a glass of ale at the Boar's Head on choir
evenings. Worthington suggested that he join them.

"Singing dries the throat," he added by way of explanation and
excuse.

"It does indeed, and I would be delighted," Ferdinand replied.
"But Miss Thornhill, did you walk here? May I escort you home in
my curricle first?"

"I brought the gig, thank you, my lord," she said, and he could tell from the stiffness of her voice that she was furious. She must feel let down by her friends, who were not repulsing him as they ought.

And so he went off to drink with six other male choristers and the realization that country life was very different from town life. More egalitarian. More genial. More to his taste—a strange thought, considering the fact that he had spent the years since Oxford kicking up every lark that fell his way and generally leading a fast, wild existence in London.

If only there were not Viola Thornhill. In some strange way he felt indignant on her behalf that the people who were her friends had allowed him within the space of one day to begin to inveigle himself into their lives. For, after all, they could not both live here, he and Miss Thornhill. One of them was going to have to leave, and that one, of course, was she. But her friends should be furious with him. They should be making life sheer hell for him.

"He could not really have enjoyed choir practice," Viola said. "Could he, Hannah?"

"I don't know, Miss Vi," Hannah said, drawing the brush in one firm stroke from the crown of Viola's head to the ends of her hair below her waist. "I just don't know."

"Well, I do," Viola said firmly. "Gentlemen like him just do not enjoy the company of people like that, Hannah. And they certainly do not enjoy singing church music with a choir like ours. He must have been excruciatingly bored. In fact, I really believe that it turned out for the best that he decided to go. After today he is sure to realize that this corner of Somersetshire has nothing whatsoever to offer a sophisticated and dissipated London rake. Do you think?"

"What I think, Miss Vi," Hannah said, "is that that man has as much charm as he has good looks and that he knows how to use both to his advantage. And I think he is a dangerous man because he will not ever admit defeat. If you had not been here when he came, he would likely have gone off again to wherever he came from within a week. But you are here, you see, and you have challenged him. That is what I think."

It was so exactly what Viola herself thought that there was nothing to add. She merely sighed as Hannah brushed back the hair from her face and began to plait it for the night.

"The thing is, Miss Vi," Hannah said when she had almost finished the task, "I thought in the village the other day that he had an eye for you. In fact, I am sure he did, him playing for your daisies and taking you onto the green to dance about the maypole and all that. And then he turned up here next morning just like fate had brought him, not knowing it was your home. And now when you have tried your best to drive him away, he has risen to the task and shown that he is your equal. I think he is *enjoying* the challenge—just because it is you, Miss Vi. Perhaps you should change your tactics, not try to drive him away, but—"

"Hannah!" Viola cut her off midsentence. "What on earth are you suggesting? That I lure that man into falling in love with me? How would that get rid of him, even if it could be done and even if I wished to do it?"

"I wasn't thinking of your getting rid of him, exactly," Hannah said, twisting a length of ribbon about the end of Viola's braid.

"You were not—"

"The thing is, Miss Vi," Hannah said, turning to put away the dress and other garments Viola had just removed, "I cannot accept that your life is over. You are still young. You are still lovely and sweet and kind and . . . Your life cannot possibly be over, that is all."

"Well, it *is*, Hannah." Viola's voice was shaking. "But at least it has been a peaceful half existence I have been living here. He is determined to drive me away. Then there will be nothing left. Nothing at all. No life, no home, no dream. No income." She swallowed convulsively. Panic had her stomach tied in knots.

"Not if he fell in love with you, he wouldn't," Hannah said. "And he is already partway there, Miss Vi. You could see to it that he fell all the way."

"Gentlemen do not house their mistresses on their country estates," Viola said tartly.

"Not mistress, Miss Vi."

Viola turned on the stool and stared incredulously at her maid. "You think he would *marry* me? He is Lord Ferdinand Dudley, Hannah. He is a gentleman, a duke's son. I am a *bastard*. And that is the kindest thing that can be said about me."

"Don't upset yourself," Hannah said with a sigh. "Stranger things have happened. He would be the lucky one to win your hand."

"Oh, Hannah." Viola laughed rather shakily. "Ever the dreamer. But if I ever were to seek a husband, you know, it would be someone far different from Lord Ferdinand. He is everything I most abhor in a gentleman. He is a *gamer*. A reckless one who plays for high stakes. I will survive somehow without even attempting to make such a dreadful sacrifice. And I have not admitted defeat yet. If he wishes to be rid of me, he will have to have me dragged away. Perhaps then everyone will think a little less of his *charm*," she added bitterly.

"That they will." Hannah was using the soothing voice she had once used on the child Viola when something had happened to make her believe her world had come to an end. Yet that had been the golden time, when really the world had been a very solid, secure place and love had been real and seemingly eternal. "You get into bed now, Miss Vi. There is nothing a good night's sleep will not solve."

Viola laughed and hugged her maid. "At least I have you, the very best friend anyone ever had," she said. "Very well, then, I will go to bed and to sleep like a good girl, and tomorrow all my problems will have vanished. Perhaps he will be so drunk when he leaves the Boar's Head that he will ride for London and forget all about Pinewood. Perhaps he will fall off his horse and break his neck."

"Lovey!" Hannah said reproachfully.

"But he did not ride to the village," Viola said. "He took his curricle. All the better. He has farther to fall."

She lay in bed a little while later, wide awake, staring up at the shadowed canopy over her head, wondering how life could have changed so completely within two days.

It was after midnight when Ferdinand returned home. The house was in darkness. *Indignant* darkness, he thought with a grin. She probably expected him to come staggering home, roaring out obscene ditties off-key and slurring his words. But the knowledge that it was not really a game they played soon wiped the grin from his face. He wished it were something that harmless. She was an interesting opponent.

Jarvey was still up. He came prowling into the hall as Ferdinand let himself in through the unlocked door, a branch of candles held aloft in one hand, its shadows across his face making him look somewhat sinister.

"Ah, Jarvey." Ferdinand handed the man his hat and cloak and whip. "Waited up for me, did you? And Bentley did too, I daresay?"

"Yes, my lord," the butler informed him. "I'll send him up to your room immediately."

"You may send him to bed," Ferdinand said, making for the library. "And go to your own too. I'll not need either of you again tonight."

But he did not really know why he had come to the library, he thought after he had shut the door behind him. It was just that soon after midnight seemed a ridiculously early hour at which to retire. He shrugged out of his coat and tossed it over the back of a chair. His waistcoat joined it there. He loosened and then removed his neckcloth. Now he was comfortable enough to settle into a chair with a book—except that he did not feel in the mood for reading. It was too late. He wandered over to the glass-fronted cabinet in one corner of the library and poured himself a brandy, but he did not particularly feel like drinking it, he realized after the first sip. He had had three glasses of ale at the Boar's Head. He had never been much of a solitary drinker. Or much of a heavy drinker at all, in fact. He was not an advocate of thick morning heads, having experienced a few of them during his youth.

There must be a solution to her problems, he thought, throwing himself into one of the chairs grouped about the fireplace. He just wished she would help him find one instead of clinging to the notion that the will would exonerate her—or that the will had been tampered with.

Why was he worrying about her problems? They were not his. They had nothing to do with him. He was giving himself a headache, a grossly unfair consequence of drinking only three glasses of ale over two and a half hours.

She had friends here. She was well liked here. If he was not much mistaken—he would know for sure when he had studied the estate books more closely and spoken with Paxton again—she had been involved in running and improving the estate. She was involved in community activities. What she should be doing was staying here.

She could stay if she married that ass and prize bore, Claypole. She could stay if . . .

Ferdinand stared at the dark painting hanging over the mantel. No! Definitely not that—*definitely!* Where the devil had that idea popped out from? But the devil that had nudged the strange idea into his mind spoke on.

She is young and beautiful and desirable.

So were dozens of other girls who had set their caps for him anytime during the past six or seven years. He had never for a moment considered matrimony with any of them.

She is fresh and innocent.

Any woman who married him would have a duke for a brother-in-law. She would be marrying into the *ton*. She would be marrying a very wealthy man. Freshness and innocence would disappear in a trice once the pleasures of society were tasted and once there were other men, more personable than Claypole, to admire her. She would be no different from any other woman in a similar marriage.

She believes in love. She trusts love, even when to all appearances it has betrayed her.

Both love and trust would disappear with innocence.

You want her.

Ferdinand closed his eyes and spread his hands on the armrests of the chair. He breathed deeply and evenly. She was an innocent. She was living unchaperoned in his house. That was scandal enough without his lusting after her.

She has a body to die for.

And he would die too before giving up his freedom merely in order to possess it.

Her problems would be solved and your conscience would be appeased if you married her.

Damn Bamber, Ferdinand thought vehemently. And damn Bamber's father. And damn Leavering for having impregnated his wife just when he had, so that *he* had not been the one to play for Pinewood instead of Ferdinand. Damn Brookes's.

He was *not* going to play the gallant by offering her marriage. The very idea had him reaching up to tug at his overtight neck-cloth—only to discover that he had removed it before he sat down. He was in a bad way, indeed.

He was going to go to bed, Ferdinand decided, getting determinedly to his feet. Not that he was going to be able to sleep, even though he had ordered Bentley to find him different pillows or, failing that, to set a block of marble at the head of his bed, since marble could not be less comfortable than what he had slept on last night. But there was nothing else to do *except* go to bed.

He snuffed the candles, having decided that there was quite enough moonlight beaming through the windows to light his way upstairs. With one finger he hooked his coat and waistcoat over his shoulder and left the room.

He fervently hoped he would rise in the morning in a more sensible frame of mind.

8

❀

The upper corridor was darker than the hall and staircase. There was only one window at the far end. But, preoccupied with his thoughts as he was, it did not occur to Ferdinand to regret not bringing a candle with him until he went plowing into a table, the corner of which caught him painfully in the middle of the thigh.

"Ouch!" he exclaimed loudly before letting loose with a few other, more profane epithets and dropping his coat and waistcoat in order to rub his leg with both hands. But even in the near-darkness he could see that further disaster was looming in the form of a large urn, which was wobbling on the table in imminent danger of toppling to its doom. He roared and lunged for it—and then whooped with self-congratulatory relief when he righted it. He pressed a hand to his injured leg again, but his absorption with the pain was short-lived. Somehow a large painting in a heavy, ornate frame had been dislodged from the wall and crashed to the floor, its descent made more spectacular by the fact that it brought the urn down with it, smashing it to smithereens, and overturned the table into the bargain.

Ferdinand swore foully and eloquently at the mess around him, though he could scarcely see the full extent of it in the darkness. He stepped back from the debris and rubbed his leg. And then suddenly there *was* light, illuminating the scene and momentarily dazzling him.

"You are *drunk!*" the person holding the candle informed him coldly.

Ferdinand put up a hand to shade his eyes. How *exactly* like a woman to jump to that conclusion.

"Devilish foxed," he agreed curtly. "Three sheets to the wind. And what's it to you?" He returned his attention to the disaster he could now see clearly, rubbing his thigh at the same time. The painting looked as if it weighed a ton, but he waded in among the debris and somehow hefted it back up to its position on the wall. He picked up the table and set it to rights. There was no apparent damage to it. But he could do nothing except grimace at the scattered remains of the urn, which lay in a few thousand separate pieces.

Her candle had been dazzling him the whole while. And she had been coming closer. When he looked at her, feeling still annoyed but also decidedly sheepish, he could see her clearly for the first time.

Good God! She had not stopped either to dress or to throw on a dressing gown. Not that there was anything particularly indecent about her appearance. Her white cotton nightgown covered her from neck to wrists to ankles. She wore no nightcap, but her hair was scraped back from her face and lay in a thick braid down her back.

She did not look indecent at all, even if her feet *were* bare. She looked like chastity incarnate, in fact. But still and all, it *was* just a nightgown, and one could not prevent oneself from imagining what was—or, more to the purpose, what was not—beneath it. Nothing whatsoever, at a guess. Ferdinand's temperature soared and he rubbed harder at his bruised thigh.

"What is it to me?" she asked, repeating his question, her voice tight with self-righteous indignation. "It is the middle of the *night*. I am trying to *sleep*."

"It is a downright stupid place to keep a table—in the middle of the corridor," he said, careful not to look fully at her and then noticing his coat and waistcoat on the floor. He was clad only in shirt and breeches and stockings himself. Oh, Lord, Lord, Lord, he could have done without this. They were alone together after midnight in the darkened corridor outside both their bedchambers— and he had thoughts crowding his mind that had no business being there at all.

Lustful thoughts.

She herself was safely armed with indignation—at least for the moment. She had probably never even heard of lust. "The table was standing against the wall, my lord," she pointed out with cold civility. "The painting was hanging *on* the wall. If there was any stupidity involved in what has happened here, it was yours in lurching along the corridor without a candle while you were drunk."

"Deuce take it," he said, "I suppose that urn was worth a king's ransom."

"At least that much," she agreed. "It was also unspeakably hideous."

He grinned directly at her when she said that and then wished he had kept his eyes averted. She had the sort of face—a perfect oval with high cheekbones, a straight nose, large eyes, and soft, kissable lips—that actually looked more beautiful without the distraction of curls and ringlets to dress it up. Her usual coronet of plaits gave her a regal air. Tonight's loose braid gave her a youthful look, an aura of innocence and purity. His temperature edged up another notch as he determinedly returned his attention to the sad remains of the urn.

"Where will I find a broom?" he asked. Perhaps sweeping up the pieces would restore his equilibrium.

But she did exactly the wrong thing. She looked directly up at him and laughed, her eyes dancing with merriment.

"I am almost tempted to tell you," she said. "It would be priceless to see you wielding a broom. But you had better forget that impulse. It is after midnight."

Which fact he was trying diligently—and futilely—to ignore.

"What should I do, then?" he asked, frowning.

"I think you ought to go to bed, Lord Ferdinand," she said.

If only the top could have blown off his head, some heat might have escaped harmlessly into the air above and saved him. But it did not, of course. And instead of taking her advice and scurrying off in the direction of his room and sanctuary, his eyes on the doorknob every step of the way, he made the mistake of looking down at her again and locking eyes with her and seeing that finally her mind had attached itself to the atmosphere that had been sizzling around them ever since she had ventured outside her room.

He did not notice himself taking the candlestick out of her hand, but it was definitely his own hand that was setting it down on the table. And then he was turning and cupping her chin with the same hand, which was sending impressions of warm softness sizzling up his arm.

"Ought I?" he asked her. "But who is going to put me there?"

Even at that late moment he might have answered his own question and scampered off with all haste to put himself to bed. Or she might have helped restore sanity to them both by making some caustic remark about his supposed inebriation before effecting a dignified retreat. Or she might have delivered this morning's speech about the sanctity of her person again. Or she could simply have turned and bolted on her bare feet, leaving the candle to him as a trophy.

Neither of them took any of the easy—and sensible—ways out.

Instead she did something totally unexpected. Her teeth sank into her soft lower lip, and in the flickering light of the candle it seemed to Ferdinand that the brightness of her eyes might have been attributable to unshed tears. The words she spoke confirmed that impression.

"I wish," she said softly, "you had gone away after that day and that evening. I wish I had never known your name."

"Do you?" He forgot danger. He forgot propriety. He even forgot that they were locked in an insoluble conflict. All he saw was his lovely, vibrant lass, who had once worn daisies in her hair but who now had tears in her eyes—because of him. "Why?"

She hesitated and then shrugged. "It would have been a pleasant memory," she said.

Had he been thinking rationally, he would have left her answer uncommented upon. But he really was not thinking at all.

"*This* memory?" He lowered his head, touched his lips to hers, and was irrevocably lost in sensation. Sweet, wholesome innocence and beauty. The enticing smells of soap and cleanliness and woman. And the memories of firelight and fiddle music and bright, twining ribbons. And of the laughing, lovely face of the woman he had taken behind the oak tree to kiss.

This woman.

He kissed her for only a few moments before drawing back his head and gazing down into her eyes. The candlelight flickered across her face as the firelight had done on the village green. Her eyes gazed dreamily back into his. The tears were gone. She raised one hand and set her fingertips lightly against his cheek, sending shivers of raw desire coursing downward through his body to center in his groin. And yet the hunger he felt was not purely carnal in nature. She was not just any lovely woman with whom he had found himself alone under provocative circumstances.

She was Viola Thornhill, the laughing, lovely, vibrant woman who danced with joy, as if she had drawn all the music and all the rhythm of the universe into her body, the relative of Bamber's who had been promised Pinewood and then betrayed, the child who had run to meet her father and poured out all her childhood secrets to him.

"Yes," she whispered at last in answer to the question he had almost forgotten asking. "I wanted that memory."

"When the real man is right here to provide others?" He forgot for the moment that she would remember her every association with him after May Day with a bitterness that would last a lifetime.

He set his hands on either side of her waist and drew her closer. She did not push him away. On the contrary, she cupped his elbows in her palms and arched herself in toward him, pressing thighs, abdomen, and breasts against his body. She was all soft, alluring curves. His arms slid tightly about her waist, and hers twined about his neck. Any doubt of the nakedness that lay beneath the virginal white of her nightgown was put to flight. So was any doubt that she was a willing participant in what was happening.

This time when he kissed her, he opened his mouth over hers and licked her parted lips and the soft, moist flesh behind them. He was consumed by sweet, raw hunger. Sweet because he knew with a deep, innate integrity that he would not take the embrace far enough to destroy her innocence—he would not take her virginity. Raw because he wanted and wanted and wanted. He wanted her beneath him on a bed, yes. He was already hard with arousal. He wanted to press himself deep inside her and bring her pleasure and himself ease. But more than that simple animal urge, he wanted . . . Ah, he simply *yearned*.

"Sweet," he murmured, moving his mouth from hers, feathering kisses over her closed eyes, her temples, her cheeks, drawing the lobe of one ear between his teeth and rubbing his tongue over the tip, burying his face in the warm, soft hollow between her neck and shoulder. He wrapped both arms even more tightly about her, lifting her until she stood on her toes.

"Yes," she murmured, her voice low velvet, her cheek rubbing against his hair, the fingers of one hand entwined in it. "Ah, sweet."

They clung for endless moments.

He was releasing his hold on her at the same moment as she set her hands against his shoulders and pushed him away, not violently, but firmly.

"Go to bed, Lord Ferdinand," she said before he could speak. "Alone." Yet she was not angry. There was something in her voice that spoke of a yearning to match his own. He knew that part of her—a weaker part—wanted him to argue.

"I was not headed down that road," he said softly. "Seduction was not on my mind. Your maidenhood is perfectly safe with me. But it would be best for us not to meet like this again. I am only a man, when all is said and done."

She picked up her candlestick. "I will have those pieces swept up in the morning," she said. "Leave them for now." She did not look at him again but made her way back to her room, her braid swinging back and forth across her back like a pendulum. She looked infinitely enticing.

He had lost all faith in innocence and purity and fidelity, and even love, long before he left his boyhood behind. He had never been in love or ever enjoyed anything more than a light, bantering sort of friendship with any woman. Women were for sex and children. He did not want children.

But perhaps, after all, Ferdinand thought as the door of her bedchamber closed behind her and the corridor was plunged into darkness again, there were such qualities as goodness and innocence and uncomplicated wholesomeness.

Perhaps there was even love.

And fidelity.

And perhaps he was simply tired, he thought as he located his abandoned clothes in the faint moonlight and picked them up before making his way toward his bedchamber. It had been a long day, after all, and an extraordinarily busy one.

There was a way for both of them to remain at Pinewood, he thought as he stepped inside the room and closed the door behind him. But he would not pursue that thought tonight. Or tomorrow either, if he was wise.

He was a perfectly contented bachelor.

Ah, sweet, she had just murmured to him, her voice throaty with passion, her cheek resting softly against his head.

Yes. Sweet, indeed.

He strode purposefully into his dressing room.

Viola greeted the absence of Lord Ferdinand Dudley from Pinewood the following morning with both relief and dismay. Through a long, almost sleepless night, she had not known how she was going to face him over the breakfast table. On the other hand, his absence was due to the fact that he had ridden out with Mr. Paxton to visit the home farm. It seemed that he was interested in the running of the estate, at least at present. Viola felt his absence on such a mission as a huge intrusion. From the first she had been personally involved in making Pinewood an efficient, prosperous concern. She had done rather well at it, with Mr. Paxton's help and advice. She had loved it.

There were no great schemes to put into effect today. Only the one this afternoon, which already seemed lame and doomed to failure. Just to accentuate her mood of depression, the lovely warm, sunny spell seemed to have deserted Somersetshire. There was a light drizzle misting the windows and heavy gray skies to darken the breakfast room.

The trouble was, she did not know for which of two evils she must blame herself more. She had capitulated to the enemy, allowing him to hold her and kiss her. And partly—oh, more than partly—that had happened because he had looked irresistibly attractive in his shirtsleeves, with his evening knee breeches skintight about his long, muscled legs, and because she had felt unbearably lonely and loveless. How could she excuse herself for giving in to desire for such a man? And yet she would prefer to accuse herself of unbridled lust than the other.

For even though she had been half lost in passion while she was in his arms, she really had been *only* half lost. The other half of herself had watched dispassionately as she arched against him, bringing her breasts against his hard chest, her thighs against his, her abdomen against the hard bulk of his erection. She had known the effect she was having on him, the power she had over him. She could have enticed him into bed with almost no effort at all. But though the passionate woman had longed for just that, to lie spread beneath him, brought to pleasure by his clean, youthful virility, the calculating woman had weighed the possibility of enticing him in an entirely different direction—toward love and even marriage.

Viola was deeply ashamed of that half of herself.

"Yes," she said when the butler stepped closer to her, "you may clear away, Mr. Jarvey. I am not hungry this morning."

She went to the library and seated herself behind the desk. She would write home. At least she need not fear interruption for the rest of the morning.

How could she even be tempted to try to make him fall in love with her? She disliked and despised him. Besides, it was impossible. Not to engage his feelings, perhaps, but to marry him. Though it was not that practical consideration that made her feel slightly nauseated, but the moral implications of trying to trick a man into marriage. She picked up the quill pen from the desk, tested the nib, and dipped it in the inkwell.

Beware of a tall, dark, handsome stranger. He can destroy you—if you do not first snare his heart.

Why had those words of the gypsy fortune-teller chosen to pop into her mind at this particular moment?

She would not do it, she thought with firm resolve. She would not do a single thing deliberately to attract his admiration—or lust. But what if she did not have to do a thing? What if his obvious attraction to her person developed quite freely into something deeper? What if . . .

No, not even then, she thought, writing, "Dearest Mama, Claire, and Maria," with a flourish across the top of a blank sheet of paper. She forced her attention onto her letter.

He had *not* been drunk, she thought after writing five words. She had tasted ale on his tongue, it was true, but he had not been drunk. And he had told her that he had not been bent on seducing her, that she was quite safe with him. Worse, she had *believed* him. Still did.

No, she would not be distracted, she thought, writing doggedly on. And she would *not* allow herself to like him.

But later that afternoon she knew there was no danger of that at all. He was, in fact, quite the most contemptible man she had ever known.

It had been her idea, more than a year before, to begin a sewing circle for the women of the village and neighborhood. There were several places and events to bring the men together, but very few for the women. They had met weekly in the church hall ever since. But Viola had hit upon the happy idea two days ago of inviting the group to meet in Pinewood's drawing room instead. There could surely be nothing, she had thought then, more calculated to send a town tulip hastening back to London than to discover a few dozen women gathered over their needlework and conversation in the drawing room he considered his property.

"This is really a remarkably good idea of yours, Miss Thornhill," Mrs. Codaire said as she spread her embroidery threads about her. "Even apart from your main motive, this is a far more convenient meeting place than the church hall. No offense to you, Mrs. Prewitt."

"None taken, Eleanor," the vicar's wife assured her graciously.

"I must say, though," Mrs. Codaire added, "that his lordship seemed a perfectly amiable gentleman when I called here with Mr. Codaire and the girls yesterday."

"He insisted upon escorting me home after choir practice last evening," Miss Prudence Merrywether said breathlessly. "I would have preferred to walk alone, for I could not think of a single intelligent thing to say to a duke's brother and would have been quite tongue-tied if he had not asked me to explain what soil is best for planting roses in. But it was very obliging of him to consider my safety, even though it is quite absurd to think of *not* being safe in Trellick. And who would think of assaulting me, anyway, when I am neither young nor beautiful nor rich?"

"It was just his cunning, Prudence," her sister said firmly, to Viola's satisfaction. "He wants us all to *like* him. I have no intention of falling for his charms."

"Quite right too, Miss Merrywether," Mrs. Claypole said. "No proper gentleman would insist upon living at Pinewood before Miss Thornhill has had a chance to move out. It is quite scandalous, and I blame him entirely. He is not a man of breeding."

"He flatly refused to allow me to stay here as dear Viola's chaperon two evenings ago," Bertha added. "He was remarkably rude."

"He smiles too much," Mrs. Warner said. "I noticed that at the village during the fête."

"Though it *is* a lovely smile," Miss Prudence said, and blushed.

Miss Faith, better organized than most of them, was already hard at work. "If Lord Ferdinand Dudley does not like having us here today, Miss Thornhill," she said, "and comes in here and orders us to leave, we will inform him that we are here to chaperon our friend and intend to remain for the better part of the afternoon."

"You always were braver than I, Faith," Miss Prudence said with a sigh. "But you are right. You are always right. Never fear, Miss Thornhill. If Lord Ferdinand chooses to scold you in our hearing—well, we will scold right back. Oh, dear, if only we dare."

They all settled to their work after that, and half an hour passed while the room hummed with the usual feminine conversational topics—the weather, everyone's health, household tips, the newest fashions as displayed in fashion plates received from London itself, the next assembly.

Then the drawing room door opened and Lord Ferdinand stepped inside. He was looking quite immaculate, Viola saw when she glanced up from the bridal kneeler she had undertaken, dressed in a green superfine coat of expert cut with buff-colored pantaloons and tasseled, highly polished Hessian boots and his usual white linen. His hair had been freshly brushed and looked thick and shiny. He must have been warned, she realized. But instead of hiding away until all the ladies had left, he had gone upstairs to change and had come back down to make his entrance with all the appearance of easy good humor.

"Ah." He included everyone in his graceful bow. "Good afternoon, ladies. Welcome to Pinewood for those of you I did not meet here yesterday."

Viola set her work aside and rose to her feet. "The ladies' sewing circle is meeting here this week," she explained. "When one is privileged enough to own a manor of this size, you see, one must be prepared to use it for the common good and give up some of one's privacy."

He turned his eyes—his *laughing* eyes—on her. "Quite so," he agreed.

"I believe," she said pointedly, "the library is free."

"It is," he said. "I have just been in there finding a book of which I have heard many good opinions."

He was holding a book in one hand, Viola noticed for the first time.

"It is called *Pride and Prejudice*," he said. "Has anyone heard of it?"

"I have," Mrs. Codaire admitted. "But I have not read it."

Viola had—more than once. She thought it easily the best book she had ever read. Lord Ferdinand strolled farther into the room and smiled about him with easy charm.

"Shall I read some of it aloud," he asked, "while you ladies sew? We men are not nearly as diligent or as skilled with our hands, you see, but perhaps we are good for something after all."

Viola glared indignantly at him. How dare he bring his charm into this female preserve instead of slinking about outside working himself into a temper as any decent man would?

"That would be very kind of you, I am sure, Lord Ferdinand," Miss Prudence Merrywether said. "Our papa used to read to us, particularly on dark evenings when time might otherwise have hung heavily on our hands. Do you remember, Faith, dear?"

He did not need further encouragement. He seated himself on the only remaining seat, an ottoman almost at Viola's feet, smiled about him once more as the ladies settled back to their work, opened the book, and began to read:

" 'It is a truth universally acknowledged that a single man in possession of a good fortune must be in want of a wife.' "

Three or four of the women laughed, and he read on—surely knowing that more than three or four of them were thinking of how that opening statement of the novel applied to him. Not that he had a good fortune in all probability. But he had Pinewood. And she, Viola, had made it prosperous. She gazed bitterly down at him for a few minutes before resuming her work.

He read well. Not only did he do so clearly and with good pacing and expression, but he also looked up at frequent intervals to reveal his reactions to the narrative with his facial expressions. He was enjoying both the book and his audience, his manner said—and his audience was enjoying *him*. A glance about the room assured Viola of that.

How she hated him!

He stayed after he had read for half an hour to discuss the book with the ladies and to take tea with them and examine and admire their work. By the time the sewing group dispersed for another week, he had all but the strong-minded few veritably eating out of his hand. He even accompanied Viola out onto the terrace to see them all on their way. The rain had stopped, but the clouds still loomed gray and cheerless overhead.

Viola could have cried, and perhaps would have done so except that she was not going to give him the satisfaction of knowing that he had bested her—again.

"What a charming group of ladies," he said, turning to her when they were alone on the terrace. "I must see to it that they are invited to meet here each week."

"So must I." Viola turned sharply away and hurried back into the house, leaving him standing on the terrace.

9

❦

Ferdinand would have enjoyed the following week if it had not been for Viola Thornhill. He had not anticipated the intense sense of belonging he felt at Pinewood. He had considered several careers after university—the army, the church, the diplomatic service—but nothing had appealed to him. But the result of doing nothing had been inevitable boredom and involvement in all sorts of madcap escapades and a general sense of purposelessness. He had not even realized it until he came to Pinewood and discovered that the life of a country landowner fit him like a glove.

But there was Viola Thornhill. He assiduously avoided any further encounter like the one the night he broke the urn. He even more firmly avoided all thoughts of matrimony. That would be a solution bought at too dear a price. And so they continued to inhabit Pinewood together.

He began to return his neighbors' calls. He continued to make friends of them and tried not to admit to himself that he was disappointed to discover how easy it was in most cases. They ought to have been more loyal to Miss Thornhill. He heartily disliked the tedious, pompous Claypoles and believed he would have disliked them under any circumstances. But their stiff, cold civility won his respect. Claypole fancied himself to be Miss Thornhill's suitor, Miss Claypole was her friend, and Mrs. Claypole doted on her children. To them Lord Ferdinand Dudley was simply the enemy.

He set about familiarizing himself with the workings of his estate. He had little knowledge and no experience, having never expected to be a landowner. But he was determined to learn rather than leave everything to a steward. Besides, he might soon be without a steward. Paxton was Miss Thornhill's loyal employee. He made that clear when Ferdinand called on him at his office over the stable block one morning, the estate book tucked under one arm.

"The books are very well kept," Ferdinand said after exchanging greetings with the steward.

"She keeps them herself," William Paxton said curtly.

Ferdinand was surprised, though he might have guessed that the small, neat handwriting was a woman's. It was not a pleasant surprise, though, to know that she had had a direct part in the running of the estate. Worse was to come.

"You have done remarkably well," he said. "I have noticed how everything has changed for the better during the last two years."

"*She* has done well," the steward replied, passion vibrating in his voice. "*She* has performed the miracle. She tells me what to do and I do it. She often asks my advice, and she usually takes it when I offer it, but she does not need it. She could have done it all without me. She has as good a head on her shoulders as any man I have ever known. If she goes from here, I go too, I am here to tell you right now. I'll not stay to see the place go to wrack and ruin again."

"But why should it?" Ferdinand asked.

"We all saw you betting recklessly on almost certain failure in

the village," Paxton said, not even trying to disguise the bitterness
in his voice. "And we all know how you acquired Pinewood through
another wild wager."

"But I did not fail," Ferdinand pointed out, "at either venture. I
do not deal in failure. I find it too depressing."

But Paxton was launched on mutiny. "You promised all sorts of
things the other morning when we went to the home farm," he said.
"The estate cannot afford them yet. *She* understands that. She does
things gradually."

"The laborers need new cottages, not just repairs upon repairs,"
Ferdinand said. "The estate will not pay for them. I will."

Paxton looked at him suspiciously. Doubtless with the label of
gambling wastrel put upon his person went that of impoverished
aristocrat, Ferdinand thought.

"However," he added, "I will need the advice and assistance of a
good steward. Was it Bamber who hired you?"

"The old earl," Paxton said, nodding. "He sent me here, but he
made it clear to me that I would be *her* employee, that Pinewood was
hers, not his."

Viola Thornhill was not the only one who had been given that
impression, then? The late earl really had intended that the property
be hers.

Paxton, like the Claypoles, was someone he came to respect during that week.

He involved himself with other neighborhood concerns. The
church choir was one. The school was another. The roof of the
schoolhouse leaked during wet weather, he learned during a visit to
the schoolmaster. There was still not enough money in the village
fund to have it replaced, even though Miss Thornhill had made a
generous donation. Ferdinand put in what remained to be raised,
and immediate arrangements were made for the job to be done. So
that classes would not have to be interrupted, he offered Pinewood

as a temporary schoolhouse for the appointed day. He told Viola Thornhill about it at dinner.

"But how can it be done?" she asked. "There is not enough money. I was hoping that within the next three or four months—" But she clamped her lips together and did not complete her sentence.

"You could afford it?" he suggested. "I have contributed what remains."

She stared mutely at him.

"I *can* afford it," he told her.

"And so of course you *will*." There was annoyance in her voice. "You will do anything to make a good impression here, will you not?"

"I suppose," he suggested, "I could not be doing it because I believe in education?"

She laughed derisively. "And school is to be held here while the work is being done?"

"Will that inconvenience you?" he asked.

"I am surprised you ask," she told him. "Pinewood is yours—according to you."

"And to law," he added.

He hoped Bamber would not simply ignore his plea to send a copy of the will. He even sent another letter, urging him not to delay. The present situation was ridiculous and impossible—and definitely dangerous. He was compromising the woman by living in this house with her. But it was not just that. He only had to set eyes on her to feel his temperature take an upward swing. Indeed, he did not even have to set eyes on her.

The nights in particular were a trial to him.

Once the will had arrived and she could see for herself that Bamber had left her nothing, she would have no choice but to leave.

It could not be soon enough for Ferdinand.

*　*　*

It was a week of near-despair for Viola. One by one she had to let go of her comfortably negative illusions about Lord Ferdinand Dudley. He was a wastrel who would care nothing about the well-being of the estate or neighborhood, she had thought. His actions proved her wrong on both counts. He was an extravagant, impoverished younger son, she had thought, a man who gambled recklessly and probably had huge debts. But he was going to build new cottages for the farm laborers, Mr. Paxton reported—out of his own money. He was going to pay half the cost of a new schoolhouse roof.

He was not to be driven away either by foolish pranks or by boredom. She suspected that he genuinely liked most of her neighbors. And it was obvious that he was winning their friendship. Under other circumstances, she thought grudgingly, she might even like him herself. He seemed good-natured. He had a sense of humor.

He was idle and empty-headed, of course. She clung to that illusion after all the others. But even that she was forced to abandon before the week was out.

The schoolmaster had marched the children in an orderly crocodile from the village to Pinewood on the appointed morning, and classes had been set up in the drawing room. As she often did, Viola helped out by supervising some of the younger children as they practiced their penmanship. But when a history lesson began, involving all the children, she went downstairs to the library to see if there were any letters.

The library was occupied. Lord Ferdinand sat on one side of the desk, one of the older boys on the other.

"Excuse me," she said, startled.

"Not at all." Lord Ferdinand got to his feet and grinned at her—with the sunny smile that was beginning to play havoc with both her digestion and her sleep. "Jamie is late for the history lesson. Off you go, then, lad."

The boy hurried past Viola, bobbing his head respectfully as he passed.

"Why was he here?" she asked.

"To learn a little Latin," Lord Ferdinand explained. "Not necessary for the son of a tenant farmer destined to take his father's place one day, one might think. But there is no accounting for the desires of the intellect."

"*Latin?*" She knew all about Jamie's brightness and scholastic ambitions, for which his father had neither sympathy nor money. "But who can teach him?"

Lord Ferdinand shrugged. "Yours truly, I am afraid," he said. "An embarrassing admission, is it not? It was my specialty at Oxford, you see. Latin and Greek. My father would have been ashamed of me if he had still been alive."

Gentlemen went to Oxford or Cambridge almost as a matter of course, unless they went into the army instead. But they went mainly to socialize and carouse with their peers—or so she had heard.

"I suppose," she said more tartly than she intended, "you did well."

"A double first." He grinned sheepishly.

A double first. In Latin and Greek.

"My brain," he said, "is so full of dry matter that if you knock on my skull you can watch the dust wafting from my ears and nostrils."

"And *why*," she asked him, "have you been wasting your time climbing over wet roofs at night and gambling?"

"Sowing my wild oats?" His eyes smiled into hers.

She did not want him to be intelligent, studious, wealthy, generous, good-humored, conscientious. She wanted him to be a wild, indigent, unprincipled hellion. She wanted to be able to despise him. It was bad enough that he was handsome and charming.

"I am sorry," he said meekly.

She turned without a word and left the library. She went back to the drawing room to hear about Oliver Cromwell and the Roundheads and the Interregnum. Music was to follow history. She usually helped out with that too.

But the drawing room door opened just as the history lesson was nearing its end, and the schoolmaster clapped his hands for everyone's attention. Viola turned her head to see Lord Ferdinand standing in the doorway.

"We will dispense with the usual music class," the schoolmaster said. He frowned ferociously when someone was unwise enough to begin applauding. "For today *only*, Felix Winwood. Lord Ferdinand Dudley has suggested that since we have the lawns of Pinewood at our disposal and it is a sunny day, we should have a games lesson instead."

"We are off outside for a cricket game," Lord Ferdinand Dudley added. "Is anyone interested?"

It was a foolish question, if ever Viola had heard one. "These children do not even know how to play cricket," she protested.

He turned his eyes on her. "But this is to be a games *lesson*," he said. "They will be taught."

"We do not have the necessary equipment," she said.

"Paxton has bats, balls, and wickets among his things," Lord Ferdinand said. "Long gathering dust, it would seem. He is fetching them."

"But what are *we* going to do while the boys play cricket?" one of the girls asked plaintively.

"What?" Lord Ferdinand grinned at her. "Girls cannot hold a bat or throw a ball or catch one or run? No one ever told my sister that, which was probably just as well. He would without a doubt have ended up with a black eye and a beacon for a nose."

One minute later the children were filing two by two down the staircase, bound for the outdoors, Lord Ferdinand leading the way, the schoolmaster bringing up the rear. Viola trailed downstairs after them. Even the children were coming over to his side.

"His lordship has been down to the kitchen this morning, ma'am," Mr. Jarvey said from the back of the hall. "He has wheedled Mrs. Walsh into making up a batch of sweet biscuits. They are to be served to the children with chocolate to drink before they go home."

"*Wheedled?*"

"He smiled and said please," the butler said sourly.

Yes, he would. He would not be content until he had all the servants worshiping and adoring him too.

"He is a dangerous gentleman, Miss Thornhill," the butler added. "I have said it from the start."

"Thank you, Mr. Jarvey." Viola wandered to the front doors, which stood open. They were down on the lawn beyond the box garden. There was a great deal of noise and commotion, but order was being created out of chaos, she could see, without Mr. Roberts having to step in with his loud schoolmaster's bellow. Lord Ferdinand Dudley was gathering everyone about him. He was explaining something and gesticulating with both arms. And everyone was listening.

She might have guessed that he would be good with children, Viola thought bitterly. After all, he was good with everyone else. She stepped outside, drawn as if by a magnet.

By the time she had descended the steps to the box garden and taken a meandering route through its gravel paths to the low hedge dividing the garden from the lawn, the children had been divided into groups. Mr. Roberts was throwing the ball out to a widely scattered group, who were practicing catching it and throwing it back as quickly and accurately as possible. Mr. Paxton—the traitor!—was leading a group in batting practice. Lord Ferdinand Dudley was showing another group how to bowl.

Viola watched him lope up to the near wickets, throw the ball in one fluid overarm motion, and shatter the far wickets every time. He had stripped down to his shirt and breeches and boots again, she could not fail to notice—he was wearing the same tight black leather breeches he had worn when she first saw him in Trellick. He was patiently and good-naturedly instructing his group, none of whom displayed the smallest suggestion of talent. Then he spotted her.

"Ah, Miss Thornhill." He strode toward her, his right hand extended. "Allow me to help you over the hedge. Have you come to join us? We need another adult. How would you like to take the schoolmaster's place while he instructs the batters and Paxton sets out the pitch ready for a game?"

Viola had very little experience with physical sports. But she had been caught by the gaiety of the scene. She set her hand in his and stepped over the hedge, smiling gaily before she could think of reacting any other way. A few minutes later she was throwing the ball underhand, silently lamenting her inability to throw it nearly as far as Mr. Roberts had done, but nonetheless enjoying the fresh air and exercise.

"You will have more success if you throw overarm," a voice said from directly behind her.

"But I have never been able to throw that way," she told Lord Ferdinand Dudley. To prove her point, she bent her arm at the elbow and hurled the ball with all her might. It hurtled ahead at a downward angle and landed with a thud on the grass perhaps twelve feet away.

He chuckled. "The motion of your arm is all wrong," he said. "You will do better if you do not clutch your upper arm to your side and tighten all your muscles as if for a feat of great strength. Throwing has little to do with strength and everything to do with timing and motion."

"Huh!" she said derisively. The children, she half noticed, were all running toward Mr. Paxton, who was about to explain some of the basic rules of the game to them.

"Like this," Lord Ferdinand said, demonstrating first without a ball in his hand and then with. The ball arced out of his hand and landed some distance away. He went and got it and held it out to her. "Try it."

She tried and achieved perhaps thirteen feet. "Huh!" she said again.

"Better," he said. "But you let go of the ball too late. You are also locking your elbow. Let me help you."

And then he was right behind her, holding her right arm loosely just below the elbow and making the throwing motion with her.

"Relax your muscles," he said. "There is nothing jerky about this."

The heat of his exertions radiated from his body. His vitality somehow wrapped about her.

"Next time open your hand as if throwing," he said. He chuckled softly again a moment later. "If you had had the ball that time, it would have bounced right at your feet. Throw when your arm is just coming to the highest point. Ah, yes, now you are getting it. Try it on your own—with the ball."

A few moments later she laughed with delight as the ball arced upward out of her hand and sailed an impressive distance before curving in for a landing. She turned to share her triumph with him. His eyes were smiling into hers from a mere few inches away. Then he went striding after the ball and she crashed into reality.

She did not join in the noisy, vigorous game that followed. But she did stay out on the lawn, cheering batters and fielders with indiscriminate enthusiasm. After the first few minutes Lord Ferdinand took over the bowling when it became obvious that none of the children could pitch the ball anywhere near the batter. He threw with gentle ease, not to shatter the wickets, but to give each batter a chance to hit the ball. He laughed a good deal and called out encouragement to everyone, while the schoolmaster and Mr. Paxton were more inclined to criticize.

Viola unwillingly watched Lord Ferdinand. She could tell that he had a real zest for life. And he was genuinely kind. It was a bitter admission.

A procession of servants was coming from the house, she could see at last, surely long before the hour could be up. But the game was over, and everyone sat down on the grass, enjoying the rare luxury of steaming chocolate and sweet biscuits. Lord Ferdinand seated himself cross-legged right in the middle of a dense mob of children and chatted with them while they ate.

Then the schoolday was over and the long crocodile of children, walking in orderly pairs, was marched off down the driveway by Mr. Roberts while the servants carried the empty cups and plates inside and Mr. Paxton disappeared back in the direction of his office. Lord Ferdinand was pulling on his coat when Viola turned back to the house.

"Miss Thornhill," he called, "would you care to join me in a stroll? Along the avenue to the hill, perhaps? It is too lovely a day to be spent indoors."

They had been avoiding each other since the night when they had kissed and her attraction to him had warred with the temptation to lure him into falling in love with her. Neither had referred to the incident since. The broken pieces of the urn had been swept up before she left her room the morning after. Another vase had appeared on the table in its place.

It would be as well if they continued to avoid each other. But they could not go on indefinitely like this, inhabiting the same home, each claiming ownership. She just feared that when one of them left, as one of them inevitably must, it was going to be her.

She would never be able to prove that the will had been changed or lost.

His eyes were smiling at her. It was another of his gifts—the ability to smile with a straight face.

"That would be pleasant," she said. "I'll go and put on a bonnet."

10

❧

rawing her into the cricket lesson had been a mistake. So had teaching her how to throw a ball overarm, especially cozying up behind her to demonstrate the correct motion of the arm with her. Suddenly it had felt like a mid-July day during a heat wave. But even more dangerous than her sexual appeal had been her laughter and her exuberant glee when she had finally hurled the ball correctly. When she had turned her sparkling smile on him, he had only just stopped himself from picking her up, twirling her about, and laughing with her.

And now he had invited her to walk with him.

She was wearing a straw bonnet when she came back outside. It fit snugly and attractively over her coronet of braids. The pale turquoise ribbons, which matched the color of her dress, were tied in a large bow beneath her left ear. She looked purely pretty, Ferdinand thought.

They conversed about trivialities until they were on the avenue behind the house. It was already Ferdinand's favorite part of the park. Wide and grassy, it was bordered on both sides by straight lines of lime trees. The turf was soft and springy underfoot. Insects were chirping in the grass, birds singing in the trees.

She walked with her arms behind her back. He could scarcely see her face beyond the poke of her bonnet. The devil of it was, he thought unexpectedly, he was going to miss her after she left.

"You have been helping teach at the village school for some time," he said. "Where were you educated?"

"My mother taught me," she said.

"I understand from Paxton," he said, "that you have been keeping the account books."

"Yes."

"And have taken an active role in the running of the estate."

"Yes."

She was not going to be forthcoming on that topic, he could see. Or perhaps on any topic. But she turned her head to look up at him just as he was thinking it.

"Why do you want Pinewood, Lord Ferdinand?" she asked. "Just because you won it and believe it to be yours? It is not a large estate and it is far from London and the sort of life you appear to have been enjoying there. It is far from any intellectual center too. What is there for you here?"

He breathed in the smells of nature as he considered his answer.

"A sense of fulfillment," he said. "I have never resented my elder brother. I always knew that Acton Park and all the other properties would be Tresham's and that I would be the landless younger son. I considered various careers, even an academic one. My father, had he lived, would have insisted on a commission with some prestigious cavalry regiment. It is what Dudley second sons have always been expected to do. I have never known what it is I want to do with the rest of my life—until now. I know now, you see. I want to be a country squire."

"Are you wealthy?" she asked. "I think you must be."

It did not occur to him to consider the question impertinent.

"Yes," he said.

"*Very* wealthy?"

"Yes."

"Could you not buy land elsewhere, then?" Her head was angled away from him so that he could not see her face.

"Instead of remaining at Pinewood, do you mean?" he asked. Strangely enough, buying land and settling on it was something he had never considered. "But why should I? And what would I do with this property? Sell it to you? *Give* it to you?"

"It is mine already," she said.

He sighed. "I hope within the next day or two that question will finally be settled beyond doubt," he said. "Until then, perhaps the least said, the better. Why are you so attached to Pinewood? You grew up in London, you told me. Do you not miss it and your friends there? And your mother? Would you not be happier back there?"

For a long time it seemed she was not going to answer at all. When she spoke, her voice was low, her head still averted.

"It is because *he* gave it to me," she said. "And because the difference between living here and living in London is the difference between heaven and hell."

He was startled—and not a little disturbed.

"Is your mother still in London?" he asked.

"Yes."

She was not going to elaborate on that monosyllabic answer, he realized. But going to live with her mother seemed to be another solution.

They were almost at the end of the avenue. The hill rose steeply in front of them.

"Shall we climb?" he asked.

"Of course." She did not even break stride, but lifted the hem of her dress with both hands and trudged upward, her head down, watching where she set her feet. She paused for breath when they were still not quite at the top, and he offered a hand. She took it, and he drew her up the rest of the slope until they stood on the bare grassy top.

He made the mistake of not immediately releasing her hand. After a few moments it would have been more awkward to let go than to hold on to it. Her fingers were curled firmly about his.

"When I stood on top of the highest hill in Acton Park as a boy," he said, "I always imagined it as the roof of the world. I was master of all I surveyed."

"Imagination is the wonder and magic of childhood," she said. "It is so easy to believe in forever when one is a child. In happily-ever-afters."

"I always believed happily-ever-after could be earned through honorable deeds of heroism and derring-do." He laughed softly. "If I killed a dragon or two, all the treasures of the universe would be mine. Is not childhood a gifted time? Even though disillusion and cynicism must follow?"

"Is it?" she asked, gazing about at the wide view over fields and river and the house below, centered perfectly between the trees of the avenue. "If there were no illusions, there would be no disillusionment. But then one would have no fond memories either, with which to fortify oneself against the pain of reality."

Her hand was soft and warm in his. A light breeze fluttered the poke of her bonnet and the ribbons that dangled from the bow beneath her ear. He wanted desperately to kiss her and wondered if he was in love with her. Or was it the tenderness of pity that he felt? Or merely lust? But he did not feel particularly lustful at the moment.

She turned her head to look at him. "I have wanted to hate and despise you," she said. "I wanted you to be all the nasty and dissolute things I thought you must be."

"But I am not?"

She answered with another question. "Is gaming your *only* weakness? Even if it is, though, it is still a serious one. It was the vice that ruined my mother's health and happiness and destroyed my life. My stepfather was a compulsive gambler."

"I never wager more than I can afford to lose," he said gently. "Gaming is not a compulsion with me. It was only because a friend of mine was called away by his wife's confinement that I played against Bamber that night."

She laughed, though there was no amusement in the sound. "And so the last of my illusions must be abandoned?" It was not really a question.

He gazed into her eyes and then raised her hand and held it to his lips. "What am I going to do with you?"

She did not answer, but then he had not really expected her to. He bent his head closer to hers, his heart thumping painfully, not so much with the knowledge that he was about to kiss her as with the realization of what he was about to say and seemed powerless *not* to say. There was really only one solution to this situation he had found at Pinewood, and at the moment it was looking like a rather desirable one. It was time perhaps to trust again, even to love again, to take a leap of faith.

"Miss Thornhill—" he began.

But she snatched her hand from his and turned her back on him.

"Gracious," she said, "luncheon must have been ready ages ago. I forgot all about the time when you invited me for a walk. I suppose it was because of the chocolate and biscuits. I am glad you thought of refreshments. Some of the children have a long walk home from the village."

She did not want to be kissed. She did not want to listen to any sort of declaration. That was perfectly clear. Perhaps she would feel differently once she knew she had no other option except to leave Pinewood. But he felt a certain sense of relief, Ferdinand admitted to himself. A huge sense, in fact. He had no wish to marry. He had always been very firm in his intention never to do so. And pity was not a strong enough reason for changing his mind. It must be pity that had impelled him. It could not be love. *Love* was a word his father had always used with contempt—it was for females. His mother had used the word all too frequently. For her, Ferdinand had learned in his formative, impressionable years, love was self-absorption and manipulation and possessiveness.

He must avoid being alone with Viola Thornhill in the future. He had just had a narrow escape. Yet a part of himself gazed at her with a certain yearning. He would miss her when she left Pinewood. She was the only woman he had come close to loving.

"Shall we return to the house, then?" he suggested. "Do you need a hand?" The slope down to the avenue seemed even steeper when viewed from the top.

"Of course not," she said, gathering her skirts above her ankles with both hands and beginning a gingerly descent.

Ferdinand loped down ahead of her and turned close to the bottom to watch her progress. She was running with small steps, and even as he watched she came faster, shrieking and laughing. He stepped in front of her and caught her as she came hurtling down. He lifted her off her feet, both arms about her waist, and swung her around in a complete circle before setting her down on her feet. Both of them were laughing.

Ah, he was a weakling indeed, he thought a moment later as he kissed her, first lightly, then fiercely. He was a man who could not force his emotions and behavior to his will. But she did not resist him as she had done at the top of the hill. She clutched his shoulders and kissed him back.

They released each other after a while, their eyes averted, their laughter gone, and began the walk back to the house side by side, not talking. Ferdinand's mind was in turmoil again. Should he or should he not? Did she wish him to or did she not? Would he regret it or would he not?

Did he love her?

It was on that question that his mind stuck. He knew so little about love—about *real* love, if there was such a thing. How could he recognize it? He liked her, he respected her, admired her, wanted her, pitied her—ah, yes, he *pitied* her. Pity was not love. He knew that much, at least. But was pity the dominant emotion he felt for her? Or was there more?

What was love?

He was still pondering the question when they circled the house to enter by the front doors. Jarvey was in the hall, looking important.

"You have a visitor, my lord," he announced. "From London. I have put him in the salon."

Ah, at last! Was it Bamber's solicitor or Bamber himself? Finally the question of ownership was to be settled. But even as Ferdinand turned toward the salon, the door opened and the visitor stepped out into the hall.

"Tresham!" Ferdinand exclaimed, striding toward his brother, his boots ringing on the tiles, his right hand extended. "What the devil are *you* doing here?"

His brother shook his hand, raised his eyebrows, and grasped the handle of his quizzing glass with the other hand. "Dear me, Ferdinand," he said, "am I not welcome?"

But Ferdinand was not to be cowed by the ducal hauteur, which could have almost every other mortal on the face of the earth quailing in terror. He squeezed his brother's hand and slapped him on the shoulder.

"Did you come alone?" he asked. "Where is Jane?"

"In London with the children," the Duke of Tresham replied. "Our younger son is a mere two months old, you may remember. Being away from them is a severe trial to me, Ferdinand, but your need sounded greater than mine. What *is* this coil you have got yourself into, pray?"

"No coil at all," Ferdinand assured him heartily, "except that it did not occur to me when Bamber lost the property that there might be someone already in residence here."

He stepped aside and turned to make the introductions. He noticed that Tresham was already looking at Viola Thornhill across the hall and even raising his glass to his eye, the better to peruse her.

"Miss Thornhill," Ferdinand said, "allow me to present my brother, the Duke of Tresham."

Her face was an expressionless mask as she dipped into the slightest of curtsies. "Your grace," she murmured.

"This is Miss Viola Thornhill," Ferdinand said.

"Ah." Tresham spoke with faint hauteur. He inclined his head but did not bow. "Your servant, ma'am."

There! Ferdinand thought indignantly. Now if only he could have behaved like that on the very first morning, she would have been gone within the hour. But at the same time he felt annoyed. This was *his* house and *his* problem. He did not need Tresham coming here to bedeck the poor woman with icicles at a single glance.

She was half smiling, Ferdinand saw before he could step into the breach and create a more civil atmosphere. It was a strangely chilling expression and made her look quite different from usual.

"Excuse me," she said. She disappeared upstairs with straight spine and uplifted chin, very much on her dignity.

Tresham was gazing after her with narrowed eyes.

"Dear me, Ferdinand," he muttered, "what *have* I walked in upon?"

Viola went straight to her room and rang for Hannah. She stood at the window while she waited and gazed along the avenue where she had walked just a few minutes ago.

She felt cold through to the very heart.

As soon as she had known who Lord Ferdinand Dudley was, she had thought he resembled his brother. She had met the Duke of Tresham once. They had been at the same dinner party—it must be four or five years ago. Both brothers were tall and dark and slender and long-legged. But there the resemblance ended, she realized now after seeing them side by side. While Lord Ferdinand was handsome, with an open, good-humored countenance, the duke was none of those things. His face was harsh and cold and arrogant. It was easy to understand why everyone feared him.

Just there, she thought, her eyes on the distant hill, Ferdinand had held and kissed her hand and begun to ask her to marry him. She had not allowed him to speak more than her name, but she was convinced that that was what he had been about to do, presumptuous as it might be to believe it. For a moment she had been very, very tempted. It had taken all her willpower to snatch away her hand and turn the moment.

He can destroy you—if you do not first snare his heart.

She had not been able to bring herself to do it.

And there, just there, she thought, moving her eyes lower, she had run shrieking and laughing into his arms and had kissed him with all the passion she had ruthlessly denied just a few minutes before. It had been one of those magical moments, like the throwing contest at the fête and the maypole dance and the kiss behind the oak. One more brief memory to tuck away for future comfort. Except that comfort would be all mingled up with pain.

It would have been easy to snare his heart. And easier still to lose her own.

The door opened behind her.

"Hannah," she said, "the Duke of Tresham has just arrived from London."

"Yes, Miss Vi." Hannah did not sound at all surprised.

"He recognized me."

"Did he, lovey?"

Viola drew a slow, deep breath. "You might as well pack my things," she said. "I think you might as well, Hannah."

"Where will we be going?" her maid asked.

Again the slow breath. But it did not keep the tremor from her voice when she spoke. "I don't know, Hannah. I'll have to think."

"Come into the library," Ferdinand said, leading the way. He felt a little embarrassed being caught returning from a walk with Viola Thornhill as if it were the most proper thing in the world to be sharing a house with a single young lady and living on amicable terms with her. He poured his brother a drink.

Tresham took the glass and sipped from it. "You get yourself into the most unbelievable scrapes," he said.

Ferdinand felt irritated again. He was three years younger than his brother, and Tresham had always been autocratic, especially since inheriting the title and all the responsibilities that went with it at the age of seventeen, but Ferdinand was no longer a boy to be criticized and scolded—especially in his own home.

"What was I supposed to do?" he asked. "Throw her out on her ear? She is convinced that Pinewood is hers, Tresham. Bamber— Bamber's father, that is—promised it to her."

"Are you sleeping with her?" his brother asked.

"Am I . . . Good Lord!" Ferdinand's hands closed into fists at his sides. "Of *course* I am not sleeping with her. I am a gentleman."

"My point exactly." Tresham had his quizzing glass in hand again. If he raised it to his eye, Ferdinand thought, he would be sorry.

"It was rash of her to insist upon staying here with me, of course," Ferdinand said. "But it is also a measure of the trust she has placed in me as a gentleman. She is an innocent, Tresham. I would not sully that." He thought guiltily of the kisses he had shared with her.

His brother set down his glass on a library shelf and sighed. "You really don't know her, then," he said. "You have not recognized her. I suspected as much."

And Tresham *did* know her? Ferdinand stared as him transfixed, a premonition of disaster holding him motionless.

"She has looked familiar from the start," he said. "But I just cannot place her."

"Perhaps," the duke said, "if she had introduced herself by her real name, Ferdinand, your memory would not have played such tricks on you. She is better known in certain London circles as Lilian Talbot."

Ferdinand stood where he was for a moment longer before turning sharply and crossing the room to the window. He stood there with his back to the room, all the cloudy layers ripping away from his memory.

He had been at the theater in London one evening several years ago, sitting in the pit with some friends. The play had already begun, but even so, there had been a sudden noticeable stir from the boxes and a buzz from the predominantly male preserve of the pit. Ferdinand's nearest companion had dug him in the ribs with an elbow and pointed with his thumb toward the party arriving late in one of the boxes. Lord Gnass, an aging but still notorious roué, was removing the russet satin cloak of his female companion to reveal a shimmering gold gown beneath—and a daring amount of the voluptuous flesh of the woman inside the gown.

"Who is she?" Ferdinand had asked, raising his quizzing glass to his eye, as a large number of other gentlemen were doing.

"Lilian Talbot," his friend had explained.

It was the only explanation necessary. Lilian Talbot was enjoying enormous fame even though she was rarely seen in public. She was said to be lovelier and more desirable than Venus or Aphrodite or Helen of Troy all rolled into one. And almost as unattainable as the moon.

Ferdinand had been able to see that reports of her had not been exaggerated. Even apart from her glorious, shapely body, she had a classically beautiful face and hair of a rich dark red set in elaborate but elegant curls high on her head and trailing down onto her long, swanlike neck. She sat down, set one bare arm along the velvet edge of the box, and directed her gaze toward the action on the stage as if she were unaware that the attention of almost the entire audience was on her.

Lilian Talbot was London's most celebrated, most sought-after, most expensive courtesan. But part of her allure was the fact that no one, not even the wealthiest, highest ranked, most influential lord of the *ton*, had ever been able to persuade her to become his mistress. One night was all she would grant of her favors to any man. Some said that no one could afford more than that anyway.

Lilian Talbot. Alias Viola Thornhill.

I am no man's mistress.

"I saw her only once at the theater," Ferdinand said, staring at the fountain in the box garden without seeing it. "I never met her. Did you?"

"Once," Tresham said.

Once? "Did you—"

"No," his brother replied coolly, without waiting for the question to be completed. "I preferred to mount mistresses for long-term comfort rather than one-time-only courtesans for sensation and prestige. What the devil is she doing here?"

"She is a relative of Bamber's," Ferdinand said, bracing both hands on the windowsill. "His father must have been fond of her. He sent her down here and promised to leave her Pinewood in his will."

The duke laughed derisively. "She must have serviced him well if he was prepared to offer her such an extravagant gift after one night," he said. "Doubtless he paid her outrageous fee as well. But he came to his senses in time. It is why I am here, Ferdinand. You might wait until doomsday for Bamber to exert himself. I called on his solicitor and persuaded him to let me see the will. There is no mention in it of either Viola Thornhill or Lilian Talbot. And the present Bamber has never heard of the former, though perhaps he has of the latter. He was clearly unaware that she was living here. Pinewood Manor is without a doubt yours. I am pleased for you. It appears to be a pretty enough property."

Not a relative, but a satisfied customer.

He loved me. Ferdinand could hear her voice down on the river-bank as if she were still speaking. *And I loved him.*

Pinewood had been the impulsive gift of a grateful, dazzled man, who had just been well serviced in bed.

I will never lose my trust in him because I will never stop loving him or knowing beyond any doubt that he loved me.

Even the most experienced courtesan could be naïve on occasion, it seemed. Bamber had changed his mind. Her trust had been misplaced.

"You can order her off the premises without further ado," the duke said. "I daresay she is even now packing her trunks— she knows the game is up. She could see that I recognized her. I will be eternally thankful that I did not bring Angeline with me. She wanted to come since Jane had to remain with the baby, but it has long been my practice to endure our sister's incessant chatter only in small doses. Besides, I believe Heyward said no even before I did, and for some reason I still have not fathomed—it is certainly not fear—Angeline obeys him."

But Ferdinand was not listening.

It is because he gave it to me, she had said only an hour or so ago when he had asked why she loved Pinewood. London's most celebrated courtesan had fallen in love with one of her clients—and had made the cardinal mistake of believing that he loved her in return.

"Where will she go?" he asked, more of himself than his brother. If she was no relative of Bamber's, her options were cut down considerably.

"To the devil, for all I care," Tresham said.

Ferdinand's hands closed more tightly about the sill.

"Good Lord, Ferdinand," his brother said, "you have not conceived a *tendre* for the woman, have you? If this does not beat all—my brother infatuated with a whore!"

Ferdinand gripped the sill as if for dear life. "Whatever she is," he said without turning, "she is under my protection while she is beneath this roof, Tresham. You will not use that word either of her or to her while you remain here, or you will answer to me."

"Good God!" the Duke of Tresham said after a short, pregnant silence.

11

*V*iola dressed carefully for dinner in a pale blue silk evening gown, fashionably high-waisted and low at the bosom, but neither overdaring nor dowdily demure. It was one Mrs. Claypole herself had commended. Viola had Hannah dress her hair in a smooth, elegant chignon. She wore no jewelry, but only an evening shawl about her shoulders.

She had no idea whether Lord Ferdinand and the Duke of Tresham intended to dine at home. She had no idea if she would be denounced and banished from the dining room if they were there. But she was no coward. She would not hide away in her room. Neither would she go quietly if they tried to rid themselves of her company for dinner. After all, she was still living here under the assumption that she belonged here, that it was they who were the usurpers. No proof to the contrary had yet been shown her.

They were both in the dining room, both wearing black evening clothes with white linen, looking very much like the sons of Satan. They rose and bowed at her entrance.

They dined together, the three of them, in a strange charade of civility. Both gentlemen were meticulously polite, making sure that she had everything she needed, careful not to choose any topic of conversation that might exclude her. Under other circumstances, Viola thought, she might have enjoyed herself. But these were not other circumstances. She was scandalously alone with two gentlemen. One of them knew who she was—or who she had been. It was impossible to tell if the other did too. But he would soon.

Viola did not afterward know quite what had been served for dinner or how many courses there had been. All she took away with her was the impression that Mrs. Walsh had excelled herself in deference to the presence of a duke at Pinewood. She found the meal interminable and rose to her feet as soon as she decently could.

"I will leave you to your port, gentlemen," she said. "If you will excuse me, I will bid you good night and go straight to my room. I have a slight headache. I trust you are happy with your room and have everything you need, your grace?"

"Everything, thank you, ma'am," he assured her.

"Miss Thornhill." Lord Ferdinand Dudley drew a folded piece of paper from a pocket of his evening coat. "Would you oblige me by reading this in your own time?"

The will? But it was just a single sheet. The Earl of Bamber's will would surely be a fat document.

"Yes." She took it from him.

It was not the will, she discovered when she had reached her room. It was not really a letter either. It was some sort of declaration, written in a bold, black hand. It stated that although the will of the late Earl of Bamber was not for copying or perusal by anyone unconnected with its contents, it had been produced and read in its entirety by the Duke of Tresham, his claim to an interest in its contents having been acknowledged. The paper asserted that beyond any doubt the will made no specific mention of Pinewood Manor in Somersetshire and none of Miss Viola Thornhill. It was signed by the duke in the same bold, black hand, and by George Westinghouse, solicitor of the late Earl of Bamber.

Viola folded the paper and held it in her lap for a long time while she stared into space. He simply would not have changed his mind. And he would not have delayed. He had known that his health was poor. He had not expected to live more than a month or two longer. He would not have forgotten.

She would not lose faith in him—not again.

The will must have been changed without his knowledge. But there was no way on earth she was going to be able to prove that, of course. And so she had lost Pinewood. How sad he would be if he could know! She felt as sad for him at that moment as for herself—she could feel only numbness for herself. He had thought she was safe and secure for life. He had been cheerful, even happy, as he had bidden her good-bye forever—they had both known it was forever.

A tear plopped off Viola's cheek and darkened the fabric of her skirt.

The Duke of Tresham stayed only until early afternoon of the following day. He was interested in seeing the house and park and home farm, all of which Ferdinand showed him during the morning, but he was eager to return to London and his family. The baby was colicky, he explained, and Jane needed his support during the nights of disturbed sleep. Ferdinand listened to the explanation in some fascination but without comment. Was it not a nurse's job to stay up with a fussy baby? Did Tresham really allow his sleep to be disturbed by a child?

Was it really possible that a marriage that had begun four years ago as an apparent love match had continued as such? With Tresham, of all people? Could he possibly be steadfast in his devotion? And faithful to Jane? Could she be faithful to him? Even now, after she had dutifully borne Tresham two sons—an heir and a spare, to use the vulgar parlance? Jane was a beautiful woman, and a spirited one too.

Was there really such a thing as true, lasting marital love? Even within his own family?

But it was too late to take any real interest in learning the answer. One day too late. Yesterday she had been Viola Thornhill, wholesome, lovely, innocent. Today she was Lilian Talbot, beautiful, experienced—and deceitful to the core of her cold heart.

"I wish you had let me have a word with her this morning, Ferdinand," the duke said as they stood together outside his traveling carriage. "You lack the necessary resolve for performing unpleasant tasks. And you are emotionally involved. I could have had her out of here by now."

"Pinewood is mine, Tresham," Ferdinand said firmly. "And everything concerned with it, even its problems."

"Take my advice and don't allow her to spend another night here." His brother laughed shortly. "But Dudleys have never taken well to advice, have they? Will we be seeing you in London before the Season is over?"

"I don't know," Ferdinand said. "Probably. Maybe not."

"A decisive answer indeed," Tresham said dryly, and took his seat in the carriage.

Ferdinand raised a hand in farewell and watched until the carriage disappeared among the trees. Then he turned and walked back into the house with firm strides. It was time to get rid of the intruder. It was time to harden his heart and behave like a man. Like a Dudley.

The butler was hovering in the hall.

"Jarvey," Ferdinand said grimly, "have Miss Thornhill in the library within the next two minutes." But he paused when his hand was on the doorknob and the butler was already on the second stair.

"Jarvey, ask Miss Thornhill if she will wait upon me in the library at her earliest convenience."

"Yes, my lord."

He stood at the library window, looking out, until he heard the door open and close behind him. He had not even been sure she was at home. He turned to look at her. She was dressed very simply in a light muslin day dress. Her hair was in its usual neat coronet of braids. He looked her over from head to toe. Perhaps after all Tresham had been mistaken, and his own memory had played tricks on him.

"Good afternoon, Miss Talbot," he said.

She did not answer immediately. But his foolish hope died an instant death. A faint smile played about her lips. It was just the expression she had worn at the theater—and in the hall yesterday when he had presented her to Tresham.

"You address me by a name that is not my own," she said.

"You knew very *well* where I had seen you before," he said, his eyes raking her again, with anger this time. How dare she look just so at him! He had been kind to her. But then, she would despise kindness. Good Lord, he thought as if realizing it for the first time, he had been sharing a house with *Lilian Talbot*.

"On the contrary." She raised her eyebrows. "Where *did* you see me, Lord Ferdinand? It was not in any bed you have ever occupied. I believe I might have remembered that. Of course, despite your claim to be wealthy, you probably could not have afforded me, could you?"

Her eyes were sweeping over him as she spoke, giving him the peculiar notion that he was being stripped naked and found wanting—rather as if he had regressed ten years or so to the time when he had shot up to a gangly, spindly height, all legs and sharp elbows and teeth too large for his face.

"At the theater," he said. "With Lord Gnass."

"Ah, yes, Lord Gnass," she said. "He *could* afford me and liked demonstrating the fact."

He could hardly believe how she had been transformed before his eyes.

"I suppose," he said curtly, "Viola Thornhill is an alias. No wonder Bamber has never heard of you. I suppose no one at Pinewood or in the neighborhood knows your real identity."

"Viola Thornhill is my real name," she said. "Lilian Talbot died a natural death two years ago. Are you disappointed? Were you hoping to sample her favors before you toss me out? I was always too expensive for you, Lord Ferdinand. I still am, no matter how large your fortune is."

She was regarding him with that sensuous, scornful half smile. He was repulsed by it and by her words. But he felt his temperature rise despite himself.

"I would waste not a penny of my fortune on purchasing the favors of a whore, Miss Talbot," he told her. He probably would have felt instant shame at his choice of words if she had shown any sign of mortification or even anger. But the look on her face merely deepened to amusement.

"I could not be tempted," he added.

She came closer then, stopping just beyond touching distance—and after he had taken an involuntary step back until his heels clicked against the base of the wall behind him. Her eyes had become heavy-lidded. Bedroom eyes, he thought. With a voice to match, he observed a moment later when she spoke again.

"That sounds very much like a challenge," she said. "I am very, very skilled, my lord. And you are very, very male."

She seemed somehow to have sucked half the air out of the room, leaving precious little to supply the need of his lungs.

"Would you care to make a wager?" she asked him.

"A wager?" He felt deuced uncomfortable, though he would not take another step back even if he could. He was already trapped against the window, looking like a bloody idiot. How had he maneuvered himself into this awkward position anyway? He was the one who had summoned her. He had been going to give her a piece of his mind before ordering her to leave before sundown.

"That I can seduce you," she said. "Or not. However you want it phrased. Bed you. Pleasure you. Cater to all your deepest and darkest sexual fantasies."

Fury held him speechless. *This* was the woman he had pitied? Grown to like? Even fancied himself half in love with? Considered marrying? Was he indeed so gauche? Such a dupe? So easily manipulated? For he could see clearly now that he had been clay in her hands from the first. She had soon realized that she could not drive him away and so had planned a different solution to her problems. She had accomplished her goal with humiliating ease—humiliating for him. If Tresham had not arrived when he had and recognized her, there was no knowing what the rest of the day might have accomplished for her. He might be betrothed to her now. He might at this moment be at the vicarage, arranging to have the first banns read on Sunday.

Now, without a blink, she had changed tactics yet again, but this time she was comfortably within the realm of her expertise. She had made a handsome living on her back. Famed for her beauty and her seductive charms and her prowess in the sexual arts—and for the clever ploy of granting each client only one night of her favors— she had been in greater demand than any other courtesan within living memory.

She chuckled low in her throat. "I *can* seduce you, you know." She moved another step closer, set one forefinger lightly against his chest, and traced a light path upward with it, over his neckcloth toward his bare throat.

He clamped a hand about her wrist and returned her arm to her side. Anger and desire and revulsion all warred within him. "I think not, ma'am," he said. "I prefer to make a free choice of my bed partners."

"Ah, but you do enjoy a wager," she said. "Especially when the stakes are high."

"If you are suggesting that I wager Pinewood," he said, "you are wasting your breath. You would lose."

"But according to you, I already have lost," she said, turning away and crossing the room to run her fingers over the bare surface of the desk. "You really appear to have won, do you not?"

"I dashed well have," he said, glaring at her. "And you have diverted me from my purpose in summoning you down here."

"Ah," she said, turning her head to smile at him, "but you changed your summons to a request, Lord Ferdinand. Mr. Jarvey told me so. You like to think of yourself as a gentleman, do you not? And you consider yourself weaker than your brother, who does not care what anyone thinks of him."

She was uncannily perceptive. But then, an understanding of men must have been necessary in her career.

"I want you out of here before nightfall," he said. "I do not care whether that gives you enough time to pack your things or not. You will leave. Today."

She was still looking at him over her shoulder. "What, Lord Ferdinand?" she said, amusement in her voice when he had steeled himself for either tears or anger. "You are afraid to accept a wager? Afraid that you will lose? How you would be derided in all the gentlemen's clubs if word were to get out that you were afraid of being bested by a woman. By a whore!"

"Don't call yourself that," he said before he could stop himself.

Her smile deepened and she turned to face him fully, her fingertips still lightly stroking the desktop.

"Give me one week," she said. "If I cannot seduce you within that time, I'll never again challenge the authenticity of that will. I will go away and never trouble either your person or your conscience again—I *do* trouble your conscience, do I not? If you lose, of course"—she caught him completely off guard by smiling dazzlingly at him—"then *you* will be the one to leave. You will also relinquish your claim to Pinewood in my favor—and in writing. With witnesses."

"Nonsense!" he said. But the thought struck him at the same moment that it would be an easily enough won bet and that in one week he—and his conscience—would be permanently rid of her.

"But before you left, Lord Ferdinand," she told him softly, her voice sultry again, "you would enjoy a night of such exquisite pleasure that you would spend the rest of your life pining for more."

Despite the revulsion her boast caused him, he also felt an unwilling surge of pure lust. Had she been dressed like a harlot—as she had been at the theater—he would more easily have resisted her. One *expected* an expensive harlot to speak in such a way. But she was clad in a dress of virginal white. Her hair was dressed for elegance and practicality. She was Viola Thornhill, for God's sake. Talking about going to bed with him.

"I never disappoint," she said, lifting her hand away from the desk, moistening her forefinger slowly with her tongue and running it along her lower lip. More of the air seemed to have gone from the room, leaving Ferdinand gasping for breath and fighting to disguise the fact.

"By God!" he blurted, his temper snapping. "I want you out of here. Now. *Sooner.*"

"Would it not be better to have me leave quietly after one week than screaming and biting and kicking and shedding copious tears today?" she asked him. "And stopping in the village to scream and weep some more?"

"Do they *know?*" He frowned at her and for the first time took a few steps farther into the room. "Do these people know who you are?"

"Who I *am?* Yes, of course," she said. "I am Viola Thornhill of Pinewood Manor. They know that I am a connection of the Earl of Bamber's."

"They believe a lie, in fact," he said indignantly. "They do not know you are a whore."

"Present tense?" She laughed softly. "But no, they do not *know*. And what a weapon I have just handed you. You may reveal my dreadful secret, Lord Ferdinand, and doubtless they will gather behind you in a righteous mob to run me out of Somersetshire."

He glared at her, white with fury. "I am a *gentleman*," he reminded her. "I do not go about spreading such unsavory tidings. Your secret is safe with me."

"Thank you," she said with mocking carelessness. "Is that a promise, my lord?"

"Devil take it!" he retorted. "I have said it is so. A gentleman does not need to promise."

"And yet," she reminded him, "it would be an easy way to rid yourself of me for all time, would it not?"

"That is already done," he said. "I daresay you read the declaration signed by both Tresham and Westinghouse that I handed you last evening. Bamber changed his mind, if ever he intended to make you a permanent gift of Pinewood. I daresay he thought it too extravagant a gift for the services you had rendered him."

She stood very still, her finger still resting against her lower lip, staring at him blankly, her faint, contemptuous smile fading. And then she returned her hand to the desk and smiled again.

"You will never know," she said, "unless you avail yourself of those services, Lord Ferdinand. You can only take my word for it that you will not consider Pinewood too extravagant a wager at all. I am very, very good at what I do. But you are convinced, of course, that you can resist me. And perhaps you can. Or perhaps not. It would be an interesting wager. You will forever consider yourself a coward if you refuse to accept it. Come." She walked toward him, her right hand extended. "Shake my hand on it."

"You would lose," he warned her weakly instead of simply repeating his order that she leave before nightfall.

"Perhaps. Perhaps not." She held her hand steady. "Are you *really* afraid of losing to a woman? Having won Pinewood at cards, are you now afraid of losing it at love?"

"*Love?*" he asked with undisguised revulsion.

"A euphemism," she admitted. "Lust, if you prefer."

"I am not afraid of losing anything at all to you, ma'am," he told her.

"Well, then." She laughed and looked for a disconcerting moment like the Viola Thornhill with whom he was more familiar. "You have nothing to fear. This will be the easiest won wager you have ever agreed to, Lord Ferdinand."

"Dammit!" He slapped his hand onto hers and squeezed it so hard that she visibly winced. "You have your wager. One that you will lose, I do assure you. You have one more week here. If I were you, I would use the time wisely and begin to pack and make plans. You will not be staying one day longer than a week. That is a promise."

"On the contrary, my lord," she said, drawing her hand free of his. "It is you who will be leaving—the morning after you bed me and turn over the deed of Pinewood and sign the necessary papers."

She turned then and left the room. Ferdinand stood where he was, looking at the door through which she had disappeared. What in thunder had he just agreed to? Another week spent under the same roof as Viola Thornhill? No—Lilian Talbot.

He had just made a wager with *Lilian Talbot*. A wager that she could seduce him within a week, Pinewood as the prize if she succeeded.

His temper had got the better of him, as it often did. And his inability to resist a wager.

He would win, of course, as he always did.

But he did not want to share a house with Lilian Talbot. Especially when she looked almost identical to Viola Thornhill—to whom he had come within a whisker of offering marriage just yesterday. What a fortunate escape he had had, he thought suddenly.

But he did not feel fortunate. He felt somehow bereft.

Viola made her way upstairs, thankful that the butler was not in the hall as she passed through it. Her hands were shaking, she noticed when she held them before her, her fingers spread. She really had thought Lilian Talbot was dead, consigned forever to the dust. But how very easily she had been resurrected. How quickly she had bundled all that was herself deep inside so that he would not see her raw pain in confronting her past.

He had called her a whore—after objecting to her calling herself that.

She had begun—oh, yes, there was no point in denying it—to fall a little in love with him.

He had called her a whore.

Hannah was still in her dressing room, packing the large trunk Viola had brought with her from London two years before.

"What happened?" she asked sharply. "What did he want?"

"Only what we expected," Viola told her. "He gave me until nightfall to leave."

"We will be ready long before then," Hannah said grimly. "He *knows*, I suppose. That duke told him?"

"Yes." Viola sat down on the dressing table stool, her back to the mirror. "But we are not leaving after all, Hannah. Not now or ever."

"Is there any point, Miss Vi?" her maid asked. "You read me that paper last night. There is no court in the land that will believe you."

"We are not leaving," Viola said. "I am going to win Pinewood from him. I have a week to do it."

"How?" Hannah straightened up from the half-packed trunk, her expression suddenly suspicious. "*How*, lovey? You are not going back to work?"

"I have talked him into a wager," Viola said. "One I intend to win. Never mind about the details, Hannah. Put my clothes back in the wardrobe. They will get creased in the trunk. And have the trunk put away in the attic again. We are staying."

"Miss Vi—"

"No, Hannah." Viola looked at her with set jaw and hard eyes. "No! This is where I belong. This is where he wanted me to be. I *will* not give in just because there has been some fraud. Lord Ferdinand Dudley has made a wager with me, and he will abide by its terms. That at least I can be sure of. He is a gentleman, you see—almost to a fault. It is a wager I will not lose."

Hannah came and stood in front of her, her head tipped to one side. "I don't think I want to know exactly what you are up to," she said, "but I do know you need to lie down for an hour or so. You are as white as any ghost. Turn around and I will brush out your hair for you."

That had always been Hannah's solution to any problem. Viola could not remember a time when her former nurse had not soothed her by brushing her hair. She turned on the stool and felt Hannah's capable hands unpinning and then unraveling her braids.

Just yesterday, Viola thought, closing her eyes, she had run down the hill into his arms, and he had twirled her about and kissed her with a fierce passion to match her own. Today he had called her a whore and ordered her to get out of Pinewood.

Tomorrow or the next day or the next she was going to entice him into bed and pleasure him there with the cold sensual arts she had learned and practiced to perfection.

She was going to do those things with Lord Ferdinand Dudley. *To* him.

One more time.

And then she was going to have to live with herself for the rest of her life. At Pinewood. It would be hers—indisputably and forever.

But would there be any dreams left to dream?

12

❦

During the next two days Ferdinand began to think that perhaps the week would pass faster and more painlessly than he had expected after agreeing to that mad wager. Perhaps she had come to regret it herself. Certainly if she intended to win it, she was going a strange way about it. He scarcely saw her.

He had a dinner engagement the first evening. It was only when he returned that he learned she had been out too, and still was. He went to bed, taking a book up with him. He heard her walk past his room an hour or so later. Her footsteps did not slow outside his door.

He saw her briefly at breakfast the following morning. She was finishing her meal as he entered the dining room after an early ride. She was looking her usual neat, wholesome self. She would be gone most of the day, she informed him. It was her regular day for visiting the sick and elderly. It struck him that it was not the way one would expect Lilian Talbot to spend her time, but he was happy enough that she would not be going to the school to help out. He had already promised that he would go there himself to give another lesson to Jamie, the would-be Latin scholar.

He intended to call on the boy's father afterward to see what could be arranged for the boy's future education. Jamie needed to be at a good boarding school. Ferdinand was quite willing to finance the whole venture himself, but he had a parent's pride to deal with. He would have to talk of scholarships, Ferdinand thought, rather than financial assistance.

"Will you be attending the assembly tomorrow evening?" Viola Thornhill asked before she left.

There was to be a dance at the assembly rooms above the inn. He had heard about it wherever he went. He certainly planned to attend. It was important to him to be an active participant in village life.

"Yes, indeed," he said. "You may ride in my carriage with me."

"Thank you." She smiled. "But I will be dining at Crossings and will go to the assembly with the Claypoles."

The Claypoles, he thought, would have a heart seizure apiece if they knew the truth about her.

He did not see her again for the rest of the day. He dined at home, but she did not. He went to choir practice at the church, but she did not. He learned when he returned home that she had been delayed at the cottage of one of the laborers, helping to care for five young children while their mother delivered a sixth.

She was going to be missed when she left Pinewood, Ferdinand knew. His neighbors treated him politely. A few had even warmed to him. But he sensed that most of them still resented the fact that he had come to turn their Miss Thornhill away.

This time he did not hear her come home. He fell asleep with his book open and his candle still alight. She had returned at four o'clock in the morning, he learned at breakfast—from which meal she was absent.

When he came back to the house after a session with Paxton, she had already left for the school.

He did see her during the afternoon, when the ladies' sewing circle gathered in the drawing room again. She was sitting demurely sewing when he went in there, shamelessly to charm the ladies and to read them another few chapters of *Pride and Prejudice*. Viola Thornhill stitched on through it all, just as if he were not there, her neck arched delicately over her embroidery frame. The sunlight pouring through the windows picked gold and auburn highlights out of the predominantly dark red braids of her hair. She was wearing one of her simple, pretty muslins.

If Tresham had not said it, he thought, he would be doubting the evidence of his own eyes now. How could she be the same woman as that voluptuous courtesan in Gnass's box, with her haughty, contemptuous half smile? Or the same woman who had forced a wager on him two days ago?

He dined alone before proceeding to the assembly. She had gone off with the Claypole ladies. Five more days after this one was over, he thought. Then he would be free. She would be gone, and he would never see her again.

Five more days.

But the thought did not cheer him nearly as much as it ought.

During her working years, men—titled, wealthy, powerful, influential men—had pursued Lilian Talbot relentlessly. Viola Thornhill had no idea how to entice a man who was determined not to have her. It was not that Lord Ferdinand did not want her. She knew he did. He had kissed her on four separate occasions. On the night he had broken the urn, he had come very close to going beyond mere kisses. No, it was not lack of desire that would make him difficult to seduce. It was his love of a wager, his determination to win it at all costs.

She could use none of her more obvious seductive arts on him. They just would not work. He would resist them. The best way to proceed, she had decided that very first day, was to convince him that she was not proceeding at all. It would be best to confuse him with the illusion that she was Viola Thornhill, that Lilian Talbot was indeed dead and gone. It would be best to tease him with only the occasional glimpse of her when he must expect to be bombarded with her company and full-blown sexual allure.

She would win the wager. She was determined to do so. Her resolve strengthened after she received a letter from Maria, telling her how much Ben was enjoying school, how much he wanted to work hard and become a lawyer when he grew up, how very kind it was of Uncle Wesley to pay his school fees.

There would be no more money to send. Pinewood's income was now Lord Ferdinand Dudley's. The little money Viola had brought with her to Pinewood had gone into the estate and to her family. What the estate had earned in two years had gone back into further improvements—and to her family. Uncle Wesley would continue to care for them, of course. They would not be destitute. But Ben would have to leave school, and there would be very little money for all the extras that added comfort to life.

There would be no more money to send unless she won her wager. She was determined to win it.

She dined at Crossings the evening of the assembly. Mr. Claypole took her aside before they left for the village and proposed marriage to her yet again. For a moment she was tempted, as she never had been before. But only for a moment. Marrying Thomas Claypole would not really solve her problems. She would live in comfort and security as his wife, but she could not expect him to pay for Ben's schooling or to help support her family. Besides, he did not know the truth about her, and she would not so deceive him as to marry him.

She refused his offer.

Soon she was in the carriage with the Claypoles, on the way to the assembly. Lord Ferdinand Dudley would be there, she thought. She would see him for a few hours at a stretch.

She wished—oh, she wished, wished, *wished* she had not been forced to make that wager with him. But there was no other way.

The village assemblies were always jolly affairs. All the sets here were country dances, performed in circles or lines, some slow and stately, others fast and vigorous, all with precise, intricate patterns, which everyone knew from long practice.

Ferdinand danced every set. So did Viola Thornhill. He talked and laughed with his neighbors between sets. So did she. He ate supper in company with a group of people who had invited him to take a seat at their table. So did she.

They scarcely looked at each other. He was aware of almost no one else. They did not exchange a word. Yet he heard her low, musical voice and her laughter even when the whole room separated them. They did not share a table, yet he knew that she ate only one-half of a buttered scone and drank only one cup of tea. He did not ask her to dance, yet he noticed the light, graceful way in which she performed the steps and pictured her with a maypole ribbon in one hand.

This time next week she would be gone. The next time there was an assembly he would be able to concentrate the whole of his attention on the pretty girls with whom he danced. He hated this constant awareness, this constant alertness for the move she must surely make soon if she hoped to have any chance at all to win her wager before time ran out. He wished fervently that she had assaulted him with all her tricks on that very first day. He had been angry enough then to resist her with ease.

He was talking with the Reverend Prewitt and Miss Faith Merrywether when Viola touched his arm. He looked down and was somewhat surprised to see that her fingers had not burned a hole through the sleeve of his evening coat. He looked into her face, flushed from the exertions of dancing.

"My lord," she said, "Mr. Claypole has had to take his mother home early. The heat has made her feel faint."

"Mrs. Claypole does not have a strong constitution," Miss Merrywether commented disapprovingly. "She is fortunate indeed to have such a doting son."

But Viola Thornhill had not removed her eyes from Ferdinand's. "They were to escort me home," she said. "But Mr. Claypole thought it wise not to take such a wide detour on his way to Crossings."

"I would be delighted to call out my carriage for your convenience, Miss Thornhill," the vicar assured her. "But I daresay his lordship will squeeze you into his."

She looked mortified and smiled apologetically. "Will you?"

Ferdinand bowed. "It would be my pleasure, ma'am," he said.

"Not just yet, though," she said. "I would not drag you away early from the dancing. There is still one more set. I was to dance it with Mr. Claypole."

"I would lead you out myself," the Reverend Prewitt said with a hearty laugh, "if I had any breath and any legs left, but I confess I have neither. His lordship will see to it that you are not a wallflower, Miss Thornhill. Will you not, my lord?"

The color in her cheeks deepened. "Perhaps his lordship has another partner in mind," she said.

But there was that glow of color in her face, and her eyes were still sparkling from an evening of dancing. Her hair, dressed in curls tonight rather than the usual coronet of braids, was still tidy, but a few wavy tendrils of hair teased her neck and temples. There was a slight sheen of perspiration on her cheeks and on her bosom above the neckline of her evening gown.

I have been waiting for a suitable partner, sir. He could hear again the low, saucy words she had spoken to him when he had sought her out to dance about the maypole with him. *I have been waiting for you.*

"I was prepared to be a wallflower myself," he said, offering her his arm, "believing that your hand had already been engaged."

She set her hand on his sleeve and he led her onto the floor to join the long lines that were forming for the Roger de Coverly.

The dance consumed all their energy and concentration. There was no chance to talk, even had they wished to. But she glowed and laughed with delight when it was their turn to twirl between the lines and lead the procession around the outside to form an arch with their arms for everyone else to dance beneath. He could not take his eyes off her.

He was still more than halfway in love with her, he realized. How could he not be? What he should do on the way home was tell her to forget that outrageous wager. He should just marry her so that they could both remain at Pinewood. Forever after. Happily ever after.

But she had been Lilian Talbot. And the courtesan in her still survived—he had seen it for himself just two days ago.

He could not simply forget and pretend that she was Viola Thornhill as he had known her for the first week. She had deceived him.

A great heavy sadness seemed to lodge itself suddenly in the soles of his dancing shoes.

Fortunately, the music drew to an end within the next few minutes. Less fortunately, it was the final set. He was handing her into his carriage only minutes later. What did all the neighbors think of the situation at Pinewood? he wondered. He would not have to worry about it for much longer, though, would he?

Five more days.

Viola was beginning to hate herself. Or perhaps it would be more accurate to say that she was beginning to hate herself *again*. There had been two years of healing, but really, she had discovered in the past few days, the gaping wound of her self-loathing had only filmed over, not knitted into wholeness at all.

It was so easy to play a part, to send herself into deep hiding and become someone else. The trouble was that this time the part she played and her real self were so similar to each other that sometimes she got them confused. She was wearing down his defenses by playing the part of Viola Thornhill. But *she was Viola Thornhill.*

Mr. Claypole really had decided to take his mother home early, but he had wanted to escort Viola home on their way. She had refused by lying. She had told him it was all arranged for her to return to Pinewood in Lord Ferdinand Dudley's carriage.

She had wanted to dance with Lord Ferdinand. She had wanted to remind him of the evening at the fête. But acting had got all jumbled up with reality. She had enjoyed herself immensely and been hopelessly miserable at the same time.

She sat silently beside him until the carriage wheels had rumbled over the bridge.

"Do you ever feel lonely?" she asked him softly.

"Lonely?" The question seemed to surprise him. "No, I don't think so. Alone, sometimes, but that is not the same thing as loneliness. Aloneness can actually be pleasant."

"How?" she asked.

"One can read," he said.

It had surprised her to realize that he did enjoy reading. It seemed out of character somehow. But then, so did the fact that he had graduated from Oxford with a double first in Latin and Greek.

"What if there are no books?" she asked.

"Then one thinks," he said. "Actually, I have not done a great deal of that for many years. I have not been much alone either. I used to be when I lived at Acton. So was Tresham. It used to be like an unspoken conspiracy sometimes—he would go off to his favorite hill and I would go to mine. It was furtive. Dudley males admitted only to being hellions, not to being thinkers, brooding on the mysteries of life and the universe."

"Is that what you did?" she asked.

"Actually, yes." He chuckled softly. "I used to read a great deal, though not openly when my father was at home. He did not approve of bookish sons. But the more I read, the more I realized how little I knew. I used to gaze out at the universe feeling all the frustration of my smallness—especially the smallness of my brain. And then I would gaze at a blade of grass and tell myself that if only I could understand *that*, then perhaps I could penetrate the larger mysteries too."

"Why have you not done that for many years?" she asked.

"I don't know." But he had obviously thought more deeply about her question before he spoke again. "I have been too busy being busy, perhaps. Or perhaps I realized when I was at university that I could never know everything and so gave up the attempt to know anything. Perhaps I have been in the wrong place. London is not conducive to thought—or wisdom."

The interior of the carriage became a little lighter as it moved clear of the trees. The conversation had not taken the course she had expected. More and more she was realizing that Lord Ferdinand Dudley was not at all the man she had taken him for when he first arrived at Pinewood. She wished she did not like him. Liking him was making things very difficult for her.

"What about you?" he asked. "Are you ever lonely?"

"No, of course not," she said. Why were people so reluctant to admit to loneliness? she wondered. It was almost as if it were something shameful.

"That was a hasty answer," he said. "Too hasty."

"Loneliness can be a balm to the soul," she said, "especially when one considers some of the alternatives. There are far worse afflictions than loneliness."

"Are there?" In the faint light she could see that his face was turned toward her.

"The worst thing about loneliness," she said, "is that it brings one face-to-face with oneself. That can also be the best thing about it, depending upon one's character. If one is strong, self-knowledge can be the best knowledge one can ever acquire."

"Are you strong?" His voice was soft.

She had thought she was. She really had thought so.

"Yes," she said.

"What have you learned about yourself?"

"That I am a survivor," she said.

The carriage rocked to a halt on its comfortable springs, and the door opened almost immediately. Lord Ferdinand's groom set down the steps.

Mr. Jarvey had waited up and took her cloak and Lord Ferdinand's cloak and hat when they stepped into the hall. He disappeared with the garments.

"Come into the library for a nightcap?" Lord Ferdinand asked her.

She could probably accomplish her goal tonight if she set her mind to it. They would share a drink and more conversation, and then he would escort her upstairs. She would pause outside his room and thank him for bringing her home. She would sway toward him so that he would be kissing her before he even had a chance to realize his danger. It would all be over within an hour after that. Tomorrow he would be gone. Pinewood would be hers.

She felt the soreness of unshed tears in her throat and chest and shook her head.

"I am tired," she said. "Thank you for bringing me home. Good night."

She did *not* sway toward him. Neither did she offer her hand. But there it was in his, and he was raising it to his lips, and his eyes were regarding her over the top of it, a faint smile softening their darkness.

"Thank you for the dance," he said. "But it is the maypole dance for which I will always remember you."

She fled, not even pausing to take a candle from the hall table. Had she done that deliberately? Caused him to kiss her hand and look at her like that and speak so softly about always remembering her? It was what she had set out to do. It was *exactly* what she had hoped to accomplish. But she had not really done it, had she? She had simply been herself.

Or had she been the Viola Thornhill who intended to throw him off guard sufficiently that he would not realize that when he bedded her he would be losing his wager to Lilian Talbot?

She no longer knew who was herself and who was the courtesan. She no longer knew whether she wanted to win that wager or not. She dreaded—*dreaded*—being in bed with him, feeling him coming inside her while she coaxed him to a pleasure so prolonged and so intense that he would never after feel cheated. How could Viola Thornhill hide deeply enough in the persona of Lilian Talbot to allow it to happen?

Viola Thornhill—the real Viola—wanted to join herself with him in love. It was something she had never experienced and could not really imagine experiencing. For the physical joining of man and woman was an ugly, demeaning act. But dreams were not quite dead after all, she was finding. And her dreams wove themselves about his person in a way that had nothing to do with any wager.

What she should do, Viola thought as she fled along the upper corridor in the darkness, was go back down to the library and announce to him that their wager was off, that she would leave Pinewood tomorrow. But she kept going until she was inside her room, the closed door firmly and safely between her and temptation.

13

❧

For the next two days Viola went about her daily round of activities with her usual energy and cheerful smile, but her mind and emotions were in turmoil. Perhaps, she thought sometimes, she should go away to somewhere other than London and seek employment. But Hannah and her family would have to fend for themselves, then. Why should she have to bear all the responsibility? But the thought of relinquishing her family to their own resources consumed her with guilt.

She could win Pinewood with her wager, and life would be back to normal again. But she could not bear the thought of seducing Lord Ferdinand—it nauseated her and filled her with self-loathing. He was a decent man.

But remaining at Pinewood was not just about money. It was her *home*, her legacy. She simply could not face leaving it.

On the third morning after the assembly, with two more days to go before she must either win her wager or leave Pinewood, matters were severely complicated by the arrival of another letter from

Claire. It was lying on the desk in the library when Viola returned from a morning walk along the avenue. She snatched it up eagerly and took it with her to the box garden. She sat on the bench that surrounded the fountain, after checking to see that the seat was dry. It had rained all the day before, though the sun was shining again today.

Everyone was well, Claire reported. She was working every day for their uncle. She liked serving in the coffee room best, where she met and talked with travelers and a few local people who came there regularly. One gentleman in particular had begun to come quite often. He was extremely pleasant and always thanked her for her kind service and gave her a generous tip. She had not recognized him at first, not having seen him for many years, but Mama and Uncle Wesley had.

Viola clutched the single sheet of paper with both hands and suddenly felt her heart beat faster. She sensed what was coming even before her eyes confirmed her premonition.

"He is Mr. Kirby," Claire had written, "the gentleman who used to frequent the inn when you worked here and then was obliging enough to recommend you for a governess's position with his friends. Mama and Uncle Wesley are delighted to see him again."

Viola clenched her eyes tightly closed. Daniel Kirby. Oh, dear God, what was he doing back at her uncle's inn? She opened her eyes and read on.

"He has asked about you," the letter continued. "He had heard you had left your position, though he did not know you are now living in the country. He gave me a message for you yesterday. Let me see, now. I want to get it just right. He had me repeat it after him. He said that he hopes that you will come back to town for a visit soon. He has discovered another paper that he is certain would be of interest to you. He said you would know what he meant. He also said that if you were not interested in seeing it, then he would show it to me instead. Was that not a provoking thing to say, for now of course I long to know what is in that paper. But he would not tell me no matter how much I pleaded. He would only laugh and tease me. But you see, dear Viola, we are not the only ones who long to see you again. . . ."

Viola stopped reading.

Another paper. Oh, yes, indeed, she knew what he meant. He had "discovered" another bill to be paid, even though he had sworn in writing that he had produced them all, that they had all been settled. They were her stepfather's numerous unpaid bills, most of them gaming vouchers, which Mr. Kirby had purchased after his death.

He had become a regular customer at the White Horse Inn after Viola's family moved there. He had been very amiable, very kind, very generous. And then one day he had told Viola he could help her to find more interesting employment than she had. He had friends, new to town, who needed a governess for their four children. They preferred to choose someone from a personal recommendation than go to an agency or put an advertisement in the papers. He would arrange for an interview if she wished.

If she wished. She had been ecstatic. So had her mother. And Uncle Wesley had raised no objection. Although he would be losing help at the inn, it pleased him that his niece would be in employment more suited to her birth and education.

She had gone to the interview, escorted by Mr. Kirby. And she had found herself in a dingy house in a shabby part of London, confronting a woman whose orange hair and painted face had made her look frighteningly grotesque. Sally Duke would train her for her new profession, Mr. Kirby had explained—and he had made no bones about what that profession was to be. Viola had flatly refused to proceed, of course. She could remember now the terror she had felt, the fear that she was a prisoner and would not be allowed to go free. But Mr. Kirby had assured her in his usual kindly manner that she was free to leave whenever she wished, but that her mother and her young sisters and brother faced long incarceration in debtors' prison if they were unable to pay off all their debts. He named the total to her, and she had felt all the blood draining downward until her head was cold and her ears were ringing and the room began to spin about her.

She had been nineteen years old. She had a mother who was in a state of nervous and physical collapse after the death of her husband. Claire had been nine years old, the twins six. Uncle Wesley had already paid off a few debts, which seemed trifling in comparison with these—there was no way he could pay them. And Mr. Kirby, of course, knew it. Viola had been able to see no way out but compliance with his demands.

The arrangement had been that eighty percent of all she earned was to go toward the reduction of the debt. She was to live on the remaining twenty percent. It behooved her, then, to work hard, to establish a reputation for herself, so that her twenty percent would enable her to keep body and soul together.

Later, when she was already working, she had been informed that only twenty of Mr. Kirby's eighty percent could be applied to debt reduction. The remaining sixty paid Mr. Kirby's fee for housing her, procuring clients for her, and looking after her best interests. To all intents and purposes, Viola had been a slave. But she had used the little power she had to insist upon working no more than two nights a week and to refuse to be any man's exclusive mistress. She had quickly become more sought after than any other courtesan in London.

By some strange miracle, she had kept the secret from all of her family. Only to Hannah had she rashly poured out her heart as soon as she knew the truth of what her future held. Hannah had insisted upon going with her even though Mama had warned that a governess would not be allowed to have her own personal maid. Her family still believed she had been a governess for four years before coming to Pinewood. Her mother had been furious with her for leaving such respectable employment in order to accept the gift.

The debts had not been significantly reduced in four years. The interest had eaten up the bulk of her payments. She had known Mr. Kirby would hold her in thrall for the rest of her working years, but she had not been able to think of a solution. It had seemed that she was caught in a lifelong trap. But then she had met the Earl of Bamber. And he had discovered the truth—she had poured her heart out to him one night, seated beside him on the plush sofa in her living room, his arm securely about her shoulders, her head nestled on his shoulder. She had told him everything she had kept bottled inside for four long years, and he had kissed her cheek and told her she was a good girl and he loved her.

A good girl. Love.

The words had been like a spring of pure water in the middle of a desert. Balm to an aching soul.

He loved her. She was loved. She was a good girl. She was three-and-twenty years old and a veteran at her profession. But she was a good girl and she was loved. He loved her.

He had called on Daniel Kirby and persuaded him to produce all the bills still owing. He had paid them all off and obtained a signed, witnessed note that there were no more. And then he had asked Viola if she would like to go to Pinewood Manor to live. It was a long way away, in the middle of nowhere, to use his own words, and as far as he knew it was probably shabby. Certainly it did not fill his coffers with income. But he would send her there if she wished, and he would send a good steward down to get everything sorted out for her, and a good butler to set the house to rights and hire other servants. The manor would be hers. He would leave it to her in his will.

She had buried her face in the hollow between his shoulder and neck and wrapped her arm about his portly middle. She had felt safe and loved and strangely clean for the first time in four years.

"Oh, yes," she had said. "Oh, yes, please. But I don't want to leave you." She had known he was gravely ill.

He had patted one large hand against the side of her face and kissed her temple. "I will be going home to the country to die," he had said gently. "My wife is there."

Grief and love and gratitude and happiness had soaked his cravat and neckcloth with a flood of tears.

The sound of booted feet on stone brought Viola back to the present with a jolt. She was sitting on the bench in the box garden at Pinewood, Claire's letter clutched in both her hands. Lord Ferdinand was striding toward the house from the direction of the stables. He always looked his most enticing in riding clothes, she thought. He paused for a moment, seeing her, and touched the brim of his hat with his whip. She half raised one hand in greeting. He did not come down the steps to join her but continued on his way into the house. She breathed a deep sigh of relief.

Claire was in terrible danger. The meaning of the message was very clear. Daniel Kirby wanted Viola to return. Although she was twenty-five years old, rather aged for a courtesan, she had retired at the height of her fame. She would still be remembered. There would surely be a rush of prospective clients, at least for a while, if word spread that she had returned to town—and Mr. Kirby would see to it that that happened. She could earn far more money for him, at least for a year or two, than Claire could do as a raw novice, who might never take as well as her sister even after training.

Viola swallowed once, and then again. For a minute or two she had to concentrate very hard not to vomit. The very thought of Claire . . .

If she did not return, he would use Claire. That was the threat he held over her head. He had kept back at least one of the bills. She was going to have to pay it off by going back to work.

Unless she owned Pinewood.

It was prospering. It was true that she had planned to put most of the profits back into improvements. It would be many years—if ever—before she could consider herself a wealthy woman. But the profits did not *have* to be reinvested. They were hers, to be spent as she wished. She could make payments on the debt. They would be endless payments, of course, but there was little she could do about that. She could . . .

But Pinewood was not hers. It was Lord Ferdinand's.

Unless . . .

Viola closed her eyes and crumpled the letter in her hand.

Yes, *unless.*

Ferdinand would have dined at the Boar's Head except that he had been told that Viola Thornhill was to spend the evening with the Misses Merrywether. He was counting down the days. There were two to go. He was stubborn to a fault. He knew that. He had made a decision, but even so he was going to torture himself for two more days with brief glimpses of her—like this morning in the box garden—and short encounters with her. He wanted her with every beat of his pulse, but he was determined to win his wager, to be able to throw that, at least, in her teeth.

She was being very foolish, of course. There had been no glimpse of Lilian Talbot since the day of their wager. Only of Viola Thornhill. How could she hope to seduce him like this?

He dressed for dinner even though he would be dining alone—it was the habit of a lifetime. He was humming as he entered the dining room, but he stopped abruptly. She was standing by the sideboard, talking with Jarvey, and there were two places set at the table. She was wearing a gold silk gown without any jewelry or other adornment. The garment itself was of such simple design that Ferdinand knew at a glance that it was very costly indeed. It shimmered over her curves in a way that would have made further adornment quite redundant. Her hair was a smooth, shining, dark red cap over her head. Her braids were coiled at the back, low on her neck. She was beauty and elegance personified.

Ferdinand checked his stride. For a moment he misplaced the rhythm of his breathing. She smiled, and he was not at all sure whether she was Viola Thornhill or Lilian Talbot. He suspected that she was wearing one of the latter's gowns. But it was a sweet smile.

"I thought you were dining with the Misses Merrywether," he said.

"No."

There was nothing for it, then, but to seat her at the table, take his own place, and make the best of the situation. They conversed politely on a number of topics. She told him how she had started the ladies' sewing group as a social outlet for the women of the neighborhood and observed with a smile that even when they were being sociable, women liked to be useful too. He told her about Tattersall's and the horse auctions that were held there every week.

They talked about the weather.

She told him how the river walk had been so overgrown when she first came to Pinewood that she had thought the area was mere wilderness. When she had discovered that there was a well-defined path there, she had set the gardeners to work and had even sent some of the farm laborers to help them. He told her about Oxford and the delight he had taken in the libraries there and the conversation of men who were unashamedly intellectual.

"It is a wonder," she said, "you did not stay there and become a lecturer or a professor or don."

"No." He laughed. "By the time I had finished my studies, I was vowing never to open another book in my life. I wanted to *live*."

They talked about the weather.

She told him that her one real extravagance since coming to Somersetshire had been buying books. She sent to London and Bath for them. Several of the books in the library had been added during the past two years, including the copy of *Pride and Prejudice* from which he was reading to the ladies. He talked about the book, and they embarked on a brief but spirited discussion of its merits.

They talked about the weather.

When she rose at the end of the meal and announced that she would leave him to his port, he breathed a silent sigh of relief. It was over for another day. She was incredibly beautiful. She was also charming and intelligent and an interesting companion. It was easy to relax into the pleasure of her company and forget that after two more days he would never see her again.

He found it a rather depressing thought.

He left the dining room a mere ten minutes later, not having drunk any port, and made his way to the library. But Jarvey intercepted him.

"I have carried a tea tray up to the drawing room, my lord," he said, "at Miss Thornhill's request."

Did she expect him to join her there? But it would be churlish of him not to.

"She asked me to inform you," the butler added.

She was pouring a cup of tea for herself when he entered the room. She looked up, smiled, and poured another for him.

"You did not stay long," she said.

She took her own cup and saucer and sat down to one side of the fireplace. She had had the fire lit, he saw, even though it was not a cold night. But it was almost dark outside and the candles were lit. The fire added coziness to the room. He took the chair at the other side of the hearth.

She did not speak. She was drinking and gazing rather dreamily into the flames. She looked relaxed and elegant at the same time.

"Why did you become a courtesan?" he asked, and could have bitten out his tongue as soon as the words were spoken.

She transferred her gaze to his face and her expression changed so slowly and so subtly that for a while he was unaware of it. He was aware only of acute discomfort.

"Why else does one work?" she asked him. "For money, of course."

He had been pondering the question a great deal during the past few days. He had never thought much about whores and their motivation. But when he *did* think about them, he concluded that they must enter their profession for one of two reasons—love or money. Which had it been for her? She had answered the question. But she had been London's leading courtesan for a long time, and she had charged a fortune for a fee. Surely after the first year or so she had not needed to continue to work for money. She must have made enough on which to retire quite comfortably.

"Why did you need the money?" he asked.

Her smile, he realized suddenly, was not Viola Thornhill's. "Asked like a true son of the aristocracy," she said. "I had to eat, my lord. Food is necessary to survival. Had you not realized that?"

"But you must have made a fortune," he said.

"Yes," she agreed. "Yes, I did."

"Did you *enjoy* it? Your profession, I mean?" He understood now that he was talking to Lilian Talbot—the amusement in her eyes was faintly mocking. Her voice had become lower pitched, more velvet in tone.

She laughed softly and began to run one finger lightly along the neckline of her gown, beginning at one shoulder. "Everyone, male and female, hungers for sex," she said. "Is it not a dream profession to work and earn one's living doing what one most enjoys? It is far preferable to making up beds and emptying chamber pots for a pittance."

He was slightly shocked. He had never heard a lady use the word *sex* or speak openly about sexual hunger.

"But with so many different men?" He frowned.

"But that is part of the allure," she told him. "It is said, you know, that no two men are identical, that each has unique gifts. I can vouch for the truth of that."

Her finger had paused at the slight shadow indicating the valley between her breasts. She hooked the fingertip down inside the fabric of her dress. He felt an uncomfortable tightening in his groin.

"And it was the challenge of my profession," she said, "to satisfy the individual needs of each client. To give so much pleasure that each man would plead for more. And never forget me."

Who had started this? he wondered, leaning farther back in his chair as if to put more distance between himself and her. And why the devil had the fire been lit on such a warm night?

She seemed to be having the identical thought. "It is very warm in here, is it not?" she asked, and she reached down a little farther into her décolletage to pull the silk of her bodice away from her flesh before returning it and sliding the finger up inside the bodice to her shoulder again.

He was mesmerized by the sight of that long finger. When he looked up into her eyes, they laughed knowingly at him.

"I should have had my maid dress my hair up off my neck," she said, raising both arms and sliding her fingers beneath the coiled braids there. She closed her eyes briefly and tipped back her head. And then he realized that her fingers were working at the braids, her movements quite unhurried. She drew out pins and set them down neatly on the table beside her. The braids uncoiled and then fell, two of them, down her back. She drew one over her shoulder and unraveled it. Thick, wavy hair spread over her bosom and down to her waist as she drew the second braid over her other shoulder and unraveled that too. She shook her head when the task was completed, and her hair fell about her in luxurious, disordered waves.

Ferdinand's mouth was dry. He had not taken his eyes from her. Neither of them had spoken a word for several minutes.

"That is better," she said, looking across at him with heavy-lidded eyes. The sharp, mocking look had gone. "Are you overwarm too? Why do you not remove your neckcloth? I will not mind. There are just the two of us. I have told Mr. Jarvey that we do not wish to be disturbed."

He was not so dazzled that he did not know exactly what was happening. She had decided that tonight was the night, and she had gone into action. She intended to bed him within the next hour and banish him tomorrow. For all the heavy sensuality of her eyes, he could not miss noticing their essential emptiness. She was working. This was business to her. And she was an experienced worker.

But very, very good. Every bit as good as she had promised. She had not even touched him yet. She was sitting several feet away from him. She was fully clothed; so was he. But he was wearing silk evening breeches. It would have been foolish to try to disguise his arousal. How would he do it? Grab a pillow and set it on his lap? He made no such attempt. Her eyes had not dipped, but he felt no doubt at all that she knew very well what effect her voice and actions would have on any red-blooded male.

He might have fought her. He might have jumped to his feet, fully aroused though he was, and walked from the room. He had always had good control over his sexual urges. But it was perhaps part of her skill, he thought as he reached up and unknotted and removed his neckcloth, that she could seduce even a man who knew he was being seduced and had sworn it could not happen.

The point was that perhaps it would be better this way. He had decided that he was going to give her Pinewood, that he was going to walk away from it, figuratively as well as literally, and buy himself property elsewhere. He would give her what was rightfully hers— the old earl should never have promised and broken his promise. A gentleman just did not act that way. The trouble was, she might spurn the gift from him. There was no predicting her reaction when he told her.

Perhaps he should simply let her win her wager.

And he wanted her. Desire had become indistinguishable from

pain. His erection pressed against the tight, confining fabric of his breeches.

"Open your shirt at the neck," she said, leaning back in her chair and laying her head against its rest so that it looked in the candle-light as if she were already laid back against pillows, her hair spread in a dark red cloud of waves about her. "You will feel cooler."

He doubted it, but he did as she suggested and ran one hand inside his shirt. His chest was damp. She was watching him and moistening her lips, the tip of her tongue moving slowly across her upper lip.

"Has anyone told you how beautiful you are?" she asked him.

No one had. He was deeply embarrassed. What man would enjoy being called beautiful? At the same time, it felt as if Jarvey must have crept in invisibly and built the fire halfway up the chimney.

"You *are*, you know," she said. "Incredibly beautiful. Even with your clothes on."

He shot out of his chair then and closed the distance between them in a few strides. He held out a hand for hers, and she placed her own in it and allowed him to draw her to her feet and straight into his arms.

"Witch!" he said, before fastening his open mouth to hers.

But she drew back her head and set her two forefingers against his lips.

"You are impatient," she said. "I wanted to make love to you with words for an hour or longer, but I cannot do that when you are touching me. Do you not like making love with words?"

"I think we had better go to bed," he said. "I want action, not words. I am conceding defeat, you see. You win. I will pay dearly for you. Pinewood in exchange for one night in bed with you. You have promised that I will never regret it. Live up to your promise, then."

He tried to kiss her again, but she cupped his face with both hands, holding it away from her, and gazed into his eyes. An extraordinary thing happened then. Lilian Talbot gradually dissolved into Viola Thornhill. He tried to draw her closer again. He was desperate for her. But she broke from his grasp and turned to run with stumbling steps toward the door.

"Viola—" he called.

But she was through it and gone before he could say any more.

14

❧

Viola did not stop running until she was inside her bed-chamber, the closed door against her back.

She could have won the wager within the hour. Indeed, he had already conceded defeat.

She had just not been able to do it.

She did not understand why. He was merely one more man; it was merely one more night of work.

She had not been able to do it.

She pushed herself away from the door and moved toward her dressing room, peeling off her gold silk gown as she went. She reached for her nightgown, but her hand stilled before she touched it. She could not bear to lie down here, to try to sleep, knowing that in time he would come up to his own room, not far from hers. She dressed quickly in one of her day dresses. She drew a warm cloak about her shoulders and as an afterthought pulled down the blanket that was always kept folded on top of the wardrobe.

The hard part was leaving her room again. She set her ear to the edge of the door and listened. There was no sound. She opened the door a crack and peeped out. Nothing and no one. She darted along the corridor, her heart thumping, ready to run back to her room if she should see him on the stairs. But they were deserted and she ran down, pausing when she reached the drawing room floor and gazing warily at the closed door. It remained shut. She darted down to the hall, which was mercifully deserted, slid back the bolts on the front doors as quickly and quietly as she could, and slipped outside. She pulled the door closed slowly, trying not to make a sound.

A minute later, she was half running along the terrace and down the sloping lawn until the trees that shaded the river walk hid her from view. Then she slowed. She had to. The moonlight did not penetrate here and she had to find her way to the path by touch and memory. Even the path itself was dark—almost frighteningly so. But she made her way along it, telling herself that ghosts and goblins were preferable to the inside of Pinewood Manor tonight. Soon enough she had walked past the trees and there was light by which to see where she was going. It was even sparkling on the surface of the river.

She sat down in the exact spot where she had made a daisy chain a week or ten years ago. It was not a chilly night, but she wrapped both her cloak and the blanket about her—she was shivering. She hit the black depths of despair as she sat. There was no glimmering of hope left. She drew her knees up, wrapped her arms about them, and rested her forehead on them.

The fight had gone out of her and she did not know how she would ever find the energy to get up from where she was. But it would not take a great deal of energy, she thought fleetingly, to move the few feet from where she was to the riverbank. The water was deep and fast-flowing. All she would have to do . . .

But even escape into oblivion was not an option. If she died, Claire would have to take her place. . . .

A twig snapped and her head shot up from her knees.

"Don't be alarmed," a voice said. "It's just me."

She would have preferred the ghosts and goblins. *Far* preferred.

"Go away," she said wearily, returning her forehead to her knees.

He did not answer her. Neither did he go away. She sensed rather than heard him sitting on the bank beside her.

"How did you know I was here?" she asked.

"I saw you," he said, "from the drawing room window."

And he had pursued her, his lust unsatisfied. But he was all out of luck. Lilian Talbot was dead. Oh, she would have to be resurrected soon enough, but not tonight. Not here. And never with him.

She sat in silence. So did he. He would go away eventually, she thought, and she would be left to concentrate on her despair. It frightened her. Even at her darkest moments, she had never been much given to self-pity.

And then every muscle in her body tensed. His hand had come to rest on her head, his touch so light that for a moment she was not sure that her senses were not playing tricks on her. But then she felt his fingertips, feather-light, massaging her scalp through her hair.

"Shhh," he said, though she had not spoken a word.

She dared not move. She did not *want* to move. His touch felt so very good, so very soothing. She had always been the pleasure giver. None of her clients had ever considered her pleasure. Why should they? Besides, personal gratification had always been the farthest thing from her mind while she had been at work. She let go of despair and accepted the brief gift of the present moment. She was relaxed in every muscle when his hand lifted and brushed her hair over to the side farthest from him. Then his lips were against the back of her neck, warm, soft, light. She should have felt threatened—he had also moved closer to her side—but instead she felt immeasurably comforted.

"I am Viola Thornhill," she said without lifting her head. She had not intended to speak. But it was as well that he know, just in case he had come with any idea of resuming what she had abandoned in the drawing room.

"Yes." His voice was a whisper of sound against her ear. "Yes, I know that, Viola."

The sudden yearning she felt was as piercing, as painful as the despair that had preceded it. She lifted her head and turned her face to him. He was only inches away. She could not see his expression in the darkness.

"I know," he said again, and then his mouth was on hers.

She hugged her knees and allowed the kiss. She did not participate except to relax her lips and teeth. She stood back mentally and emotionally, rather as she had done the night of the fête, except for different reasons, to observe. And to take the kiss to herself as a gift. She felt gifted.

He was not fierce and impatient, as he had been earlier in the drawing room. He kissed her slowly and with infinite gentleness, his mouth open, warm, and moist, his tongue tracing the line of her lips and then penetrating slowly, exploring, touching, teasing, sending darting spirals of sensation down into her throat and even into her breasts. One of his hands cupped the side of her face and then smoothed the hair back from her temple.

She had little previous experience with gentleness. She was helpless against it.

"Viola," he whispered when he finally drew back his head.

"Yes."

A question had been asked and answered. But she was no longer outside herself, observing. She had spoken the one word from a deep inner need—for someone gentle and tender, for someone who asked the question with her name, for someone who did not demand that she perform for him.

He touched her then, drawing her upward until they were both on their knees, facing each other. He unbuttoned her cloak and let it fall. She lifted both arms as he drew her dress off over her head. He did not immediately remove her shift too. He set his hands on either side of her waist—they were trembling, she noticed—and lowered his head to kiss her beneath one ear, at the base of her throat, on the rise of one breast. When his mouth closed over the nipple and suckled her, she tipped back her head, closed her eyes, and buried her fingers in his hair.

And then she lifted her arms again while he removed her shift.

She was almost a total stranger to physical desire. She felt it now in the almost painful tightening of her breasts and in the raw, pulsing ache in her womb and down between her thighs. She was pressed to him from her waist to her knees, and through the thin silk of his knee breeches she could feel again the hard bulk of his erection.

She would do nothing except surrender. She knew exactly what to do to bring him crashing to pleasure, but she would do nothing. She was Viola Thornhill tonight, not that other woman. But she did not know what to do with her own desire.

Please. Please, please.

"Please."

He had been suckling her other breast, but he lifted his head at the sound of her voice and gazed into her eyes.

"Yes," he whispered. "Let me spread your cloak on the grass. And roll my coat for a pillow."

He was taking it off as he spoke. He arranged their bed while she knelt and watched, and then stood to undress while she lay down and waited for him. He was even more beautiful without his clothes, she saw as first his waistcoat and shirt and then his stockings and breeches came off. But she said nothing and made no move to touch him. She rested her hands palm-down on either side of her naked body. He removed his underdrawers and knelt down beside her. He was large. She could see that even in the near-darkness. A pulse throbbed between her legs. She did not want to wait any longer. She willed him not to want any more foreplay.

"Viola." He leaned over her and spoke against her lips. "I want to be inside you. Now."

"Yes." She spread her legs on the cloak as he came over her. He settled between them and on top of her. He was heavy. His weight was almost robbing her of breath. The ground was hard against her back. She had never before done this anywhere except on a bed, but she was glad the whole experience was to be different. She was glad the ground was hard. She was glad there were stars above. She was glad she could hear the sound of rushing water.

He slid his hands beneath her, and she raised her knees and braced her feet on the ground. He came into her with one deep, hard thrust. He held very still in her for a few moments before sliding his hands away and lifting some of his weight onto his forearms. He looked down into her eyes and touched his mouth to hers.

She was aching and throbbing from her thighs up to her throat. She wanted to wrap her legs about his, tighten her inner muscles about his hardness, and spread her hands against his back so that she could arch upward and touch his chest with her hardened nipples. But she lay still and relaxed.

"Tell me it feels good," he whispered.

"It feels good."

"I want to go now," he said, his voice tense and breathless. "I *must* go. But I want it to be good for you."

"It will be good." She lifted her hands from the cloak and spread them lightly over his buttocks. "It *is* good."

He came hard and fast then. It was over within moments. But it did not matter. Her pain reached a point beyond which it could not be borne. She cried out and the stars above her shattered into a million shards of light. At the same moment she heard him call out his own release.

The sense of peace and well-being that followed negated any discomfort the hard ground at her back and his full relaxed weight might have brought. She listened to the water flowing past the bank and watched the stars re-form themselves above her head and hugged the moment to herself with all her will.

He inhaled deeply and released the breath on a sigh before rolling to one side of her. She thought it was over, but he reached for the blanket, pulled it over them, and drew her against him, one arm pillowing her head. She breathed in the scents of cologne and sweat and man and relaxed. His body was warm and damp against hers. She thought she might sleep if she just concentrated upon the moment and did not allow her thoughts to drift to tomorrow or any more distant future. *The present moment is, after all, the only moment we ever have,* she thought.

She was at the point of dozing when one reality of what had just happened struck her with absolute certainty.

He had been a virgin.

Ferdinand did not sleep. He had been a dismal failure, he thought. If he had timed himself—he had not done so, thank God—he would surely have discovered the humiliating truth that the whole thing had been over within one minute. Less than a minute from mount to release. He felt mortified indeed. He just had not fully imagined what it would be like to feel her soft, wet heat sheathing him. He had thought he knew, but his expectations had fallen lamentably short of reality.

He had wanted to be gentle with her. He had wanted her to feel that he was doing something for her, not just for his own pleasure. He had wanted her to feel less like a whore and more like a woman.

Instead he had gone off half-cocked, like a damned schoolboy.

She had burrowed her head into the hollow between his neck and shoulder and appeared to be sleeping, which was at least a promising sign. He kissed the top of her head and twined his free hand into the luxurious thickness of her hair.

There was a certain feeling of relief despite his embarrassment. He was twenty-seven years old. He had known when he was still a boy that he could never marry, since there was no such thing as marital fidelity among his own class. The idea of marital infidelity had always sickened him. But it was only when he was older—when he was at university, in fact—that he had learned to his alarm that while he had perfectly healthy sexual urges, he could not satisfy them with a whore. He had tried a few times. He had gone to brothels with his friends and ended up paying the girl of his choice on each occasion for nothing more than her time. The thought of the physical act without any emotional component had chilled him. The thought of doing it with a whore, who knew no sentiment at all, gave him the shudders.

He had begun to think there must be something wrong with him. At least now he knew he could do it. In under one minute—he grimaced. He had probably broken some record, for God's sake.

He wished he could have made it better for her. She had needed comforting, and he had offered comfort. It had been more than just sex. Yes, he was sure it had.

"Mmmm," she said on a long sigh as she moved and stretched against him.

He felt the stirrings of renewed desire and smiled when she tipped back her head to look up at him, the moonlight on her face.

"Viola."

"Yes."

He half expected her to berate him with his inadequacy as a lover, but she looked almost happy. He could feel himself growing hard again. She must feel it too—her body was against his—but she did not draw away. He wanted to be inside her again, to feel that feeling again, to see if he could make it last longer than one minute.

And then she did move—to kneel up beside him. He felt foolish. Once had obviously been more than enough for her.

"Lie on your back," she said.

At first he felt alarmed. The moonlight showed her in all her glorious beauty—firm, voluptuous breasts, small waist, very feminine hips, shapely legs, her hair a dark, loose cloud about her face and down her back. But the moonlight lit her face too, and there was nothing there of the contemptuous half smile he feared to see. She was not playing the part of courtesan.

He turned onto his back and she came astride him and leaned over him, setting her hands flat on the grass beside his head. Her hair fell about him like a fragrant curtain. He felt the tips of her breasts touch his chest as she kissed him openmouthed, and he hardened into full arousal.

He kissed her back, his hands spread over the outsides of her thighs. He did not know what else to do. He did not know where to touch her or how. Had she been a novice, like him, he could have experimented until he learned what best pleased her. But he was afraid of being gauche.

She knelt upright even as he was thinking it, spread her legs wide, caressed him lightly with both hands, and brought herself down onto him until she was sitting on him, fully impaled. He inhaled slowly, fighting for control.

Then she moved, her fingertips light against his stomach, her head tipped back while she rode to a rhythm that pulsed with the beating of his blood. He bent his legs at the knee to brace his feet on the ground, and he rode with her.

There could be no greater sensual delight. While he pulsed with desire, with the urge to drive up into her until his seed sprang, he also felt powerful, detached from his need, in control of it. He wanted the act to last a long, long time. All night. He wanted this to go on forever. He wanted *her* forever. He watched her. Her eyes were closed, her lips parted. He was giving her pleasure, he thought, and the realization made him happy. He was redeeming himself.

He listened to the rhythmic suck and pull of their mating, to her labored breathing and his own, and wondered how she could hold her legs wide for so long without cramping. He massaged his hands over her thighs, and she lifted her head to smile down at him. Somehow it was the most intimate moment of all.

And then she did something that had him gripping her thighs. She clenched inner muscles about him as he reached the peak of his thrust and then relaxed them as he withdrew . . . and clenched again as he entered. He had never in his life known such exquisite agony. The rhythm became faster and more frenzied until she broke it suddenly, holding still when he expected her to move, relaxing her muscles when he expected her to clench them.

He spilled in one hot thrust and fell off the edge of the world.

Somewhere out in the vast reaches of the universe came the echo of her wordless cry. And two spoken words.

"My love."

In his voice.

When he awoke, they were both tangled in her cloak and the blanket. His feet were chilly, though the rest of him was warm—he had her for an extra blanket. She was still on top of him. He was still inside her. A strand of her hair was tickling his nose.

"Are you awake?" he asked.

"No." Her voice was sleepy.

"Well." He chuckled. "You have won our wager in fine fashion, have you not?"

He knew he had made a mistake as soon as the words were out. She did not stiffen. She did not move at all or say anything. But he knew he had said the wrong thing. He tried again, his voice more gentle.

"Pinewood is yours," he said. "I could not deprive you of it, you see. I will give you the deed in the morning. I'll have the legalities attended to in London and then it will be official. Your home is yours, Viola. For the rest of your life. Your nightmare is over." He kissed the top of her head.

She still said nothing.

"I'll be relinquishing every claim to Pinewood," he said. "Winning it at cards does not quite match the promise you were made, does it?"

"But the winning of wagers is more important to you than almost anything else," she said, speaking at last. "This is one you have lost. I have won. I knew I had a better chance to seduce you as Viola Thornhill than as Lilian Talbot. But I could have done it as either one tonight, could I not? You did not stand a chance. It was a foolish wager to agree to."

He felt a lurching of doubt. But dammit, he had hurt her. He had said the wrong thing. They had been making love, for God's sake. The wager had been the farthest thing from his mind. And from hers too, he was quite sure.

"I was not thinking of the wager when I came out here after you, Viola," he said.

"Then the more fool you." She disengaged herself from him as she spoke and pushed up onto her knees to lift herself off him. She gathered up her clothes, stood up, and began to dress. "I had a week. I did not need that long. I could have bedded you anytime during the past five days. You have lost, Lord Ferdinand. I wonder." She looked down at him, pushing her hair to one side so that her face would not be in shadow. "Do you feel cheated? Or do you feel that what you have had from me tonight more than compensates you for the loss of Pinewood?"

The devil! Dammit! It was Lilian Talbot who was looking down at him as she straightened her dress at the shoulder. That ghastly half smile was playing about her lips. And her voice had become a velvet caress.

"I believe," he said curtly, "we were making love."

She laughed softly. "Poor Lord Ferdinand," she said. "It was the illusion of love. What it was in reality was very good lust. Very good for you, that is. Men always like to believe that their prowess in bed can crumble the defenses of even the most hardened whore. It is necessary for their pride's sake to give the impression that one has received as much pleasure as one has given. Did I do well?"

"Viola—" he said sharply.

"I am a *very* hardened whore," she said. "You were foolish to tangle with me."

It had been an act? The whole if it? And in his foolish inexperience he had thought they were making love? Was it possible? Or was she merely covering up for the hurt of being told that she had won their wager? He had intended to follow up by telling her that it had been his intention all day simply to give her Pinewood.

He watched her go without even attempting to call after her or follow her. He had already stuffed one of his shoes into his mouth. He would doubtless ram the other one in too if he tried to rectify the situation. He had so little experience in dealing with the sensibilities of women. He had expected her to be amused at the reminder of their stupid wager. He had expected her to laugh.

Dammit, was he *mad*?

He was going to have some major humble pie to eat in the morning, he thought ruefully. He had better sit up for what remained of the night composing some speech that would mollify her and keep his footwear out of his mouth. Not that her good opinion should matter a great deal to him. It would not take long, after all, to hand over the deed and the note he would sign and have his valet witness even before he went down to breakfast. He would leave right after breakfast. He might even eat at the Boar's Head. It would not really matter what she thought of him.

Except that it mattered one devil of a lot.

And the prospect of leaving tomorrow and never seeing her again caused his stomach to clench into knots of panic.

Dammit!

He had never expected to fall in love. He had never wanted to. By what joke of fate, then, had he fallen in love with a notorious ex-courtesan?

And fallen hard too.

Goddammit all to hell!

15

❧

*V*iola had left her cloak and the blanket behind. But she did not feel the chill of the night air as she hurried along the river path, scrambled up through the trees and over the lawn, and half ran along the terrace.

You have won our wager in fine fashion, have you not?

And she *had* won it. Except that the wager had been that she would *seduce* him. That had not been seduction.

But to him it had. To him what had happened had been nothing but sex. What had she expected?

My love, he had said against her ear.

So what? That was just the sort of nonsense many men babbled in sexual climax. Oh, Sally Duke had been quite right. One must never, *never* equate sex with love. No matter what passionate declarations a man might utter while in bed, sex was simply physical gratification to him, the woman only the instrument of his pleasure.

Viola made her way to the servants' quarters as soon as she had entered the house.

He was going to give her the deed to Pinewood in the morning. Her winnings, her pay for the services she had rendered twice down by the river. She would no longer owe her home to the dead Earl of Bamber, but to Lord Ferdinand Dudley, satisfied client.

No!

She tapped on Hannah's door and eased it open, hoping not to startle her maid into screaming.

"Don't be alarmed," she whispered. "It's just me." Exactly the words he had used a few hours ago, she remembered, wincing.

"Miss Vi?" Hannah shot up in bed. "What is it? What has he done to you?"

"Hannah," she said, still whispering, "we are leaving. You will need to get dressed and pack your things. If you finish before I do, you may come and help me, if you please. But come quietly."

"Leaving?" Hannah said. "When? What time is it?"

"I have no idea," Viola admitted. "One o'clock? Two? The stage-coach passes above the village very early, and it does not stop unless there are passengers waiting by the side of the road. We must be there."

"What happened?" Hannah peered at her in the darkness. "Did he hurt you? Did he—"

"He did not hurt me," Viola said. "There is no time for talk, Hannah. We must catch the stage. I cannot stay here another day. We will take only what we can carry. I do not want anyone to know we are leaving."

She left before Hannah had a chance to ask any more questions, and hurried in the direction of her own room. There was no sign of him as she went. Perhaps he had remained down by the river. Perhaps he was sleeping again. Perhaps she had serviced him that well, she thought bitterly.

She would not cry. There was nothing on this earth worth shedding a tear over, least of all her own foolish heart.

*   *   *

It was surprising how quickly one could become attached to a place, Ferdinand thought. He was standing at the window of his bed-chamber, looking out over the box garden and the lawns and trees beyond. Over the tops of the trees he could just see the spire of the church at Trellick.

He did not want to leave.

But his bags were packed, and he was dressed in his riding clothes. Bentley had just shaved him. While he was having breakfast—though he was not at all hungry—his carriage would be loaded up and would set off for London with Bentley. His groom would accompany it on Ferdinand's horse. He himself would drive his curricle.

He should perhaps have left earlier. She probably would not want to see him again, and it would be just as well if he did not see her. But he owed it to her to place the deed of the manor in her hand and also the letter he had written, assuring the world in case of his sudden death within the next few days that he had given her Pinewood Manor. He needed to explain that even if last night had not happened he would still be giving it to her and would still be leaving, never to bother her again.

He did not want to leave.

It pained him to think that he would see her only once more. It was just that she had been his first sex partner, he tried to tell himself, and that he could not imagine bringing himself to do it with anyone else after her. But he was not sure he was being truthful.

He moved resolutely from the window and went down for break-fast. It was early, but she was usually an early riser. He was disap-pointed not to find her in the dining room. He had steeled himself for meeting her there. He had planned exactly how he would look at her and exactly what he would say.

He forced himself to eat two slices of toast and drink a cup of coffee. He dawdled over a second cup, but she still did not come down. Perhaps she was avoiding him, he thought. Undoubtedly she was, in fact. Perhaps he should simply leave. Even so, he paced the hall, his boots ringing on the tiled floor, for half an hour or so after leaving the dining room. His carriage and servants and baggage had left long before.

She had had a late night. It had been after two o'clock when he came back to the house not long after her. She was sleeping late. Or more likely, she was deliberately keeping to her room until he left. He had told her last night, had he not, that he would be going away today? He had offended her with his foolish notion of a joke, and she was not going to forgive him.

Well, he would wait no longer, he thought eventually. The morning was already well advanced. He was wasting precious traveling time. He strode into the library. He would leave the deed and the letter on the desk. He knew she looked there every morning for incoming mail. He would tell Jarvey to make sure she checked there.

There was a letter already lying on the otherwise bare surface of the desk. Had this morning's post already come, then? It was addressed to him, he saw as he picked it up—and recognized the small, neat hand that kept the estate books. What the devil? She could not face him this morning and so had written to him instead? He unfolded the letter.

"We each conceded victory to the other in the drawing room last evening," she had written. "It was a stalemate. Our wager was void. What happened afterward had nothing to do with any wager. Pinewood is yours. I am leaving." There was no signature.

Ferdinand strode to the door.

"Jarvey!" he bellowed. For once the butler was not hovering in the hall. He came soon enough, though. Probably everyone in the house had heard the summons. "Go fetch Miss Thornhill *now*."

The butler retreated in the direction of the stairs, but Ferdinand knew it was hopeless. She would not have put that letter there before going to bed. She would have put it there, as he had been going to put his, as she was leaving the house.

"Stop!" he called, and the butler turned on the bottom stair. "Never mind. Find her maid. And fetch Hardinge from the stables. No, forget it, I'll go there and talk to him myself." He did not wait to see Jarvey's reaction to such confused and conflicting orders. He hurried from the house to the stables.

There was no carriage missing but his own. No horse either. And the groom looked as blank as Jarvey had when Viola Thornhill's name was mentioned. So did young Eli. Damn the woman. Goddamn her! Unless he had missed something in her letter—but how could he have, when it was as terse a letter as any he had ever seen—she had given no clue to her destination. She had simply gone. Probably to London.

"Is there a stagecoach that stops in Trellick?" he asked.

"It used to come right down to the Boar's Head, m'lord," Hardinge explained, "but there were too few passengers getting on and off there, so now it passes on by and just stops to drop off the odd passenger on the main road."

"Or pick up the odd passenger who happens to be standing there?"

"Yes, m'lord."

Goddammit!

She had escaped. She had slipped through his fingers. She had punished him in the worst possible way for what he had said last night—*as a joke,* for God's sake. He had made light of what had happened between them by telling her she had won their wager. She had punished him by disappearing without a trace, leaving him in possession of an estate he no longer wanted. Neither did she, it seemed.

Did anyone in this godforsaken place know where she might have gone? How the deuce was he going to find her so that he could stuff the deed down her throat? Before he throttled her, that is.

Devil take it, he had been *joking.* They had been making love—at least that was what he had been doing. He could not speak for her—he was pathetically low on experience. But surely she would not have taken such stupid offense if she had not been making love too. If she just had a spark of humor in her body she would have been crowing all over him long before he made his stab at a joke. She would have been teasing him to death about one of the few wagers he had lost in his entire life—and to a woman. She could have made much of that.

One did not joke with a woman, he guessed, wincing inwardly as he strode back to the house, when one had just finished making love to her. It was probably wiser to whisper sweet nothings. He would remember that next time.

Next time—ha!

The stagecoach guard riding up behind the coach blew his yard of tin as a signal of something—that they were approaching an inn for a change of horses or that someone was about to pass them in one direction or the other or that there were sheep or cows or some other obstruction on the road ahead or that they were approaching a tollgate. The horn had been blasting at frequent intervals throughout the long, uncomfortable day. Sleep was impossible. Whenever Viola had come close to nodding off, she had been rudely jolted awake again.

"What is it this time?" Hannah mumbled from beside her. "I'll give that man a piece of my mind, I will, when we stop next."

A fellow passenger agreed. Another hoped that the sound meant an inn and refreshments ahead—he was starved. They had been allowed only ten minutes at the last stop. The cup of tea and meat pasty he had ordered had not come in time. A spirited litany of complaints followed.

Viola looked out through the window beside her. There was no sign of any town or village ahead. But there was another vehicle passing them—from behind. The road was not wide at this point, and the coachman did not draw his vehicle to one side or even slacken its speed to let the other pass. This happened all too often, she thought, holding her breath and involuntarily shrinking back from the window as if to allow the curricle more room to pass. The road abounded with discourteous stagecoach drivers and reckless, impatient gentlemen with their sporting vehicles.

This particular curricle passed at high speed. It remained clear of the stagecoach by a mere few inches. The gentleman plying the ribbons drove with consummate skill and with criminal disregard for his own safety and that of the stagecoach passengers. Viola glanced up to the high seat of the curricle. Its driver glanced down into the interior of the coach at the same moment and their eyes met for the merest fraction of a second.

Then both he and his curricle were past.

Viola sat sharply back in her seat and closed her eyes.

"The fool!" someone said. "He might have killed us all."

What on earth was he doing on the road to London? Had he not read her letter? Had he seen her? *Of course he had seen her.*

Viola kept her eyes firmly closed as her thoughts and emotions swirled. All day she had been remembering the night before and trying desperately not to remember. But the only other thing to think about was the future and all it would hold for her. . . .

The guard blew the horn again and a passenger cursed. Hannah scolded him and reminded him that there were ladies present. The coach was slackening speed. It was an inn this time. And the first thing Viola saw as the stagecoach drew into the crowded yard was the curricle that had passed them on the road ten minutes earlier. An ostler was changing the horses.

"Hannah!" Viola grabbed her maid's wrist as the steps were set down and the passengers scrambled to get out and make the most of the short time they would be allowed. "Stay here, please. You are not desperate for anything, are you? We will wait until the next stop."

Hannah looked surprised, but before she could question Viola's strange request, someone had come to stand in the doorway and was extending a hand toward Viola.

"Allow me," Lord Ferdinand Dudley said.

Hannah drew in a sharp breath.

"No," Viola said. "Thank you. We do not need to get out."

But he was not the smiling, good-natured gentleman she was most familiar with. He was the grim, hard-jawed, arrogant, demanding aristocrat he had been that first morning at Pinewood. His eyes looked very black.

"Hannah," he said, "get down, please. Go inside the coffee room and order yourself a meal. You need not hurry. There will be plenty of time to eat it. The stagecoach will be continuing on its way without the two of you."

"It most certainly will not." Viola bristled with indignation. "Stay where you are, Hannah."

"If you wish to scrap with me in the inn yard with a score of people looking on, I am game," he said grimly. "But you will not be continuing your journey on this stagecoach. I suggest we go inside to the private parlor I have reserved and scrap there. Hannah, please?"

Hannah took his hand without further argument and scrambled down from the coach. She disappeared in the direction of the inn without even looking back at Viola.

"Come." He had reached his hand back inside.

"Our bags——" she said.

"Have already been taken down," he assured her.

She was angry then. "You have no right," she said, brushing aside his hand and descending to the cobbled yard without his assistance. Her bag and Hannah's were indeed standing side by side on the ground. "This is bullying. This—" She encountered the grinning face of an interested groom and clamped her mouth shut. He was not the only one who had stopped work in the obvious hope of witnessing a fight.

"Runaway wives need firm handling," Lord Ferdinand remarked cheerfully, obviously for their further amusement. He took her elbow in a firm grasp and propelled her toward the inn while she listened indignantly to the purely male laughter behind them.

"How dare you!" she said.

"It's dashed fortunate I caught up to you before you reached London," he said. "What the devil did you mean by running off like that?"

He led her down a long, low-beamed corridor to a small room at the back of the inn. There was a fire crackling in the hearth. A table in the middle of the room had been set with a white cloth and laid for two.

"I would be obliged if you would watch your language," she said. "And my movements are none of your business. Or my destination in London. Excuse me. I have to fetch Hannah and have our bags put back on the coach before it leaves without us."

He ignored her. He closed the parlor door and stood against it, his long, booted legs crossed at the ankles, his arms folded across his chest. He was looking less grim now.

"Was it that stupid joke I made?" he asked her. "About your winning our wager? It was a *joke*."

"It was *not* a joke," she said, taking up her stand on the far side of the table. "You said you were going to give me the deed to Pinewood today. Don't tell me you were going to do it out of the goodness of your heart. Or out of a pang of conscience."

"But I was," he said.

"Was I *that* good?" She glared scornfully at him.

"I decided it yesterday," he said, "long before I knew whether you were good or not."

Her eyes flashed. "Liar!"

He stared at her for such a long time that her fury evaporated and a cold chill crept up her spine in its place.

"If you were a man," he said at last, "I would call you out for that."

"If I were a man," she retorted, "I would accept."

He reached into a pocket of his coat and drew out some folded papers. He held them out to her. "Yours," he said. "Come and take them. We'll eat, and then I'll reserve a room here for you and your maid tonight and hire a private chaise to take you both home tomorrow."

"No." She stayed where she was. "I don't want it."

"Pinewood?"

"I don't want it."

He stared at her for a few moments before striding toward the table and slapping the papers down on it.

"Goddammit!" he said. "If that doesn't beat all. What the devil *do* you want?"

"Watch your language!" she said again. What she *did* want was to rush around the table, cast herself into his arms, and sob out all her misery. But since that was not an option, she regarded him coldly. "I want you to go away and leave me alone. I want you to take those papers with you. And if it is not too late, I want to get on the stagecoach."

"Viola," he said, his voice so gentle suddenly that he almost broke her reserve, "take Pinewood. It is yours. It was never mine. Not really. I daresay the old earl meant it to be yours but just forgot to change his will."

"He did *not* forget," she said stubbornly. "He would not have done so. He did it. It was the wrong will that the Duke of Tresham read."

"Well, then." He shrugged and she knew she had not convinced him. "All the more reason for you to take the papers and go back home. I'll continue on my way to London and make the transfer right and tight. Let me tell the landlord we are ready for dinner."

"No!" He had already taken a couple of steps toward the door. He turned to look at her in some exasperation. "No," she said again. "It would be a gift from you. Or the prize for a wager won. I will not accept it either way. Things would never be the same. It was a gift from *him*."

"Very well, then." He was definitely annoyed now. "We will just say that I am setting matters right."

"No."

He ran the fingers of one hand through his hair, leaving it disheveled and unconsciously making himself look more gorgeous than ever.

"What do you want, then?" he asked her.

"I have told you."

"What are you going to do in London?"

She smiled at him even though every muscle in her face felt stiff. "That is not any of your business," she told him.

His eyes narrowed and he looked menacing again. "If you are planning to go back to whoring," he said, "it dashed well is my business. You were happy enough at Pinewood until I came along. I am not going to have you on my conscience every time I see you about town with the Lord Gnasses of this world. You had better marry me."

Her insides somersaulted, and for a moment she stared at him in utter astonishment. He looked hardly less surprised himself. She forced herself to smile again.

"I think I had better *not* marry you," she said. "The Duke of Tresham would devour you for breakfast."

"I don't care a tuppenny toss what Tresham says," he said. "Or anyone else. I'll marry whomever I want to marry."

"Unless she says no." She felt engulfed in a huge wave of sadness as she continued to smile. "And she does say no. You think you know the worst about me, Lord Ferdinand, but you do not know all. I am a bastard, you see. When my mother married my stepfather, it was her first marriage. Thornhill was her maiden name. You do not want to be marrying a bastard *and* a whore."

"Don't do that." He frowned. "Don't smile like that and call yourself names like that."

"But they are true names," she said. "Come, admit that you are relieved by my refusal. You spoke entirely without forethought. You would be horrified if I said yes."

"I would not," he said, but he spoke without conviction.

Viola smiled again.

"You are not going back to whoring," he told her.

"How vulgar!" she said. "I was never a whore. I was a courtesan. There is a world of difference."

"Don't *do* that," he said again. "Do you have any money?"

She stiffened. "That is none—"

"And *don't* tell me it is none of my damned business," he said. "You don't, do you?"

"I have enough," she told him.

"Enough for what?" he asked. "Your fare and your maid's to London? A few meals along the way?"

That was about it.

"If you won't go home to Pinewood and if you won't marry me," he said, "there is only one thing left for you."

Yes, she knew that. But she felt as if the weight of the universe had settled on her shoulders again. Had she really been hoping that he would be more persuasive over one of the other options?

"You are going to have to be my mistress," he said.

16

❖

They were driving into London in Ferdinand's carriage, everyone else in their entourage having been banished to horse or curricle. They were sitting side by side, as far apart as space allowed, gazing out of opposite windows. They had not spoken to each other for more than an hour. It was early evening.

Ferdinand did not feel as he imagined a man ought to feel with a new mistress. Not that she had yet agreed to accept the position. But she had adamantly refused to go back to Pinewood. She had insisted upon paying for her own room at the inn and had tried to purchase tickets for herself and her maid on today's London stage. That was after breakfast. He had threatened to revive the story about her being a runaway wife if she tried it. He would take her over his knee in some very public place and wallop her a good one, and there would not be a man or woman at the inn who would not applaud him.

She had retaliated with an icy stare and an assurance that if he laid so much as a fingernail on her she would inform everyone within earshot exactly *why* she had run away from her husband. He would not care to discover how very inventive she could be, she warned him, but he was welcome to find out, if he so desired. However, she *would* accept a ride in his carriage to London, since he had caused her to miss yesterday's stagecoach, for which she had paid.

"I suppose," she said now, breaking the long silence between them, "you have not thought this thing through, have you? I suppose you do not know where you would take me. We cannot go to a hotel. It would not be respectable. You cannot take me to your rooms. Your neighbors would be scandalized. I have no rooms of my own—I gave them up two years ago."

"There you are wrong," he told her. "Of course I know where I am taking you. You are going to be my mistress, and I intend to house you in style. But I have just the house in mind for tonight and the next few days."

"I suppose," she said, "it is where you always house your mistresses."

"Well, it is not," he said. "I am not in the habit of mounting mistresses. I prefer to . . . Well, never mind." She had turned to look at him, her expression faintly amused. She was such an expert at that look, and it never failed to irritate him and make him feel like a gauche schoolboy. "The house is Tresham's."

"Your brother's?" She raised her eyebrows. "It is where he houses *his* mistresses? Are you sure there is no one in residence?"

"It is where he *did* house them," he said, "before his marriage. I don't know why he has never sold the house, but to my knowledge he still has it."

"How long has the duke been married?" she asked.

"Four years," he said.

"Are you quite sure, then, that the house is not occupied?" she asked.

It had damned well better not be. If it was, he would rearrange

Tresham's nose for him so that it projected inward instead of outward. Not that one could really challenge one's brother for being unfaithful to one's sister-in-law. But Ferdinand had not realized until that moment how much he was depending upon his brother to restore some of his faith in love and marriage. Tresham's had almost certainly been a love match. But could it stand the test of time? Tresham had always changed mistresses dizzyingly often.

"You really are not sure, are you?" Viola Thornhill asked him. "You had better let me down at a clean, cheap hotel, Lord Ferdinand. You can go back to Pinewood or back to your usual life here in London and forget all about me. You are not responsible for me."

"I am," he said. "I played cards with Bamber and turned your life upside down." Not to mention his own.

"If it had not been you," she said, "it would have been someone else. You are not responsible for me. Set me down and I will get on with my life. I will not be destitute. I have work awaiting me."

"As a whore?" He frowned fiercely at her. "You could do better than that. There are all sorts of other things you could do."

"But whoring is so lucrative," she said, her voice pure velvet amusement. He *hated* it when she did that.

"You are going to be my mistress," he said stubbornly. "It was settled yesterday. It has been settled again today. I don't want to hear any more arguments."

"It was settled and is being settled unilaterally," she said. "Do I have no say in the matter? Because I am a woman, perhaps? A nonentity? A thing? A toy? You do not want a mistress, Lord Ferdinand. And I have never been one. I have always belonged to myself."

"There is no point in telling me yet again that you are no man's mistress," he said. "You are now. And you are going to be for some time to come. You are *my* mistress. Look at me."

She looked at his chin and smiled as she settled her shoulders across the corner of the carriage.

"Into my eyes. Look into my eyes."

"Whyever should I?" She laughed softly.

"Because you are not the sort to enjoy being called a coward," he said. "Dash it all, look into my eyes."

She did.

"Now tell me," he said. "Would you prefer to go whoring with a different man each night than to be my mistress?"

"It would be the same thing," she said.

"It would *not*." He did not know why he was arguing with her. She kept insisting she was not his responsibility. Why not take her at her word? "Being a man's mistress is respectable employment. And it would not be uncongenial to you to be *my* mistress, would it? You did not mind two nights ago. I believe you even enjoyed it."

"I am very skilled at feigning enjoyment, Lord Ferdinand," she said.

He turned his head away. Yes, of course she was. He had doubtless been mortifyingly fumbling and awkward and ignorant. What did he know about pleasing any woman, not to mention a skilled, experienced courtesan? And why was he trying to pressure such a woman into accepting regular employment from him? How would he hold her interest—or incite it in the first place? Not that a man was required to do that with his mistress, of course. She was the one being paid. It was her job to hold *his* interest. Except that he did not believe he would be able to do those intimate things with a woman who did them with him only because she was being paid.

She touched his arm then. "But I did not have to feign it two nights ago," she said.

Well, there. He felt absurdly pleased, though she might well have said so just out of kindness.

"You will stay at that house of Tresham's until I can find a place of my own for you," he said.

"Very well," she said quietly. "Take me there. But I will stay only as long as we both wish to continue the liaison. We must both be free to end it at a moment's notice."

It chilled him to think of ending the affair even before it had begun, but he had no objection. Of course she must be free to leave when she tired of him. He must be free to leave when he tired of her. It would happen at some time, he supposed. He could not imagine ever tiring of Viola Thornhill, but he was naïve and inexperienced.

"We have a deal, then," he said, and he reached out and took her hand in a firm clasp. She did not return the pressure of his fingers, but neither did she pull away. "You will be my mistress and under my protection. All we have left to discuss is your salary."

He could not bear the thought of paying her to bed with him. But dammit, he had offered her Pinewood and she had refused. He had offered her marriage and she had refused. What other choice had she left him?

"Not now," she said, turning her head away to look out through her window. "We can talk about that tomorrow."

There should be some definitive moment, he thought, to mark the beginning of their liaison. He should draw her into his arms and kiss her soundly. But the carriage was well into London already. Indeed, they would be stopping outside Dudley House within a minute or two. He would wait until he had her inside Tresham's house—the other house, that is. He would kiss her soundly then. No, he would take her to bed and consummate their new relationship—employer and employee, man and mistress.

Lord, but there was something strangely depressing about the thought. He was not at all sure . . .

The carriage turned onto Grosvenor Square and rolled to a halt outside Dudley House.

"Stay here," he said, releasing her hand as his coachman opened the door and set down the steps.

"Ferdinand!" The Duchess of Tresham came hurrying toward him as soon as he strode into the drawing room in the wake of the butler's announcement. "What a delightful surprise!" She set both her hands in his and kissed him on the cheek.

"Jane." He squeezed her hands and looked her over. "As lovely as ever. Have you fully recovered your health after your confinement?"

She laughed. She was a golden beauty, whose figure looked just as good to Ferdinand now as it had four years ago, when he first met her.

"Jocelyn warned me before he married me that Dudley babies give their mothers a hard time even before they are born," she said. "He said it to shock me at the time, but he was perfectly right. I have, however, survived the ordeal twice."

His brother was in the room too, Ferdinand saw then. He was holding a tiny baby against one shoulder and patting its back.

"I never thought I would live to see the day, Tresh," Ferdinand said with a grin, strolling closer to admire his newest nephew, whose eyes were open but fixed, as if he were very close to sleep.

"Yes, well, Dudley babies are not finished with giving their parents a rough time once they are out of the womb, Ferdinand, as we should well remember," his brother said. "Don't waggle your fingers at him like that, if you please. I do believe he is about to nod off after deafening me with his cries for all of an hour past. Have the joys of country living palled already? I thought you had found your vocation at last. I came home from Somersetshire and told Jane so."

"What Jocelyn means," Jane said, "is that we are delighted to see you, Ferdinand. You must join us for dinner, which will be ready as soon as Christopher is returned to the nursery. Nicholas is already asleep. You must come and see him tomorrow."

"I am not here to stay," Ferdinand said. "I wondered if I might have a word with you, Tresh."

"Alone?" his brother asked. "With something that is not for the duchess's ears? Dear me. Did you rid yourself of that woman, by the way? I hope she did not persuade you into paying her a large bribe."

"Miss Thornhill is no longer at Pinewood," Ferdinand said stiffly.

"Then I am proud of you," his brother said. "Particularly if you did *not* bribe her. I'll take Christopher up to his bed, Jane. Ferdinand may accompany me and divulge his secret."

"I'll say good night, Jane," Ferdinand said, bowing to her, "and call on you tomorrow at a more proper hour, if I may."

"You may call here at any hour you please, Ferdinand," she said, smiling affectionately at him. "I want to hear all about Pinewood Manor."

"Well, speak," Tresham said when they were on the stairs. "What scrape are you in now? And do not waste your breath assuring me that there is no scrape. Your face has always borne a distinct resemblance to an open book."

"I would like a loan of your house," Ferdinand said abruptly. "Your other house, that is. If you still own it, but I believe you do. And if there is no current occupant."

"There are two," his brother said. "Mr. and Mrs. Jacobs, butler and housekeeper. No mistress, Ferdinand, if that is what you meant, and I daresay it was. I have a wife. Now, let me guess and let me hope I am well wide of the mark. You *do* have a mistress. Lilian Talbot, by any chance?"

"Miss Thornhill," Ferdinand said. They turned in the direction of the nursery, but Tresham made no move to go inside. "She needs somewhere to live. She won't take Pinewood and I won't be responsible for her returning to whoring."

"She won't take Pinewood." Tresham did not make the remark

into a question. "I suppose you developed a chronic case of bleeding heart, Ferdinand, and offered it to her free of charge. And she had too much pride to accept. Good for her."

"She won it," Ferdinand said. "We made a wager. But she would not accept her winnings. Then she ran away. What was I to do? A gentleman cannot lose a wager and then retain what he wagered. It would just not be honorable."

The baby, whose eyes were now closed, made stirring noises, but Tresham patted him on the back and he settled again.

"I am not going to ask what the wager was," the duke said. "And please do not volunteer the information, Ferdinand. I have a strong suspicion that I do not want to know. She ran away, you ran after her, and now she is your mistress—but you have nowhere to take her. It all makes perfect sense," he added dryly.

"I need the house for a night or two," Ferdinand said. "Until I can get something of my own."

"If you want my advice, Ferdinand," his brother said, "which of course you do not because you are a Dudley, you will pay her handsomely and turn her off. She will not starve. She will be mobbed by prospective protectors as soon as it is known that she is in town. Go back to Pinewood so that you will not have to listen to all the men who will boast of having had her. I believe you belong at Pinewood. I was surprised to realize it, but realize it I did."

"All I want," Ferdinand said through his clenched teeth, "is permission to use your house for a day or two. Will those servants let me in?"

"They will if I write a note," his brother said, "which I will do as soon as I have turned Christopher over to his nurse's care. Have *you* had her yet, Ferdinand? No, don't answer. I suppose you are still besotted with her?"

"I was never—"

But Tresham had opened the nursery door and proceeded inside. Ferdinand followed him. The children slept in the same room,

Nicholas in a bed, the baby in a crib. Ferdinand went to look at the sleeping boy while his brother set the baby down and the children's nurse hurried in from an adjoining room and curtsied.

Just a few years ago, Ferdinand thought, gazing down at the tousled head of his sleeping nephew, one could not have imagined Tresham domesticated. It would certainly have been impossible to picture him with a baby in his arms or bent over a crib as he was now, tucking a blanket warmly about the tiny form.

All appearances suggested that his elder brother was a contented family man. Ferdinand felt an unexpected pang of envy as he bade the nurse a good evening and led the way out of the nursery.

But why the devil had Tresham never sold that house? Did Jane even know about it?

"Come to the library for a moment," Tresham said, "and I'll write that note for you. Where have you left her?"

"Outside in the carriage," Ferdinand said.

His brother did not comment.

Viola did not move from the carriage even though after Lord Ferdinand disappeared inside the Duke of Tresham's house she was very tempted to get out. His curricle had come to a stop behind the carriage and Hannah sat there with his groom. It would be easy enough to call her maid, find their bags among all the other luggage, and walk away into the gathering dusk.

But perhaps not. Perhaps after all she would discover that she was a type of prisoner. Perhaps one of his servants would make a fuss, try to stop her, knock on the house door to raise the alarm. Not that any of them could or would detain her for long against her will, of course. But she would embarrass Lord Ferdinand in front of his servants and the duke's—perhaps in front of his brother too.

She would not do that to him.

She might at this moment be back at Pinewood, Viola thought. Alone. The undisputed owner. She was a fool to be here instead. But Pinewood would no longer have the power to bring her any sort of peace or security. She had thought, after she first read Claire's letter, that Pinewood rents would pay off the debt to Daniel Kirby even if the estate was impoverished in the process. But she had realized since that he would not accept that arrangement. He wanted her back working for him, earning him a fortune. If she failed to come, he would punish her by using Claire.

Lord Ferdinand would agree to pay her a large salary as his mistress. She had no doubt about that. But Viola knew Daniel Kirby would not accept a share of that either. He wanted to control her career.

All the way to London she had pondered the situation and all the possible choices she had. But however her mind approached the problem, it always ended up with the same conclusion—the only possible one. She had to go back to her life as a courtesan.

Besides, she could not bear the thought of being Lord Ferdinand's mistress. She did not want to do with him what they had done by the river as a condition of employment. She did not want to earn her living by lying with him. Ah, dear God, not with Ferdinand.

The carriage door opened and interrupted her train of thought. Ferdinand took his seat beside her again. She turned her head, but darkness was already falling and the interior of the carriage was dim. Even so, she shivered at the sight of him and wished after all that she had had the courage to make her escape with Hannah while he was inside the house. She could not bear this.

"We will be there in a few minutes," he said as the carriage lurched into motion. "You must be weary after such a long journey."

"Yes."

He took her hand in his, curling his strong fingers about her

own. But he made no attempt to draw closer to her, to kiss her, or
even to converse with her. His hand did not relax. She wondered if
he regretted what he believed they had agreed to. She wondered if
the Duke of Tresham had tried to talk him out of it. But it did not
matter. Nothing mattered. Tomorrow he would be able to go back
to Pinewood. He belonged there—it was a bitter admission. He
would soon forget her.

Tomorrow she would set the future in motion.

That left tonight. She closed her eyes and rested her head
against the squabs of the carriage. Oh, yes, she would allow herself
tonight.

The house in which the Duke of Tresham had housed his
mistresses was in a quiet, respectable neighborhood. The manser-
vant who answered Lord Ferdinand's knock also seemed like the
kind of servant one might find in any respectable home. So did
his wife, who came into the hall to discover who the late callers
were, and curtsied first to Lord Ferdinand and then to Viola after
he had introduced her and explained that she would be living there
for a short while. They looked at her as she had become accustomed
to being regarded, as if she were a lady worthy of respect. They would
have been trained to behave that way, of course. The Duke of
Tresham would not tolerate servants who treated his mistresses like
doxies.

"I will show Miss Thornhill around," Lord Ferdinand informed
the butler. "Have her bags taken up and her maid shown to her
rooms, will you?"

"Have you been here before, then?" Viola asked him as he ushered her into a room to their left.

"No," he admitted. "But it is not a large house. I do not expect I
will get lost."

The sitting room in which they found themselves was tastefully
furnished and decorated in delicate shades of gray and lavender. It
was a very feminine room, even if it lacked some warmth. It was a

good place, she decided, looking about with a practiced eye, for a mistress to entertain her employer before they adjourned to the bedchamber.

The room next door was less pretty, but far cozier. There were some comfortable armchairs arranged about the fireplace as well as a small but elegant desk and chair. There was a pianoforte and a bookcase filled with books. There was an empty embroidery frame before one of the chairs and an artist's easel propped against one wall.

The Duke of Tresham's mistresses, Viola thought, or one of them, at least, had been people in their own right. How strange, that she of all people should feel some surprise at that fact. This room had an air of having been lived in, perhaps even happily. Maybe, after all, being a mistress was preferable to the sort of life she had led for four years. Perhaps there was a chance of some relationship. But whoever the poor woman was who had been happy here with the duke, she was gone now. He had married the duchess.

"I like this room," she said. "Someone made a home here."

Lord Ferdinand was looking about too, his eyes pausing on each object, a slight frown between his brows. But he did not comment aloud. He ushered her into the dining room and then upstairs.

The bedchamber took her quite by surprise. Although it was opulently decorated in satins and velvets and had a thick carpet underfoot, it did not look like a typical love nest. Men invariably liked scarlet as an accompaniment to their sensual delights. Lilian Talbot's bedchamber had been predominantly scarlet. This one was decorated in varying shades of moss green, cream, and gold.

One would feel less like a mistress in this room and more like a lover, she thought. She was glad it was here she would spend her last hours with Lord Ferdinand. She would not be his mistress, because she was not going to be paid, but she was glad their surroundings would help her see him as a lover rather than as a client.

The door that must lead into the dressing room, slightly ajar when they entered the bedchamber, was pulled firmly closed from the other side.

Viola turned to look at Lord Ferdinand. He was hovering in the doorway, his hands at his back, his long legs slightly apart. He looked handsome and powerful and slightly dangerous—and very obviously uncomfortable. This, of course, she realized, was all new to him.

"Will it do until I can find something else?" he asked.

"Yes, it will do."

His eyes shifted away from hers. "You must be very tired," he said.

"Yes, rather."

"I will leave you, then," he said. "I will return tomorrow to see that you have settled comfortably. I daresay the rest of your belongings will arrive within the next few days. I sent a message back to Pinewood yesterday."

He was going to leave her out of deference to her weariness after two days of travel. She had not expected this. How easy it would be. She could see the last of him forever now, within the next few minutes, before she had time to think. But she could not bear to be alone tonight. It was too soon. She had not had a chance to steel her mind to it. Tomorrow she would be ready, but tonight . . .

She crossed the room and set her fingertips against his chest. He did not move as she smiled into his face and arched her body inward until she touched him from her hips to her knees.

"I *am* tired," she said, "and ready for bed. Are you?"

He flushed. "Don't do that," he said, frowning. "Don't *do* it, do you hear me? If I wanted a damned whore, I would go to a brothel. I don't want Lilian Talbot. I want *you*. I want Viola Thornhill."

She had donned her other persona without conscious thought, she realized, desperate to shield herself from pain. It was strange, she thought, and just a little frightening, to realize that Lilian Talbot repelled him, that it was Viola Thornhill who drew him to intimacy. It was Viola he wanted as his mistress. She drew away from him and let her arms fall to her sides. Without her customary mask, all her emotions felt naked.

"Let us at least be honest with each other," he said. "Must there be artifice and tricks and games just because we are embarking on a sexual relationship? You *know*, do you not? I suppose it was embarrassingly obvious that you were my first woman. Let me be Viola Thornhill's first man, then. Let us look for some comfort from this relationship as well as pleasure. Perhaps even some companionship? Will it be possible, do you suppose?"

But she could only shake her head, while unshed tears balled themselves into a lump in her throat and welled into her eyes.

"I do not know," she whispered.

"I am not interested in Lilian Talbot," he said. "She would make me feel gauche and inadequate, you see. And rather dirty. I want you or no one at all. Take it or leave it."

It was time for the truth. Time to tell him that she had tricked him earlier in the carriage, getting him to agree that she was free to end the liaison at a moment's notice. Time to tell him that she intended to use that freedom tomorrow morning.

She stepped against him again and pressed her face into his neckcloth.

"Ah, Ferdinand," she said.

17

He was in deep waters. His instinct was to wade out so that he could stand upon the shore and view the situation from a safe distance. If he went back to his own rooms, he would be able to digest what was happening to him. It was not even late. He could change his clothes and go to White's, find some of his friends, discover what entertainments the evening offered, and pick one or two to attend. Life would be familiar and comfortable again.

Was this how all men felt about their mistresses at first? As if their very souls yearned for union, for comfort, for peace? For love? Did all men suffer from the illusion that the woman was the other half of their soul?

He must be naïve indeed to be feeling as he was feeling. But he knew with blinding clarity that what had happened between him and Viola two evenings ago on the riverbank at Pinewood had merely confirmed what he had known about himself most of his life. He would rather go celibate through life than engage in sex for its own sake.

He wrapped his arms about her and kissed her mouth when she raised her face to his.

"Do you want me to stay?" he asked her. But he set one finger over her lips before she had a chance to answer. "You must be honest. I'll never bed you unless you want it too."

Her lips curved beneath his silencing finger. "What if I never want it?"

"Then I'll have to find some other solution for you," he said. "But you are not going back to your old life. I'll not allow it."

Her smile was purely Viola's, not that other woman's, he was glad to see. It seemed to be tinged with sadness. "Do you have any say in the matter?" she asked him.

"I dashed well do," he told her. "You are my woman."

Not mistress—*woman*. There was a difference. He had spoken without forethought, but he knew that he had spoken a true thing. He was responsible for her. He had no legal obligation to her and no legal right to demand obedience from her. Nevertheless, she was his woman.

"Stay with me," she said. "I do not want to be alone tonight. And I do want you."

She could trust him, he almost told her. Through most of his life he had trusted no one but himself, knowing that even those people nearest and dearest to him could let him down at any moment and make the firm earth beneath his feet feel more like quicksand. He had trusted in himself and had never done anything he considered truly shameful or dishonorable. She could trust him too. He would be the Rock of Gibraltar for her. But how could he say the words without sounding like a foolish, boastful boy?

He would have to *show* her that he was to be trusted, that was all. Only time would accomplish that.

In the meantime, she had told him that she wanted him. And by God, he wanted her too. She had been pulsing like a fever in his blood all day long. And yesterday too when he had come chasing after her.

He drew her into his arms and kissed her hungrily. She wrapped her arms about him and kissed him back in the same way. But he remembered suddenly that until less than half an hour before she had been sitting in his carriage since their last posting stop.

"Go into your dressing room and make yourself comfortable," he said. "Come back in ten minutes' time."

She smiled slowly at him. "Thank you," she said.

He was glad almost fifteen minutes later that he had done it. He was sitting on the side of the bed, the covers turned back, when she returned. He had stripped down to his riding breeches. She was wearing a nightgown, perhaps the same one she had worn the night he broke the urn. It was white and virginal and covered her from neck to wrists to bare feet. Her hair had been unbraided and brushed until it shone like copper. It was loose and billowed down her back almost to her bottom. She could not have looked more desirable if she had come to him naked. Or if the single candle had been gleaming off the scarlet trappings he had half expected to find in this bedchamber.

She came toward him, and he spread his knees and reached out his hands so that she could come right to the edge of the bed and stand against him. He set his hands on either side of her small waist and rested his face in the valley between her breasts. The nightgown had a freshly washed smell. So did she. The most enticing feminine perfume, he discovered in that moment, was soap and woman. Her fingers smoothed lightly through his hair.

"Do you want me to undress?" she asked him. "I was not sure."

"No." He got to his feet and pulled the bedcovers back farther. "Lie down. Let me see you there before I blow out the candle."

"You want to blow it out?" she asked him as she lay down and smoothed her nightgown over her knees.

"Yes."

It was not that he did not want to see her. It was certainly not that he would be embarrassed by his own nakedness. After all, they had been naked together just two nights before in moonlight. He was not quite sure why he wanted darkness. Or why he wanted her to keep her nightgown on. Perhaps there would be more of fantasy in it—the illusion that they were not man and mistress having sex for his pleasure, but a couple, finding warmth and comfort in each other's bodies in the bed where they slept together.

He blew out the candle, removed his breeches and drawers, and lay down beside her. He slid one arm beneath her head, and she turned against him and found his mouth with her own.

"Make love to me, Ferdinand," she said. "As you did two nights ago. Please. No one else had ever made love to me. Just you. You were the first."

His hands moved over her warm curves, on top of the nightgown. "I don't know how to please you," he said. "But I'll learn if you will be patient with me. I want to please you more than anything else in life."

"You pleased me," she told him. "More than anyone or anything ever has done before. And you please me now. You feel good. You smell good."

He laughed softly. He had washed, but he did not have any of his colognes with him. She did not mind his inexperience, he realized. Perhaps it was something that appealed more than expertise would have to Viola Thornhill.

It was Viola Thornhill with whom he was making love. In some strange way she had come virgin to him. He felt gifted—and vaguely disturbed. But he pushed back the latter feeling. It was only as his mistress that he could keep her safe.

She did not mind his inexperience and so he relaxed and did not mind it himself any longer. He explored her with his hands, learning every curve of his woman, while desire heated his blood and tightened his groin and stiffened his erection. He began to discover the places—some of them unexpected—that drew soft purrs of pleasure or slow gasps of desire from her. He began to know her.

And then he slipped his hand beneath her nightgown and moved it upward, along her slim, smooth legs to the heart of her. She was hot and moist. She parted her thighs and her hands fell still on his body as his fingers explored her, learned the folds and the secrets of her, slid inside her. He hardened to almost unbearable arousal as her inner muscles clenched about his fingers.

And then by some instinct the pad of his thumb found a small part of her at the mouth of her opening and rubbed lightly over it. He knew immediately that he had discovered perhaps her most intense pleasure spot. She trembled, her hands gripping his sides, and cried out as she shuddered into what could only be a feminine orgasm.

He laughed softly after she had finished. "Can I possibly be that good?" he asked her.

She laughed with him, her voice breathless and a little shaky. "I think you must be," she said. "What did you *do?*"

"That is my secret," he said. "I find that I have hidden talents. I am one devil of a fine lover, in fact."

They laughed together as he raised himself on one elbow and leaned over her. They had not drawn the curtains across the window. He could see her faintly, her face surrounded by a cloud of dark hair on the pillow.

"And enormously modest," she said.

"Well. Enormous, anyway." He rubbed his nose across hers.

She tutted. "I rest my case."

The laughter was unexpected. And unexpectedly good.

"Give me a moment," he said, "and I'll show you that I speak only the truth."

He did not peel her nightgown all the way off. The fantasy felt more erotic than nudity. He moved over her and settled himself between her thighs.

"Show me, then," she said, "and I'll pass judgment. I *think* you are merely boasting."

He thrust hard and deep—and fought the urge to bring himself to a fast completion. But he had known what to expect this time. It was a little easier. He wanted to take his time. He wanted to give her time to enjoy it with him.

"No," she said, her voice sounding startlingly normal, "it was no boast."

Minx. Jade. Witch. Woman.

He raised himself onto his forearms and grinned down at her. "Five minutes?" he said. "Or ten? Which do you think me capable of?"

"I do not wager when I have no hope of winning," she said. "But which do I *think* you capable of? Let me see. Both added together, I believe. Fifteen." She laughed.

He moved in her then, settling much of his weight on her, working her with slow, rhythmic strokes, enjoying the feel of her, the smell of her, the sounds of their coupling, the knowledge that she was enjoying the same things about him and what they did together.

Together. It was the key. United. As one. Bodies joined in the deeply intimate, infinitely pleasurable dance of sex. And not just bodies. Not just any man with any woman.

"Viola," he whispered against her ear.

"Yes."

They kissed openmouthed without breaking the rhythm of their loving. But she knew—of course she knew—what he had said to her with the single word of her name. She said it back to him timeless moments later.

"Ferdinand."

"Yes."

They kissed again. And then he buried his face in the silky fragrance of her hair and quickened and deepened his pace until he felt her tighten every muscle and strain closer to him and closer and closer until . . .

The thing was, he thought some time later, a moment before he realized he was lying on top of her like a dead weight and lifted himself off—the thing was that there was only a before and an after and a knowledge of a placeless, nameless, eventless somewhere and sometime in between that left one peaceful and exhausted and utterly convinced that it was heaven one had spied and forgotten all in the same eternal momentless moment.

It had happened to them together. He had not consciously heard her, but he knew she had cried out. So had he. He had little experience, but instinct told him that what they had shared was rare and precious. They had glimpsed heaven together.

His friends would cart him off to Bedlam and leave him there if ever he started spouting such embarrassing nonsense in their hearing, he thought. His acquaintances' conversations about women were altogether more earthy and bawdy.

He lowered Viola's nightgown and cradled her against him. He kissed the top of her head.

"Thank you," he said.

The night had been sweet agony. They had been hungry after making love and had dressed and gone downstairs for a cold supper Ferdinand had asked for earlier. It was late after they had finished and talked for a while. Viola had expected him to leave. But he had asked her, reaching across the small round table to set one hand over hers, if she wanted him to stay, and she had said yes.

They had slept together. They had also made love twice more, once when they went back to bed, once before they got up in the morning. But it was the actual sleeping together that Viola had found most agonizing. She had slept in fits and starts, and every time she awoke she was aware of him, sometimes turned away from her, more often with his arms about her, the bedcovers all tangled about them. Simply being together like that had seemed more intimate to her than the sex. And more seductive.

Her head was aching now as they sat at breakfast. He was wearing yesterday's clothes and was not turned out as immaculately as usual. His hair was still looking rather tousled, even though it had been combed. He was unshaven. He was looking altogether adorable.

"I have a number of things to do today," he was saying, "not least of which is to go home and change my clothes." He grinned and rubbed a hand over his jaw. "And get rid of this beard. Perhaps I'll be able to call in here this afternoon, though. We need to discuss your salary, and then we will be able to forget about it and not mention it again. I do find that part of our arrangement a little distasteful, don't you?"

"But quite essential." She smiled at him and memorized him with her eyes—the restless, rather boyishly eager manner that was so typical of him, the ready grin, which she had at first thought was rakish, the confident air, tinged with an unconscious arrogance that came from his birth and upbringing, the hint of reckless danger that always saved him from being a soft touch.

"I daresay Jane—the duchess, that is—will invite me for dinner tonight," he said. "I have promised to call sometime today to see the children—they were sleeping last evening. Or if it is not Jane it will be Angie—Lady Heyward, my sister. She will ferret me out fast enough once she knows I am back in town."

Viola held on to her smile. He had family, of whose members he was fonder than he realized. His voice told her that he was looking forward to seeing them again. The gulf between her and him was enormous, insurmountable. As his mistress she would be on the very periphery of his life, performing a base, if essential, service. And even that would be just for a few weeks or months, until he tired of her. His family was his forever.

Such thoughts confirmed her in her resolve.

"I won't stay late, though." He reached across the table, as he had the evening before, and took her hand in a warm clasp. "I won't let them persuade me to go off with them to whatever balls or soirees or concerts are scheduled for tonight. I'll come back here after dinner." He squeezed her hand. "I can hardly wait."

"Me neither." She smiled at him.

"Really, Viola?" His dark eyes were gazing into hers. "It really and truly is not just a job to you? You really—"

"Ferdinand." She raised their clasped hands and brought his against her cheek. His uncertainty and vulnerability, in such contrast to the image he presented to the world, broke her heart. "You cannot believe that. Not after last night. Please don't believe that. Not ever."

"No." He chuckled. "I won't. I just don't like this setup, though, Viola, and I don't mind telling you so. You ought to be back in the country—Miss Thornhill of Pinewood Manor. Or my wife—Lady Ferdinand Dudley. You really ought. I don't care that you have no father or that you did what you did because you had to eat. And I don't care what people might say. I'm the sort of fellow everyone expects to get into scrapes anyway."

"Marrying me would hardly be a scrape, Ferdinand," she said past the great lump in her throat.

"Let's do it," he said eagerly. "Let's just *do* it. I'll purchase a special license and—"

"No!" She turned her head to kiss the back of his hand before releasing it and standing up.

"It is what Tresham and Jane did," he said quickly, getting to his feet too. "They just went off one morning and got married while Angie and I were devising schemes for getting him to offer for her. He announced their marriage in the middle of a ball that night. I don't think they have ever regretted it. I think they are happy."

To be Ferdinand's wife. To be able to go back to Pinewood with him . . .

"It would not work for us, dear," she said gently, and then was jolted by the realization that she had spoken the endearment out loud. "You must be on your way. You have things to do."

"Yes." He took both her hands in his and raised them one at a time to his lips. "I wish I had met you six or seven years ago, Viola. Before . . . well, *before*. What were you doing then?"

"Probably serving coffee at my uncle's inn," she said. "And you were in the dusty depths of a library somewhere at Oxford studying Latin declensions. Go now."

"Later, then." He was still holding her hands. He leaned forward and touched his lips to hers. "I could become addicted to you. Be warned." He grinned at her as he turned and strode from the room.

It was appropriate, she thought, that her final sight of him was almost identical to her first—or nearly the first. He had been smiling just like that when her eyes had met his across the village green at the conclusion of the sack race.

A handsome, dashing stranger then.

The love of her heart now.

She stood where she was beside the dining room table until she heard the front door open and then shut behind him. She closed her eyes tightly and clutched the back of her chair.

Then she took a deep breath and went in search of Hannah.

18

*I*t was midmorning by the time Ferdinand set off for the offices of Selby and Braithwaite. Fortunately, Selby was free to see him no more than five minutes after he arrived.

"Ah, my lord." The solicitor met him at the door of his office and shook his hand warmly. "Come up to London for the rest of the Season, have you? I hope you found Pinewood to your taste. I heard from his grace about the spot of bother you had when you arrived there, but that has all been cleared up, I trust. Have a chair and tell me what I may do for you."

Matthew Selby, middle-aged, genial, woolly-haired, looked like everyone's image of an upright, respectable father figure. He was also one of London's toughest solicitors.

"What you may do, Selby," Ferdinand said, "is transfer ownership of Pinewood Manor to Miss Viola Thornhill. I want it done legally and in writing so there can never be any argument about it."

"She is the lady you found living there," the solicitor said, frowning. "His grace mentioned her by name. She has no legal claim on the estate, my lord. Even though his grace insisted upon calling at Westinghouse and Sons in person, I did conduct my own investigation too, since you are a valued client of mine."

"If she had a legal claim I would not need to come, would I?" Ferdinand said. "Draw up any papers that are necessary and I will sign them. I want it done today."

Selby removed the spectacles that were usually perched halfway down his nose and regarded Ferdinand with paternal concern, as if he were a boy who could not possibly make a rational decision on his own.

"Might I respectfully suggest, my lord," he said, "that you discuss the matter with the Duke of Tresham before doing anything hasty?"

Ferdinand fixed him with a stare. "Does Tresham have any claim on Pinewood?" he asked. "Is he my guardian?"

"I beg your pardon, my lord," Selby said, "I merely thought he might help you reach a wise decision."

"You are agreed," Ferdinand continued, "that Pinewood is mine? You have just said so. You investigated the matter and discovered that there can be no possible doubt."

"None whatsoever, my lord. But—"

"Then Pinewood is mine to give away," Ferdinand told him. "I am giving it away. To Miss Viola Thornhill. I want you to do the paperwork for me, Selby, so that I will know everything is done properly. I don't want anyone else to ride up to Pinewood in two years' time, claiming to have won the damned property in a card game and kicking her out. Now, can you do it for me, or shall I go elsewhere?"

Selby looked across the desk at him with gentle reproach as he put his spectacles back on his nose.

"I can do it, my lord," he said.

"Good." Ferdinand sat back and crossed his booted legs at the ankles. "Do it, then. I'll wait."

He thought about Pinewood and Trellick while he waited—

about choir practice proceeding without him this week, about Jamie going without his Latin lessons, about the ladies straining their eyes sewing in the poorly lit church hall instead of in the drawing room at Pinewood, about the building of the laborers' cottages being delayed. About a certain spot on the riverbank where the river rushed past and daisies and buttercups grew in the grass, about a hillside down which a woman had run out of control, laughing and shrieking. About a village lass with daisies in her hair.

Well, he decided later as he strode away from the offices, there was no point in thinking about it all any longer. It had nothing to do with him. This time she would have to accept the gift. She would have no choice. He would take her the deed this afternoon. Of course—his footsteps lagged and some of the spring went out of his step—it would mean that she would no longer need to be his mistress. But that had been very much a last-resort offer on his part anyway.

He did not really want Viola Thornhill as his mistress. He wanted her . . . well, he simply wanted her. But he would damned well have to learn to do without her, wouldn't he? That was all there was to it. Of course . . .

"Wool-gathering, Ferdinand?"

He looked up to see his brother on horseback, riding along the street in the opposite direction from the one he was taking.

"Tresham," he said.

"And looking decidedly glum," the duke said. "She would not agree to terms, I suppose? Women of her sort are not worth brooding over, take my word for it. Do you want to come to Jackson's boxing saloon and try your luck sparring with me? Throwing a few punches can be a marvelous cure for bruised pride."

"Where is Jane?" Ferdinand asked.

His brother raised his eyebrows. "Angeline took her shopping," he said. "This will mean one new bonnet at the very least, I daresay.

For our sister, that is. One wonders why Heyward is still complaisant enough to pay the bills. She must have a bonnet for every day of the year, with a few to spare."

Ferdinand grimaced. "It is to be hoped that Jane will steer her away from her usual garish choice," he said. "Our sister was born with the severe handicap of no taste whatsoever."

"She was wearing a puce monstrosity today," his brother said, "with a canary yellow plume at least a yard tall nodding above it. I made the mistake of looking at it through my quizzing glass. I was thankful it was my duchess who was to be seen in public with her and not me."

"I'll say," Ferdinand agreed fervently. He continued without giving himself time to think. Tresham was not the most comfortable person in the world to be telling such things to, even though it was none of his business. "I called on Selby just now. I have made Pinewood over to Miss Thornhill."

His brother looked down at him with an inscrutable stare. "You are a fool, Ferdinand," he said at last. "But one must look on the bright side. She will return there and be out of your life. It is not wise, you see, to fall in love with one's mistress. Especially one of such notoriety."

Something clicked in Ferdinand's brain. That room last night—the one with the pianoforte and the easel—and the embroidery frame. There was something about it that had teased at his mind. Tresham played the pianoforte. He also painted. But they had both been hidden, repressed talents until Jane had gone to work on him. Their father had brought his sons up to believe that art and music were effeminate pursuits. He had made his heir ashamed of indulging his talents. Even now Tresham rarely played for anyone but Jane. And he painted only when she was with him, sitting quietly in a room with him, working on her embroidery. She was wonderfully skilled with her needle. *That room.*

"But *you* did it," he said, looking up with narrow-eyed intensity into his brother's eyes. "You fell in love with *your* mistress, Tresham. You married her."

He found himself at the receiving end of one of Tresham's famous black stares.

"Who told you that?" Tresham's voice was always at its quietest and most pleasant when he was at his most dangerous.

"A certain room in a certain house," Ferdinand told him.

But it was not just the one room. There was the bedchamber too, with its unexpectedly elegant green and cream colorings. He would bet a pony Jane was responsible for that room. She had exquisite taste in design and color. She had been Tresham's *mistress*. He understood now at least why his brother had not sold the house.

"I had better rent the house from you, Tresham," he said while his brother continued to gaze at him, tight-lipped. "It won't be for long, I daresay. She will probably go back to Pinewood once she knows that it is hers whether she likes it or not. You will be able to relax then. Your little brother will be safe from the clutches of a notoriously wicked woman. Unlike you. Everyone thought *your* mistress was an ax murderer."

"By God, Ferdinand." Tresham leaned one arm across the pommel of his saddle and tapped his whip against one boot. "Are you deliberately courting death? Some advice, my dear fellow. Point a pistol between my eyes and pull the trigger if you must, but cast no aspersions on the good name of my duchess. It is not allowed."

"And I, *damn* you, will have none cast on that of Miss Thornhill," Ferdinand said.

His brother straightened up. "What is this all about, Ferdinand?" he asked. "Will it upset you so very much to see her go?"

Life was going to be empty without her, that was all. There was not going to seem much point to it. But he would soldier on, he supposed. One did not die of such a ridiculous malady as a broken heart. And when had he started to feel quite this way about her, anyway? After sleeping with her? It was probably just lust that was bothering him. Nothing more serious than that.

"The thing is," he said, "that I can't help thinking that if I had not made over the property to her this morning or if I failed to hand her the deed, she would stay and be my mistress. I can't help being tempted. But it would be wrong. It would, Tresh. I don't care what she has done in the past. I daresay she had her reasons. But *now*, you see, she is Miss Thornhill of Pinewood Manor. She is a lady. And I can't bear it because I have already defiled her and because I want to keep on doing so when she belongs back there. And I damned well can't *bear* the thought of her going. And make one sneering remark about this babbling drivel that is spouting out of my mouth and I'll drag you down from your horse and punch out all your teeth. I swear I will."

His brother stared broodingly at him for a few moments before dismounting to stand beside him. "Come to Jackson's," he said, "and pound the stuffing out of me, if it will make you feel better—and if you can. Preferably not my teeth, though, if it's all the same to you. Strange—I did not think you were into the petticoat line, Ferdinand. But perhaps that is the whole point. Perhaps I should have guessed that when you eventually fell, you would fall hard."

It was much later in the afternoon before Ferdinand went back to the house. He had gone home with Tresham after they had sparred to a stalemate at Jackson's. Angie had been there and had talked his ear off and forced both him and Tresham to view her new bonnet. He had played a vigorous wrestling game with his nephew, whom Tresham had brought down from the nursery for tea. Angie and Jane had vied for his company at dinner. Angie had won, though he had assured her that he would not go on to the Grosnick ball with her afterward—Heyward was to accompany her, she had explained, but Ferdie knew how much he danced, provoking man, which was absolutely not at all, while Ferdie was a divine dancer and would make her the envy of every other lady present.

Finally he arrived at the house. He was not really sure how he was going to proceed. Hand her the deed immediately and tell her Pinewood was hers whether she wanted it or not? Or keep the news until tonight? Perhaps they could go to bed this afternoon. Would it be dishonorable? Dash it, but honor could sometimes be a dreary killjoy of a weight on the conscience.

"Tell Miss Thornhill that I am here," he instructed Jacobs after he had been admitted to the house. "Where is she?"

"She is not in, my lord," the butler said, taking his hat and cane.

Damnation! He had not considered the possibility that she might be out. But it was a pleasant afternoon. She must have felt the need for some air and exercise.

"I'll wait," he said. "Did she say when she would be back?"

"No, my lord."

"Did she take her maid?" Ferdinand frowned. She was in London now. He would not have her walking about outside without a chaperon.

"Yes, my lord."

He went into the room with the pianoforte and looked about him. How on earth had he not realized the truth yesterday as soon as he set foot in here? he wondered. It had Jane and Tresham-with-Jane written all over it. It was a strangely cozy room, even though the embroidery frame and the easel and music stand were all empty. He would enjoy spending time here with Viola. She would feel like his companion as well as his mistress in here. They would talk and read and be comfortable together. She would feel almost like a wife.

But he did not want a wife, he reminded himself—or mistress either. He wanted Viola to be back at Pinewood, lady of the manor again. Even if it meant never seeing her again, because that was what she wanted.

He wandered restlessly from the room and upstairs to the bed-chamber. He sat on the side of the bed and ran one hand over the pillow where her head had lain last night. He hoped—he swallowed the lump that had formed in his throat—he hoped she would go back home. Perhaps after some time had passed he could go down there, stay at the Boar's Head, call on her, court her. . . .

He wandered into her dressing room. It looked empty. She had brought only the one bag with her from Pinewood, it was true, but there surely should have been a comb or brush or something on the dressing table. All that was there, propped against the mirror, was a folded piece of paper. He crossed the room with hesitant steps, knowing very well what it was. It had his name written on the outside in the now-familiar neat handwriting.

It was as terse as the last one.

"We agreed that we were both free to end our liaison at a moment's notice," she had written. "I am ending it now. Go back to Pinewood. It is where you will find the fulfillment for which you have been searching all your adult life, I believe. Be happy there. Viola."

So she had escaped after all. She had intended it from the start, he realized. Now that he thought about it, he could recall that she had never said explicitly that she would be his mistress, only that she would come here with him and must be free to go whenever she chose. She had disappeared into the vastness of London. Last night had meant nothing to her. *He* meant nothing to her. She preferred the life of a courtesan. It made no sense whatsoever to him. But did it need to?

Would he never learn?

He crumpled the paper and dropped it to the floor.

"Goddamn you," he said aloud.

And then he surprised and embarrassed himself—almost as if there were an audience—by sobbing once and then again and finding it impossible to stem the flow of his grief.

"Goddamn you to hell," he said between sobs. "What do you *want* from me?"

The silence answered him loud and clear.

Nothing at all.

Viola was going home. Home to her uncle's inn to see her mother and sisters. And to meet Daniel Kirby and come to some arrangement with him about her future. But even though she would not put herself through the agony of hoping, she intended to fight as far as she was able. Bag in hand, Hannah beside her, she made her way first in the opposite direction to the inn. She had a call to make.

She sat and waited stubbornly for three hours in a dingy outer office of Westinghouse and Sons, Solicitors, before being admitted for one whole minute into the presence of the most junior partner and assured that the late Earl of Bamber's will made no mention whatsoever of Miss Viola Thornhill.

"Well, Hannah," she said as they were leaving, "I did not expect anything different, you know. But I had to hear it with my own ears."

"Where are we going now, Miss Vi?"

Hannah had been disapproving of last night's destination. But this morning she had disapproved of their leaving. She had wanted Viola to throw herself upon Lord Ferdinand's mercy, to tell him everything, to beg him to lend her the money with which to pay Daniel Kirby. Ferdinand was more than halfway in love with her, according to Hannah. He could be brought to offer for her if Miss Vi just played her cards right.

Never! She would not beg money from him, she would not burden him with her problems, and she would not entice him into a marriage he would bitterly regret for the rest of his life.

"We are going to call on the Earl of Bamber," she said in answer to Hannah's question.

It was halfway through the afternoon by the time they arrived there. It was very probable he would not be home. It was even more probable that she would be denied admittance even if he were. It was a shocking thing for a lady to call upon a single gentleman, even though she was accompanied by her maid. The look with which the earl's butler regarded her when he opened the door to her knock confirmed her fears. She probably would not have succeeded in setting so much as a foot over the doorstep if chance had not brought the earl home while she was standing there arguing.

"Who do we have here, then?" he asked, coming up the steps behind her, his eyes raking over her.

He was short, portly, fair-haired, and florid of complexion. He bore no discernible resemblance to his father.

"I am Viola Thornhill," she said, turning to face him.

"Well, damn me." His brows snapped together. "The woman herself, standing on my doorstep. I am mortally sick of hearing your name. I'll not have you bothering me, I say. Take yourself off. Shoo!"

"My mother was once your governess," she said.

For a moment she thought he was going to tell her again to shoo, but then an arrested look came over his face.

"*Hillie?*" he said. "I only ever had one governess—before I went to school. She was Hillie."

"Rosamond Thornhill," Viola said. "My mother."

She watched the glimmer of understanding come into his rather bloodshot eyes.

"You had better come inside," he said ungraciously, and he led the way into the house and across the hall to a small salon. Hannah followed them and stood quietly inside the door after the earl had shut it.

"Who the devil are you?" he asked.

"My mother was your father's mistress for ten years," she said. "He was my father too."

He stared at her, his expression grim.

"What do you want from me?" he asked her. "If you have come here begging for money—"

"I met him shortly before he died," she said. "He was determined to provide for me. He sent me to Pinewood Manor. It was one of his smaller, unentailed holdings, he said. He had never even been there himself. But he thought it was in a suitably secluded corner of England and could offer me a decent living if it was well managed. He was going to change his will so that it would always be mine."

"Well, he did not do so," he said. "The very idea—"

"He loved me," she said. "He always loved me. I never doubted his affection while I was a child, before my mother married. I doubted it afterward because suddenly he did not come anymore or even write. But that was my mother's fault, I learned later. She had broken off her relationship with him and refused to let him even see me. She destroyed all the letters and gifts he sent me. It was quite by chance that I saw him in the park. . . . But no matter. The details can be of no interest to you. Did you persuade Mr. Westinghouse to erase the new clause from his will?"

The explosive blasphemy that was his first reaction convinced her that he was not the villain of this piece. "Get out of here," he told her, "before I throw you out."

"Could he have made a new will with someone else?" she asked, ignoring his wrath. "You see, it is not only Pinewood that is at stake. There was another paper, which he said he would file officially with his solicitor so that the matter could never be disputed. He paid off some debts to release me from an obligation and keep my mother out of debtors' prison. He had the man who held the debts sign a paper stating that all the bills had been paid in full, that there were no more, and that he waived the right to claim for any other unpaid bill that preceded the date of the agreement."

"What the devil!" the Earl of Bamber said.

"That man has now discovered other debts," Viola said, "and is demanding payment."

"And you expect me—"

"No!" she said. "My father rescued me . . . from the life of prostitution I had been forced into so that I could pay back the debt. He provided for my future so that I could live in peace and security for the rest of my life. I ask nothing of you, my lord. I ask only that my father not be denied his dying wish. That paper is of vital importance to me. Your father loved me. I was as much his daughter as you were his son, you see, even though I was born on the wrong side of the blanket."

He stared at her for a while and then ran the fingers of one hand through his hair before turning abruptly away to stare into the unlit coals of the fire.

"Damn me," he said. "Why did I go to Brookes's that night? I have had nothing but trouble over that worthless property ever since. Well, he didn't change his will, and that's all about it. And there is no paper. Westinghouse would have said so. He would at least have recognized your name, wouldn't he?"

"And there is no possibility there was someone else?"

He drummed his fingers on the mantel above his head. "I wonder if m'mother knew about Hillie," he muttered. "And about you. I bet she did. M'mother always knows everything."

Viola waited.

"I'm sorry," he said eventually, turning abruptly to face her. "I can't help you, you know. And I can't send you back to Pinewood even if I wanted to—which I don't particularly. Why should I? You are just m'father's by-blow. Pinewood is Dudley's. Go beg from him. I'm expected somewhere for dinner. You will have to leave now."

There was nothing further to say. Viola left with Hannah. There was no way to save herself from her inevitable future, it seemed.

They began the long walk home.

19

❧

I have never known you so out of sorts, Ferdie," Lady Heyward complained. "I expected you to be bubbling over with stories about Pinewood and your two weeks in the country. But whenever one asks you a question, you say nothing whatsoever of any significance."

"Perhaps, Angie," he said irritably, "it is because trying to get a word in sideways in your company is an exercise in futility. Besides, the dinner is good and to be savored. Convey my compliments to your cook, will you?"

"Unfair!" she cried. "Is he not being unfair, Jane? Tell me, have I or have I not plied Ferdie with enough questions to get him talking about Pinewood? And have I or have I not paused each time to allow him all the time in the world to answer?"

"There really is not—" Ferdinand began.

"Of *course* there must be a great deal to say," she said. "Who are your neighbors there? What—"

"Angie," Ferdinand said firmly, "Pinewood no longer belongs to me. It is hardly worth talking about the place."

"Jocelyn told me you have legally made over the ownership to Miss Thornhill, Ferdinand," the Duchess of Tresham said. "I *do* admire you for doing something so very honorable."

"You have done *what*, Ferdie?" His sister's eyes were wide with astonishment.

"He has given Pinewood back to Miss Thornhill," Jane explained, "because he believed it was more hers than his. I am very proud of you, Ferdinand. Jocelyn told me that it is a lovely place."

"Was that wise, Ferdinand?" Lord Heyward asked. "It might have been a prosperous estate for you."

"Now everything makes perfect sense!" Angeline cried. "Ferdie is in *love!*"

"Oh, good Lord!" he was startled into saying.

"You are in love with this Miss Thornhill," she said. "How absolutely splendid. And so of course you have made the magnificent gesture of returning Pinewood to her. But you *must* go back there. She is sure to fall into your arms and dissolve into tears of gratitude. I simply must be there to see it. Do take me with you. Heyward, *may* I go? You spend all your days at the House of Lords anyway, and you know it will be a relief not to have to escort me to evening entertainments for a week or two. There will be time before the Season ends to organize a grand wedding at St. George's. We will have a great squeeze of a ball here. Jane, you must help me. I was deprived of the opportunity of doing it for you and Tresh when he whisked you off to marry you one morning with absolutely no one in attendance but his secretary and your maid. What a waste that was. For Ferdie I am determined to do much better."

"Angie!" Ferdinand said firmly. "Take a damper." He caught his brother's eye across the table. Tresham merely raised his eyebrows, pursed his lips, and addressed himself to the food on his plate.

"I do believe you are embarrassing your brother, my love," Lord Heyward said.

"Men!" Angeline exclaimed. "Always embarrassed at any mention of love and marriage. Are they not ridiculous creatures, Jane?"

"I have frequently said so," the duchess agreed, looking with some amusement at Tresham, who did not rise to the bait. "But Ferdinand, who *is* Miss Thornhill? Jocelyn did tell me she is beautiful."

"It was, of course," Tresham said, "the first question Jane asked when I returned home."

"Oh, not the *first*, you odious man," she protested.

"She is the most irritating female I have ever known," Ferdinand said. "She talked me into making a wager with her, Pinewood as the prize—and she won. She would not take it. Then I gave it to her as a gift. She ran away. I followed her and caught her before she reached London. Today I had Selby make the change of ownership legal, but when I went to tell her so, she had disappeared again. It seems she really does not want it."

"How extraordinary!" Jane said.

"You must go back tomorrow, then, and get Selby to reverse the procedure," Heyward said. "You ought to have come to me or Tresham before you did it anyway, Ferdinand. You have a strong tendency to act impulsively. It is the Dudley blood in you."

"People are always impulsive when they are in love," Angeline said. "Ferdie, you must find her. You must comb London for her. Hire a Bow Street Runner. How very romantic."

"I have no wish to find her," he said.

"Do you have no idea where she is?" Jane asked.

"None," he said curtly. "And I have no wish to know. Pinewood is hers. If she does not want it, that is her concern. It may rot, for all I care."

And then a thought popped into his head as if from nowhere—a thought spoken in her voice . . .

Probably serving coffee at my uncle's inn.

He had asked her what she would have been doing six or seven years ago if he had met her before she became a courtesan. At the time his mind had scarcely registered her answer.

"I believe her uncle owns an inn," he said.

Angie was all eagerness to know what kind of inn, where in London it might be situated, what the uncle's name was. She—and Jane, to a lesser degree—seemed determined to find in the whole situation a romance that must be given a happy ending. He could stand it no longer after a few minutes.

"There is no question of finding her," he said. "I offered her Pinewood and she would not take it. I offered her marriage and she would not accept me. I offered her . . . protection and she ran away. She would prefer to return to her old way of life."

"What is that?" Angeline asked.

Ferdinand was aware of his brother's black stare across the table.

"She was a courtesan," he said. "A very successful one until she went to Pinewood two years ago. And she is illegitimate into the bargain. So you might as well take a damper, Angie, and go match-make for someone else. Now let's change the subject, shall we?"

"Oh, the poor lady," Jane said softly. "I wonder what is driving her back to her old life."

"Me," Ferdinand said.

"No." She shook her head, frowning. "No, Ferdinand. Not that."

"A lady with a scarlet past and a murky secret," Angeline said, clasping her hands to her bosom. "How irresistibly intriguing. You can be sure she loves you as desperately as you love her, Ferdie. Why else would she have run away from you twice?"

Women! he thought as Heyward launched into a long, dry monologue about a speech he had delivered in the House that very day. The older he grew, Ferdinand thought, the less he understood women. Angie and Jane should be in the middle of a fit of the vapors apiece.

An innkeeper. He dared not even guess how many inns there

might be in London. Her uncle—maternal or paternal? How slender was the chance that he bore the same last name as she? He had been an innkeeper six or seven years ago. Was he still?

She had no wish to be found—until she surfaced again as Lilian Talbot, he supposed. And he had no wish to find her. She had deceived and rejected him one time too many.

How many inns *were* there?

He was not really going to waste his time searching, was he?

I wonder what is driving her back to her old life.

Jane's words echoed and reechoed in his mind.

A coach was leaving the White Horse Inn with a great deal of din and bustle. Viola and Hannah stood aside to let it turn out onto the street before stepping into the cobbled yard. The innkeeper was standing outside the door, bellowing something to a distant ostler. But he turned and saw the two women, and his scowl was replaced by a broad smile.

"Viola!" he exclaimed, spreading his arms wide.

"Uncle Wesley!"

Soon she was enveloped in his strong arms and crushed against his broad chest.

"So you *did* come," he said, holding her at arm's length. "But why did you not let us know when? Someone would have met you. Hello, Hannah. Rosamond and the girls are going to be delighted." He called through the open door of the inn, "Claire! Come and see what we have here."

Viola's sister came rushing through the door a moment later. She was looking remarkably pretty, Viola noticed at once. She had blossomed into a slender, shapely beauty with shining blond tresses. Then they were in each other's arms, hugging and laughing.

"I *knew* you would come!" her sister exclaimed. "And Hannah is with you. Oh, do come upstairs. Mama will be ecstatic. So will

Maria." She took Viola by the hand and turned back toward the inn door. But then she stopped and looked anxiously at her uncle. "*May* I go up with her, Uncle Wesley? Everything is quiet now that the coach has left."

"Up with you both," he said jovially. "Away you go."

Viola was led up to the private living quarters on the upper floor and into her mother's sitting room. Her mother was seated by the window sewing, while Maria sat at the table, a book open before her. But a moment later, all was movement and squeals and laughter and hugs and kisses.

"We *knew* you would come," Maria cried when some sanity had been restored to the scene. "Oh, I do hope you will be living here now."

Maria had changed from a child to a young girl with some promise of beauty to come.

"You must be weary," their mother said, linking an arm through Viola's and leading her to a love seat, where they seated themselves side by side. "Have you just traveled up from Somersetshire? I wish we had known it was today we were to expect you. We would have come to meet you. Maria, dear, run downstairs and bring up a tea tray and some cakes, there's a good girl."

Maria went obediently, even though she looked reluctant to miss even a moment of her eldest sister's homecoming.

"It is so lovely to be back here and to see you all," Viola said. For the moment she allowed home and family to wrap themselves about her like a cocoon, where she could be safe from all the menaces of the outside world. And from all the memories. She wondered if Ferdinand had returned to the house yet and discovered her gone.

"All will be well." Her mother took her hand and patted it.

"But it seems that you were all expecting me," Viola said, puzzled.

Her mother squeezed her hand. "We have heard," she said, "about Pinewood's turning out not to belong to you after all. I am so sorry, Viola. You know I was opposed to your accepting it from—f-from Bamber when you were doing so well at your governess's post, but I am sorry he deceived you so."

Despite the bitter quarrel they had had before she left for Pinewood, Viola had had enough experience of life not to pass too severe a judgment on her mother. She had been got with child—with her, Viola—while she was governess to the Earl of Bamber's son. The earl had whisked her off to London and kept her there as his mistress for ten years before she fell headlong in love with Clarence Wilding and married him. The change in Viola's life was total and severe. There was no more contact with her father, whom she had adored. There was the impatience and contempt of her stepfather instead. Sometimes, when he was drunk and her mother was not present, he called her "the bastard." She had had to ask Hannah the meaning of the word.

It was not until almost thirteen years later, when she recognized her father driving in the park one afternoon while she was walking and had impulsively hailed him, that she had discovered the full truth. Her father had not abandoned her. He had tried to see her. He had written to her and sent her presents. He had sent money for her support. He had wanted to send her to a good boarding school before arranging a respectable marriage for her. Everything had been returned to him.

And so he had discovered the truth about his daughter and the life she was living and the reason for it. He had arranged a meeting with Daniel Kirby and paid off all the remaining debts of the man who had taken his mistress and his daughter from him. And then he had given Viola the precious gift of a new life. He had given her Pinewood.

Her mother had been incensed. At first Viola had been much inclined to blame her. What right had she to keep Viola from her own father? But she had learned enough about life by that time to know that the human heart was a complex organ and frequently led one in the wrong direction without any really cruel intent. Also she recognized that her mother was reacting without full knowledge of all the facts. Her mother believed that Viola had respectable employment as a governess.

She had forgiven her mother long ago.

"He did not deceive me, Mama," she said. "But how did you know about Pinewood?"

"Mr. Kirby told us," her mother said.

Just the sound of his name made Viola's stomach lurch.

"Do you remember him?" her mother asked. "But of course you must. He comes to the inn to take coffee quite frequently, does he not, Claire? He is still very amiable. I have gone down once or twice to converse with him. He commiserated with us over your loss. Naturally, we were mystified. That was when he told us about the Duke of Tresham's brother winning the property from the earl and going down to Somersetshire to claim it. What is the brother's name? I cannot recall."

"Lord Ferdinand Dudley," Viola said.

Daniel Kirby had heard, then. But *of course* he would have heard. He made it his business to know everything. This explained why he suddenly discovered a new debt. He knew she would be returning to London. He knew he could exercise power over her again.

"What is Lord Ferdinand like, Viola?" Claire asked.

Handsome. Full of laughter. Gregarious, charming, impossibly attractive. Daring and dashing. Kind. Honorable. Innocent—strangely innocent.

"I did not know him long enough to form any lasting impression," she said.

Maria came back then, carrying a tray, which she set down on a table close to the love seat.

"Well," their mother said as she poured the tea, "you are home now, Viola. That part of your life is in the past and best forgotten. Perhaps Mr. Kirby will help you again. He knows a great many influential people. And of course your former employers may be willing to give you a good recommendation even though you left them rather abruptly."

Viola shook her head when Maria offered the plate of cakes. She felt quite nauseated. For that, of course, was just what was going to happen. Daniel Kirby would come here soon and the two of them would talk and come to some arrangement for the resumption of her career. They would set about spinning a suitable yarn for her family so they would never know the truth.

Perhaps, Viola thought as she sipped her tea and listened to Maria's prattle about the latest news from Ben, she should tell them herself—now, before her life became a web of lies and deceit again.

But she simply could not do it. All their lives would be ruined. Uncle Wesley had been enormously kind to them over the years. He had never remarried after his young wife died giving birth to their stillborn child only one year into their marriage. His sister and her family had become his own. He had supported them cheerfully and without complaint. Viola could not see him destroyed. And there were Claire and Maria and Ben, who must be allowed a future of pleasant prospects. Her mother's health was not strong. She would not be able to support the burden.

No, she could not do it.

20

❦

I t was Ferdinand's second day of riding from inn to inn on a
search that he fully expected to be futile. He would waste a
week or so in this way until finally he would either see her—
in the park or at the theater—or hear of her from his acquaintances. Lilian Talbot was back, the story would go, as beautiful,
as alluring, as expensive as ever. Lord So-and-so had been the fortunate one to secure her services first, Lord Such-and-such second . . .

If he was wise, Ferdinand kept telling himself, he would return
to Selby and get him to tear up the papers transferring ownership of
Pinewood, and he would go back there himself—and stay there for
the rest of his life.

He never had been renowned for his wisdom.

He had arrived at the White Horse Inn at just the wrong time,
he thought as he rode into the cobbled yard. A stagecoach was
preparing for departure. There were people, horses, and baggage
everywhere, and a great deal of noise and commotion. But one sta-

blehand recognized him as a gentleman and hurried toward him to ask if he could take his horse.

"Perhaps," Ferdinand said, leaning down from his saddle. "But I am not sure I have the right place. I am looking for an innkeeper by the name of Thornhill."

"He is over there, sir," the lad said, pointing to the densest throng of people close to the coach. "He is busy, but I'll call him if you like."

"No." Ferdinand dismounted and handed the boy a coin. "I'll go inside and wait."

The innkeeper was large in both height and girth. He was exchanging pleasantries with the stagecoach driver. His name was Thornhill. Could the search possibly end this easily? Ferdinand wondered.

He ducked through the doorway and found himself in a dark, beamed porch. A slender, pretty young girl with a tray of used dishes in her hands curtsied to him and would have proceeded on her way if he had not spoken.

"I am looking for Miss Viola Thornhill," he said.

She looked far more directly at him then. "Viola?" she said. "She is in the coffee room, sir. Shall I call her?"

"No," he said. He was feeling almost dizzy. She was *here?* "Which room is that?"

She pointed and stood to watch him as he proceeded toward it.

There must still be some time left before the stagecoach was due to depart, he thought as he stood in the doorway. It was still half full. But he saw Viola immediately, seated at the far side of the room, facing toward him. Opposite her sat a man, to whom she was talking.

Ferdinand stood watching them, torn between feelings of relief, anger, and uncertainty. He never had decided how he would proceed if he found her. He could stride toward that table now, if he chose, place the papers beside her saucer, make his bow, and leave without saying a word. He could then get on with his life, his conscience appeased.

But two things happened before he could make up his mind to do it.

The man turned his head sideways to look out through the window. Ferdinand could not see him full-face, but he could see enough to realize that he knew him. Not personally, but he supposed there were not many men of his class who would not recognize Daniel Kirby. He was a gentleman, though not a member of the *ton*. He hung about places like Tattersall's and Jackson's and various racetracks—places frequented primarily by men. A small, round-faced, jovial fellow, he was nevertheless well known for the weasel he was. He was a moneylender, a blackmailer, and other unsavory things. Wherever there was money to be made by shady means, Daniel Kirby was there.

And Viola Thornhill was in conversation with him.

The other thing that happened was that she looked beyond the shoulder of her companion and her gaze locked with Ferdinand's for a moment. But although she stopped talking for that moment, her expression did not change. There was no look of surprise, anger, embarrassment—or anything else. Then she returned her attention to Kirby and continued with what she was saying as if nothing had happened.

She did not want Kirby to know he was there, Ferdinand concluded. Only seconds must have passed, he realized, when he turned to find the young maid still standing where she was, holding her tray.

"Does she live here?" he asked.

"Yes, sir," the girl said.

"And her mother too?"

"Yes, sir."

"What is her name?"

"My mother's?" She frowned.

"*Your* mother's?" He looked more intently at her. "Is Miss Thornhill your sister?"

"My half-sister, sir," she said. "I am Claire Wilding."

He had not even known that she had a sister. The girl was small and slender and blond. He made an impulsive decision.

"Will you ask Mrs. Wilding if she will receive me?" he asked. He drew out one of his visiting cards from his coat pocket.

She looked at it as he set it on the tray.

"Yes, my lord." She curtsied and blushed. "I'll ask her."

She spoke with a refined accent, he noticed, just as Viola did. Clearly she could also read.

Life could get no bleaker, Viola thought as Daniel Kirby took his leave. When her uncle had come upstairs earlier to announce his arrival, he had been smiling. Her mother had smiled too and insisted on coming down to the coffee room with Viola to pay her respects to him.

The conversation had turned to business once the two of them had been alone together, of course. The terms were the same as they had been before. Viola had not given in without protest, but she had known it was hopeless. When she had mentioned the receipt Mr. Kirby had signed and given to her father, he had regarded her kindly but blankly.

"Now, what receipt would that be?" he had asked her. "I recollect no such thing."

"No, of course. You would not," she had replied coldly.

He was to find her rooms. He was to put about the word that she was back in town. He was to engage clients for her. He granted her a week's holiday to spend with her family while he made all the arrangements.

"After all," he had said, "your family might find it strange if I were to find you a governess's post too soon. And we would not wish to upset your family, would we?"

But if the interview with Daniel Kirby was not trouble enough for one morning, there was the other ghastly thing that had happened while she was sitting talking to him. She had looked up, conscious that someone was standing in the doorway, and for a moment had completely lost the trend of what she was saying.

In the split second before she had pulled herself together, all she had thought of was that he had *found* her, that he had come for her, that she could rush into his arms, and he would hold her there safe forever. Then she *had* pulled herself together and looked away. When she had glanced up again a few seconds later, he had gone.

She had felt enormous relief.

She had also hit the depths of despair.

She got up from the empty table. She had promised to help out in the office with some of the paperwork Claire so abhorred. But first, she thought, she must go to her room to spend some time alone.

How had he found her?

Why had he come?

Why had he gone away again without a word?

Would he come back?

Hannah was in her room, hanging up her newly laundered and ironed traveling dress.

"Your mother asked that you go to her as soon as *that man* left," she said.

Viola sighed. "Did she say what she wanted, Hannah?"

"No," her maid said, though Viola had the feeling that she knew very well.

She sighed again. Her mother probably wanted to share her delight at Mr. Kirby's promise to help her daughter find employment, Viola thought as she opened the sitting room door and stepped inside.

Lord Ferdinand Dudley was sitting by the fireplace.

"See who has come to call upon me this morning, Viola," her

mother said, getting to her feet and hurrying closer. "He needs no introduction to you, of course."

He rose and bowed as her mother turned to smile warmly at him.

"Miss Thornhill," he said.

"Lord Ferdinand has just traveled up from Somersetshire," her mother explained, "and has come to pay his respects to me. Is that not a kind courtesy, Viola? He has been telling Maria and me how highly thought of you are at Pinewood."

Viola looked at him with silent reproach. "It was kind of you to call, my lord," she said. *How did you find me? Why did you find me?*

"Do sit down again," her mother told their guest as she drew Viola to sit beside her on the love seat. "I have been explaining, Viola, why you could not join us immediately." She looked back at their visitor. "My father was a gentleman, you see, but he lost his fortune in some unwise investments, and so my brother had to forge his own way in the world, as did I. I was a governess too. Viola's father was a gentleman. So was my late husband."

Her mother was on the defensive, Viola thought.

"No one who saw Miss Thornhill manage a country fête could possibly doubt that she is a lady, ma'am," Lord Ferdinand said, his eyes smiling into Viola's.

He proceeded to tell her mother and Maria about the May Day celebrations at Trellick. He soon had both of them laughing and exclaiming in delight. The ability to charm almost any audience was one of his personal gifts, of course. It had annoyed her at Pinewood. It annoyed her now.

"We are glad to have Viola home with us again," her mother said at last. "Of course, she will probably be teaching again soon. Mr. Kirby has promised to help her find a respectable position, as he did once before."

Viola watched Lord Ferdinand, but he gave no sign of knowing the name.

"I came to town just in time, then, ma'am," he said. "I might have missed Miss Thornhill if I had postponed my visit to a later date."

"Yes, indeed," her mother agreed.

"I wonder if I might beg the favor of a private word with your daughter, ma'am?" he asked.

Viola shook her head imperceptibly, but no one was looking at her. Her mother got to her feet without any hesitation.

"Of course, my lord," she said, sounding inordinately pleased. "Come along, Maria. We will see what help we can offer downstairs."

Mama thought he had come *courting*, Viola thought as her mother, her back to their visitor, gave her a significant look. Then she left, taking Maria with her.

The clock ticked with unnatural loudness on the mantel.

Viola spread her hands in her lap and looked down at them.

"How did you find me?" she asked.

"You said your uncle was an innkeeper," he said.

Had she told him that?

"I started searching yesterday morning," he said. "I began with the coaching inns and the slim hope that your uncle was still in business and bore the name of Thornhill."

She looked up at him. "Why?"

He had got to his feet when her mother rose. He stood now in front of the fireplace, his hands at his back. He looked large and powerful. She felt at a distinct disadvantage. She saw him draw a deep breath and release it slowly.

"Mainly for this reason, I suppose," he said, reaching into his coat pocket and bringing out a sheaf of papers.

"How many times do I have to say no before you will believe me?" she asked.

"Pinewood is yours," he said. "I have had the title legally transferred to you. It is yours whether you want it or not, Viola."

He held out the papers, but she made no move to take them. It was too late. Daniel Kirby had heard about his winning Pinewood and had concluded that if her father had not changed his will, he had probably not kept that receipt either. He had guessed that he had her in his power again. Pinewood would not be able to help her now. He would make sure that the rents were not quite enough to cover payment on the debts.

Lord Ferdinand moved toward the table and set the papers down beside Maria's books.

"It is yours," he said again.

"Very well," she said, her eyes on her hands again. "Your task has been successfully accomplished. Good day to you, my lord."

"Viola," he said softly, and she heard him sigh with exasperation.

The next moment, she saw his riding boots almost toe-to-toe with her slippers, and then he came down on his haunches and captured both her hands in his own. She had little choice but to look into his eyes, on a level with her own.

"Do you hate me so much?" he asked her.

The question almost broke her heart. Perhaps she had not realized until this precise moment just how much she loved him. Not just how much she was *in* love with him, but how much she *loved* him.

"Do you find it so hard to believe," she asked in return, "that I could wish to be my own person rather than your mistress?"

"I offered you Pinewood," he said. "You told me it meant so much to you only because the late Earl of Bamber gave it to you. Did you love him so much more than me, then? He must have been old enough to be your father."

His words might have been funny under other circumstances.

"Fool!" she said, but she spoke gently. "Ferdinand, he *was* my father. Do you think I would have accepted a gift like that from a lover?"

His hands tightened about her own and he stared at her in astonishment. "Bamber was your *father?*"

She nodded. "I had not seen him since my mother married Clarence Wilding. He had been in poor health for years. He did not come to London often. He came then to consult a physician, but it was hopeless. He knew he was dying. I will forever be thankful that I saw him and recognized him in Hyde Park and called out to him before I could stop myself. He explained why I had not heard from him during all those years. And he tried to atone, to do for me what he would have done if we had not been estranged by my mother's marriage. It was too late for him to arrange a decent marriage for me—I had been working for four years. But he gave me Pinewood and the chance of a new life. It was a precious gift, Ferdinand, because it came from my father. It was a gift of pure love."

He bent his head and closed his eyes. "This explains why you will not believe that he neglected to change his will," he said.

"Yes."

Ferdinand lifted her hands one at a time to his lips. "Forgive me," he said. "I behaved like a prize ass when I came to Pinewood. I should have gone away immediately. You would still be happy there now."

"No." She gazed earnestly at him. "You behaved quite reasonably under the circumstances. You might have thrown me out that very first day."

"Go home," he urged her. "Go back there. Not because I want you to but because your father did. And because that is where you belong."

"Perhaps I will," she said.

"No, dash it." He got to his feet and drew her to hers. "I can tell by the look on your face that you are humoring me. You have no intention of going there, have you? Because it comes from *me*. It brings me back to my original question. Do you hate me so much?"

"I don't hate you." She closed her eyes.

It was a mistake. He stepped closer, wrapped his arms about her, and set his mouth, open, over hers. She was powerless to end the embrace, even though he did not hold her imprisoned. She twined her arms about his neck and allowed all the defenses she had erected about herself in the past few days to crumble away. She kissed him back with all the yearning, all the passion, all the love in her heart.

For those few moments, impossibilities seemed possible. But passion did not have the power to drown out reality for very long.

"Ferdinand," she said, drawing back her head, though she kept her arms about him, "I cannot be your mistress."

"No, you dashed well cannot," he agreed. "The position is no longer open. It was all wrong anyway. I was not made to have mistresses. I cannot bed a woman and carry on with the rest of my life as if she did not exist. I want you to marry me."

"Because I am the daughter of the Earl of Bamber?" she asked, her hands slipping to his shoulders.

He clucked his tongue. "*Illegitimate* daughter. You forgot that juicy detail," he said scornfully. "No, of course not for that reason. I asked you once before, long before I knew who your father was. I want to marry you, that is all. I miss you."

He had not said he loved her, but he did not need to. It was there in the way he looked at her, in the way he held her, in the words he spoke. Viola knew a few moments of intense temptation. For she knew that with one word—*yes*—she could turn her whole life around. He loved her. He wanted to marry her. She could tell him everything—he already knew the worst about her. She had no doubt that he could and would pay off all of Clarence Wilding's debts and so free her family from the threat of ruin. She herself would be freed forever from the power of Daniel Kirby and a life of prostitution.

But she *loved* him. He could not marry her without sacrificing everything that was dear to him—his family, his position in society, his friends. He might think now that he did not care—he always had that reckless, dangerous eagerness to take up any challenge— the more outrageous, the better. But this was a challenge he could not win. He would be unhappy for most of the rest of his life. And therefore, so would she.

"Ferdinand," she said, and she retreated behind the contemptuous half smile that was second nature to her whenever she needed to protect herself from hurt, "I refused to marry you because I have no wish to marry you or any man. Why should I, when I can have any man I please whenever I please and still retain my freedom? I never did agree to become your mistress. I slept with you the night we arrived in London because you seemed to want it so badly. And it was pleasant, I must admit. But you really do not know yet—forgive me—how to please a woman in bed. I would become restless within a week or two if I stayed with you. I have been feeling restless at Pinewood for some time. You did me a favor by coming there and forcing me into doing what I have been wanting to do—resuming my career, that is. I find the life exciting."

"Don't *do* that." He was gripping her arms hard enough to leave bruises. He was also glaring into her eyes, his own suddenly very black. "Goddamn you, Viola. Don't you *trust* me? If you loved me, you would. I thought perhaps you did love me."

"Oh, Ferdinand." She smiled and spoke softly. "How foolish of you."

He swung away from her and picked up his hat and his cane from a chair inside the door.

"You could have trusted me, you know." He looked back at her when his hand was on the doorknob. "If he has some sort of power over you, you could have told me so. Dudley men know how to protect their women. But I can't force you, can I? And I can't make you love me if you don't. Good day to you."

The door was closing behind him as she reached out one arm toward him. She clapped her hand over her mouth so that she would not call after him. The ache in her throat was almost too painful to bear.

He *did* know who Daniel Kirby was.

You could have trusted me . . . you could have told me so. Dudley men know how to protect their women.

She did not know where he lived. She would not know where to find him if she changed her mind.

Thank God she did not know. Temptation was beyond her reach.

21

Ferdinand had still not quite adjusted his mind to thinking of his brother as a family man. But when Tresham's butler led him all the way up to the nursery of Dudley House and announced him, he walked in to find Tresham actually down on the floor building a precarious-looking castle out of wooden blocks with his three-year-old while the baby lay on a blanket beside them—out of range of falling masonry—kicking his legs and waving his arms. Their nurse was nowhere in sight. Neither was Jane.

The arrival of an uncle was more appealing, at least for a few minutes, it seemed, than the castle. Nicholas came hurtling across the room, and Ferdinand scooped him up and tossed him at the ceiling.

"Hello, old sport," he said as he caught the shrieking child. "By gad, I almost missed you. You weigh a ton."

"Again!"

Ferdinand tossed him again, made a great to-do about staggering and roaring with alarm as he caught the boy, and then set him down before bending to tickle the baby's stomach.

"Where is Jane?" he asked.

"Calling on Lady Webb—her godmother," Tresham explained, in case Ferdinand had forgotten. "Angie went with her and so I did not. About the only common sense our sister has ever shown is her attachment to Jane. This notion that during the Season it is bad *ton* for husbands and wives to be seen anywhere together, or at least to remain together for longer than two minutes after their arrival at any entertainment, is damnably irritating, Ferdinand. I am taking my duchess back home to Acton at the earliest opportunity."

This was what his brother had become? Ferdinand thought, looking at him in some fascination. A man who spent much of his time with his children and grumbled when his wife was not with him? After four years, Tresham was still not fretting against his leg shackle?

"I need some information," Ferdinand said with deliberate casualness. "I thought you might know."

"Well, the devil!" his brother exclaimed as the castle suddenly came crashing down. "Was that my fault, Nick? Or was it yours? Did you poke it with your finger again? You did, you rascal." He caught his giggling son before he could escape and wrestled with him on the floor.

Ferdinand watched with some wistfulness.

"Now." Tresham got to his feet and brushed at his clothes, even though he looked as immaculate as ever. "What is it, Ferdinand?"

"You know Kirby, I suppose," Ferdinand said. "Do you know where I might find him? Where he lives, I mean?"

His brother paused midbrush and looked up in obvious surprise. "Kirby?" he said. "Good God, Ferdinand, if it is a woman you want, there are far more direct—"

"Did he manage Lilian Talbot's career?" Ferdinand asked.

The duke looked sharply at him. "Pick up the blocks and put

them away, Nick," he said, "before Nurse comes back." He glanced at the baby, who appeared contented enough, before crossing the room to stand facing the window. Ferdinand joined him there.

"They were talking together this morning," Ferdinand said. "Kirby and Viola Thornhill, that is. And then her mother told me that he is helping her daughter find a governess's position, as he did once before. She seemed to believe it too."

"I assume, then," Tresham said, his hand closing about the handle of his quizzing glass, though he did not raise it to his eye, "that your question about his being her former manager was rhetorical?"

"I need to find him," Ferdinand said. "I need to ask him none too gently what hold he has over her."

"Has it occurred to you," his brother asked, "that *she* might have contacted *him* because she wishes to return to work?"

"Yes," Ferdinand said curtly. He gazed down at his brother's crested town carriage, which had drawn to a stop outside the front doors. His sister and his sister-in-law were descending from it. "But that is not the way it is. She knows Pinewood is hers, but she will not go back there. She was *happy* there, Tresham. You should have seen her the first time I did, organizing a sack race on the village green, flushed and laughing, her hair in a plait down her back, a bunch of daisies here." He gestured to a point above his left ear. "She was *happy*, dammit. And now she insists she does not love me." It was a non sequitur that he did not even notice.

"My dear Ferdinand—" His brother sounded genuinely concerned.

"She is lying," Ferdinand said. "Devil take it, Tresham, she is *lying*."

But their conversation was cut short by the opening of the nursery door and the appearance of Jane and Angeline. For a few minutes there was a great deal of noise and confusion as the children were picked up and hugged and Nicholas prattled loudly to his mother and his aunt about building a castle as tall as the sky and

Uncle Ferdie throwing him up so high that he almost dropped him—and the baby set up a loud wailing. Fortunately, the children's nurse arrived on the scene to rescue the adults, and they were able to retreat to the drawing room for tea.

"Well, Ferdie," Angeline asked as soon as they were settled there, "have you found her yet?"

"Miss Thornhill?" he said warily. He was not sure how willing Heyward would be to have Angie fed information about one of London's most notorious courtesans. "Yes. At the White Horse Inn. Her uncle owns it. Her mother and half-sisters live there too."

"How splendid," she said. "Are they dreadfully vulgar?"

"Not at all," he said stiffly. "Thornhill is actually a gentleman by birth. So was Wilding—Miss Thornhill's stepfather."

"*Clarence* Wilding?" Tresham said. "I remember him. Got himself killed in some brawl, if I remember correctly."

"But a gentleman nonetheless," Ferdinand said, realizing even as he spoke that he was on the defensive, just as Mrs. Wilding had been earlier. "Miss Thornhill is the natural daughter of the late Earl of Bamber."

Tresham raised his eyebrows. Angeline looked ecstatic.

"Oh, Ferdinand," Jane said, "that would explain why she was at Pinewood Manor. Now I am more glad than ever that you have given it back to her."

"An *earl's* daughter!" Angeline exclaimed. "How utterly splendid. It will be quite unexceptionable for you to marry her, Ferdie. The very highest sticklers may frown upon natural sons and daughters, but perfectly respectable people marry them all the time. And Miss Thornhill was recognized by her father before he died. He gave her property—I am sure he meant to do it even if he forgot to say so in his will, and now that you have given it back to her, no one will be any the wiser anyway. She will be known simply as Miss Thornhill of Pinewood—until she becomes Lady Ferdinand Dudley, of course. Jane, we must waste no more ti—"

"Angie!" Ferdinand said sharply. "Her illegitimacy is not the worst charge the *ton* would level against her. Not that I would care the snap of two fingers, and I would defend her honor against anyone who chose to argue the point. But *you* would care. At least you would by the time Heyward had finished with you."

"Pooh!" she said. "Heyward does not rule me. Besides, he would not be so stuffy."

"Ferdinand." Jane leaned forward in her chair. "You *are* fond of her, are you not? Are you going to marry her? *We* will never disown you if you do. Will we, Jocelyn?"

"Will we not?" he asked, looking at her with one of his black stares.

Her eyes sparked. It had always fascinated Ferdinand to see that not only was Jane uncowed by that look, which could cause even the strongest man to quake in his boots, but that it provoked her into giving as good as she got. Perhaps, he had concluded long ago, that was why Tresham had married her.

"You claim to be a *Dudley* and yet ask such a question?" she cried. "I will not disown Ferdinand, even if *you* do. And I will not disown Miss Thornhill either if he should choose to marry her. She cannot help her birth. And who knows why she chose the career she did? Women become courtesans and mistresses and . . . and *whores* for a number of reasons. But it is *never* from personal choice. No woman would freely choose such degradation. If Miss Thornhill has won Ferdinand's respect and admiration and love, then she is worthy of recognition by his family. She will have *my* recognition, if no one else's."

"Indeed, my love!" Tresham said softly before turning his eyes on his brother. "So there you have it, Ferdinand. We are Dudleys. And if society tells us that something is impossible, then of course we have been provoked into proving that we do not care *that* much for society's good opinion." He snapped his thumb and middle finger with a satisfyingly loud crack.

"Bravo, Tresh!" Angeline said. "The White Horse Inn, did you say, Ferdie? Jane, we must call on Mrs. Wilding and Miss Thornhill there. I cannot wait to see her, can you? She must be extremely beautiful, to have caught Ferdie's eye. Heyward says he has never been in the petticoat line, which of course he ought not to have said in my hearing, but I persuaded him years ago that I am no delicate bloom and will not faint away at the merest provocation. What we will do, Jane, is invite them here for some grand reception to introduce them to society. Ferdie can announce his betroth—"

"Angie!" Ferdinand was on his feet. "Take a damper, will you? She won't marry me."

For a rare moment she was speechless. She stared at him, her mouth still open. But she recovered quickly.

"Why not?" she asked.

"Because she does not *want* to," he said. "Because she would prefer to retain her freedom and live her own life. Because she does not care for me. Because she does not *love* me." He ran the fingers of one hand through his hair. "Deuce take it, I cannot believe I am discussing my personal life with my family."

"Is she going back to Pinewood, then?" Jane asked.

"No," he said. "She dashed well won't do that either. She is going back to her old way of life, if you must know. There! End of discussion. For all time. I will take my leave now. Thank you for tea, Jane." He had not touched a drop of it.

"Angeline." Jane spoke to their sister-in-law, but she was looking at Ferdinand. "I like your idea. We will call at the White Horse Inn tomorrow morning. I think we ought not to delay any longer than that. Don't forbid me to go, Jocelyn. I would simply defy you."

"My love," he said, his voice deceptively meek, "I cannot have it said that I am one of those sad men who cannot control their own wives. I issue commands only when I have a reasonable expectation that they will be obeyed."

Ferdinand heard no more. He had left the room and closed the door behind him. But he had not had an answer to the question he had come to ask, he thought as he ran down the stairs.

He would just have to find Kirby himself. It should not be impossibly difficult. He just hoped Kirby would be reluctant to talk. He hoped the man would need considerable persuasion, in fact.

Viola was in the small office of the White Horse Inn the next morning bringing the account books up to date, making sure that the columns of figures balanced. She had dressed in one of her plainest morning gowns, one she had left behind at the inn years ago. It was not particularly out of fashion, simply because it had never been *in* fashion. She had had Hannah dress her hair in a tight coronet of braids.

She wanted to feel, at least for the rest of this week, as if she were nothing more than her uncle's secretary and bookkeeper. She did not want to look either ahead or back. She kept her mind ruthlessly focused on the figures before her.

Yet the mind is a strange thing. It can concentrate on a mechanical task while at the same time wandering in the most undisciplined way.

To her meeting with Daniel Kirby.

To the upsetting confrontation with Ferdinand.

To all that had happened afterward.

Her mother had come back to the sitting room soon after he had left. So had Maria and Claire and Uncle Wesley. They had all been beaming expectantly.

"Well?" her mother had asked.

"He brought me the deed of Pinewood," she had told them, indicating the papers on the table. "He has had ownership transferred to me. It was always more mine than his, he said."

"That is all?" her mother had asked, clearly disappointed.

"Oh, Viola," Maria had said, "he is so *handsome.*"

"He offered me marriage," Viola had told them. "I refused."

She had not been able to explain any of her real reasons, of course, and so had been forced to allow her mother to draw the conclusion that it was her illegitimacy that had led her to refuse. Mama had wept. But she had not been able to understand why that fact should mean so much to Viola when clearly it did not to Lord Ferdinand Dudley.

"Mama," Viola had said at last, "I do not love him."

"Love? *Love?*" Her mother's voice had risen. "You refuse a lord, the son of a *duke*, when you might marry him and be secure for life? When you might do something for your sisters? How *can* you be so selfish?"

"How can you not love him," Maria had wailed, "when he is so *gorgeous?*"

"Hush, Maria!" Claire had said sternly. "Mama, do dry your eyes and let me bring you some tea."

"Oh," their mother had said after blowing her nose, "I am the selfish one. Forgive me, Viola. You always sent us money from your governess's salary. You were kind to us."

"And since then too, Rosamond," Uncle Wesley had said. He had continued despite Viola's shake of the head. "I am not the one who has been paying Benjamin's school fees, you know. Viola has. And other things too that you have thought came from me. It is time you knew. You do not have to marry any wealthy aristocrat you do not even like, niece. And you do not have to go out as a governess again either if you do not want to. The inn will support my sister and her children just as it would have supported Alice and our children if she had lived."

They had all ended up in tears, except Uncle Wesley, who had slipped off back downstairs. No one had mentioned Ferdinand again—except Hannah, who had still been in Viola's room when she returned there.

"Well?" she had asked. "Did he come to take you back to that

house? Or has he come to his senses and offered you something
better?"

"Something better, Hannah," Viola had told her. "He has given
me Pinewood. Perhaps one day, when Mr. Kirby can make no more
money out of me and decides that the debt is paid off, we will go
back there, you and I. Everyone needs some hope. Lord Ferdinand
Dudley has given it to me."

"And he didn't offer to make an honest woman of you?"
Hannah had asked. "I thought better of him, I must confess."

"An honest woman." Viola had sighed and then laughed. "He *did*
offer, Hannah, and I refused. No, don't look at me in that mulish
manner. You of all people must know why I refused, why I could
never marry him or any other man. I could not do that to him."

"Why not, lovey?" Hannah had asked.

It was really a rhetorical question, but Viola had answered it anyway.

"Because I *love* him, that is why," she had cried. "Because I l-l-
love him, Hannah." She had sobbed in her old nurse's arms, which
were wonderfully comforting but which had somehow lost their
magical ability to make all better.

She had definitely added up that column correctly, she thought
now, her head bent over the account book. She had added it three
times and arrived at the same total each time. The trouble was that
there was no more paperwork to do and she did not want it to be at
an end. She wanted to lose herself in work.

But the door opened suddenly and Maria's flushed, excited face
appeared around it.

"Viola," she said, "you are to come up immediately to Mama.
She has sent me to fetch you."

"Why?" Viola was immediately suspicious.

"I am not going to say." Maria smirked importantly. "It is a
secret."

Viola sighed in exasperation. "He has not come back, has he?"

she asked. "Tell me if he has, Maria. I do not want to see him and you may go back and tell Mama so."

"I am not saying," her sister said.

As Viola made her way upstairs, it suddenly occurred to her that perhaps it was Daniel Kirby who had called. But Maria would not be so excited about that, surely.

"You will never guess," she said from just behind Viola.

There were two ladies in the sitting room with her mother, who was looking almost as flushed as Maria. Two very grand ladies, both dressed in the first state of fashion, the one quietly and expensively elegant, the other brighter and more flamboyant.

"Viola." Her mother stood, as they both did too. "Come and make your curtsy to these ladies, who have been kind enough to call upon me and ask to make your acquaintance too."

Maria slipped past her into the room, but Viola stood just inside the door.

"This is my eldest daughter, Viola Thornhill," her mother said. "Her grace, the Duchess of Tresham, and Lady Heyward, Viola." She indicated first the elegant, golden-haired lady and then the other.

Viola was never sure afterward if she curtsied or not. She did know that somehow her hands found the doorknob behind her back and gripped it as if for dear life.

Both ladies were smiling at her. The duchess spoke first.

"Miss Thornhill," she said, "I do hope you will forgive us for calling on you and your mama without any warning. We have heard so much about you from Ferdinand, you see, and longed to make your acquaintance."

"I am his sister," Lady Heyward said. "You are every bit as lovely as I expected. And younger."

Did they know? *Did they know?* Did Ferdinand know they were here? *Did the Duke of Tresham?*

"Thank you," Viola said. "How very obliging of you to call upon Mama."

"Her grace has invited us to take tea with her at Dudley House tomorrow afternoon, Viola," her mother said. "Do come and sit down."

Did they know?

"Actually, Mrs. Wilding," the duchess said, "we would like to take Miss Thornhill for a drive with us today. It is far too lovely a day to be spent indoors. Can you spare her for an hour?"

"I am working on my uncle's books," Viola said.

"But of *course* you can be spared," her mother said. "Run and change into one of your pretty dresses. I cannot imagine where you found that old thing you are wearing. Whatever will her grace and Lady Heyward think of you?"

"Please come," the duchess said with a warm smile for Viola.

"Yes, please do," Lady Heyward added.

There seemed to be no other choice but to go and change. Ten minutes later Viola was seated in a very luxurious open barouche beside Lady Heyward while the duchess sat on the seat opposite, her back to the horses.

Please not to the park.

But the barouche turned in the direction of Hyde Park.

"We have disturbed and upset you," the duchess said. "Please do not blame Ferdinand, Miss Thornhill. He did not send us. He told us you had refused his marriage offer."

"You must have seen from your visit to my uncle's inn how unsuitable such a match would have been," Viola said, clasping her gloved hands in her lap so that she would not fidget.

"Your mother is a real lady," the duchess said, "and your younger sister delightful. We did not meet the older girl. You have a half-brother at school too, I believe?"

"Yes," Viola said.

"We were so very curious, you see," Lady Heyward said, "to meet the lady who has stolen Ferdie's heart. You *have* stolen it, Miss Thornhill. Did you know that? Or did he neglect to tell you, as gentlemen so often do? They can be such foolish creatures, can they not, Jane? They will make a perfectly decent marriage proposal in which they list all the considerable advantages of making a match with them and neglect to mention the only one that really matters. I refused Heyward when he first offered for me, even though he went down on one knee very prettily and looked very foolish, the poor darling. Everyone says he is just a dry old stick—at least Tresham and Ferdie say it, because of course he is so very different from them. He is not really stuffy, at least not when one is private with him, but when he first offered for me he made not the slightest hint of a mention of love. He did not even try to steal a kiss. Can you imagine anything so provoking? How could I have accepted him, even if I *was* head over heels for him? Now, what was it I set out to say?"

"You wondered how I could have refused Lord Ferdinand," Viola said. The barouche was turning into the park, and her heart was beating faster. Of course, this was not the fashionable hour, which would draw the whole of the *ton* into the park in a few hours' time, but even so, she might be recognized at any moment. "There are very compelling reasons, believe me, none of which have anything to do with the regard in which I hold him. Not the least of those reasons is that I am not a daughter of my mother's marriage. Perhaps you wondered why my name is different from hers. It is her maiden name, you see."

"You are a natural daughter of the late Earl of Bamber," Lady Heyward said, taking Viola's hand in her own. "Which is nothing to be ashamed of. Natural sons cannot inherit their fathers' titles and entailed property, of course, but apart from that it is as respectable to be a natural child as to be one born within wedlock. *That* need not keep you from wedding Ferdie. Do you love him?"

"There is a reason," Viola said, turning her head away so that her face would be hidden by the brim of her straw bonnet, "why that question has no relevance at all. I cannot marry him. And I will not explain to you. You must take me back to my uncle's inn, please. You would not wish to be seen with me. The duke and Lord Heyward would not wish it."

"Oh, Miss Thornhill, do not distress yourself," the duchess said. "I am going to tell you something that very few people know. Even Angeline will be hearing it for the first time now. Before I married Jocelyn, I was his mistress."

Lady Heyward's hand slipped away from Viola's.

"He kept me in the house where Ferdinand took you on your return to London," the duchess said. "Jocelyn has kept the house. We always spend an afternoon or two there when we are in town. It holds many fond memories. It was there we learned to be happy together. But that does not alter the fact that I was a mistress. A fallen woman, if you will."

"Jane!" Lady Heyward exclaimed. "How utterly, splendidly romantic. Whyever have you never told me?"

So they *did* know, Viola thought. How rash of them to bring her out with them like this, in an open carriage.

"It was always a matter of pride with me," she said, her head averted again, "to keep on asserting that I would be no man's mistress. You knew one man, your grace. During the four years I worked, I knew so many men that I lost count. I never even tried to keep count, in fact, or wanted to. It was work. It was entirely different from your situation. I was famous. I was much in demand. I might still be recognized at any moment. Take me back home."

"Miss Thornhill." The duchess leaned forward and took Viola's hand in both her own. "We three are women. We understand things that men will never understand, even the men we love. We understand that what brings men pleasure by the very nature of the act can bring us none unless it is more an emotional than a physical experience, unless there is some sort of love commitment from and to our partner. We understand that *no* courtesan embarks on her career with a free or joyful heart. We know that no woman could enjoy such a life. And we know too—as men most certainly do not—that the woman, the *person,* is something quite distinct from what she does for a living. You are uncomfortable with us. You probably resent us. But I know—I sense—that I will like you very much indeed if you will allow me to. Do you love Ferdinand?"

Viola turned her head sharply to glare at the duchess and pulled her hand away. "Of course I love him," she said. "*Of course* I do. Why else would I have refused him? It would be a magnificent coup, would it not, for an illegitimate whore to marry the brother of a duke? Well, this illegitimate whore will not do it. I can do only one thing in my life to demonstrate how very much I love him. *One thing*—I can refuse him. I can make him believe that the prospect of returning to my old life is more enticing than the possibility of marrying him. If you love him, you will take me home now and go back and tell him how coldly and disdainfully I received you. I have feelings. I have *feelings,* and I cannot stand much more of this. Take me home."

The duchess turned her head and called new instructions to the coachman. Then she turned back to Viola.

"I am so sorry," she said. "We are such meddlesome creatures, Angeline and I. But we both love Ferdinand, you see, and hate to see him miserable. Now it breaks my heart to see that you are every bit as unhappy as he. We chose the park deliberately as our destination. We *wanted* to be seen with you. We want to make you respectable."

Viola laughed bitterly. "You do not understand."

Lady Heyward touched her arm. "Oh, yes," she said, "we do. But Jane chose the wrong word. We are not going to make you respectable, Miss Thornhill, but *respected*. We Dudleys have never been respectable, you see. I would never be a simpering miss. Tresham was forever fighting duels before Jane intervened one time and caused him to get shot in the leg—and it was always over women. Ferdie can never resist the most outrageous and dangerous challenges. But we never wanted to be respectable—how dull that would be! We are respected, though. No one would dare *not* respect us. We could make you respected too if you would give us the chance. How exciting it would be. I would give a grand ball—"

"Thank you," Viola said quietly but firmly. "You are both very kind. But no."

Conversation lapsed until the barouche turned into the inn yard again. The duchess's coachman jumped down from his perch to assist Viola to alight.

"Miss Thornhill." The duchess smiled at her. "Please come for tea with your mother tomorrow. I believe she would be disappointed if you refused."

"I am delighted," Lady Heyward said, "to have met Miss Thornhill of Pinewood Manor at last."

"Thank you." Viola hurried into the inn before the barouche turned to leave again.

She had a new plan. It had come to her full-blown after they had left the park. It filled her mind with dizzying hope and bleak despair both at the same time. She needed to think through a few details.

22

❦

Ferdinand rose from his bed the following morning much later than he had intended. Of course, he had been out most of the night, dragging John Leavering and a few of his other friends from party to party—not the sort he normally attended—and even to a couple of the more notorious gaming hells. But there had been no sign at any of them of Kirby.

He intended to spend the day at Tattersall's and a few other places where the man was likely to be. He would have to be patient, he decided, though patience was not a virtue he had much cultivated. If Kirby was seeking clients for Viola, then he must do so in the places Ferdinand intended to haunt.

He was just finishing breakfast when his valet announced that a visitor had called. He handed his master a calling card.

"Bamber?" Ferdinand frowned. Bamber up and about before noon? What the devil? "Show him in, Bentley."

The earl strode into the dining room a few moments later, looking as ill-natured as ever and more dissolute than usual. His hair was disheveled and his eyes bloodshot. He was unshaven. He must surely have been up all night, but he was not wearing evening clothes. He was dressed for travel.

"Ah, Bamber." Ferdinand got to his feet and extended his right hand.

The earl ignored it. He strode up to the table, reaching into a capacious pocket of his carriage coat as he did so. He pulled out a couple of folded papers and slapped them down.

"There!" he said. "It was an ill wind that blew me to Brookes's that night, Dudley. I wish I'd never set foot there, and that's the truth, but I did, and it can't be helped. Damn you for all the trouble you have caused me." He was reaching into an inner pocket as he spoke. He brought out a sheaf of banknotes and set them down beside the other papers. "Here is an end of the matter, and I hope not to hear another word about it for the rest of my days—from *anyone.*"

Ferdinand sat back down. "What is this?" he asked, gesturing to the papers and the money.

Bamber picked up one of the papers and unfolded it before shoving it under Ferdinand's nose.

"*This,*" he said, "is a copy of the codicil m'father made to his will a few weeks before he died and left with m'mother's solicitor in York. As you can see for yourself, he left Pinewood to that chit, his by-blow. The property was never mine, and so it was never yours, Dudley." He tapped his forefinger on the money. "And *this* is five hundred pounds. It is the amount you set on the table against the promise of Pinewood. It is in payment of my debt to you. Are you satisfied? It is not one fraction the worth of Pinewood, of course. If you want more—"

"It is enough," Ferdinand said. He took the paper and read it. His eyes lingered on four of the words written there—"my daughter, Viola Thornhill." The late earl had made this public acknowledgment of his relationship to her, then. Ferdinand looked curiously at the other man. "Have you just come from Yorkshire, Bamber? It looks as if you have been traveling all night."

"I damned well have," the earl assured him. "I may be a ramshackle fellow, Dudley. I may be known as something of a loose screw, but I'll not have it said that I have been a party to any fraud or cover-up. As soon as the chit said she had met m'father here just before he died—"

"Miss Thornhill?"

"She had the effrontery to come calling on me," Bamber said. "You could have knocked me over with a bald feather. I didn't know she existed. Anyway, I knew as soon as she said it that if he *had* been going to do anything to his will he couldn't have done it that week he was here. I remember because I asked him to go to Westinghouse to have my allowance raised. I was living on *pin* money, for the love of God, and old Westinghouse always made a great to-do about giving me an advance on the next quarter. Anyway, m'father told me he had been to see Westinghouse the day before but he had not been there. His mother had died in Kent or something inconvenient like that and he had gone off to bury her. M'father left London the same day. He sometimes went to my mother's solicitor on small matters. It struck me that he might have gone to him about this— and that other matter the chit mentioned too. In fact, she seemed more concerned about that than about the will." He tapped the other folded paper.

"Why did these not come to light before now?" Ferdinand asked.

"Corking is not the brightest light," Bamber said carelessly. "He forgot all about them."

"*Forgot?*" Ferdinand looked at him incredulously.

The earl leaned both hands on the table and looked narrow-eyed at Ferdinand.

"He *forgot*," he repeated with slow emphasis. "My questions jolted his memory. Leave it at that, Dudley. He *forgot*."

Ferdinand understood immediately. The York solicitor was

primarily the Countess of Bamber's. The late earl had used him out of desperation because Westinghouse had been gone from London and Bamber had known he did not have much time left in which to make all secure for his newly restored daughter. The countess had found out about the codicil, and she had persuaded her solicitor to say nothing about it. Whose decision it had been not to destroy the papers, Ferdinand could not even guess. He could merely feel grateful that one or both of them had not been prepared to go that whole criminal length.

"I don't know where to find the chit," Bamber said. "And quite honestly, I don't intend to put myself out trying. I don't feel any obligation whatsoever to her even if she is m'half-sister. But I won't do her out of what is rightfully hers either. I daresay you know where she is. Will you take her these?"

"Yes," Ferdinand said. He had no idea what the content of the other paper was or why she had said it was more important to her than the will. She was going to be ecstatic to learn that her unwavering faith in Bamber had not been misplaced. So she did not owe Pinewood in any way at all to him, he thought wryly.

"Good," Bamber said. "That is it, then. I'm going home to sleep. I hope never to hear the names Pinewood or Thornhill ever again. Or Dudley either, for that matter. Corking has sent a copy of the codicil to Westinghouse, by the way."

He turned to leave.

"Wait!" Ferdinand said, an idea popping into his head. "Sit down and have some coffee, Bamber. I haven't finished with you yet."

"Devil take it!" the earl said irritably, pulling a chair out from the table and plumping himself down onto it none too elegantly. "I would set a light to Brookes's with m'own hands today, and stand around to watch it burn to the ground too, if it were not somewhat akin to shutting the stable door after the horse had bolted. What now?"

Ferdinand looked assessingly at him.

Viola felt horribly exposed as she approached the front doors of Dudley House on Grosvenor Square. She was terrified that they would open and the duchess would step out—or that the duchess would be looking out through one of the many windows that overlooked the square. After she had lifted the knocker and let it fall against the door, she was afraid the duchess might be in the hall.

A very superior-looking butler opened the door. His eyes alit on her and then went beyond her to note that there was no carriage and no companion, not even a maid. He looked back at her.

"I wish to see his grace," she said. She felt as breathless as if she had run a mile uphill. Her knees were unsteady.

The butler raised his eyebrows and looked at her as if she were a little lower on the social scale than a worm. Viola had realized, of course, that the very strong chance the duke was away from home so close to the middle of the day was not the least of her worries.

"Kindly inform him that Lilian Talbot wishes to speak with him," she said, holding his gaze with a confidence she did not feel. She reminded herself that she was still wearing the clothes she had worn for the drive in the park. They were the clothes of a lady, the clothes Viola Thornhill of Pinewood Manor had worn for afternoon visits.

"I believe," she said, "he will agree to see me."

"Step inside," the butler said, after such a lengthy pause that she feared any moment to have the door slammed in her face. "Wait here."

She had hoped he would show her into a room to wait. At any moment one of the doors that lined the hall might open to reveal the duchess. Or she might come down the grand staircase that the butler was now ascending. Viola stood just inside the front doors with one silent liveried footman for company. She stood there for what felt like an hour at the very least but was perhaps five minutes. Then the butler came back downstairs.

"This way," he said as frigidly as he had spoken before. He opened a door to her right, and she stepped into what was obviously a reception room—a square, elegant apartment with chairs arranged about the walls. "His grace will be with you soon." The door closed.

Another five minutes passed before he came. Viola thought a dozen times at least of bolting, but she had come this far. She would see it through to the end. If the Duke of Tresham was the man she thought he was, he would agree to her suggestion. Then the door opened again, and she turned from the window.

She felt a strange shock as soon as he stepped into the room. He was as austere, as forbidding, as . . . frightening as he had been at Pinewood. Yet he was holding a tiny baby. The child was against his shoulder, making fussing noises and sucking loudly on one fist. The duke was patting its back with one long-fingered hand.

"Miss . . . Talbot?" he said, raising his eyebrows.

She curtsied and lifted her chin. She would not be cowed. "Yes, your grace."

"And how may I be of service to you?" he asked her.

"I have a proposition to make to you," she said.

"Indeed?" His voice was soft, but all her insides jerked with alarm.

"It is not what you think," she said hastily.

"Am I to feel flattered or . . . shattered?" he asked her. He cupped his hand over the back of the baby's head when the child fussed in an obvious attempt to find a more comfortable position. There was gentleness in that hand, she thought. But there was none whatsoever in his face.

"I do not know," she said, "if you are aware that Lord Ferdinand Dudley has restored Pinewood Manor to me. Or that he has offered me marriage."

His eyebrows rose again. "But do I need to be aware?" he asked her. "My brother is seven-and-twenty, Miss . . . Talbot."

She hesitated before continuing. "And I do not know," she said, "if you are aware that the duchess and Lady Heyward called upon my mother this morning and then took me driving in the park. Or that the duchess has invited my mother and me to tea here tomorrow. I do not wish to cause any trouble for them," she added.

Two of his long fingers were rubbing lightly over the baby's neck. "You need not fear," he said. "I do not make a habit of taking a whip to my wife. And my sister is Lord Heyward's responsibility."

"I am aware," she said, "that my presence in London can be nothing but an embarrassment to you."

"Are you?" he said.

"I might have been seen in your barouche this morning," she said. "I might have been seen coming here. I might be seen tomorrow when I come with my mother. And recognized."

He appeared to consider for a moment. "Unless you wear a mask," he agreed, "I suppose that is a distinct possibility."

"I am prepared to go back to Pinewood," she said. "I am prepared to live there for the rest of my life and repel any attempt Lord Ferdinand may make to write to me or to see me there. This I will swear to—in writing, if you will."

His stare was as black as his brother's, she thought during the silent moments that followed. No, blacker. For Ferdinand's stare always gave evidence of some emotion behind it. This man seemed as cold as death.

"This is extremely magnanimous of you," he said at last. "I assume there is a condition attached? How much, Miss Talbot? I suppose you are aware that I am one of the wealthiest men in England?"

She named the sum baldly, without any explanation or apology.

He strolled farther into the room and turned half away from her. The baby—its eyes were blue—stared sleepily at her. The neck-rubbing was putting it to sleep.

"Apparently," the duke said, "you do not realize *how* wealthy, Miss Talbot. You might have asked for considerably more. But it is too late now, is it not?"

"It is a loan I ask for," she said. "I will pay you back. With interest."

He swung around to look at her again, and for the first time his eyes looked less than opaque. She had sparked his interest, it seemed.

"In that case," he said, "I am ensuring the respectability of my name and my family at remarkably small cost. You surprise me."

"But you must do something else for me," she said.

"Ah." He tipped his head to one side to note that his child was sleeping. Then he looked back at Viola. "Yes, I am sure there is. Proceed."

"The money is to be used in payment of a debt," she said. "I want you to pay it for me—in person. I want you to get a receipt stating that the debt has been paid in full and that there are no others. I want you to send me a copy at the White Horse Inn, signed by both you and him."

"Who?" His eyebrows were raised again.

"Daniel Kirby," she said. "Do you know him? I can give you his direction."

"Please do." He spoke softly. "Why, if I am permitted to ask, can you not pay him yourself if I give you the money?"

She hesitated. "It will not be enough," she explained. "He will discover other unpaid bills or he will claim that I was mistaken about the interest rate. If *you* go to him, the amount will be right. You are a powerful man."

He stared at her for a long time while his child slumbered peacefully against his shoulder.

"Yes," he said at last. "I believe I am."

"You will do it?" she asked him.

"I will do it."

She closed her eyes. She had not really expected him to agree. She had not been sure if she would be more relieved or disappointed if he would not. She was still not sure. She had not yet permitted herself to look ahead to the rest of her life, when she must keep her side of their bargain.

"I will wait for that receipt to be delivered to my uncle's inn, then," she said after giving him Daniel Kirby's address. "Do you wish to say now, your grace, in what installments you will expect the loan to be repaid? And what interest will be acceptable to you? Shall I sign something now?"

"I think that will be unnecessary, Miss Talbot," he said. "I am sure I can trust you to repay your debt in a timely manner. I know where you may be reached at any time during the rest of your life, after all, do I not? And I am, as you observed a short while ago, a powerful man."

She shivered.

"Yes. Thank you," she said. "I will leave for Pinewood on the next stagecoach after the receipt has been delivered into my hands."

"I am sure you will," he said.

She hurried across the room and opened the door. The butler was in the hall. He opened the front doors, and a few moments later she was out on the steps, gulping in fresh air. It had been so very easy.

She had just been saved from what had appeared to be an unavoidable future.

Mama and Uncle Wesley had been saved.

So had Claire.

She hurried out of the square, her head down, the warmth of

bright sunlight soaking into her. Why did life still appear bleaker than bleak? Why was she cold through to her very soul?

The Duchess of Tresham looked around the open door of the reception room before stepping inside.

"She has gone?" she asked unnecessarily. "Why did she come alone and ask to speak with *you*, Jocelyn? Why did she use a false name?" The duchess had been looking out through the nursery window earlier while nursing the baby and had observed the arrival of Viola Thornhill. She had remarked on it to her husband, who had been reading their elder son a story.

"Lilian Talbot was her working name," he said.

"Oh." She frowned.

"She has persuaded me," he said, "to pay her off so that she will go back to Pinewood and never be seen or heard from again."

"And you *agreed*?"

"Ah, but it is only a loan, you see," he said. "We will not be permanently impoverished, Jane. She is to pay me back."

"She thinks this is what is best for Ferdinand?" she asked. "How foolishly noble."

"She did apologize for letting me know that you and Angeline took her driving in the park this morning," he said. "But I promised not to whip you, you will be relieved to know."

"Jocelyn!" She tipped her head to one side. "You have been terrifying the poor lady. You are not serious about this, are you? You are not going to be odious and break Ferdinand's heart?"

"It is just the effect I have on people, you see," he said. "You are the only one who has ever defied me, Jane. I married you so that you would be forced to obey me, but we both know how successful I have been at that."

She smiled with amusement despite herself. "I see that Christopher is asleep," she said. "How do you *do* it, Jocelyn? I resent it. I am his mother, but he does nothing except squirm and wail when I try to rock him to sleep."

"He is wise enough to understand that he can expect no meal from me, you see," he said. "There is nothing else to alleviate his boredom than to nod off. Dudleys are never so foolish as to waste negative energy. They merely fall asleep and store it up for future mayhem. Christopher is going to be more of a handful than Ferdinand and I were combined—with Angeline thrown in. I believe Nick may prove to be more biddable."

She laughed but then sobered.

"Are you really going to send her back to Pinewood?" she asked. "Ferdinand may well challenge you if he discovers what you have done."

"That would make a change," he said. "I have not been challenged for over four years. I have forgotten the peculiar excitement attached to gazing down the wrong end of a pistol. I had better go and find him and give him the opportunity."

"Jocelyn, do be serious," she said.

"I was never more so," he assured her. "I must find Ferdinand. I have to confess that being head of the family has never been more interesting. Take this rascal, will you, Jane? If I am not much mistaken, he has dampened my sleeve. Not to mention the soggy patch on my shoulder."

He kissed her swiftly as she took their sleeping son from him.

Ferdinand wasted a good part of the afternoon looking for Daniel Kirby—without success—before deciding that as usual he was allowing impetuosity to lead him by the nose instead of harnessing his wrath and using it in a measured and effective way.

There was sure to be a *much* more effective way. He would need some assistance, though. He did not have to think too deeply before deciding that his brother was his best possible choice. And so he made his way to Grosvenor Square.

Both the duchess and his grace were away from home, Tresham's pokerfaced butler informed him. The duchess was attending a garden party with Lady Webb. His grace was simply out.

"Damnation!" Ferdinand said aloud, flicking his riding whip impatiently against his boot. "I'll have to go searching for him, then."

Fortunately he did not have to look far. Tresham's curricle turned into the square just as he was swinging himself up into the saddle.

"Ah," Tresham called, "just the man I have been looking for. And you were on my doorstep all the time."

"You have been looking for me?" Ferdinand dismounted, and his brother vaulted down from the high seat of his curricle and tossed the ribbons to his groom.

"Combing the streets of London," Tresham said, setting a hand on his brother's shoulder and walking back up the steps to the house with him. He took Ferdinand into his library, closed the door, and poured them both a drink. "I have a confession to make, Ferdinand. My duchess believes it highly probable that you will slap a glove in my face as soon as I tell you." He handed Ferdinand one of the glasses.

Ferdinand was bursting with his own news, but his brother's words arrested him. "What?" he asked.

"I have agreed to pay Miss Thornhill a largish sum to withdraw to Pinewood and never communicate with you again," Tresham said.

"By God!" Ferdinand's fury finally found an available target. "You might have heeded Jane's warning. I'll kill you for this, Tresham."

His brother sat down on a leather chair beside the hearth and crossed one booted leg over the other. He looked damnably unconcerned. "Actually," he said, "it was Miss Thornhill's suggestion. And it is to be a loan rather than a gift. She will repay every penny plus interest. It is the additional request she made of me as part of our bargain that will be of particular interest to you."

"Well, it will not be," Ferdinand said, setting his glass down. "I do not want to hear it. I don't care what sum you have bribed her with, and I do not care what promises she has made you. I will pay your damned money back, and then I am going to release her from her promise. Maybe she will never have me. But she is going to be free to say yes if she means yes and no if she means no. Damn you, Tresham. I'll never speak to you again after today. I am too disgusted even to kill you, damn you." He turned toward the door.

"She wants me to deliver the money personally into Kirby's hands," Tresham said, ignoring the outburst. "And to extort from him a written statement to the effect that all debts have been fully and permanently paid off. Jane was right, you see. That scoundrel had her working off debts for a number of years. And having heard that she was returning to London, he no doubt discovered other debts—the ones I have agreed to pay off for her by advancing her a loan. I have told you all this with the greatest reluctance, Ferdinand, merely because it seemed selfish to hoard to myself all the pleasure of dealing with Kirby. I thought perhaps you might consider your claim to take the first, er, *shot* at him superior to my own."

Ferdinand looked over his shoulder at his brother for a few moments before reaching into a pocket and drawing out the second of the two papers Bamber had put on his breakfast table earlier. He had hesitated about reading it at first, since it belonged to Viola, but it had been unsealed and he had been unable to resist the temptation. He crossed the room and handed it to his brother, who read it carefully from beginning to end.

"Where did you get this?" he asked.

"From Bamber," Ferdinand said. "It was put into the safekeeping of the countess's solicitor in York together with a codicil to the late

Bamber's will leaving Pinewood to his daughter. The solicitor, doubtless encouraged by the countess, conveniently *forgot* about both documents until Bamber went up there and reminded him. He arrived back in town this morning and came straight to me."

"Bamber Senior paid off all the debts two years ago," Tresham said, looking back at the paper. "*All.* And this is an interesting detail, Ferdinand. They were debts incurred by Clarence Wilding. Having had a slight acquaintance with the man, I can believe they were large enough. They became as deep as the ocean, no doubt, by the time Kirby acquired them and added interest of several hundred percent. Does *Mrs.* Wilding know of these debts? Do you know?"

"I don't think so," Ferdinand said. "She seems genuinely to believe that Kirby found Viola a governess's job once upon a time and is finding her another now."

"She took the whole burden on her own young shoulders, then," Tresham said. "There are younger half-brothers and -sisters, I seem to recall?"

"Three of them. They must have been mere children at the time," Ferdinand said. "Viola was a young lady by birth and education. Her illegitimacy would have been no great barrier to a decent future. Her father was an earl, after all. She could have expected to make a respectable match. Kirby took that chance from her and plunged her into hell instead."

"You must understand," Tresham said, "what a great sacrifice I am making, Ferdinand, in granting you precedence in this matter. I would offer to be your second, but I do not believe this man has earned the right to an honorable challenge, do you? Let me assist you, though. And a suggestion? I will not call it advice or you must reject it out of sheer principle. A bullet between the eyes is too easy. Besides, it will involve you in all sorts of annoying complications and you may find yourself obliged to spend the next year or two kicking your heels on the Continent. Pick up your drink again and have a seat and together we will contrive some suitable punishment."

"Even death would not be *suitable* for what he has done," Ferdinand said savagely. "But it is the best substitute I can think of."

"Ah," his brother said softly. "But we must think of what is best for your Viola too, Ferdinand. You cannot afford to make a mistake there or she will lock herself behind Pinewood doors and never come out again."

Ferdinand picked up his glass and sat down.

23

Viola sat reading the next morning while her mother gave Maria an arithmetic lesson. At least she held an open book in her lap and even remembered to turn a page now and then. But her hands were like ice and her heart was thudding and her mind was in turmoil.

All she needed was that piece of paper in her hands. There was a stagecoach leaving for the west country from another inn during the afternoon. She could be on it. Hannah already had their bags packed. Her mother would be disappointed, of course. She had her heart set on going to Dudley House for tea. She firmly believed that Lord Ferdinand would renew his addresses and that this time Viola would have the good sense to accept. But Mama's disappointment would have to be borne.

Surely his grace would call on Daniel Kirby this morning. Or perhaps he had gone yesterday but had waited until today to send her the receipt. Surely he would not let her down when the alternative for him might be acquiring Lilian Talbot as a sister-in-law.

She turned a page with a cold, clammy hand.

And then the sitting room door opened to admit Claire, waving a letter. Viola leaped to her feet, and her book clattered to the floor.

"Is it for me?" she cried.

"It is. A messenger brought it." Claire was smiling. "Perhaps it is from Mr. Kirby, Viola. Perhaps he has found you a position."

Viola snatched the letter from her sister's hand. Her name on the outside was written in bold black letters, like the duke's writing as she had seen it at Pinewood.

"I'll read it in my room," she said, and hurried away before anyone could protest.

Her hands were shaking as she sat down heavily on her bed and broke the seal. She and Hannah would be in time to catch the afternoon stage.

She would never see him again.

Two papers fluttered into her lap. She ignored them while her eyes scanned the brief note that had enclosed them.

"With my compliments," it said. "Both papers were filed with a solicitor in York shortly before the late Earl of Bamber's passing. F. Dudley."

It was Ferdinand's handwriting, then.

She picked up the top paper from her lap and unfolded it.

Oh, God! Oh, God, oh, God! Her hand shook so violently that she had to grip the paper with the other hand too. It was the receipt her father had made Daniel Kirby sign, declaring that the late Clarence Wilding's debts had been paid in full and for all time. There were the two signatures as plain as could be. And the signatures of two witnesses too.

She was free. They were all free.

But there was the paper lying folded in her lap. She set aside the one she had just read on the bed beside her and unfolded the second. She stared down at it until her vision blurred and one tear plopped onto a corner of it. She had not doubted him. Not even for a moment. But it was sweet—ah, it was sweet indeed—to hold the documentary evidence in her hands.

Father. Oh, Papa, Papa.

She was weeping openly when her bedroom door opened and her mother first peeped around it and then came hurrying inside.

"Viola?" she said. "Oh, what is it, my dear? Is the letter from the duchess? Has she changed her mind about this afternoon? It really does not matter. Oh, goodness me, what *is* it?"

She had come close to the bed and would have gathered her daughter in her arms, but Viola held out the codicil to her father's will.

"He *did* love me," she wailed. "He *did*."

Her mother read it before folding it and returning it to Viola's lap. "Yes, of course he did," she said softly. "He adored you. Long after our relationship turned sour he came just to see you. I truly believe he loved you more than anyone else in the world. When I married your stepfather, I wanted nothing more to do with him. I was in love and I was very proud. I ignored your needs. He was my lover, but he was your father. There is a world of difference—I know that now. I suppose my anger with you for accepting Pinewood Manor from him arose from my guilt. I am so sorry. Can you ever forgive me? I am glad you were right and he really did leave Pinewood to you. I *am* glad, Viola."

Viola pulled a handkerchief out of the pocket of her dress and held it to her eyes, but for the moment at least she could not seem to stop crying.

"What is *this*?" her mother asked suddenly in a strange voice.

The other paper. Viola slapped a hand onto the bed beside her, but it was too late. The paper was in her mother's hands, and she was reading it with wide, dismayed eyes.

"Bamber paid off Clarence's debts?" she said. "What debts? To Mr. *Kirby*?" She lifted her gaze to Viola's face.

Viola could think of nothing to say.

"Explain this to me." Her mother sat down beside her.

"I did not want to worry you," Viola said. "You were so ill after my stepfather died. And it would not have been fair to Uncle Wesley to have burdened him. I—I tried to pay the bills myself, but there were so many of them. M-my father was kind enough to pay them all off for me."

Leave it at that, Mama.

"*You* were paying Clarence's debts, Viola?" her mother said. "*Gaming* debts? Out of a governess's pay? *And* you were helping to support us?"

"I needed very little for myself," Viola said. *Please leave it at that.*

But her mother had turned noticeably paler. "What *did* you do during those years?" she asked. "You were not a governess, were you? He was not our friend, was he?"

"Mama—" Viola laid a hand on her mother's arm, but her mother shook it off and gazed at her in horror.

"What did you do?" she cried. "Viola, *what did he force you to do?*"

Viola shook her head and bit her upper lip as her mother clapped a shaking hand over her mouth.

"Oh, my child," she said, "what have you done for us? What did you do *for four years?*"

"Uncle would have been ruined," Viola said. "Please try to understand. The children would have ended up in debtors' prison with you. Mama, *please* try to understand. Don't hate me."

"*Hate you?*" Her mother grabbed her, held her tightly, and rocked her. "Viola. My sweet child. What have I done to you?"

Some time passed before Viola drew away and blew her nose firmly. "I think I am glad you know," she said. "It is horrid to have dark secrets from one's own family. But it is all over now, Mama. He has no more power over me—or Claire."

"Claire?" her mother cried.

"He would have used her if I had not come back to London," Viola explained. "But she is safe now, Mama. The receipt has been found. And Pinewood belongs to me. I am going to go back there. After I have settled again, perhaps you and the children will come and live with me. All is well that ends well, you see."

"Where did these papers come from?" her mother asked.

"Lord Ferdinand Dudley sent them," Viola said. "He must have gone looking for them."

"Oh, my love." Her mother touched her arm. "He knows? Yet he still cares for you? Surely you must feel some affection for him."

Viola got to her feet and turned her back on her mother. "You must understand now, Mama," she said, "why such a match is a total impossibility. Besides, he will not renew his addresses. He sent these papers with a messenger." And signed himself F. Dudley.

Her mother sighed. "It is his loss, then," she said. "Did Bam— Did your father know everything, Viola?"

"Yes."

"And so he freed you from your burden and gave you Pinewood so that you could start a new life," her mother said. "He was always a generous man. I cannot deny that. My complaints must have seemed cruel indeed to you. Come to the sitting room and we will have a cup of tea together."

But Viola shook her head. "I have a letter to write, Mama," she said. "And Hannah and I will be leaving for Pinewood this afternoon."

She had to write to the Duke of Tresham first. If the letter arrived in time, she would save him some effort and herself some money. But the letter would assure him that she would keep her part of their bargain regardless.

She was going home.

Daniel Kirby settled himself in the high seat of the curricle that had long been the envy of the male half of the *ton* and smiled genially at the man beside him. "I always did suspect you had an eye for the best, your grace," he said.

"The best in sporting vehicles?" the Duke of Tresham asked.

"That too." Kirby chuckled.

"Ah." His grace flicked the ribbons and his horses stepped smartly out onto the street, leaving Kirby's lodgings behind in a matter of moments. "You were referring to female charms. Yes, I have always had an eye for the very best."

"Which is precisely what you will get with Miss Talbot," the other man said. "She is more alluring than ever after a two-year absence. But perhaps your grace's brother has informed you of that, since he must have met her at Pinewood."

"Indeed," the duke said.

"She will be ready to start entertaining within the week," Kirby said. He clung to the rail beside him as the curricle turned into Hyde Park. "Of course, you must know that she is expensive, but one must always be prepared to pay for the best."

"I have always said so," his grace agreed.

Kirby chuckled. "And there will be an extra charge to her first client," he said. "It will be worth it, your grace. You will acquire considerable prestige in the eyes of your acquaintances as the first to bed the delectable Lilian Talbot in two years."

"One always likes to bolster one's prestige in a worthy cause," Tresham said. "Miss Talbot is, ah, eager to return to work?"

"Work!" Kirby laughed heartily. "She calls it pleasure, your grace. She would start tonight if I would let her. But I wanted to give her to someone . . . ah, shall we say, *special,* the first time?"

"I do like to consider myself special," the duke said. "Dear me, whatever is going on up ahead of us, I wonder?"

Up ahead of them, on the grass to one side of the path along which they drove, there was a considerable gathering of people. It was strange, really, as all were on foot and this particular part of the park, shaded by trees and hidden from much of the rest of it, was not one of the most frequented. As they drove closer it became clear that all the people were men. One of them, a little apart from the others and lounging at his ease against a tree trunk, his arms crossed over his chest, was in a shocking state of semi-undress. He wore a white shirt with tight leather riding breeches and boots, but if he had worn a waistcoat and coat and hat into the park, there certainly was no sign of them now.

"A fight?" Kirby suggested, his voice brightening with interest.

"If so, there seems to be only one participant," Tresham said. "And dear me, it appears to be my brother." He slowed the pace of his horses until they came to a halt altogether beside the relaxed figure of Lord Ferdinand Dudley.

"Ah," he said with a grin, "just the man I want to see."

"Me?" Kirby asked, pointing to his own chest when it became obvious that Lord Ferdinand's gaze was not directed at his brother. He eyed the gathered throng, all of whom had fallen silent. "You wished to see me, my lord?"

"You *are* Lilian Talbot's manager, are you not?" Ferdinand asked him.

Daniel Kirby smiled jovially, if a little self-consciously. "If *that* is what you wish to see me about," he said, "you are going to have to stand in line behind his grace, your brother, my lord."

"Let me understand you," Ferdinand said. "You manage Lilian Talbot, whose real name is Viola Thornhill."

"I like to grant her some privacy, my lord, by keeping mum about that second name," Kirby said.

"Natural daughter of the late Earl of Bamber," Ferdinand added.

There was a murmuring from the spectators, to whom that detail appeared to come as news. For the first time, Kirby looked uneasy.

"Bamber." Ferdinand had raised his voice. "Is this true? Lilian

Talbot is really Miss Viola Thornhill, your father's natural daughter?"

"He acknowledged her as such," the Earl of Bamber agreed from close by.

"I did not—" Kirby began.

"Miss Thornhill lived quietly and respectably with her mother and half-brother and -sisters at her uncle's inn until you bought up the debts of Clarence Wilding, her late stepfather?" Ferdinand asked.

"I don't know what this is about," Kirby said, "but—"

He was about to clamber down from his seat, but the duke set four gloved fingertips lightly on his arm, and he changed his mind.

"You offered her the chance of saving her family from debtors' prison?" Ferdinand asked.

"Here, here," Kirby said indignantly, "I had to recover that money somehow. It was a large sum."

"And so you created Lilian Talbot," Ferdinand said, "and put her to work and took her earnings. For *four years*. They must have been astronomical debts."

"They *were*," the other man said indignantly. "And I did not take more than a small fraction of her earnings. She lived in the lap of luxury. And she enjoyed what she did. There are men here who can vouch for the fact."

"Shame!" several of the gentlemen present murmured. But Ferdinand held up a staying hand.

"Miss Thornhill must have been disappointed, then," he said, "when Bamber, her father, discovered the truth, paid off all the debts, received a written receipt to that effect from you, Kirby, and gave her Pinewood Manor in Somersetshire, where she could live out her life in a manner suited to her birth."

"There was no such receipt," Kirby said. "And if she says so—"

But Ferdinand had held up his hand again.

"It would be wise not to perjure yourself," he said. "The paper has been found. Both Bamber and I have seen it—and Tresham too. But when I won Pinewood from Bamber, you assumed that the late earl had played her false, did you not, and that the receipt had been discarded or lost. A foolish assumption. Bamber has discovered that his father did indeed change his will. Miss Thornhill is mistress of Pinewood."

There was a smattering of applause from behind him.

"You discovered more debts when you believed her to be destitute," Ferdinand said. "You have been attempting to force her return to prostitution, Kirby."

The murmur behind him was louder and uglier now.

"I have not—"

"Tresham?" Ferdinand asked coolly.

"I was to have her within the week," the duke said. "At something over and above her usual high fee, since apparently it would add to my prestige and make me appear, ah, *special* to be her first client after two years."

Ferdinand's jaw tightened.

"I was about to decline when I spotted this interesting gathering," Tresham continued. "The duchess, it is to be understood, would carve out my liver without bothering to kill me first."

There was a burst of laughter from the spectators. But Ferdinand did not join in. He was gazing at a clearly nervous Daniel Kirby, his eyes very black, his jaw hard, his mouth a thin line.

"You have terrorized and ruined a gently born lady, Kirby," he said, "whose only fault has been love of her family and a willingness to sacrifice her honor and her very self for their freedom and happiness. You are looking at her champion, sir."

"Look," Daniel Kirby said, his eyes darting about as if to search out a friendly face or an escape route, "I don't want any trouble."

"Quite frankly," Ferdinand said, "I do not care what you want, Kirby. It is trouble you have found this morning—six years too late for Miss Thornhill. Get down from there. You are going to be punished."

"Your grace." Kirby turned frightened eyes on Tresham. "I must call upon you to protect me. I came with you in good faith to arrange an assignation."

"And an assignation has been arranged," the duke said, vaulting down from his seat and tossing the ribbons to his groom, who had been up behind the curricle. "This is it. Get down from there or I will come around and help you down. You will be given five minutes to strip to the waist and prepare to defend yourself. No, don't look so alarmed. We are not all about to pounce upon you like a pack of wolves. The idea has considerable appeal, it is true, but most of us *gentlemen* are constrained by a damnable sense of honor, you see. All the pleasure of the encounter falls to Lord Ferdinand Dudley, who has appointed himself Miss Thornhill's champion."

There was loud jeering from the spectators while Daniel Kirby sat where he was. There was laughter and then cheers as the Duke of Tresham stalked around his curricle and Kirby scrambled hastily down. Ferdinand pulled his shirt off over his head and tossed it to the grass. Kirby cast one horrified glance at his hard torso and rippling muscles and looked away again. Even though no one touched him, he was being herded onto the grass by the sheer menace of a few dozen gentlemen moving purposefully to form a ring about an ominously empty area of lawn.

"Strip down," Ferdinand said tersely, "or I'll do it for you, Kirby, and I'll not stop at your waist. It will be a fair fight. If you can fell me, you are free to go. No one here will stop you. I am not going to kill you, but I *am* going to thrash you within an inch of your life—with my bare hands. If you imagine that going down will save you, you are mistaken. It will not. You will be unconscious by the time I have finished with you. So I will say the rest of what I have to say now. After you have recovered from your beating well enough to travel—it may take a week or two—you are to travel until there is

an ocean between you and me. That ocean will remain between us
for the rest of your life. If I ever hear of your returning, I will hunt
you down and punish you all over again—to within *half* an inch
of your life. I will not ask if you understand me. You are a weasel,
but you are obviously intelligent too—intelligent enough to choose
a young, vulnerable, loving girl as your victim. This is going to be
for her—to restore her honor in the sight of these witnesses. *Get*
that shirt off."

A moment later, Daniel Kirby, small, pudgy, and pasty-skinned,
stood shivering within the hostile, jeering ring of spectators. He
was visibly shaking as Ferdinand strode toward him. He fell to his
knees and clasped his hands together.

"I am not a fighter. I am a peaceable man," he said. "Just let me
go. I'll be gone from London before the day is out. You'll never see
me again. I'll never trouble you again. Just don't hit me. Arrgghh!"

Ferdinand had reached out and grasped Kirby's nose between the
middle and forefinger of one hand. He twisted and raised his arm
until Kirby was standing on his toes before him, his hands flailing
helplessly, his mouth wide open to gasp in air. There was a roar of
mirth from the spectators.

"For God's sake, man," Ferdinand said in the utmost disgust,
"stay on your feet and throw at least one punch. Show some self-
respect."

He released his hold and for a moment stood before the other
man, within arm's length, his own arms at his side, unprotected. But
Kirby merely covered his injured nose with both hands.

"I am a peaceable man," he wailed.

And so it was punishment pure and simple. And coldly and sci-
entifically meted out. It would have been easy to render him unconscious with a few powerful blows. And it would have been easy to
pity a man whose physical stature and condition gave him no chance
whatsoever of winning the fight. But Ferdinand did not allow himself either the luxury of fury or the weakness of pity.

This was not for himself or for the spectators. This was not sport.

This was for Viola.

He had said he was her champion. He would avenge her, then, in the only way he could, inadequate as it was—with his physical strength.

She was his lady, and this was for her.

The spectators had grown strangely quiet and Ferdinand's knuckles on both hands were red and raw by the time he judged Daniel Kirby to be within the proverbial inch of his life. Only then did he draw back his right fist and drive it up beneath the man's chin with enough force to send him into oblivion.

He stood looking down at the plump, unconscious body, his hands still balled into fists at his sides, his mind bleak with sorrow and near-despair as the men around him, his friends and acquaintances, his peers, clapped slowly.

"If anyone," he said without looking up—there was instant silence so that everyone could hear what he had to say—"has any doubt in his mind that Miss Viola Thornhill is a lady deserving of the deepest honor and respect and admiration, let him speak now."

No one spoke until Tresham broke the silence.

"My duchess will be sending out invitations within a day or two to a reception at Dudley House," he said. "It is our hope that the guest of honor will be Miss Thornhill of Pinewood Manor in Somersetshire, natural daughter of the late Earl of Bamber. She is a lady we wish to have the pleasure of presenting to society."

"And it is my hope," the Earl of Bamber said unexpectedly, "that she will arrive at Dudley House under my escort, Tresham. M'half-sister, you know."

Ferdinand turned and walked away to where he had left his clothes in the keeping of his friend John Leavering. He dressed in silence. Although there was now an excited buzz from those who had watched the punishment, no one approached him. His black mood, so uncharacteristic of him, was too obvious to them all. But his brother clasped his shoulder as he pulled on his waistcoat.

"I am prouder of you today than I have ever been before, Ferdinand," he said softly. "And I have always been proud of you."

"I wish I could have killed the bastard," Ferdinand said, pushing his arms into the sleeves of his coat. "Perhaps I would feel better if I had killed him."

"You have done much better than that," his brother told him. "You have restored life to someone deserving of it, Ferdinand. There is not a man here who would not gladly kneel to kiss the hem of Viola Thornhill's garments. You have shown her as a lady who sacrificed all for love."

"I have done damn all," Ferdinand said, gazing at his raw knuckles. "She suffered for four years, Tresham. And again in the last few weeks."

"You will have to spend a lifetime soothing the pain of those four years, then," Tresham said. "Shall I come with you to the White Horse?"

Ferdinand shook his head.

His brother squeezed his shoulder hard and comfortingly once more before turning away.

24

❧

T he guard had already blown one long blast on his horn—the final warning for any laggards among the passengers to scramble on board the stagecoach before it pulled out of the inn yard and began its journey west. But only one outside passenger had yet to board. The guard slammed the door on the inside passengers and moved to take his place at the rear of the coach.

Mrs. Wilding stepped back, a handkerchief pressed to her lips. Maria clung to her free arm. Claire, smiling bravely, raised one hand in farewell. Viola, seated beside the window, smiled back. Farewells were so hard. She had tried to persuade them not to come with her and Hannah from the White Horse Inn, but they had insisted.

She would see them all again, of course, perhaps soon. Her mother had declared adamantly that her home was with her brother, that it was with him she would stay. But she had agreed to come to Pinewood for a visit later in the year. Maria and Claire could stay longer if they wished, she had said. Maybe Ben would wish to spend a part of his summer holiday there.

But the moment of parting was still hard.

She was leaving London behind forever. She would never see him again. He had sent her those precious papers this morning, but he had not seen fit to bring them in person. And in the accompanying note he had signed himself merely F. Dudley.

She had heard nothing from the Duke of Tresham. It did not matter. If he had already paid Daniel Kirby, then she would repay the loan.

She was going *home*, she reminded herself as the guard blew another deafening blast on his yard of tin as a warning to anyone on the street outside to make way. She had been happy there and would be happy again. Soon the memories would begin to recede, and she would start to heal once more. All she needed was time and patience.

Ah, but the memories were fresh and raw now.

Why had he not come? She had not wanted him to, but why had he not? Why had he sent the papers with a servant?

Ferdinand.

The coach lurched into motion and the *clop-clop* of the horses' hooves drowned out all other sounds. Mama was crying. So was Maria. But they were all smiling too and waving. Viola smiled determinedly and raised her hand. Once the coach had turned onto the street and she could not see them anymore, she would feel better.

But just when she expected it to begin its turn, it jerked to a sudden halt and there was a great deal of shouting and general commotion from the direction of the street.

"Lord love us," Hannah said from beside Viola, "what now?"

The man opposite them, who was facing the horses, pressed the side of his head against the glass and peered forward.

"There be horses and a carriage of some sort drawn across the entrance," he announced to his fellow passengers. "He'll be in trouble, that driver will. Be he deaf?"

It might be to his benefit if he was, Viola thought, noting that her family were no longer looking at her but at the cause of the delay. Even the walls and windows of the coach could not keep out the blistering profanities with which the coachman, the guard, and several of the outside passengers were berating the hapless man who had driven his carriage across the entryway of the inn yard despite the horn's warning and had apparently stopped there, blocking the stagecoach's path.

And then the sounds of merry laughter and another voice dominated all others.

"Come, now," the voice called gaily, "you can do better than that, my fine fellow. You have not yet turned the air blue. I have business with one of your passengers."

Viola scarcely had time to feel shock before the carriage door was wrenched open.

"In the nick of time," Lord Ferdinand Dudley said, peering inside and then reaching up a gloved hand to her. "Come, Viola."

A moment ago her heart had felt as if it were breaking in two because she would never see him again. Now she was furiously angry. How dare he!

"What are you doing here?" she asked. "How did you know—"

"I went to the White Horse Inn first." He grinned. "I have just put terror into half of London by springing my horses through its streets. Come down."

She clasped her hands firmly in her lap and glared at him. "I am going home," she said. "You are holding up the coach and making a spectacle of us both. Please shut the door, my lord."

If the coachman had not turned the air blue before, he must surely be doing it now. Other men were shouting indignantly too. Only the inside passengers remained quiet, their attention focused on the interesting scene before them.

"Don't go," he said. "Not yet. We need to talk."

Viola shook her head while one of the female passengers informed the others in an awed whisper that the gentleman was a *lord*.

"There is nothing more to say," Viola said. "*Please* go away. Everyone is terribly angry."

"Let them be," he said. "Come down and talk to me."

"You go with him, love," the same passenger advised aloud. "He's a right handsome gent, he is. I'd go with him myself if he would take me instead."

There was a burst of appreciative laughter from those within hearing distance.

"Go away!" Viola said, angry and embarrassed.

"Please, Viola." He was no longer smiling. He was compelling her shamelessly with his dark eyes, which gazed very deeply into her own. "Please, my love. Don't go."

The other passengers awaited her reply with bated breath.

Hannah touched her arm. "We had better get out, Miss Vi," she said, "before we are thrown out."

The coachman and a few other men were still swearing ferociously. The guard had jumped down from his place and was advancing menacingly on Lord Ferdinand.

"If you insist upon staying where you are," Ferdinand said, grinning suddenly again, "I'll follow the coach, Viola, and accost you at every tollgate and every stop between here and Somersetshire. I can make a very public nuisance of myself when I choose. Take my hand now, and get down."

He had made it impossible for her to remain in the coach. How would she look her fellow passengers in the eye during the long hours ahead? How would she be able to face the coachman and guard at the various stops along the way? She stretched out her hand slowly until it was resting in Ferdinand's. He grasped it tightly, and the next moment she was descending to the inn yard while all the inside passengers, a few of the outside ones, and a sizable ring of spectators cheered and applauded.

"Toss down the lady's bags and her maid's, if you will, my man," Ferdinand said, grinning at the guard and pressing a gold coin into his hand. With one glance at it, the guard forgot his wrath and did as he had been bidden. Ferdinand, meanwhile, was assisting Hannah to alight and then stretching up an arm to appease the coachman with another coin. His curricle and horses, Viola noticed, were still blocking the gateway, his groom holding the horses' heads.

She stood mutely watching while the curricle was pulled ahead and the stagecoach finally rumbled out of the yard—without her— and turned onto the street. The grooms and other spectators were dispersing.

"Ma'am." Lord Ferdinand was addressing her mother. "May I have your leave to take Miss Thornhill for a drive?"

She did not *want* to drive with him. At this particular moment she hated him. The worst should be over now. She should be on her way home.

"Of course, my lord," her mother said warmly. "Hannah will return to the White Horse with us."

They were all smiling, Viola saw when she looked from one to the other of them—just as if they were witnessing the beginning of a happily-ever-after. Even Hannah was beaming. Did they not *understand*?

He was offering her his arm. She took it without a word and went with him out to the street, where he handed her up to the high seat of his curricle before striding around to the other side and climbing up beside her. He took the ribbons from his groom's hand.

"I am very vexed with you," she said curtly when the curricle was in motion.

"Are you?" He turned his head to look briefly at her. "Why?"

"You had no business stopping me from doing what I had decided to do," she said, "and what I *wanted* to do. This morning, when there were important papers to deliver to me, you sent them with a servant and a note signed *F. Dudley.* Now suddenly this afternoon you need to speak with me urgently enough to drag me from a stagecoach."

"Ah, this morning," he said. "I had a very important commitment this morning that made it impossible to call on you in person. But it struck me that you had a right to see those papers at the earliest possible moment. I had time only to dash off a quick note. Did I really sign myself that way? Were you offended?"

"Not at all," she said. "Why should I be?"

He merely flashed her a grin.

"There is nothing more to be said," she told him. "I have already sent a letter thanking you for the papers. Where did they come from, by the way?"

"Bamber," he said. "He went to Yorkshire to call upon the countess's solicitor. It seems that his father used his services occasionally. He did so just before his death because Westinghouse was away from London when you left for Pinewood. The York solicitor neglected to bring the papers to light afterward, though, probably at the countess's urging. Bamber did not know where to find you with them, and so he came to me."

"I would have expected him to keep his mouth shut too," she said tartly. "He cannot feel kindly toward me, after all."

"He is a ramshackle fellow," Ferdinand said, "but not dishonest."

"Everything has been said, then." She turned her head away from him. "It could have been explained just as well in a letter. You did not need to see me again. I wanted to be on that stagecoach. I wanted to go home. I did not want to see you again."

"We have to talk," he said—and then was silent.

"Where are we going?" she asked after a few minutes.

"Somewhere where we can talk," he said.

Her question had been rhetorical. It was clear that they were headed in the direction of the Duke of Tresham's house—the one where his grace housed his mistresses. The curricle drew to a stop there a couple of minutes later and Ferdinand jumped down before coming around to her side.

"I won't," she said firmly as her feet touched the pavement.

"Sleep with me?" he said, grinning down at her. "No, you dashed well won't, Viola. Not today anyway. We need to talk."

Alone together. Here, of all places, where they had spent one night of delirious happiness.

She hated him with an intense anger.

He took her to the room he liked best—the back room with the pianoforte and books, where Jane and Tresham must have spent a great deal of time. She took off her outdoor garments and went to sit primly in the armchair beside the hearth. Her face was pale and expressionless. She had not once looked at him since they entered the house.

"Why didn't you trust me?" he asked her. He stood some distance from her, his hands clasped at his back. She had lost weight and bloom since that day of the village fête. But somehow she looked as beautiful as ever. Or perhaps it seemed so because he was no longer able to see her objectively. "Why did you go to Tresham instead?"

She looked up at him sharply then. "How do you know that?"

"He told me so," he said. "Did you think he would not, Viola?"

She stared at him. "Now that I think of it," she said, "I can see that it is something he *would* do. He would want to tell you how I was willing to bargain with him and take money from him in exchange for refusing to marry you. Yes, I can see that he would get satisfaction from telling you how calculating and mercenary I am. Does he know about the receipt the Earl of Bamber brought you? How disappointed he must have been—and how terrified that after all I might accept a marriage offer from you."

She was still angry, he could see. He had learned early that Viola Thornhill was not easily dominated. She would not readily forgive him for forcing her to get down from that stagecoach.

"Why did you not trust me?" he asked her again. "Why did you not ask me for the money, Viola? You must know that I would have helped you."

"I did not want you to," she said. "I did not want you to know why I worked for Daniel Kirby. I wanted you to believe that I was Lilian Talbot because I liked being her and doing what she did. I wanted you to abandon the foolish notion that we could marry. I still wish it. I *was* Lilian Talbot, even though I hated every moment of her life. And I remain what she was. I wish the Duke of Tresham had not told you. Better yet, I wish I had not gone to him or had waited another day. That receipt has set me free, you see. But not free to live here or to associate with people like you."

"I can never ever be worthy of you, you know," he said. She looked at him in astonishment, but he continued. "When I learned as a boy of the life my mother and father lived, as well as most of their friends, I was so disillusioned with love that I shrank from it forever after and withdrew into cynicism. Apart from my studies I have done nothing worthwhile in all the years since. Certainly I have not given love. You, on the other hand, have stuck steadfastly by love even though it has hurt you immeasurably. And you keep on sticking by it. You are intent upon not hurting me, are you not?"

She turned her head away. "Don't make a saint of me," she said. "I did what I had to do. But I am a whore nonetheless."

"I think," he said, "that I have done *one* worthwhile thing in my adult life."

"Yes. You gave Pinewood back to me before you knew it was mine anyway," she said. "I will always remember you kindly for that."

"Kirby won't be troubling you again," he said.

"No." He saw her shudder.

"I would have killed him for you, Viola," he said quietly. "I would *like* to have killed him."

"Oh, no." She was on her feet then and closing the distance between them. She set one hand on his sleeve and looked earnestly into his face. "Don't get into any trouble on my behalf, Ferdinand. He has no more power over me."

He covered her hand on his arm with his own. "Oh, I did not say that he has gone unpunished," he said.

She looked at his hand as he spoke, and then she looked down at the other, her eyes widening. "Oh, Ferdinand, what have you done?"

"I have punished him," he said. "No punishment could be adequate for what he has done to you, not even death. But I believe it will be several days before he can get up off his bed. Once he *is* up, he will be taking himself beyond these shores for the rest of his life."

She raised his hand and set her cheek gently against his raw knuckles. "How dreadful of me to feel glad," she said. "But I do. Thank you. But I hope no one else hears of this, especially the Duke of Tresham. You should not be seen to have any involvement with me. But no matter. I will leave for home tomorrow, and no one will ever hear from me again. I did not want to see you today, Ferdinand, but I am glad after all that you caught up to me in time. I will have this as a last memory of you."

"Actually, Tresham does know," he said. "He is the one who brought Kirby to me in the park."

She looked at him in horror. "He *knows*? In the *park*?"

"With fifty or so other chosen witnesses," he told her. "By now there is probably no one in the *ton* who does not know."

She stepped back from him, her face suddenly pale. Then she tried to rush past him to the door, but he caught her arm and held her.

"By now," he said, "everyone knows of your courage and selfless devotion to your family when you were little more than a girl. Everyone knows that the villain who preyed upon you has been publicly humiliated and punished. Everyone knows that the powerful and influential Dudleys, led by the Duke of Tresham himself, have taken your part and devoted themselves to restoring your good

name and celebrating your heroism. And everyone knows that Lord
Ferdinand Dudley has appointed himself your champion."

"How could you?" she cried. "How *could* you? To have exposed
me to such public..." She could not seem to think of the right
word. Her eyes flashed at him.

"Do you not see that it is the only way?" he asked her gently.
"Tresham is going to invite the *ton* to a reception at Dudley House.
He wants you to be the guest of honor. Everyone will come, Viola.
They will all be agog to catch a glimpse of you. But it is our version
of you they will come to see. It is the real Viola Thornhill they will
meet. You will become all the rage."

"I don't want to be all the rage," she snapped at him. "Ferdinand,
I was a courtesan for four years. I am illegitimate. I—"

"Bamber hopes to escort you to the reception and present you to
the *ton* as his half-sister," he said.

"What?" She stared at him. *"What?"*

"He was in the park too," he told her.

"So were a dozen or more of my former clients, I daresay." She
glared indignantly at him.

"Yes." He drew a slow breath and tested the idea in his mind. It
really did not matter to him. "But not one of them will reveal the
fact by so much as a flicker of an eyelash, Viola. You will be the acknowledged half-sister of the Earl of Bamber. You will be the pro-
tégée of the Duke and Duchess of Tresham. You will be my
lady—or so I hope."

He could see the moment at which anger drained out of her and
a certain wistfulness took its place, parting her lips and making her
eyes more luminous.

"Ferdinand," she said softly, "it cannot be, my dear. You must
not do this." Tears welled into her eyes.

He possessed himself of both her hands. What he was about to
do might look ridiculous, but he felt an overwhelming need to pay

homage to her courage and loyalty and unfailing love—to her superiority over him. He went down on one knee and set his forehead against the backs of her hands.

"My love," he said. "Do me the honor of marrying me. If you truly do not love me, I will understand. I will send you home to Pinewood in my own carriage the day after the reception. But I love you. I'll always love you. It is my dream that you will marry me and that we will go home to Pinewood together and raise a family there."

She drew her hands free of his, and he waited for rejection. But then he felt them come to rest lightly on his head, like a benediction.

"Ferdinand," she said. "Oh, my dear love."

He was on his feet then and scooping her up into his arms with a whoop that had her laughing. He twirled her about and carried her to the chair by the fireplace, where he sat with her cradled in his arms, her head nestled in the warm hollow between his neck and shoulder.

"Of course," he said, "everyone will be expecting our betrothal announcement at Tresham's reception. Angie will want to insist upon a grand wedding in St. George's and a lavish breakfast for five hundred or so afterward. All of it preceded the night before by a great ball."

"Oh, no," she said, real horror in her voice.

"Ghastly thought, is it not?" he agreed. "She will be even more eager this time because Tresham foiled all her grandiose plans by marrying Jane quietly by special license."

"Can *we* marry quietly?" she begged him. "At Trellick, perhaps?"

He chuckled. "You don't know my sister," he said, "though I daresay you soon will."

"Ferdinand." She tipped back her head and gazed up at him. "Are you sure? Are you quite, quite—"

There was only one way to deal with such foolishness. He covered her mouth with his own and silenced her. After a few moments her arm crept up about his neck and she sighed her surrender.

Ferdinand found himself thinking all sorts of mindless drivel—about being surely the happiest man in the world, for example.

25

iola was seated in the Earl of Bamber's opulent town carriage, her mother beside her, the earl opposite. They were on their way to Dudley House.

It had been a turbulent week. The Duchess of Tresham had called at the White Horse Inn the day after Ferdinand stopped Viola from leaving on the stagecoach. She had issued a formal invitation to Viola and her mother to attend the reception she and her husband were giving. She had stayed for twenty minutes and had shown an interest in Claire, who was not working downstairs at the time. Her grace had mentioned that her godmother, Lady Webb, was considering employing a companion to live with her—she spent half the year in London and the other half in Bath. The duchess had wondered if Claire would be interested in the position.

The day after, Claire had gone with their mother, by invitation, to call upon Lady Webb, and the two had appeared delighted with each other. Claire was to begin her new position in two weeks' time and had looked during the past few days as if she were walking on air.

"This is very kind of you, my lord," Viola's mother said to the earl.

He was looking stout and florid and very fine indeed in his evening clothes. He must be eight or nine years her senior, Viola guessed. She had not asked her mother how it had come about that she had progressed from being the boy's governess to becoming his father's mistress. That was her mother's private, secret life.

"Not at all, ma'am," he said, stiffly inclining his head.

He too had called on them during the week. His manner to his former governess had been distant, but not discourteous. With Viola herself he had been scrupulously polite. He had requested the honor of escorting both ladies to the Duke of Tresham's reception. Viola wondered now why he was doing it. Her mother had been his father's mistress, and she was the offspring of that illicit union. But he answered her question even as she thought it.

"M'father wanted Miss Thornhill to be recognized as a lady," he said. "I will have no part in thwarting his wishes."

"She *is* a lady," Viola's mother said. "My father . . ."

But Viola was not listening. She was nervous. Yes, of course she was. It would be pointless to deny it. Even without her scarlet past—and even if she had been Clarence Wilding's legitimate daughter—she could never have hoped to be on her way to a *ton* party. Although both he and her mother were of the gentry class, they were not high enough on the social scale to mingle with the *beau monde*.

But she refused to give in to her nerves. She had decided to trust Ferdinand and his family to know what they were doing. In a sense, it was a relief to have everything out in the open. To have no more secrets. No more hidden fears. And no more doubts.

She was wearing a white satin gown with a delicately scalloped hem and short train but with no other adornment. She had been to several tedious fittings during the week with one of Bond Street's most prestigious dressmakers. The gown, as well as the silver slippers and gloves and fan she had chosen to wear with it, had been exorbitantly costly, but the loan she had asked of Uncle Wesley until she could send the money from Pinewood had turned into a gift. Her mother had told him everything and he had been angry with Viola—but in a tearful, hugging sort of way. It had hurt him that she had borne the burden of her stepfather's debts instead of going to him.

She had scarcely seen Ferdinand all week. He had called once formally to ask her mother's and her uncle's permission to marry her, even though she was twenty-five years old and he need not have asked at all. She had seen him only once—briefly—since then. Her hands closed firmly about her fan, and she smiled.

Tomorrow she was going home.

The carriage turned into Grosvenor Square and rolled to a halt before the doors of Dudley House.

She looked like Miss Thornhill of Pinewood Manor. That was Ferdinand's thought as he watched her through much of the evening. She was the picture of understated elegance in her deceptively simple white gown. She wore her hair in the familiar braids, but they were looped and coiled in an intricate design. She bore herself with regal grace. If she was nervous—and she undoubtedly was—she did not show it.

He kept his distance. Everyone at Dudley House—and the drawing room and the adjoining salons beyond it were thronged with the crème de la crème of society—would know what he had done on her behalf in Hyde Park the week before. He would not have it said, then, that she had to cling to him tonight, that without him she could not have done what she clearly was doing quite magnificently.

She was mingling with the *ton*. She was conversing with ladies whom one might expect under other circumstances to avert their faces from her and gather their skirts about them lest they rub against her. She was talking and laughing with gentlemen who had known her in her other, now-dead persona.

And she was doing it alone.

It was true that Bamber, distinguishing himself by his good manners as he had perhaps never done before, hovered at her elbow for the first hour until he had personally introduced her to every guest as his half-sister. And Jane, Angie, Tresham, and even Heyward made sure that one of them was always in any group that gathered about her.

But she behaved like Miss Thornhill of Pinewood. However she was feeling inside, she appeared to be perfectly at her ease.

Ferdinand watched her, at first with some anxiety, then with pride.

He had not been at all sure that day he had stopped her from leaving London that she would agree to the daring scheme he and Tresham had conceived. Perhaps in her own way, he thought, Viola was as drawn to a difficult challenge as irresistibly as he ever was. Nothing had been more chancy than her appearance here tonight.

But she had done it, and it had worked. Oh, he knew she had no wish to mingle with the *ton* after tonight. He knew she longed to go home to Pinewood and to resume her life there. But she had done this first, and now it would be known that society had accepted her and she could return anytime she wished.

"Well, Ferdie." His sister had come up beside him without his noticing. "I can see now why she was always so celebrated for her beauty. If I were a few years younger and still on the marriage mart, I would doubtless hate her." She laughed merrily. "Heyward said you were mad, you and Tresh, and that you could never pull this off. But you have, as I told him you would—and of course Heyward is pleased about it. He says he always knew that when you finally did fall in love, it would be with someone wildly ineligible, but that he was going to have to throw his support behind you because you are my brother."

"That is magnanimous of him." He grinned.

"Well, it *is*," she agreed. "There is no higher stickler than Heyward, you know. I believe it is why I decided the first time I set eyes on him that I would marry him. He was so *different* from us."

It had always been a source of amusement to Ferdinand and his brother that their shatterbrained, chatterbox Angie and a dry old stick like Heyward were locked up tight in a love match.

"Ferdie." She set one gloved hand on his arm. "I simply *must* tell you, even though Heyward said I must not because it would be vulgar to talk about such a thing at a public event. Just you, though. I have already whispered it to Jane and Tresh. Ferdie, I am in an *interesting condition*. I saw a physician today and it is quite, quite certain. After *six years*."

Her eyes were swimming with tears, he saw when he looked down at her and set his hand warmly over hers.

"Angie," he said.

"I hope," she said. "Oh, I *do* hope I can present Heyward with an heir, though he says that he does not mind if it is a girl as long as both she and I come safely through the ordeal."

"Of course he will not mind," Ferdinand said, raising her hand to his lips. "He loves you, after all."

"Yes." She searched out her husband with her eyes and beamed at him while he looked back with an expression of pained resignation—he knew very well, of course, that she was spreading the embarrassing news of his impending fatherhood. "Yes, he does."

She chattered on.

There was a formal supper later in the evening, during which Ferdinand sat with Mrs. Wilding and Lady Webb, who had taken Viola's mother under her wing during most of the evening. Viola was at the opposite side of the room with Bamber and Angie and

Heyward. But they were very aware of each other. Their eyes met halfway through the meal, and they smiled at each other—though it was more a smile of the eyes than of the face.

I am so proud of you, his look said.

I am so happy, hers replied.

I love you.

I love you.

And then Tresham was touching his shoulder and bending his head to speak quietly.

"You want the announcement made, then?" he asked. "And you still want me to make it?"

"It is your house and reception," Ferdinand said. "And you are the head of the family."

His brother squeezed his shoulder, straightened up, and cleared his throat. The Duke of Tresham never needed to do more than that to command the attention of a large number of people. The room was silent within moments.

"I have an announcement to make," his grace said. "I daresay most, if not all of you, have half guessed it."

There was a murmuring as all eyes moved between Ferdinand and Viola. His own were on her. She was flushed, her gaze lowered.

"But only half," Tresham continued. "Lord Ferdinand Dudley asked me several days ago if I would announce his betrothal to Miss Viola Thornhill this evening."

There was a swell of sound and a smattering of applause. Viola was biting her lower lip. Tresham held up one hand for quiet.

"I prepared a suitable speech," he said, "of congratulation to my brother, of sincere welcome to our family of my future sister-in-law. But we Dudleys can never behave ourselves as we ought, you know."

There was laughter.

"My sister and my duchess were already planning a grand wedding at St. George's and a breakfast and ball," Tresham continued. "It was to be the event of the Season."

"What do you mean by *were* and *was*, Tresh?" Angeline cried, her voice filled with sudden suspicion. "Ferdie has not—"

"Yes, I am afraid he has," Tresham said. "This morning I was informed an hour after the event that Ferdinand and Miss Thornhill were married by special license, his valet and her maid the only witnesses. Ladies and gentlemen, I proudly present to you my brother and sister-in-law, Lord and Lady Ferdinand Dudley."

Viola had found the courage to look up while the duke spoke. She gazed across the room at Ferdinand, handsome and elegant in his crisp black and white evening clothes, and so very, very dear.

Her husband.

How she had longed for him all day. But she had had the reception to prepare for, and he had had business to attend to so that he could be ready to leave with her for Pinewood tomorrow morning. And they had wanted no one to know except her mother and the duke, whom they had told after their brief, achingly beautiful wedding early in the morning.

How she had longed all evening to go to him, to have him come to her. But she had insisted, and he had agreed, that this evening was something she must do for herself, in her own person. She would not hide behind anyone's coattails. The evening had been incredibly hard, but she had felt his powerful, comforting presence at every moment of it, and she had done it—for herself and for him. He had taken a great gamble, marrying her this morning before he knew for sure that the *ton* would not spurn her and turn its back on him.

She gazed at him now across the room and rose to her feet as he came striding toward her, his dark eyes alight, one arm lifting as he drew close. She set her hand in his, and he raised it to his lips.

It was only then that she became fully aware of the noise about them—voices and applause and laughter. But then the noise died away again. The Duke of Tresham—her *brother-in-law*—had not finished speaking.

"There has not been a great deal of time," he said, "but my duchess is a resourceful lady—I did share the secret with her, of course. And we have able servants. We ask you all to join us in the ballroom after supper. But before we adjourn . . ." He lifted his eyebrows in the direction of his butler, who was standing in the doorway, and the man stood aside for two footmen, who were carrying between them a white and silver three-tiered wedding cake.

"The devil!" Ferdinand murmured, gripping Viola's hand and drawing it through his arm. "I might have known it would be fatal to say anything before tonight." His eyes were dancing with merriment when he looked down at her. "I hope you won't mind too much, my love."

For the next half hour she felt too overwhelmed to know if she minded or not. Her mother came to hug them both, as did Jane and Angeline—who each insisted that she must now call them by their first names—and even the duke. Lord Heyward and the Earl of Bamber hugged her and shook hands with Ferdinand. But then Jane insisted it was time to cut the cake and carry it around on a silver platter so that all the guests could have a chance to congratulate them and wish them well.

It was the very fuss they had hoped to avoid by marrying quietly.

It was wonderful.

Gradually the guests drifted away from the dining room until only Jane and Angeline and Viola's mother were left apart from the newlyweds. Angeline was complaining bitterly about two brothers who had foiled her dearest wish to organize a grand wedding. But interspersed with the complaints were tears and hugs and an assurance that she had never been happier in her life.

"Besides," she added, "if I have a daughter I will be able to give her the grandest wedding anyone has ever seen. Then you will know what you and Tresh missed, Ferdie."

"We should go and join everyone else," he suggested, smiling so warmly into Viola's eyes that her heart turned over.

"Why the ballroom?" she asked.

"A question I have been trying not to ask myself," he said with a grimace. "First, though, a matter of importance that I should have seen to as soon as Tresham made his announcement, love." He drew her wedding ring out of a pocket of his evening coat and slid it onto her finger—where it had lain for such a brief spell during the morning. He kissed it. "For all time, Viola."

The ballroom was large, imposing, and quite breathtaking, Viola saw. The guests stood about the edges of the dance floor. An orchestra occupied a dais at the other end of the room. Three large chandeliers overhead glistened with all their candles alight. The walls and windows and doorways were adorned with masses of white flowers, greenery, and silver ribbons.

There was renewed applause as Viola and Ferdinand appeared in the doorway. The Duke of Tresham stood on the dais, waiting for quiet.

"An impromptu ball, ladies and gentlemen," he said, "in celebration of a marriage. Ferdinand, lead your bride into the opening waltz, if you please."

Ferdinand turned his head and looked down at Viola as the orchestra began to play. He looked embarrassed and pleased—and also slightly amused.

"Now, what are you doing hiding here," he murmured to her, "when you should be out there dancing?"

She was struck by the familiarity of the words and then remembered where and when he had spoken them before. She smiled back at him.

"I have been waiting for the right partner, sir," she replied. And, more softly, "I have been waiting for *you*."

She set her hand on his and he led her onto the dance floor and set one arm about her waist. He moved her into the lilting rhythm of the waltz while their wedding guests watched. His eyes smiled into hers.

And then she remembered something else from that fateful May Day about the village green in Trellick. ————————————

Beware of a tall, dark, handsome stranger. He can destroy you—if you do not first snare his heart.

About the Author

Bestselling, multi-award-winning author Mary Balogh grew up in Wales, land of sea and mountains, song and legend. She brought music and a vivid imagination with her when she came to Canada to teach. Here she began a second career as a writer of books that always end happily and always celebrate the power of love. There are over three million copies of her Regency romances and historical romances in print. You can learn more about her novels at her website: www.marybalogh.com.